D1140367

Please renew/return items by last date shown. Please call the number below:

Renewals and enquiries: 0300 1234049

Textphone for hearing or speech impaired users: 01992 555506

www.hertfordshire.gov.uk/libraries
L32

Hertfordshire

'A dark and engrossing tale set against a glittering backdrop of shifting power and dangerous ambition. A *Throne of Swans* is utterly magical and completely entranced me – I couldn't put it down!' – Isabel Strychacz, author of *Starling*

532 038 90 4

A CROWN OF TALONS

KATHARINE
& ELIZABETH CORR

HOT
KEY
BOOKS

First published in Great Britain in 2021 by
HOT KEY BOOKS
80–81 Wimpole St, London W1G 9RE
Owned by Bonnier Books
Sveavägen 56, Stockholm, Sweden
www.hotkeybooks.com

A CIP catalogue record for this book is available from the British Library.

ISBN: 978-1-4714-0887-8
Also available as an ebook and in audio

1

This book is typeset using Atomik ePublisher
Printed and bound in Great Britain by Clays Ltd, Elcograf S.p.A.

Hot Key Books is an imprint of Bonnier Books UK
www.bonnierbooks.co.uk

It is a fearful kind of fury, and fatal,
When lover and beloved wage war.

δεινή τις ὀργὴ καὶ δυσίατος πέλει,
ὅταν φίλοι φίλοισι συμβάλωσ᾽ ἔριν.

Euripides, *Medea*, vv. 520–21, trans. Georgie
Penney

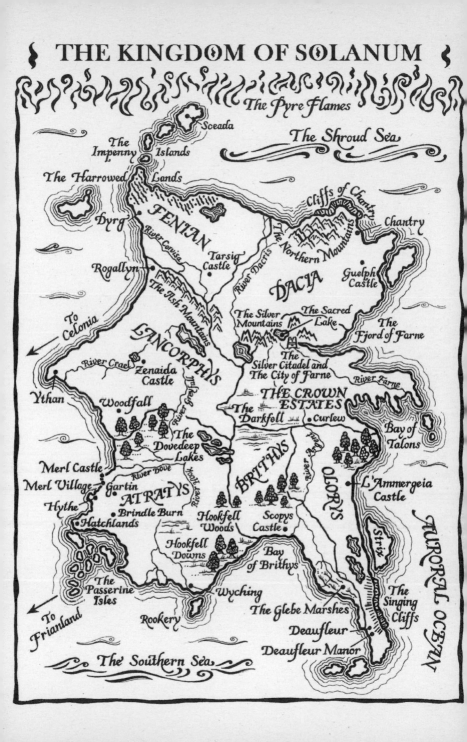

THE KINGDOM OF SOLANUM

The Pyre Flames

The Shroud Sea

Sceada

The Impenny Islands

The Harrowed Lands

Cliffs of Chantry

Dyrg

FENTAN

Chantry

River Corvisa

The Northern Mountains

River Dacris

Tarsig Castle

DACIA

Guelph Castle

Rogallyn

The Ash Mountains

The Silver Mountains

The Sacred Lake

The Fjord of Farne

To Celonia

LANCORPHIS

The Silver Citadel and The City of Farne

River Crael

Zenaida Castle

River Farne

Ythan

Woodfall

River Ruah

THE CROWN ESTATES

The Darkfell

Curlew

Bay of Talons

The Dovedeep Lakes

BRITHYS

River Hethil

L'Ammergeia Castle

Merl Castle

River Dove

River Hook

OLORIS

Merl Village

Gartin

ATRATYS

Hythe

Brindle Burn

Hookfell Woods

Scopys Castle

AURORAL OCEAN

Hatchlands

Hookfell Downs

Bay of Brithys

Strix

The Passerine Isles

Wyching

The Glebe Marshes

The Singing Cliffs

To Frianland

Rookery

Deaufleur

Deaufleur Manor

The Southern Sea

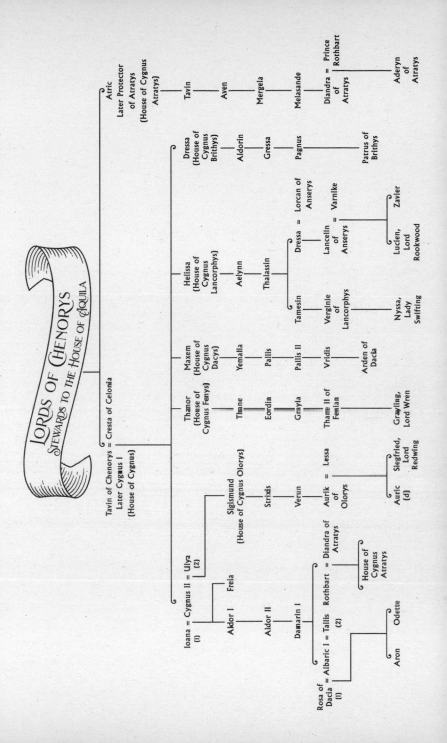

LORDS OF CHENORYS
STEWARDS TO THE HOUSE OF AQUILA

Prologue

Winter has caged my kingdom in ice.

For the last month the snow has been relentless: an endless fall of frozen feathers, too thick to fly through. The glass-panelled octagon of the great hall creaks with the white weight of it. But this evening, at least temporarily, the clouds have dispersed, and beneath the cold gaze of the stars the inhabitants of the Silver Citadel are celebrating the midwinter feast of the Deep Dark, the first Solstice of my reign. Pine logs crackle in the fireplaces. The scented smoke mingles with the aroma of the delicacies heaped upon the tables. Roasted venison, still sizzling from the spit; winter roots tossed in spiced flour and fried in salted butter; sugar-iced plum cake and thirty or more other dishes. A thousand candles blaze in ornate crystal chandeliers, attempting to dispel the darkness of this long, frostbitten night.

Dressed in a cloth-of-gold gown, with a gold and diamond circlet set in my dark hair, I'm dancing with Aron, my cousin and co-ruler. My husband, at least in name. I'm surrounded by servants and courtiers, all of whom have sworn loyalty to me.

Many of whom claim to love me. But in this glittering throng, my thoughts and feelings are focused entirely on one man. A man who has been ignoring me, and flirting with others, for the last three hours.

With every laugh, with every look, Lucien Rookwood drives another dagger into my heart.

Aron takes advantage of a pause in the music to lean forward and whisper to me, 'You seem tired.'

'I slept badly,' I reply. I haven't slept well for weeks. The violence of this winter is bringing sickness and fear of famine to my people. I'm tired of being cooped up by bad weather, unable to take to the sky. And I'm tired of the Protectors and the nobles through whom I rule. Of their stubborn resistance to the reforms Aron and I want to introduce that would grant greater protection to our flightless population. Of their blind insistence that Siegfried and Tallis, the Oloryan half-siblings who nearly succeeded in seizing the throne, are no longer a threat, merely because no one currently knows where they are. I cannot forget for a single day Tallis's promises: that she and her brother would return to exact revenge upon Aron and me. That the whole of Solanum would pay the price for our defiance . . .

I've plenty of reasons to worry.

But tonight, at least, every other concern is consumed by my misery over Lucien.

My feet take me through the steps and turns of the minuet while I concentrate on not allowing myself to look at the man who was – so briefly – my lover. Three months have passed, but my heart fractures a little further whenever I think about the one night we spent together, or about our last meeting. Lucien left court straight after my coronation. He came back a week ago, but that was only because of the Solstice. Because I specifically invited him to the celebration. Insisted, in fact, that he should come.

'Aderyn?' Aron has raised one white-blond eyebrow; the dance has ended and he's waiting for an answer to a question I didn't hear. He sighs. 'I said, do you want to dance again, or rest?'

I become aware of the flightless musicians, bows poised above strings, waiting for me to decide whether I wish to continue. Of the dazzlingly clothed nobles observing me. 'I'll rest.'

'As you wish.' Aron kisses my hand as I leave the floor. He walks over to his sister, Odette, and leads her back into the dance. As the music resumes, I return to my seat on the dais and let my eyes stray towards Lucien. His dark hair – the same iridescent blue-black as the raven into which he can transform – is longer now; it curls against the edge of his collar. But otherwise he's little altered. He's still handsome and broad-shouldered. He's even wearing the same sleeveless grey silk tunic he wore on the night we first arrived here – less than six months ago, though it seems like another lifetime. A life in which I was merely the Protector of the Dominion of Atratys, hoping to find answers about my mother's murder, hoping to survive the intrigues of my uncle's court. A life in which Lucien was merely my clerk.

But now . . . Now I am the Queen of Solanum. And Lucien seems more remote than ever.

Another pause between dances. Aron is still with Odette,

3

so I take a sip from the goblet of mulled wine a servant has placed at my elbow, grip my courage between my teeth and rise, making my way down the room to where Lucien is standing, chatting to his dance partner. Courtiers part and bow as I pass. The heavily armoured Dark Guards patrolling the edge of the room stand to attention, and household servants – now clad in the blue and silver of my house, Cygnus Atratys – drop their gaze. Yet Lucien does not appear to notice my approach. He is talking and laughing loudly, and doesn't stop until the woman he is with bows and backs away.

'Your Majesty.' He ducks his head. His expression is calm, but his dark eyes are hard, glittering too brightly. 'May the Creator guide your flight through the frozen season.'

A well-worn expression. His first words to me since he told me to leave his room, after I revealed my marriage to Aron. They are appropriate to the time of year. Still, I'd hoped for something more, given what we had been to each other. I swallow my disappointment and force a smile.

'I'm glad to see you back at court, Lord Lucien. Will you do me the honour of being my partner in the next dance?'

His face flushes – whether with surprise or vexation, I'm not sure – but he cannot refuse my request. I place my hand on the bare skin of the arm he has offered me, try to ignore the surge of desire in my belly as he leads me back to the centre of the hall.

There's a delay as the orchestra tunes up and we wait for the other dancers to assemble. Lucien makes no attempt at conversation. Instead he gazes around the hall, as if he's bored, until I can't bear the silence any more.

'How is your father?'

Lucien glances at me briefly. 'He is well, I thank you.'

'And your mother, and your brother?'

'Well enough.'

More silence, and still the orchestra is not ready. I can't ask the only question to which I actually want the answer: whether he has forgiven me. His tone and behaviour tell me he has not. My dress and diadem grow heavy with humiliation, pinning me in place, until I blurt out the only uncontroversial thing I can think of.

'You must have caught the first of the snowstorms on your flight from Atratys. I hope you didn't run into any difficulties.'

He shoots me a look of such contempt that the blood rushes into my cheeks. 'I am here, and uninjured. What difficulties do you imagine I could have had?'

The music starts, ending my agony, but anger sparks inside me as we begin to dance. I want to shake him, to ask what choice he thinks I really had. To remind him that I married Aron to save the kingdom. To save Lucien himself. But I don't. Instead, I focus on my steps, wishing that I hadn't forced Lucien to come back to court.

Aron, I know, is watching us.

Finally the dance ends. I sweep away from Lucien before he has finished bowing, making for the full-length windows that lead out onto the terrace. I need some air – clean, cold air, not stuffy with woodsmoke and the scent of wax. But before I reach the windows, the heavy doors at the far end of the great hall are flung open. There are cries coming from the entrance hall. The Dark Guards stationed at the edges of the room swarm towards the source of the commotion.

'Aderyn!' Aron is hurrying towards me, his hand held out. Together we retreat to the dais, other guards taking up position in front of us. Aron has a sword belted to his waist; I regret that I have not. Both my ceremonial swords are locked, useless, in my rooms.

We don't have to wait long. One of the guard captains runs across the ballroom towards us. 'Majesties . . .'

'Speak, Hemeth.' Aron beckons the man closer. 'What's amiss?'

'Nobles, from the Kingdom of Celonia.'

A neighbouring country, just close enough to fly to. Friendly, I had thought. My heart races. 'An invasion? Has Siegfried launched an attack?'

'No, my queen.' The captain hesitates. 'They claim there has been a rebellion. That the flightless of Celonia have risen up, and that the capital and the royal palace and many other towns are on fire. The nobles are here seeking refuge.' He gestures behind him. 'Those who survived.'

The flightless seizing control of an entire country? The word *impossible* rises to my lips. But I can't disbelieve my own eyes. People, some robed, some still naked from transformation, are crowding into the ballroom. Some are limping, many are injured – a woman with long, matted red hair clutches one hand to her face as blood wells between her fingers.

A man who seems to be leading them drops to his knees. 'Mercy . . .' He clasps a young child, bundled in a robe, to his chest. 'Mercy and shelter, we beg you . . .' Solanish words, but spoken with such a strong Celonian accent that it takes me a moment to understand him. His speech is punctuated by rapid, shallow breaths.

One of my courtiers pushes forward – Nyssa, Lady Swifting. Lucien's cousin. 'What of my betrothed? Where is Lord Bastien?'

The man stares at her, uncomprehending.

'Bastien of Verne,' Nyssa repeats. 'Where is he?'

'Behind us, I hope. We were separated . . .' The child in his arms begins to writhe and cry, a high-pitched keening that makes me wince in sympathy. I'm about to step forward and take her from him when Aron's fingers curl around my wrist. Whether to protect me or to remind me of my position, I'm not sure. Instead, Nyssa helps the noble lay the child on the floor.

'Aron . . .'

He nods, moves his hand briefly to my shoulder before turning away to begin issuing orders. The injured must be tended to. But I saw in his eyes my own fears: Solanum is about to be plunged into more uncertainty. More danger.

I leave Aron to organise the servants and summon doctors. I am the queen: my role is to be seen to rule, to be in control. So I walk briefly among the injured, dropping words of comfort here and there, counselling patience to my own nobility. Like Lady Nyssa, some here have family and friends in Celonia, but I would not have anyone fly off in rage and get killed. I remind them of the enduring nature of Solanum, of storms that we have weathered before. But I know – everyone here now knows – that the world is shifting beneath our feet. Whether we like it or not.

Finally I feel my work is done. Back in my own rooms, my maidservants help me out of my heavy gown, relieve me of the diadem, bracelets and rings that have been weighing me down. They depart. Naked – alone – I make my way out onto the private landing platform that is tucked away at the back of the royal apartments. The landing platform I prefer to use, for convenience, and to avoid exposing my scarred back more than is necessary. I need to feel the wind beneath my body, to lose myself in the consuming joy of flight. To get as close as I can to the stars that burn above the surrounding mountain peaks. Wading into the frigid water of the lake, I give in to the power that is always waiting just beneath my skin. Hair morphs into feather, muscles shift and bones lengthen and lighten as I let myself transform from human into swan.

Within a few moments I am high enough to look down upon the Silver Citadel and the city of Farne which surrounds it. The House of Cygnus has ruled here for over two hundred years; the Citadel itself has stood for many centuries more. From up here, this symbol of our power appears unyielding. Eternal. Changeless.

But it's an illusion, nothing more. The old world is fading as fire sweeps across Celonia. If we do nothing, I fear Solanum too will burn.

One

We pace the council chamber in a slow, elongated circle, almost like a dance. From the lead-latticed windows spanning one end of the wood-panelled room, to the huge stone fireplace at the other, around and around we go. Aron and me and our principal royal councillors; Lord Corvax, the leader of Convocation – the assembly that represents nobles below the rank of Protector, and the four Protectors themselves. Only four, because I am Protector of both Atratys – the dominion in which I grew up – and, for the time being, at least, of Olorys, the dominion that was previously ruled over by the family of Siegfried Redwing. By law, Siegfried should be Protector of Olorys, not me. But that was before he tried to seize the crown. Before he murdered his own father, we've since discovered, in order to smooth his path to power.

Lord Corvax's stick thumps against the carpeted floorboards, unintentionally keeping time. Meetings are usually conducted like this: a way of ensuring our leg muscles do not wither, given the amount of time we spend on the wing. The council scribe orbits us like a comet, taking notes and reminding us, if necessary, of the items we are here to discuss.

Not that we need reminding of the revolution in Celonia. Two weeks after the interruption of our Solstice feast, the stream of escaping nobles shows no sign of abating.

'. . . and it appears that some have gone straight to friends and family in the dominions. But most of those who can fly have made their way here.' Lady Finch, Warden of the Citadel, sighs and shakes her head. 'The Citadel is full, Your Majesties. My people are trying to find space for new arrivals in the city, but then there is the question of provisions . . .'

I glance, questioning, at the Steward of the Crown Estates. He pulls a long face.

'Snowfall has blocked all the main roads. I fear the grain imports we need from Lancorphys are being eaten by barn rats instead.'

The litany of troubles goes on. Celonians who were too badly injured to fly – and there are many – have started arriving by boat at our port towns. Some have brought sickness with them. No one knows the number of dead.

Thane, Protector of Fenian, launches into a ponderous and bloodthirsty description of exactly what he'd like to do to Celonia's flightless rebels, if only he could get his hands on them. I check my impatience by studying the ornately painted ceiling. It depicts mythology: the war between birds and humans, and the Firebird's creation of beings who could take both forms – us – to bring about peace and prosperity. I wonder if the flightless artist who painted it was being ironic. Finally, Thane is forced to pause for breath, and I seize my opportunity.

'Dreams of revenge are all very well, Lord Thane, but the reality is seldom as satisfactory as the fantasy. And I will not authorise any action until we have a clearer sense of the situation in Celonia. The Skein will meet in two days' time to consider what is to be done.'

'But what, Majesty, of the rumours? Unrest in flightless towns, secret gatherings and plotting . . .' Thane's eyes bulge. 'Are we to do nothing to protect ourselves?'

'Rumours, my lord, are not facts. Have you any evidence to present?'

Thane pouts, but he doesn't reply.

'Well, then. Any acts of retribution directed at our own flightless population will be severely dealt with.' My friend Letya's wedding present to me, a piece of Atratyan luckstone carved into the shape of a feather, is in my pocket. I grip it tightly. Lift my chin and stare at the circle of faces. 'Do I make myself clear?' There are murmurs of assent, some more grudging than others. The flightless, my Letya included, have no voice and little power, beyond whatever local assemblies may be allowed within each dominion. When the Skein meets, I hope to raise again the question of giving them representation – but I'm not about to mention that now. The first time I proposed it, the idea was rejected outright; I've learned it's better not to give my nobles time to prepare their objections. 'Lord Fletch, what other items of business do we have?'

The grey-skinned scribe, a junior member of one of the goose families, shuffles his papers and purses his orange-pink lips.

'Um . . . the proposal for establishing a bounty for information leading to the capture of Siegfried of Olorys and the former queen Tallis, his half-sister.'

11

Lord Pianet, our Master Secretary, outlines the plan: to set up a fund, and to put up notices in every town square – together with likenesses of Siegfried and Tallis – offering rewards for information leading to their capture.

My councillors continue pacing, silent, until Arden, Protector of Dacia, raises his hand.

'Is it necessary? Nearly four months have passed, and we've found no sign of them. Every noble household in the kingdom has been searched. Olorys has been ransacked. And still nothing. They could be dead, for all we know.' He waves his hand, dismissing them easily as his mouth curves into a smile. 'And if they're not, they don't have the resources to be a credible threat. I think there are better uses for our money.'

'True, true,' Lord Thane adds. 'And to be encouraging the flightless to inform against nobles is hardly appropriate.'

Aron, who has previously said little, stops walking so abruptly that Lady Verginie, Protector of Lancorphys, nearly runs into him. 'Must I remind you, Lord Thane, that these particular nobles are murderous traitors, and will be treated as such?' He doesn't raise his voice, but there's no mistaking the dangerously sharp edge to his tone. Thane changes colour and begins to murmur his agreement. Aron talks over him. 'And we do not require your approval, Lord Arden. The bounty will be funded by the crown. Our purpose today is merely to inform you of the ongoing efforts to bring the traitors to justice.'

'Of course, Your Majesty.' Lord Corvax bows, placating. 'You have the full support of Convocation in these efforts.'

Their support, but not their money, I notice.

Corvax continues. 'I'm sure Lord Arden's only concern is to spare Your Majesties unnecessary anxiety.'

Aron does not dignify this comment with a response. After a moment, Lord Pianet asks whether there is any further business. Patrus, Protector of Brithys – since I have yet to find a way of legally removing him – raises his hand.

'Speaking of threats to the kingdom, may I remind the council that the question of the royal succession is not yet settled. Perhaps it would be advisable for Their Majesties to name an heir, since there is no child of the royal blood. As yet.' He stares pointedly at my flat stomach with his one remaining eye; I blinded the other when he attempted to abduct me.

Aron and I glance at each other. We're both aware that there is speculation at court about the exact nature of our union. We married to keep the throne out of Siegfried's hands, and to stop the kingdom falling into civil war, but without any pretence of more than cousinly affection. Aron knows I was – am – in love with Lucien. He was in love with him too, once.

I draw breath, planning to tell Patrus exactly what he can do with his suggestion, but Aron slips his arm around my waist and speaks first.

'The question of the succession will soon be dealt with, Lord Patrus. But rest assured that whatever happens, the next ruler of Solanum will not be you.' He gives Patrus a grin that is all teeth and no humour. 'So there's absolutely no need for you to worry about how you'd cope with the responsibility. You may leave us now.'

Everyone bows, the circle disperses, and in another moment Aron and I are alone in the council chamber.

'Why did you say that, Aron? Now everyone is going to assume I'm pregnant, and it will be obvious soon enough that I'm not. I was just going to tell him to –'

'I can guess what you were about to say.' He smiles slightly, and there's affection in his wide green eyes. 'And believe me, I have every sympathy. Patrus is a monster. A rock dragon would make a better Protector; at least it would only kill people for survival and not for pleasure. But we have to proceed with caution, Aderyn. You and I both know that Siegfried and Tallis will come back, and when they do, we'll need all the support among the nobility that we can get. We have to respect the Decrees. You want to change everything, and I understand why. But we can't have tyranny.' He goes to lean against the window, his hand resting on the side of the frame. 'I saw enough of that in my father's reign.'

He's right, of course. I do want to change things. That's one of the reasons I said yes, to Aron and to the throne. I want to carry on the work my mother started in Atratys. It's wrong, that the lives of the flightless – education, freedom, everything – should depend on the whims of the nobles who rule them. Lucien's words come back to me; he described Solanum's government as a rotten edifice. At the time I didn't agree with him. I didn't know enough to know if he spoke the truth. But now . . . I don't want a revolution. I don't want bloodshed. But things have to change.

I just hadn't realised it would be so . . . complicated.

I've never even told Aron about my other dream: that of challenging the Decrees, to allow us to rule as cousins, not husband and wife. To free me to be with Lucien. If Lucien ever forgives me.

14

Aron is still staring out of the window. The fabrics he chooses now he's king are richer, more ornately embroidered, but his preference for black hasn't changed; he believes his missing arm is less noticeable in dark colours. He's currently wearing black leather trousers and boots, and a black velvet tunic over a fine linen shirt – a striking contrast to his white-blond hair, and to the scene beyond the glass. Snow is falling again, thick enough to obscure the view across the fjord that would normally be visible from here. The tumbling flakes are mesmerising, but they mean another day without flying or riding. I touch his shoulder gently.

'I'm supposed to meet with Letya, so if you'll excuse me –'

'Lucien is still at court, I see.' Aron glances at me out of the corner of his eye, questioning me with a faint lift of his brows. 'Still as devastatingly handsome as ever.'

Is that what he's been wondering about? 'True. I suppose he has friends here he hasn't seen in a while: his cousin Nyssa, and his aunt, and so on.' I shrug. 'I didn't ask him to stay, Aron. I haven't forgotten the vows we took.'

'Neither have I. Please –' he offers me his arm – 'allow me to escort you back to your apartments.'

I wonder whether Aron is happy. Whether he thinks his throne was worth the cost we both agreed to: a life lived with friendship, and the type of love that friendship may become, but without any deeper passion.

I don't ask him, of course. Just note it as another unspoken question that lies between us.

As we leave the council chamber, the snow falls more thickly than ever. Aron would never admit it, but I'm sure there must be some spark of him that is glad of this weather. For however long it lasts, he is not the only one of us who is earthbound.

We reach the royal audience chamber, only to hear raised voices coming from the sitting room that lies beyond. The voices are easily recognisable: Letya, my clerk, waiting woman and best friend – my sister, by affection though not by blood – and Lady Crump, the 'adviser' foisted on me by Convocation.

Aron clamps his lips together as if he's trying not to laugh.

I sigh. 'This is your fault. You persuaded me to agree to having that woman around.' Unlike most nobles, who spend at least two years at court before they come of age, I had no contact with the Citadel until last summer. Lady Crump is supposed to be advising me on royal protocol. Teaching me how to be a queen, though she and I have very different ideas of what exactly that entails. 'She makes me feel like –' I scrunch up my face, searching for the right words. 'Imagine if someone gets a rusty nail and a bit of slate and scrapes the one across the other, over and over and over until you want to scream. That's how she makes me feel.'

'That's how she makes everyone feel. But it will be worth it, in the end.' Aron leans down to whisper in my ear, mindful I suppose of the servants standing stiffly by the door. 'She's connected to every noble family in the kingdom, pretty much. Just put up with her for another few months. As I said, we need the support.'

I narrow my eyes. 'Fine. But you can go in there with me –' I point to the door of the audience chamber – 'and help sort this out.'

'I'd love to, my dear. But I'm sure there's something in my own apartments that requires my immediate attention.' He begins backing away. 'Paperwork. Or something.'

I put my hands on my hips. 'You're scared of her.'

Aron smiles, shrugs and executes a flawless bow. 'I have every confidence in you, my queen.' He's still smirking as he turns away.

Sharpened by irritation, the dull headache that has been coiled around my right eye socket stabs upward into my skull. But there is no avoiding it.

The servants fling the doors open ahead of me.

Letya is standing in front of one the sofas, clutching a book – my diary, I think – to her chest. Opposite her is Lady Crump, arms crossed, mouth open in an expression of horrified shock.

'What is going on here?'

Lady Crump curtsies deeply. 'I beg your pardon, Your Majesty. Mistress Letya and I were just having a discussion.'

'Is that so?' I look towards Letya. 'Is everything well?'

Letya, flushing to the roots of her ash-blonde hair, says *no* at the same time as Lady Crump says *yes*.

I turn to my friend. 'What's the matter?'

'*She* wants me to give up my position as your clerk. She says it isn't fitting, for nobles to have to ask a flightless woman for an appointment. She says I'm not deserving of the honour, by birth or education . . .'

I stare at the other woman. 'Letya shared my lessons from when she was twelve years old. Do you consider me uneducated?'

Crump forces her mouth into a smile, though she can't

conceal the disdain in her eyes. 'Absolutely not, Your Majesty. I was merely trying to point out that a queen is judged by those with whom she surrounds herself. While there is no doubt of Mistress Letya's qualification to act as your personal servant, the position of clerk has *traditionally* –' she puts such weight on the word that it becomes a thing of stone, a weapon with which to crush the life out of someone – 'been held by a noble. It is what is expected.' She fixes her gaze on the ceiling, a habit she has when she's about to deliver a statement. 'A clerk of high status, well-connected to the most important houses and families, free to move about the court and act as a bridge between the monarch and the nobles . . . Such a clerk can only enhance the status of the one whom she serves.'

'It sounds as if you have someone specific in mind for the post.'

My comment throws Lady Crump for a moment. The mossy tint of her skin – she's one of the numerous pigeon families – turns darker green. 'The selection of your staff is of course up to you, Your Majesty. But if you have no one else in mind, my eldest daughter is returning to court shortly. I'm sure she would be deeply honoured to be of service to Your Majesty.' Another curtsy and false smile accompany this suggestion.

Next to me, Letya is tense. I want to point out to Lady Crump that I've not actually agreed to replace my friend. If anything, I want to banish *her* from court, to send her back to the marshlands of Brithys, where she can preach about tradition and status to her own unfortunate dependents.

But Aron is right. We need support. We need time to convince our nobility that our plans for the future of the kingdom are

18

workable. So I grit my teeth and give Lady Crump a smile as false as the one she gave me.

'Thank you, Lady Crump. As always, you bring such an interesting perspective to matters. I will definitely give your words consideration. There will be no need for you to speak to Letya any further on this subject.'

Crump's brow wrinkles as she tries to work out my meaning.

'I'm afraid I have a headache,' I continue. 'Lady Crump, would you be so good as to send for my physician on your way out?'

She has no option but to curtsy again and go. As soon as I'm sure she's left my apartments, I turn back to Letya. 'I'm so sorry.'

'It's not your fault. That woman is a mean-spirited, jealous-natured weasel who would sour milk if she passed within three wingspans of a dairy.' My friend sighs. 'I'm not sure she's wrong though.'

'Of course she's wrong.' I grasp Letya's gloved hand briefly; the power that allows us to transform, that lingers in our skin even as humans, also means that our touch is dangerous to the flightless majority. I've seen nobles burn servants' skin in anger. I was forced by my uncle, the last king, to do so myself once. 'You're a fine clerk, Letya. Don't let her make you doubt yourself.'

'I don't doubt myself. But when nobles come to me to ask for an appointment with you . . .' She drops her gaze, shaking her head. 'I've seen how they look at me. As if they're . . . they're lowering themselves, just by talking to me.' When she looks up again, her eyes are glassy. 'As if I've got some disease they're afraid they're going to catch.'

19

A surge of anger and sorrow takes my breath away. 'I'm going to change things, Letya. I promise.' I just don't know when. Or exactly how. 'And if Crump ever talks to you like that again I'll have her thrown in the dungeons, no matter how well-connected she is.'

'Don't do that. I don't want to make things difficult for you.' She opens the diary, and for a few minutes we sit together on the sofa – close, but not touching – and go through my appointments for the next few days. But I can tell her mind is not on the ambassadors and trade delegations who fill the pages, their names and purposes noted in Letya's curving script.

'What are you thinking about?'

'Change.' She folds the corner of one of the thick pages. 'Things have changed in Celonia.'

'They have. But, surely, you don't want –'

'No, of course not.'

Silence fills the space between us. 'Letya,' I ask eventually, 'do you want to go home? You know you can, any time you want to.' Dread of what her answer will be makes my stomach twist into knots. I have Aron and Odette, and I've come to love my cousins. I've made some friends among the younger nobles. But I've spent at least part of every day with Letya since I was eleven years old, when she came to be my companion after my mother's murder. My life without her would be unrecognisable.

Still, I have to give her the choice. When we left Merl Castle late last spring, we thought we'd only be away for six weeks. It wasn't supposed to be forever.

Letya hesitates, but only for a second or so. 'No.' She shakes her head decidedly. 'I won't leave you, Aderyn. And besides –'

sly humour twinkles in her eyes – 'Lord Lancelin is still paying me to be your companion. It's good money.'

I grin. 'And still entertaining, I hope.'

She shrugs and laughs. 'Well, you've not risked your life for a while now. And though I doubt it will last, I don't mind a little less excitement for the time being.'

Her tone is light, but I know what lies behind her words. Despite the best efforts of our doctors, Letya's neck still bears the hand-shaped burn left by Siegfried's grip.

Revenge doesn't solve things. Watching my mother's murderer die didn't bring me the peace I thought it would. Whatever I do to Siegfried won't heal Letya's skin. But I have to find him. If nothing else, I have to stop him inflicting the same pain on others.

My doctor arrives with a tincture of willow for my headache. When he's gone, Letya helps me swap my silk gown for a long-sleeved tunic of padded leather, trousers and high boots, and I make my way to the new training room, eager to burn off some energy, eager to do something – anything – to distract me from this morning's dealings with my council and Lady Crump. I learned to fight with a sword after I lost my ability to shift my shape. Although that power has now returned to me, I've continued to practise; I'm not sure about Tallis, but Siegfried can handle a blade.

When I arrive, the room is busy; the endless snow is forcing many nobles to seek alternative forms of exercise. But the crowd here isn't just nobles. This is the only space in the Citadel where flighted and flightless – a privileged portion of them, at least – are on an equal footing. The training room was expanded by Aron after we were crowned, but it's run and overseen by the Dark Guards. They practise sword-fighting and axe-throwing here themselves, but now they allow nobles to use the space too, offering advice on technique and ruling on disputed matches. Despite Solanum's two hundred years of peace, the ability to use a sword is still valued by some, though too many nobles disdain it as a skill only necessary for the flightless. The guards won't fight nobles themselves though. The exception to this is Aron; when he lost his arm, nearly three years ago now, the Dark Guards befriended him and taught him, and he still values their friendship. I search the large, high-ceilinged room for his slim figure.

Hemeth – handsome, copper-haired, and Aron's closest friend in the Dark Guards – approaches me and nods respectfully. 'Madam.' There are no titles used in this room. No references to house or rank.

'Good afternoon, Hemeth. Is my husband here?'

'No. But there's a match that's just about to finish if you wish for a practice partner.' He hands me a dull-edged, blunt-tipped practice sword and leads me past the axe targets to where two men, both breathing hard, both misted with sweat, are saluting each other. One of the participants is unknown to me. He's of average height, powerfully built, with dark eyes and silvery hair that is tied back now but must fall past his shoulders. Hemeth murmurs that the man is one of the nobles who escaped from Celonia; there's a scabbed-over wound marring one of his cheekbones.

The man's opponent is Lucien.

He's had his dark hair cut short, so that he looks just like my Lucien again. The Lucien I dream about. My heart, traitor that it is, beats faster.

Hemeth steps forward. 'Gentlemen, if either of you is inclined to fight again, this lady wishes for a partner.'

The stranger narrows his eyes slightly, shooting Hemeth an incredulous glance, but he makes a sweeping bow to signal his acquiescence. Lucien, after a tiny hesitation, nods. Even smiles a little; I wonder if he's trying to make up for his behaviour the last time we met. But then he begins to walk forward. As if my choice is already made. As if I'm bound to choose him, even after he treated me with such disdain at the Solstice ball.

'This gentleman –' I gesture at the stranger instead – 'would make a worthy opponent, I believe.'

Lucien stiffens. Clamps his mouth shut and swings away from me.

I refuse to let my gaze follow him.

Hemeth is already scattering fresh sand on the floor. The silver-haired stranger salutes me and, with a slight smile playing upon his lips, raises his sword. I take a deep breath and ready my sword in response. I've no time to worry about Lucien or anything else; as soon as we are both in position, the stranger attacks.

Without hesitation I parry, quickly swinging my left arm upwards, blocking the tip of his blade with my own; we lock eyes for a moment and I am surprised by the determination, by the controlled fury I sense within him. He lunges at me again but I'm faster; I spin away from him, launch a counter-attack, land blow after blow after blow. He takes a step back, breathing heavily, and I can see that I've surprised him. Clearly he didn't anticipate that I would – or could – fight so well. We circle each other, catching our breath, but my opponent soon comes at me again. He tries to use his height and superior strength against me and I wince as the muscles in my arms and legs protest against the sheer force of his attack. A few spectators are gathering nearby. I ignore them. Although I have less experience of the court than most of my courtiers, there are few here – with the exception of Aron – who fight as well as I do. I don't intend to be beaten by this Celonian exile.

As he attacks again, I lower my sword slightly, hoping that he will think he has forced me onto the defensive. My deceit works. He moves in closer; he thinks it's over, that he's won.

But he's wrong. I drop down onto my knees, flattening my back against the ground to lower myself beneath the reach of his blade. Roll quickly onto my side. And then, with one swift movement, I sweep his legs from underneath him. My opponent lands flat on his back, grunting with the force of the impact, sending particles of sand and dust spraying upwards. Before he's had time to right himself, I'm up on my feet and pushing the tip of my blade squarely into the middle of his chest.

'Do you yield, sir?'

He stares up at me, the surprise in his eyes quickly replaced by irritation. But the next moment he's grinning broadly. 'I do indeed, my lady. That was . . . well played.'

There is a smattering of applause from the onlookers before they disperse. My opponent picks himself up off the ground and bows to me.

I nod in response, breathing hard, wincing as I return the practice sword to Hemeth and flex my fingers. The scarred skin of my back is beginning to sting; I've not fought this hard for months. Still, I'm struggling to stop myself grinning.

The stranger makes another bow and smiles briefly. 'I am delighted to have met such a challenging opponent.' He has a pleasant accent. 'May I?' He holds out his hand; when I place mine within his grasp, he kisses my fingers. 'Would you care for another bout? I'd be grateful for the distraction.'

'Thank you, but I'm afraid I have a prior engagement.' I begin to walk away.

Lucien is leaning against the wall nearby, watching me and scowling.

On impulse I turn back to the stranger. 'Perhaps another day though, when we are both at leisure.' I smile at him warmly. 'May I know your name?'

'Of course. I am Veron.' He doesn't tell me his house – Hemeth has obviously made the rules clear to him.

'Well, thank you, Veron. I've enjoyed myself.' I smile again and incline my head and leave.

I don't look back to see what Lucien's doing.

The rest of my day is taken up with yet more meetings. I have no time to relax until after the evening meal when, finally, I'm alone with Letya in my sitting room. She is knitting, while I'm curled up in the corner of one of the sofas. I've a book in my hand – an amusing tale of a young woman's discovery of a new world, and all the wonders she encounters – but although I'm staring at the words printed on the page, I'm no longer reading. Soothed by the click of Letya's needles and the crackle of logs burning in the fireplace, my mind is wandering. I'm dreaming of a different future, filled with adventure and travel instead of responsibility. Until a knock at the door jerks me back into the present.

One of the blue-and-silver-clad household servants stands on the threshold. 'If it please Your Majesty, Lady Nyssa Swifting requests a moment of your time.' His face is wooden, but I can hear someone – Nyssa? – breathing unevenly in the background.

'Very well.' I nod to Letya; she gathers her knitting and moves to wait at the edge of the room as the other woman enters. Nyssa's face is blotchy, eyes swollen with crying. I guess what has happened. 'Lord Bastien?'

She nods. 'They found his body, out on the coast at Ythan. He had lost too much blood, the doctor says, he had so many wounds, and they'd –' she gulps – 'they'd cut off one of his ears . . .' Fresh tears suspend her voice as she covers her face with her hands.

'I'm so sorry, Nyssa. Does your mother know? Let me send a servant to fetch her. Or Lord Lucien. Please, tell me how I can help you, what you need.'

'Vengeance.' The word is spoken quietly, but the next moment she clasps her hands together and drops to her knees in front of me, her voice throbbing. 'Blood for blood, that is what I desire. I beg you, as your loyal subject, and your cousin – help the nobles of Celonia regain what has been taken from them. Send a force against the flightless who now claim to rule there. Make them pay for the lives they've taken.'

'Please, Nyssa, get up.' The bare skin at the nape of my neck prickles; I can almost feel Siegfried and Tallis watching from the shadowed corners of the room, waiting for me to make a

26

mistake. To do something that leaves the kingdom vulnerable. 'The situation is complicated.'

'No, it's not.' She forces herself upright, taking a ragged breath. 'We must crush this rebellion, Your Majesty.' Her hands curl into fists. 'Or it will spread, and Solanum will fall, and our blood will run in the streets of Farne.' Nyssa looks at Letya and her face flushes as she leans forward. 'The place of the flightless is to serve, not to rule. Not to consort with kings as if they are equals –'

'Enough!' I lift my chin and allow ice to enter my voice. 'You forget yourself, Lady Swifting. Your grief has overset your reason.'

Nyssa stares at me, so much anger blazing in her eyes that I wonder whether she is about to strike me. But the moment passes; she begins sobbing, and stumbles to a nearby chair.

'Letya . . .'

My friend understands. She hurries to the door and issues instructions to the servants outside. I pace up and down while we wait, but I don't try to speak to Nyssa. I don't know what to say to her.

Eventually there is another knock at the door. Nyssa's mother, Verginie of Lancorphys, is here; so is Lucien. He helps Verginie coax her daughter out of the chair and the two women leave, Verginie murmuring apologies as she goes.

Letya ignores Lucien. 'I'll go and make sure the maids have warmed your bed, Your Majesty.' She curtsies and goes into my bedroom, shutting the door behind her.

For the first time in more than three months, Lucien and I are alone.

Two

We stare each at each other, as a clamour of unspoken thoughts and feelings fills my mouth. The silence thickens until it is stifling. Until it is heavy enough to crush the air out of my lungs. If I do not speak, I'll suffocate.

'I'm sorry.' The first words blurted out, I breathe easier.

'You're sorry . . . ?' Lucien's question is laced with scorn.

I hesitate. 'About Lord Bastien, I mean. Your cousin was distraught.'

'Oh.' Lucien turns his face away and gazes at the fire. 'What did Nyssa say to you?'

'She can tell you that, if she wishes. Will you make sure a doctor attends her?' I choose to believe – I have to hope – that Nyssa's views and wishes, as well as her grief, will be moderated by time.

He doesn't answer. Just goes on watching the dancing flames, while I watch him, absorbed by the way the firelight is reddening his lips and turning his skin to gold. I remember another night. A night when he lay in my arms, gilded by candlelight, when my body shivered at his touch, and gradually my desire edges out every rational thought. Without even meaning to, I stretch out my hand towards him. 'Lucien . . .'

'My aunt says you are offering a bounty for information about Tallis and Siegfried.'

I let my arm drop. 'Yes. I'm not going to stop hunting them. I promise.'

Lucien almost died at Tallis's hands. Would have died, if I hadn't got there in time to save him, if I had not physically fought off the guards attempting to kill him. Our kind heals quickly. Heals well from all but the worst injuries. He probably no longer bears the imprint of the whip that was used to torture him. But surely, surely he couldn't have forgotten what I did?

There's an ornament on the mantelpiece, a swan woven from spun glass. A wedding gift from the Ryskan ambassador. Lucien picks it up and turns the delicate confection over in his fingers so that it catches the light.

'And what of Celonia? Will we invade in support of its nobles?'

'The Skein meets the day after next. But I don't think so. I hope we can avoid being dragged into a conflict.' I think back to what my councillors have told me of Celonia. 'Especially since it seems possible that their nobility got what they deserved . . .'

'You surprise me.'

'Why?'

'You seemed very well pleased with the Celonian nobility earlier today.' He puts the glass swan down on a small table near the fire. 'With one Celonian noble in particular.'

I feel myself blush as I catch his meaning. 'I fought one match with him, Lucien. And I don't see why you should care –'

'But the king might care.' His mouth twists into the mockery of a smile. 'You told me we couldn't be together because of your promise to Aron. Is your commitment to your marriage vows weakening, my lady? Or were your words to me nothing more than a lie? A way of softening the truth: that I never mattered to you. Or rather, that I didn't matter to you enough. That I was nothing to you, compared to the crown.'

For a moment I'm too shocked to reply. But only for a moment. 'How can you say that? How can you be so cruel, when you know exactly what you mean to me?' I swallow hard. 'I don't know you, Lucien. I'm beginning to wonder if I ever knew you.'

His eyes widen and he takes a step forward. 'Aderyn –'

I shake my head. 'Get out.'

'But I didn't –'

'Get out!'

Lucien hesitates for a wing beat, before hurrying from the room. In his haste he knocks against the small table; the glass swan slips from the smooth wood onto the granite hearth.

I hurry to the fireplace and sink to my knees. The swan's wings are broken. And when I pick it up, try to put it back together, it just fractures further. Comes to pieces in my hands.

It was only a little thing. I've no reason to care so much. But once I start crying, I can't stop.

I sleep badly, dreaming of Lucien. Somehow, in my nightmares, he becomes Lord Bastien: it's Lucien's mangled body that

I see lying on the rocky shore of Ythan. And Nyssa becomes Tallis, laughing at me as she leads an army to invade the Citadel. I watch her fight and kill Aron before I drift back into unconsciousness. When I finally wake, bleary-eyed, the sun is shining brightly around the edges of my bedroom curtains. I push myself up and stretch, and tug on the bell pull next to the bed.

My maidservant Fris enters the room soon after and bobs a curtsy. 'Good morning, Your Majesty. May I open the curtains?'

'Please. What time is it?'

'A quarter till the fifth hour, Your Majesty. Um . . .' she twists her hands nervously, 'Mistress Letya said you weren't to be disturbed. On account of it being an Ember Day.'

Of course. No business to be conducted today. No banquets. I get out of bed and go to the tall diamond-paned windows that overlook the gardens of the Citadel and the mountains beyond. The sunlight glinting off the snow dazzles me, but I can see people down below clearing the paths between the bare-limbed trees. And when I unlatch the window, the air feels a little warmer than of late, the pale blue of the sky tempting me to lean out in the hope of feeling the sun on my face. Fris is hovering beside me with my dressing gown. 'Thank you, Fris. Fetch my breakfast, will you?' I bounce up and down on the balls of my feet, impatient to escape the Citadel even if it's only for a couple of hours. 'And ask Letya to meet me at the stables. I think we might risk taking the horses out.'

After breakfast I put on my new riding habit – a green tunic and matching long split skirt of fine, light wool, woven in

31

Dacia – and send a message to have Henga, my horse, saddled. The way to the stables lies through the magnificent entrance hall of the Citadel. My cousin Odette is there, dressed in white velvet, her white-blonde tresses curling loosely down her back, talking to a young nobleman whose name I can't recall. As I walk past, she turns from the noble and calls out to me.

'Cousin, are you going to the Sanctuary? The Venerable Sisters are singing a fire service.' She sighs. 'Poor Nyssa.'

The Sisters sing for Lord Bastien, I guess. Nyssa's fiancé's Last Flight can't yet have been arranged, but the service will allow those who wish to light a candle for the homing of his soul. I hesitate. If Nyssa is there, I'm probably the last person she'll want to see.

'Perhaps later. I'm going riding now. But if you want to walk with me . . .'

Odette tucks her arm through mine and we cross the hall. Aron has told me about her nightmares: that Siegfried or Tallis or both of them will return. Will succeed, this time, in killing her. And although she is busy, having thrown herself into projects for improving the lot of the flightless in Farne, and says she's happy, I can't help noticing how pale she is. How thin she's grown. I interrupt her description of the new hospital building.

'Cousin, are you truly well? You'd tell me, wouldn't you? If there was something –'

'I'm well, Aderyn. Honestly. And I finally have a purpose. For all I'd convinced myself that I loved Siegfried, that I wanted to marry him, I never wanted to be a queen.' She squeezes my hand. 'You know why I used to spend so much time in flight? So that I wouldn't have to think about the future that was waiting for me. But now . . .' She shrugs. 'You don't need to worry about me. Did I tell you that we've engaged the first master for the new school?'

She turns the conversation. Soon after, we part; Odette has a meeting with some of the senior nobles about establishing a hospital for the flightless, and I continue to the stables alone. Letya is waiting for me. The grooms, warned of my presence, have shut the workhorses in their stalls; the presence of shapeshifters makes them skittish at best. Aron is the only other noble I know of who has trained a horse to carry him. But my Henga is dependable and comfortable with me. She tosses her head and snorts as I approach, trying to pull away from the groom who is holding her.

'Be easy, Henga. We're going now.' I put on a pair of gloves, take an apple from the store nearby and hold it out to her on the flat of my hand; I won't risk touching her or petting her as I'd like to. While Henga enjoys the apple, I use the mounting block to get astride her. Letya brings her horse, Vasta, alongside, and we take the road that leads from the back gates of the Citadel towards the fjord. Two Dark Guards, also on horseback, follow us at a distance. A necessary but disagreeable precaution.

As the noon sun strengthens, there are signs of a slight thaw. The ground is frozen hard, but water drips from the trees. Every so often there's a muffled thump as snow slides from roofs and branches, and closer to the fjord's edge the light breeze carries the voices of the flightless fishermen, inspecting damage to their boats after weeks of storms and inactivity. Someone is singing, though I can't catch the words. I turn to Letya to make some comment about the fishing boats in Merl harbour. But my friend seems distracted. She's staring, blank-eyed, at the back of Vasta's head, her bottom lip caught between her teeth.

'Letya? What's wrong?'

'Oh . . . nothing.' She shakes her ash-blonde hair back from her shoulders. 'I was just thinking that it's been too long since we've had a proper gallop. Not since before we left Merl last spring.'

She's right; we used to ride almost every other day, before I became queen. But even then we were exploring the countryside at no more than a trot. We've not raced since that day on the beach below Merl Castle, when a sand mole spooked Henga into throwing me. The same day I met Lucien. The same day I was nearly killed by the rock dragon from which, I later discovered, my father had obtained the venom that was used to poison the king.

Letya's brow is creased again; wherever she is in her head, it's not this rocky, snow-covered path.

'Please, tell me what's worrying you. Is it Nyssa? What she said last night? Or . . .' I hesitate. '. . . or Lucien?' Letya was angry when I told her what Lucien had said. Angry enough for me to order her not to follow him and start an argument.

'Both, perhaps.' She sighs. 'Grief and loss change people. So my grandma used to say.'

Ahead of us lies a clearing ringed by dark firs and holly trees. A fallen tree trunk bars the path and we stop talking to concentrate on jumping our horses over the obstacle. Restless from too long in the stables, Henga and Vasta sail over the trunk so high and fast it leaves me grinning. But Letya barely smiles.

I nudge a little harder.

'So . . . there's something more than Nyssa and Lucien making you miserable. And it can't simply be the lack of galloping.' I glance at Letya from the corner of my eye. She's slouching in her saddle. 'Has one of the Dark Guards broken your heart? If so, just tell me his name. And how you'd like him executed.'

That makes her laugh. She shakes her head, protesting. 'My heart is still in one piece.'

'What, then? If you don't tell me, you know I'll imagine worse.'

She twists in her saddle to look at me. 'Very well. Don't be cross, Aderyn, but I don't want to be your clerk any more.'

Not what I was expecting. I raise my eyebrows. 'Because of Lady Crump?'

'In part. I hate Lady Crump. But she's only saying what everyone else thinks.'

'That's not true . . .'

Now Letya gives me a sideways glance. 'Yes, it is. And maybe I shouldn't care, but I do. I'm tired of it. I'm tired of spending all day dealing with people who despise me. If there were more flightless at court in the same position –'

'But there are doctors, and guards, and scribes –'

Vasta snorts as Letya yanks too hard on the reins. My friend stops riding, so I do too. Our breath hangs, frozen, in the winter air. 'There are lots of doctors and guards, and the nobles are used to them. And they're happy enough for flightless to do the jobs they don't want to do. But a flightless has never been clerk to a queen.' She strokes Vasta's neck, calming her. 'I don't want to be the experiment, Aderyn. It's too hard.'

There's a holly tree in arm's reach. I pluck one of the frost-withered berries, trying to remember whether I'd asked Letya if she'd like to be my clerk, or simply told her that she was. 'I just thought . . . I wanted people to see that you're important to me. That you're more than a waiting woman.'

'I know, my friend, I know.' Letya chuckles. 'Neither of us is exactly doing what we dreamed of when we were younger. Do you remember?'

'Yes.' The recollection makes me smile. 'The first thing you told me was that you wanted to be a famous dressmaker. And I wanted to be an explorer.' Shut up at Merl after my mother's death, maps and books were my only way of seeing the world. I study Letya's face. 'Will it make you happy, if I find another clerk?'

She nods.

'Then that's what I'll do.'

We start riding again. Single file: the trees crowd close together, shutting out the sky, and I have to crouch low over Henga's neck. Then suddenly the path opens out, and I'm squinting at the crystalline brightness of the fjord spread before us. Wind-ruffled water glints in the sunshine. From here we're able to look out to the mouth of the fjord and the sea, avoiding the tower that thrusts out of the water nearer the Citadel. Letya and I were confined there by Siegfried; a night neither of us wants to remember. We come to a halt at the water's edge. The two Dark Guards wait further along the shore.

There are fishing boats tacking out to sea, the colours of their sails making a sort of rainbow against the snow-clad backdrop of the mountains. I breathe the crisp air deeply. 'It is beautiful here.'

'It is. Though not as beautiful as Atratys.'

I let my mind wander back to winters at Merl. Storms whipping up the water, turning salt spray into mist, until grey sea and grey sky were almost one. Quieter days, with pale sunshine painting the frost-covered gardens in silver. Nights when snowfall muted every sound in the castle ... Until Letya brings me back to the present.

'Fris told me something strange,' she remarks. 'About her cousin.'

Fris has been one of my maidservants for the last two years. I sent for her and some others from Merl after I became queen; Letya needed help, and I would rather have my own people around me than any spy that Lady Crump might try to foist on me. Fris is hardworking and pleasant, but she has a tendency towards epic stories involving her vast extended family.

'Is this the same cousin who had a friend who heard the unearthly shrieking on the beach? Or the cousin who keeps the inn at Occifin and swears her ale was cursed by river wraiths?'

'No, this is a different cousin. She lives in Lower Farne.'

'Oh.' At its worst, Lower Farne is unimaginable. The tightly packed courts in the area nearest the fjord are overcrowded slums full of disease, poverty and death. Aron and I have set in place programmes to improve the lot of the inhabitants, but progress is slow. 'Does she need help to move?'

'No, it's not that. She's pregnant. And the father ...' Letya trails off, chewing on her lower lip.

37

'Is he shirking his responsibilities? I can give her money. Send a doctor.'

'He's disappeared. But he told her, before he left, that he wasn't exactly flightless. And he wasn't noble either, not having the ability to transform. Claimed he was different.'

'Different how?' I raise an eyebrow. 'Let me guess: magical?'

'No. A human, but not like you or me. A different type of person.'

I shake my head. 'There is no other type of person. He probably made up a story to make himself seem more exciting, to get the girl into bed. He's not the first man to spin such a lie. He definitely won't be the last.'

'But Fris says he told her cousin all sorts of details.' A sudden gust of wind whips Letya's hair back from her shoulders. 'That he came from the Impenny Islands, up in northern Fenian, and that there are lots of other people like him, and that nobles can't burn them; they're immune to their touch somehow. And he claimed that they're great warriors, far stronger than ordinary men. And she says he had a symbol carved into the skin of his shoulder, a marking that he said all his people share.' There's an edge of longing in her voice. 'Think of that, Aderyn, an entire race of people with more-than-human strength. Maybe they could help you, if it's true. They could help you find Siegfried and Tallis. And since they can't fly, maybe they'd offer to help us flightless too – to stand up for us, and be on our side. And then maybe Convocation would finally do what you've been asking. And the nobles would start to see us as people like themselves.'

There's something about Fris's cousin's story that nags at

my memory, an echo of something I've read or been told. But it's impossible; the Impenny Islands aren't even inhabited. I open my mouth to remind Letya of this fact, to assert that, sad as her situation is, Fris's cousin is simply a victim of this man's guile, combined with her own wishful thinking.

And yet, if a story can give her, and Letya, and all the other flightless, some hope to cling to, why should I take that away? We offer them little enough. I promised Letya I'd change things for the flightless, and I haven't.

'Maybe there's something in it. I'll see what I can find out.' Another gust of wind brings spots of rain with it. Behind us, to the north, dark clouds are gathering. The massive granite bulk of the Silver Citadel, its towers and ramparts, glitter for another moment or two in the sunlight, before being plunged into shadow. I shiver, and turn my horse for home.

By the next morning I've drawn up a list of nobles – definitely not including Lady Crump's daughter – who might replace Letya as my clerk. But there will likely be no time today for interviews. The Skein is meeting to discuss the crisis in Celonia, and soon after breakfast I have to dress for the occasion. Wearing gloves to protect her skin from the searing power that emanates from mine, Fris helps me into a grey, brocaded satin gown, as sober as my mood. When she's finished fastening the row of buttons that curves down my back, and pinning up my hair, Letya sets the monarch's chain of state around my neck. The gold links, formed of intricately embossed, interlacing loops, are supposed to represent the curving necks of swans. She pins up my black hair and on my head she places a gold circlet set with red firestones, gems that symbolise power. The chain is heavy, weighing uncomfortably on my shoulders, and the circlet is slightly too tight; it was taken as a trophy from a previous ruling house, and wasn't made for me. But I'm determined to wear both of these ornaments. Today I need everyone to remember exactly who I am.

Aron and I meet in the audience chamber that lies between our apartments and make our way to the throne room. The hum of voices from the Skein – and only the Skein, since the gallery is closed – fades to silence as we enter and make our way to the dais at the top end of the room. Aron hands me up to the ornately carved and gilded throne before taking his seat next to me; the kings and queens of Solanum have always ruled in mated pairs, and there is easily enough space for the both of us. Below us are set chairs for the Protectors, and below them – made smaller, and lower – are those of the members of Convocation. This may be a council, but it is not a meeting of equals.

I nod to the four Protectors who are present. The twenty-eight members of Convocation, led by Lord Semper Corvax, take their seats after the Protectors. But there are two additional empty seats, and two strangers hovering nearby. One I recognise: Veron, my fencing partner from two days ago. The other is so like him – though taller and somewhat slenderer, and younger; the same age as Aron, I would guess – that he must be his brother. Veron is gaping at me and I remember that I never told him my name.

'Your Majesties, honoured Protectors, lord and ladies of Convocation.' Lord Corvax rises again. 'May I present Lord

Veron, the Gardien of Gyr, and his brother Lord Valentin, both of the House of Falco Gyr. Their lordships have lately escaped from Celonia.'

The Celonian nobles bow to Aron and me – dipping low, extending their arms backwards to imitate wings, the correct gesture on first meeting a reigning monarch – and glance uncertainly around the table as they move towards the empty chairs. They've barely settled in their seats before Patrus of Brithys stands up.

'I trust Lord Corvax is going to provide us all with an explanation as to why strangers have been invited to witness the Skein without prior permission from the Protectors?'

'They are here because I invited them, my lord of Brithys.' Aron crosses his legs and gazes coldly at Patrus, one eyebrow raised in a disdainful arch. 'There seems little point in discussing what happened in Celonia without hearing from those who were present, wouldn't you say?'

Patrus colours, splutters something unintelligible and subsides.

'If no one else has any comments –' I glance around the circle, hoping I seem as confident as Aron – 'I suggest we allow our guests to speak. I for one would like to know how this happened. Reports from Celonia before the Solstice contained no rumours of rebellion.'

Veron stands and nods at Aron. 'I must thank Your Majesty for this opportunity, and even more for providing us sanctuary, medicine, food. Some of my people have been less fortunate; they fled to countries that we thought were our friends, and have not been welcomed.'

41

'Your people?' Aron asks. 'Do you claim leadership?'

'I regret, yes.' Emotion thickens Veron's accent. 'I understand my cousin the king and his whole family have been executed. Even the children, drowned in the lake in front of the palace . . .' He turns his head away, but I can see the tendons standing out on his clenched hands. 'By right, the throne of Celonia – what is left of it – falls to me. I was away from court when the rebellion broke out, but my brother was present. If you will allow him to address you . . . ?'

Aron nods his agreement and Valentin gets to his feet.

'Well . . .' he clears his throat and runs a finger beneath the collar of his tunic, 'I believe it began with the famine. The harvest was poor this year, poorer even than the year before. There was a – a . . .' He turns to his brother and utters a word in Celonian.

'A blight?' Veron suggests.

'Yes. A blight on what you call waxen-wheat, the crop that the flightless rely on. It became known that some nobles, members of the royal family included, were hoarding waxen-wheat to sell it abroad. And then the winter came early, and the snows fell, and the price of firewood in the towns –'

'What's the point of this?' Thane of Fenian growls, slapping his hand on his thigh. 'The flightless always suffer. It is their lot. You are here to tell us about the revolt, and the suffering of those of noble blood.'

Valentin flushes. 'You misunderstand, my lord. The suffering of the flightless directly led to the suffering of the nobles. At least –' he glances at his brother – 'that is what I believe.' He pauses, but Veron does not respond. 'Still, I will tell you only the facts, if you wish. The people began to starve in great numbers. Of those who did not starve, many froze. There was so much death that the graveyards were choked, and bodies abandoned on the streets. Plague broke out. And among all this suffering, the king . . .' He laughs a little. 'The king went to his winter retreat, and from there issued an order for a tax to be raised upon the flightless.'

'A tax?' I ask. 'To provide relief to the poorest?'

'No. To pay for the marriage of his eldest son.'

The inhumanity and stupidity of such an act must be obvious even to the most bone-headed of the assembled nobles; as I glance around the Skein, most are staring at the floor.

'And what happened?' I prompt. 'I assume there were protests against this tax?'

'Much worse.' Valentin turns his head slightly, as if he is suddenly aware of the Dark Guards stationed at the edge of the room. 'The royal guards – flightless themselves, despite their privileged position – turned on a ruler who showed so little concern for their own kind. They began the uprising. And from there . . .' He takes a deep breath. 'What began as a quest for justice quickly turned into the pursuit of vengeance. The fury of the flightless majority, when it finally broke upon us, could not be moderated. There are rumours that agents from outside Celonia encouraged the worst excesses of the mob. But whether that is true or not, most of the country was quickly engulfed in bloodshed. We barely escaped with our lives.'

Valentin sits down.

I wonder whether this future lies in wait for our own kingdom, if we don't take steps to avert it.

Arden of Dacia is shaking his head. 'The flighted rule, the flightless are ruled.' He's quoting from the Decrees. 'That is the way it has always been, in Celonia not less than here. The flightless cower before our very touch. I don't understand how the Celonian nobles allowed this to happen.'

'Were you not listening, Lord Arden?' I snap. 'Yes, we can burn the flightless by the merest brush of a fingertip. But they outnumber us. If we lose the loyalty of those we employ as guards, if the flightless are willing to die for their freedom –'

'They are,' Valentin interrupts. 'We destroyed countless thousands of them, but always there were more, willing to take their place. At least –' he rubs a hand across his face – 'they were in Celonia. I cannot tell how it may be here.'

Silence falls. Some of the Skein are scowling, shifting uncomfortably in their seats; worrying about the flightless inhabitants of their own estates and Dominions perhaps?

Veron is watching me, leaning on the arm of his chair, his chin propped on one hand.

'Do you agree with your brother's assessment, Lord Veron?'

He shrugs slightly. 'My brother speaks as he finds. For myself, I agree that the recent treatment of the flightless was self-defeating, and unnecessarily cruel. But the violence that was meted out in return . . .'

I wait, but he offers no further clarification of his views.

'And these foreign agents you speak of, Lord Valentin,' Aron asks, 'the ones supposedly encouraging the mob's thirst for blood: where are they from?'

'Our information is slight. Most say Frianland, which I can believe.' Valentin's tone is contemptuous. I'm not surprised – there were rumours last year of a possible conflict between Frianland and Celonia – but before I can pose a question, he adds, 'Although, some spoke of interference from Solanum . . .'

'Impossible. We would never authorise such activities.' I speak firmly, but in truth I have no idea what Siegfried and Tallis, or those who secretly support them, might try to do. I press my fingertips to my temples, trying to massage away an incipient headache. Everything comes back to them. As long as they are at liberty, Aron and I do not command unwavering support, no matter what the nobles may say to our faces. But without complete support, it becomes harder and harder to catch them.

Siegfried and Tallis haunt me, even though I don't for a moment believe they are dead.

The royal secretary clears his throat. 'If I may, Your Majesties?' I nod my assent, and he continues, 'Just before the Skein met, I received a letter from the Ambassador of Frianland: the Crown Prince wishes to meet with us.'

'Does he?' Aron murmurs. 'What a coincidence.'

We all look at Veron.

He shrugs. 'The vultures begin to circle the carcass. They will suggest an alliance, a joint force to be sent on a mission of mercy to Celonia. That is what they will call it, at any rate.'

I shake my head. 'Solanum will not be party to an invasion. I will not have the kingdom drawn into a foreign war.' A glance around the table tells me that most of the Skein agree with me. Or appear to. But Thane of Fenian is gazing at the Celonians speculatively, as if he's weighing up exactly what might be won and lost from becoming involved in our neighbour's difficulties.

And if he's the first to consider the profitability of warfare, he won't be the last; Solanum held large tracts of Celonia several hundred years ago, and I know there are some among the nobility who still think we should make a push to get it back.

A shiver of pain across my brow makes me wince.

Aron must notice. He says something to Veron and Valentin in Celonian – a language that I now regret not learning – and inclines his head to them, before adding, 'The Skein will reconvene the day after tomorrow. You will be notified as to the hour.' That's it: no apology, no explanation. Despite my 'lessons' from Lady Crump, he carries his royalty so much better than I. A trick he learned from his father. Aron was born to be a king and has always wanted to rule. It seems unfair that the loss of his arm means he has to rely on me for his throne.

As I lead the way from the dais, we pass a plinth of dark stone, pitted with age. This is where the ancient Crown of Talons should sit: the royal symbol of Solanum, displayed in state. But the crown is gone, stolen or destroyed by Tallis, and the empty space gapes at me, sore as a missing tooth. A constant reminder that Aron and I weren't quick enough, the day we claimed the throne; that we lost what had been successfully preserved by the long line of rulers before us.

Perhaps it was only fitting that my own coronation, in consequence, was incomplete. An imitation of the real thing. I'm sure plenty of my nobles still think I'm merely a girl, playing at being queen.

I turn my face from the empty plinth and leave the throne room.

Aron and I meet again in the training room that afternoon. Although the exercise was his idea, he seems irritable. His bad temper affects his concentration and I'm able to win the first match quickly. He does better in our second bout, eventually twisting my sword out of my grasp and bringing the point of his own blade under my chin. But if anything, his mood gets worse. Letya tells me she heard him snapping at his valet for pinning the empty sleeve of his tunic incorrectly, and during dinner he swears at the servant who is there to assist him in cutting up his meat. When we're finally alone in my sitting room I stop him before he can bid me goodnight.

'Wait, Aron. Please – won't you tell me what's wrong?'

'What's wrong?' He hesitates for a moment before letting out a harsh laugh. 'Why, nothing. Apart from this.' He slaps the empty sleeve of his tunic with his remaining hand, hard enough to make me flinch.

'Is the pain worse again?' I pause, thinking about the Skein that morning. 'Or is this about me, that you should be king in your own right but I –'

'No!' He cuts me off and begins striding across the carpet. 'It's nothing to do with you. Or the crown. And it's utterly ridiculous, in any case.' Slowing, he sighs and pinches the bridge of his nose. 'And it's irrelevant, because I'm married. But if I wasn't – who would want me, Aderyn? Crippled, flightless as I am . . . What other noble would look at me?'

I don't know what to say. He presses the heel of his hand to one eye, then the other. 'Ignore me. I'm tired.'

'My dear Aron . . .' I brush my fingers against his. 'Don't

47

say such things. You may not be able to fly, but you're clever, and handsome, and you have more true nobility than men like Patrus and Thane could ever have. More nobility than they could even understand –'

A knock; the doors open and Fris hurries into the room. I step in front of Aron, shielding him.

'Fris, not now!'

'But, Your Majesty –' Her voice is high-pitched with fear.

'What's happened?'

'It's Letya. She's been accused of treason.' Fris gulps back tears. 'She's been arrested.'

Three

'Arrested?' I curse, as coarsely as I know how. 'Where is she?'

'I thought perhaps . . .' Fris falters, glancing at Aron. 'I thought perhaps Your Majesties would wish to summon someone –'

'No. I'll deal with this myself.' Aron and I follow Fris out of the royal apartments, confused servants and guards at our heels. She leads us to the south wing of the Citadel and upwards to the top floor, and I realise where we are going: to the Sun Chamber, the same place where Lucien was questioned by Siegfried.

The Dark Guards on duty outside snap to attention as we approach.

'Open the door.'

They obey instantly, and I sweep into the room.

Letya is standing between two more guards, her hands bound in front of her. Lord Pianet, our Master Secretary, is seated behind a table, papers spread in front of him, a clerk hovering at his shoulder. At our entrance, he gasps. Stands up so quickly the chair topples backwards behind him.

'Your Majesties –'

'What in the Firebird's name are you doing?' I turn on Letya's guards. 'Release her. Now!'

They jump to carry out my command and I hurry towards my friend. 'Are you hurt?'

'No. They tied the rope loose enough.' She scowls. 'Lucky for them.'

'Your Majesties.' Pianet has emerged from behind the table. 'Please let me explain.'

There's a heavy oak chair set in the centre of the opposite wall. I sit down and beckon Aron and Letya to stand next to me. Order everyone else apart from Lord Pianet to leave.

'Well?'

'Your Majesties . . .' He pauses, fingering the golden badge of office that hangs around his neck. 'I beg your pardons, if I have offended, and if I have overstepped my authority. My concern has been, as always, the safety and well-being of Your Majesties, and indeed the safety of –'

'Get on with it, Pianet,' Aron mutters, 'before I begin to regret appointing you.'

The older man nods. 'To be brief then, we've received evidence of a flightless plot against the throne, a plan to bring down the monarchy.'

'Linked to the revolution in Celonia?' I ask.

'Well . . .' He looks up at the ceiling. 'Not exactly. The evidence itself is somewhat out of date. Lady Yara Flit, a very minor landholder in Dacia, came into the possession of some letters when she sent her people to collect death dues from a flightless tenant.'

I've heard of the custom: noble landowners going to the houses of their deceased flightless tenants and seizing the most valuable items as some sort of 'compensation' for the loss of labour. My parents banned death dues in Atratys.

Pianet continues. 'She passed the letters on to one of my agents. But, although the letters may be old, they very clearly refer to someone –' he picks up a sheet of paper from the table and scans it – 'to someone who, and I quote, "is already close to the queen, who would never be suspected, who can strike when least expected."' Our Master Secretary shrugs. 'Mistress Letya seemed like the obvious person to question.'

'So you wait until late at night, and have guards drag my clerk up to this . . . this courtroom, so you may confront her with these ridiculous charges?' I grip the arms of the chair tightly, trying to keep some control over my temper. 'You insult me, my lord. Mistress Letya may be flightless, but she is also my friend. Her loyalty is beyond question. And I will not have her dishonoured in this way.'

Aron places his hand upon my shoulder; the weight of it steadies me.

Pianet, meanwhile, has dropped awkwardly onto one knee. 'I ask forgiveness, my queen. My only defence is that I believe there is a real risk to your life. We have heard other rumours, in the last few days, of an assassination attempt being planned. But clearly, my fear for your safety has made me –' he dips his head further – 'over-hasty.'

I glance at Letya. She is flushed, her lips clamped tightly together, staring at the floor. Aron leans down to whisper in my ear.

'Pianet is over-zealous. And clearly mistaken in this case. But I don't doubt his loyalty.'

I sigh. Loyalty is not so common that Aron and I can afford to squander it. 'Where was Mistress Letya arrested, Pianet?'

'In the servants' hall, I believe, Your Majesty.'

'Then tomorrow evening, at the same time, I would like you to go to the servants' hall and publicly apologise to her for this dreadful mistake. It seems only fair.'

Pianet nods. 'As you wish, Your Majesty. My only desire is to serve.'

I've heard those words before, from my steward Lancelin, from Lucien and others. Too early yet to know whether, in Pianet's mouth, they are anything more than words.

I force myself to speak more calmly. 'I cannot condone your actions on this occasion, Lord Pianet. Nevertheless, I thank you for your efforts to keep the king and me safe.' It's late. I stand and turn to Aron. 'Do you wish to add anything, husband?'

'Only that I would like to examine those letters for myself. Bring them to me in the morning, Pianet. You may leave us.'

And then Aron and Letya and I are alone. My friend takes a deep, shuddering breath and drags the back of her hand across her eyes.

'I'm so sorry, Letya . . .' The second time I've had to apologise to her in two days. 'Are you content with what I said to Pianet? Do you want me to –'

'The only thing I want you to do, Aderyn, is keep your promises. Pianet's honest enough, I don't doubt, but in his head, flightless aren't to be trusted. And unless things change in this country . . .' She catches her breath. 'I'm sorry, Your Majesty. It's been a long evening.'

'Of course.' I stretch my hand towards hers, but she's not wearing gloves; I daren't risk even the slightest touch. 'Go and rest. Fris will help me get ready for bed.'

She goes, and I'm about to follow her out of the room when Aron stops me.

'Aderyn – I think we should take Pianet's worries seriously. He's wrong about Letya, but that doesn't mean there isn't a threat to your life.'

I already know that Tallis and Siegfried will kill me if they can. And now it seems I'm at risk from a flightless assassin too. I shiver, and wrap my arms around my body. 'And?'

'And I want you to promise me something. That you'll stay inside the Citadel. No flying or riding until we find out more.'

Stay locked up in the Citadel? 'I can't promise that.'

'Why not? You've been confined because of the bad weather. How is this any different?'

'It just is. The weather is one thing, but to be denied any escape from this place because of a rumour, to have everyone think I'm afraid . . .' My body tenses. 'I won't be trapped here, Aron. I know you need to keep me alive to remain king, but –'

'That is not the point. I told you earlier: this is not about the crown.' Anger blazes briefly in my cousin's eyes. Then he sighs. 'I'm fond of you, Aderyn. You know I am.' He takes my hand. 'If you won't stay inside, will you at least be more careful?'

I nod.

He hesitates, and I think for a moment that he might put

his arm around me. But he doesn't. Just bows and ushers me out of the room.

I know Aron avoids touching me. I know it's because he doesn't want to make me uncomfortable, given the pretence of our marriage. But in truth, I'm hungry for human contact. And I can't tell him that, can't ask him to wrap his arm around my shoulders, because he might feel uncomfortable too. Not that we talk about it. We exist in a private dance with unspoken rules, in which the most that is permitted is the occasional touch of his fingers to mine, or the weight of my hand upon his arm.

I walk in silence back to my apartment, thinking about Lucien, and the warmth of his skin. Thinking about Letya's words. *Unless things change* . . . What was she going to say after that? That Solanum might go the same way as Celonia? That there might be a revolution? And if she's right – what then? What would the rebels do to her, the flightless companion of the queen they're trying to overthrow? Should I send her away from court to keep her safe?

I go to sleep with my questions unanswered.

For the next few days I fly or ride – both with Letya and with Aron – as usual. But I take more bodyguards with me, and I add a sword belt to my riding habit; whatever I might say to Aron, Pianet's talk of plots has made me nervous. Even transformation can't entirely suppress the knife edge of tension prickling against my spine. But no assassins appear. Pianet's agents don't uncover any further information. Gradually I begin to relax. Despite the snow still lying in drifts across the Citadel gardens, the slender silver-green tips of frost-feathers have begun to appear in the flower beds, and I'm thinking of summer and my mother's rose garden at Merl when I return from a flight one afternoon to find a note from Aron on my desk. I go to his rooms without waiting to change out of my robe. Aron is lounging on a window seat, one leg dangling, staring out at the fjord, but as I cross the room, he moves to make space next to him.

'What's happened?' I sit down and curl my legs underneath me.

'Oh – nothing urgent. I just wanted to let you know that we've had another letter from the Friant ambassador.' He pulls a face, as if he's bitten into an under-ripe plum. 'He wants to meet with us urgently to discuss the lamentable situation in Celonia, and to convey his master the Crown Prince's anxiety that something more should be done to help the Celonian nobles.'

'His anxiety – really?' Prince Eorman became the de facto ruler of Frianland some months back, when his father fell ill. There have been rumours of his plans to expand Frianland's sphere of influence, if not its actual borders, ever since. 'I'm tired of playing games. Let's meet with the ambassador. Let's ask him whether Eorman is sheltering Tallis and Siegfried within his borders.'

'Let's not.' Aron holds up his hand, palm out. 'Siegfried did spend some time at the Friant court, and Pianet still has agents there, trying to establish whether there has been more recent contact. If we make accusations without evidence, we might put them at risk.'

'I suppose so.' I take a deep breath, trying to get the better of my irritation at our continued inaction. 'If that's all, then –'

'There is something else. I've asked Lords Veron and Valentin to dine with us this evening. At the thirteenth hour.'

'But it's an Ember Day . . .' I can't conceal my disappointment. I thought I'd be free to spend the evening with Letya. 'They said yes?'

'An informal meal only, just for the four of us. We'll dine in the audience chamber.' Aron's eyes brighten. 'I didn't realise, but Valentin nearly lost an arm to injury. He's been telling me how it changed him, and how he became interested in building things . . .' He colours faintly. 'Besides, a friendship with them could be useful, if Veron is someday to rule Celonia.'

'At the moment, that seems unlikely. But it was a kind thought.'

Aron is tapping his fingers on his knee, as if he has something else on his mind, so I linger.

'What will you wear, do you think?'

His question makes me raise my eyebrows. 'I don't know. Something simple, I suppose. I'll ask Letya.' My curiosity is roused; Aron rarely pays much attention to clothes. 'Why?'

'I just wondered. I had my tailor make me a new tunic.' He jumps up and leads the way into his dressing room. Hanging from the front of a wardrobe is a green velvet tunic almost the exact colour of his eyes. Fine silver thread coils in an intricate design across the front of the tunic, but, unlike most clothes designed for evening wear, this one has sleeves, and the tailor has cleverly stitched the pattern so that it will not be interrupted when Aron's empty sleeve is pinned in place. 'What do you think?' Aron waits, gazing at me anxiously, but his concern can't be for my benefit. Is it Veron, or Valentin, he wishes to impress? 'Is it too much? I could wear something else. You know how some of the older nobles are about being too fine on an Ember Day . . .'

'You're the king, Aron. You should wear whatever you like.' The fabric of the tunic is soft beneath my fingers. 'This is beautifully made. The colour will suit you, and I wouldn't be surprised if you set a new fashion for wearing sleeves in the evening. You'll look very handsome.' The relief on his face makes me smile. I bump my shoulder gently against his. 'I'll see you this evening, my lord.'

'Aderyn . . .'

'What?'

'This question of whether we should help the Celonian nobles regain their lands . . .' Aron drops his gaze and rubs at a mended patch of carpet with the toe of his boot.

'I thought you agreed that we shouldn't risk having the kingdom drawn into a war?' I straighten up. 'You heard Lord Valentin's description of what's been going on in Celonia. What kind of message do you think it will send to our flightless population, if we help the Celonian nobles go back home so they can keep starving their own people to death?'

'I'm not saying we should do that, but I . . .' He sighs and looks back at me. 'If you want our nobles to agree to reform – real reform, not just allowing the servants to learn to read, or setting up a school – then perhaps it would be better to show more sympathy for the Celonians than you feel. Remember, you're a queen now.'

Has he been talking to Lady Crump? 'Watch my tongue, you mean?'

57

'I mean, be nice.' He smiles at me, half-joking, half-pleading. 'Please?'

My anger ebbs away. 'I'll try. For you.'

I spend what's left of the afternoon with Letya, reading or playing Battle. We've played together so often, and are so familiar with each other's moves, that the game takes an age. By the time I finally capture Letya's eagle, I have only half an hour to get changed. But Fris hurries me into a plain silk evening gown, the same pale green as a newly opened leaf of a beech tree, and Letya leaves my dark hair loose, merely catching up a few tresses in a single silver comb. I enter the audience chamber only a few moments late.

Our guests are already there, standing near the fireplace with Aron.

'Lord Veron, Lord Valentin, thank you for joining us.'

Both bow, and Veron adds, 'We are honoured to be here, Your Majesty.'

Aron leads us towards the table where servants have set out food. No meat, given the day, but mackerel and potato pie, poached mere-salmon with green sauce, salads, roasted vegetables in pastry, breads, cheeses and several different types of cake and pudding. While we eat, we talk on general subjects. Local foods, wines, the differences in landscape between Solanum and Celonia; I describe experiments by engineers in Fenian to create a mechanical pump that runs on steam. It all feels very . . . artificial. Veron, in particular, seems tense. Often he and I are silent while the others chat. When Aron stands to show Valentin some of the swords displayed on the walls around us, I turn to Veron.

'Please don't feel obliged to stay, if you're tired.' He doesn't answer me; he's gazing at his brother, his brows drawn together in a frown that deepens as Valentin laughs at some comment of Aron's. Veron's absorption gives me the chance to study him more closely. His hair is not pure silver, but mingled strands of silver and pale gold; his eyes are a dark blue that is almost violet. Handsome, without a doubt. But his disapproving expression as he watches his brother makes me wonder whether his temperament is less pleasant than his face. I speak more loudly. 'It may seem odd that Aron should have invited you to dine, given the day, but my husband wishes to be hospitable.'

Veron switches his attention to me. 'To be sure.' He shrugs. 'And we all have to eat.'

His tone is mocking. I want to remind him that he is a guest in my kingdom, an uninvited guest dependent on my goodwill for the clothes on his back and the bed he sleeps in; but, as Aron reminded me, I'm a queen. And I promised I would try. So I clamp my mouth shut, keeping my words behind my teeth, and turn my back on Veron, taking my glass of wine to the window. The moon is waning; an imperfect circle hangs in the sky beyond the Citadel, adding lustre to the mountaintops and the dark waters below.

I stood by another window like this, on another night, with Lucien. He still hasn't left the Citadel. My thoughts wander through the rooms and corridors, wondering where Lucien is, what he's doing, until Veron's voice recalls me to my surroundings.

'Forgive me, Your Majesty.' He's standing at my shoulder. 'My grief for my homeland makes me . . . unreasonable.'

I incline my head, not trusting my tongue.

'This evening has been pleasant,' he continues, 'but everything reminds me how different Celonia is – or was – from Solanum. The food. The wines. The fact that you can speak of your flightless as inventors. It is all so strange.' He gives a strained laugh. 'I did not even know, until yesterday, that you are the true ruler here, that the king rules in your right. In Celonia, we have – had – no women in power. No female Guardiens – what you call Protectors. No women holding office as your clerk does. Definitely no queen who is set above all the nobles of the realm.'

And I thought Solanum was resistant to change . . . Veron is watching me, waiting for a reply, so I force myself to say something more or less neutral. 'Just as well for me, then, that I was not born in Celonia.'

'But Celonian women are protected. They are not expected to fight, or weary themselves with politics.' He smiles slightly. 'No Celonian woman could handle a sword as you do. They rule within the domestic sphere, and they find that sufficient.'

I'm about to ask whether he has confirmed his assertion with any actual Celonian women, but he continues.

'Though it must be said, Celonia is a prisoner of its past in many ways.' His gaze drifts back to his brother, who has taken one of the swords from the wall and is weighing it in his hand, exclaiming at the workmanship. 'And sometimes our inheritance is more of a burden than a joy.'

Has he learned nothing from the rebellion that drove him from his home? Whatever Aron and Lady Crump think, I can't stand here and mutely agree with him.

'If your inheritance is a burden, I suggest you abandon it. What's the point of clinging to traditions that no longer serve you or your people?' He draws back a little, his eyes widening, but I push on. 'Your brother spoke of reforms to help the flightless. Why not pursue them? Why not improve the lives of nobles too, if you're able?'

Veron frowns and turns down the corners of his mouth, doubt and displeasure plain on his face. 'You may be right,' he murmurs eventually. 'At least partially so. But change is disruptive. Even if I sat on the throne of Celonia tomorrow, I would have to be convinced that the price was worth paying. I know the Celonian nobility. If I offer them a free but uncharted future, most will cling to the old ways, merely because they are *their* ways. The pain of the past is, at least, familiar.'

I think about the endlessly frustrating debates Aron and I have already had with the Protectors and Convocation about amending the Decrees. 'True.'

Veron sighs. 'As it is, I am not ruler of Celonia. I may never be. But my first duty is still to those who follow me. I'll do whatever I can to restore their home to them. Whatever it may cost me.' He drops his gaze, swirling the wine in his glass. 'Of course, you understand that. The cost of leadership. The sacrifices that may be demanded.' When he looks back up at me there's a hint of an invitation in his eyes. To talk, or something more?

I stiffen, wondering whether someone has told him about Lucien; has suggested that my marriage is a sham.

'What do you mean?'

My sharpness brings a flush to his cheeks.

'Only that you're young to be ruling a kingdom. It's a heavy responsibility.' He runs one hand through his hair, smiling ruefully. 'Dealing with an influx of displaced nobles, if nothing else. And I imagine the nobles of Solanum are fairly set in their ways . . .'

I don't need to be reminded of my youth and inexperience, particularly by someone whose own kingdom lies in tatters. 'I've already learned, Lord Veron, that it's dangerous to judge by appearances.' The remembrance of Siegfried – smiling, caressing, black-hearted Siegfried – makes my skin prickle. 'His Majesty and I are well equipped to deal with the issues facing our kingdom. And I consider our youth an advantage. We dare to dream of a different world, and we're not afraid to try to bring it about.' Too late I remember Lady Crump, and try to soften my tone. 'I'd advise you not to underestimate us.'

Veron turns away from me, his mouth drawn into a narrow line. I'm thankful that Valentin chooses that moment to replace the sword on the wall; he and Aron join us at the window.

'Such a sword, brother!' Valentin's eyes are bright. 'Such balance, and so light.' He turns to me. 'From your own dominion, I understand, Your Majesty.'

'Indeed. Do you enjoy fencing?'

'Not particularly.' He shoves his hands in his pockets, darting a glance at his brother. 'I'm fascinated by how they are made, though. By the making and building of things in general.'

'Atratys has some fine swordsmiths. Perhaps you would care to visit them?'

'I would be delighted.' He nods enthusiastically, but his smile soon fades and he looks to Veron again. I realise that although he is Aron's age, he has not half my cousin's self-assurance. 'If we have time before we must return to Celonia.'

The tall clock across the room begins to chime the hour.

'It's late,' Aron murmurs. 'I'm sure you both need to rest.' He tugs the nearest bell pull and servants immediately enter and begin to clear the table.

'Thank you for this evening.' Veron bows to Aron. 'I honour you for your hospitality. And as for our conversation, it was most enlightening.' He flashes me a smile. 'And enjoyable. I hope we may speak again, and fight again soon.'

During the days following our supper I notice Aron showing Valentin around the Citadel; apparently our guest is interested in the architecture and history of the building. It occurs to me that the Citadel's archivist and its master mason might be better qualified to give such a tour than the king. Still, Aron seems to be enjoying himself. But I don't see anything of Valentin's elder brother until I spot him in a corner of the long gallery, one rainy morning nearly a week after our dinner. Veron is arguing with another exile, a scrawny-necked older man with the red-ringed eyes and orange-tinted skin of a vulture. They break off as I pass. Both smile and bow, but the hostility in the older man's eyes makes me shiver.

I forget about our guests when I reach my rooms. Lord Pianet is waiting in my audience chamber with a flightless man, a lower-ranking merchant, I guess by his clothes. The man stands hunched, his gaze fixed on the carpet, his hands gripping his hat in front of his chest as Pianet explains why he is here: he saw the reward being offered in the marketplace at Hythe for information leading to the capture of Siegfried and Tallis, and has come with intelligence.

I sit down and try, unsuccessfully, to dampen the spark of excitement that quickens my pulse.

'Won't you take a seat?'

The man gives Pianet a scared look, but obeys, perching on the edge of the nearest chair.

'You live in Hythe, I take it?'

He swallows. 'Just outside, Your Majesty. Village of Beeching.'

'And you are . . . ?'

'Pater Craxby, Majesty. Agent to Master Fingale, amber and gem merchant.' He falls silent again.

Pianet huffs loudly. 'Just tell Her Majesty what you saw, Craxby.'

'Well . . .' Craxby shifts in his seat, getting as far away from Pianet as he is able, 'I was in Vauban-in-the-Marches, for the amber . . .' He glances up at me, and I nod to show my understanding. My father made sure I learned all the facts and figures about Atratys that I could. I know that amber is one of our principal exports, that most of the trade flows through Vauban, and that the city itself is divided: it straddles the border between Celonia and Frianland. 'Well,' Craxby continues, 'I was agreeing terms for the next shipment with the importers. Marron and Company; they're in Vauban North, in the street that runs alongside the docks. I was looking out of the window at the ships – the room's on the first floor, so it gives a good view – while they were checking the paperwork. I was watching the crowds; the city's busy, full of Celonian refugees from Vauban South. And then I saw him. Siegfried Redwing, I mean.' He glances at the cup of water a servant has placed on the table nearby.

'Please . . .' I gesture to the cup.

Craxby drains it. 'He was in the street right below me, talking to this big grey-haired fellow who was dressed like a sailor – his hair in a plait –' Craxby reaches up to his own hair as he speaks – 'and a canvas jacket. Both of them pointing towards the ships.'

'Are you sure it was him?'

'Yes, Majesty. The wind was blowing something fierce, you see. He had a cloak on, but I could see the rich clothes he had on beneath. And though the grey-haired man was wearing gloves, he wasn't. So I could tell he was a noble. And then his hood blew down, and as soon as I saw his face, I knew.' He turns to Pianet. 'I'd studied the drawings in the marketplace. All of us in Atratys want to help Her Majesty, being as she's one of us, so to speak.'

Pianet looks as if he doesn't quite know how to swallow this comment, so I smile warmly at Craxby. 'Thank you. How long ago was this?'

'Three weeks, Majesty. I couldn't get here faster. The wind was against us on the journey back to Hythe, and then the roads are that bad after the winter we've had. Not that they were good to begin with –' He breaks off, gasping a little.

I remember Lucien's comments last summer about Solanum's roads: they're not well maintained because only the flightless use them.

'You're right, Craxby. The roads are not good. I hope in time we'll be able to improve them. One more question: the ship they were pointing at – do you know where it was bound?'

'I wasn't exactly sure which ship it was. But I was standing opposite the Atratys dock . . .'

My own dominion – I press a hand to my chest, take a breath to slow my racing heart. 'Lord Pianet, please gather the royal council as soon as possible, and send a letter to Lord Lancelin at Merl Castle, telling him Atratys is under threat and to take what steps he thinks necessary.' Craxby has given me evidence that Siegfried and his half-sister have not simply disappeared. Enough evidence, surely, to convince my recalcitrant nobility that it's time to prepare the kingdom for war.

Craxby has risen from the chair and is holding out a small package. 'A . . . a present, Your Majesty, from my master. He wished me to assure you of his undying loyalty.'

I unwrap the soft leather to find a large, beautifully cut firestone. A princely gift; I suppose the flightless as well as the nobles are worried about the repercussions of the Celonian revolution. 'From Fenian, I assume?'

Craxby nods. 'The best ones are. I brought that down from Fenian last summer.'

As he bows and begins shuffling backwards, Fris's cousin resurfaces in my memory. 'Craxby, when you've been in Fenian, have you ever heard stories about some strange people who are neither flightless nor noble?' The man glances at Pianet, hesitant. 'You may speak freely.'

'Well . . .' he swallows hard, twisting the brim of his hat through his hands, 'I have *heard* such stories. But I'd never repeat them. Nor believe them, neither.' He stands straighter, as if back on solid ground. 'Folk up in north Fenian do talk a lot of nonsense.'

Craxby and Pianet leave. I pace my sitting room, listening

to the storm raging outside the windows, wondering where Siegfried is now.

The rain continues all day. By late afternoon, unable to settle, I walk down towards the cloistered garden on the sheltered western side of the Citadel. Odette, wearing a robe, meets me in the entrance hall. Her hair is dripping onto the marble floor.

'You've been out flying in this weather, cousin?'

'I've just returned from Lancorphys. I went to visit Nyssa, to see if I could persuade her to return to court.' Nyssa went to Zenaida Castle for her fiancé's Last Flight, and has been there ever since.

'No luck, I take it.'

My cousin shakes her head. 'But she gave me a lock of her hair –' she touches the pouch hanging around her neck – 'and asked me to make an offering for him, in the Sanctuary. Yesterday was to have been their wedding day.' Odette sniffs. 'It was so sad, when she spoke of it; how they'd looked forward to it, how a wedding day is supposed to be full of joy . . .' She trails off, clutching the pouch in her hand.

Is she thinking of the wedding planned between her and Siegfried, that so very nearly took place? Or about my wedding to Aron, which was conducted in secret and in haste, an arrangement made for the security of the kingdom and to save Lucien's life? About both perhaps. I rest my hand on her arm. 'I'm in need of some peace. I'll wait for you to get changed and go with you.'

Half an hour later, we enter the Sanctuary together. The sound of chanting floats through the high, domed space. Near the entrance stands a bronze dish supported on a tripod; I linger there, running my fingers through the dried rose petals the dish contains, releasing their sweetness into the air, waiting for my eyes to adjust. The Sanctuary is dim today, lit only by two oil lamps and what little daylight is filtering through the ring of high stained-glass windows. Eventually I'm able to make out the Venerable Sisters in the gallery above the main altar. Their ceremonial surcoats are edged with feathers; plucked, my nurse told me once, from their own transformed bodies. As the melody soars around us, Odette crosses the inlaid floor to her favourite side chapel and places the lock of Nyssa's hair on the small altar there. Some of the hair has already changed into feathers, as is the way with our kind. While my cousin makes her devotions, I wander over to where the book of Litanies for this month is open upon a stand. Today's Litany is at the top of the second page: *Consider too how the leaves of the oak tree may conceal both the acorn and the eagle, yielding life one day, and death the next.*

True enough, I suppose. And if it's true of oak trees, it's even more true of people. I think back on my initial friendship with Siegfried, and the ease with which he was able to conceal his real intentions.

The last phrase of the Responsories echoes around the Sanctuary and the sisters file out of the gallery. Odette joins me.

'What are you thinking about, Aderyn?'

'Truth. Lies. How difficult it is sometimes to tell them apart.' I gesture up at the huge mosaic that forms the ceiling of the Sanctuary's central space. The image is of the Creator in the shape of the Firebird, flying out of the centre of a star. 'Even here – do you believe the literal truth of everything we're taught?'

Odette follows my gaze, staring upwards, her lips pursed. 'If you're asking me whether I believe that the land was actually formed from the Firebird's feathers, and the sea from her blood, then no. But I believe something – or someone – might exist, who is wiser and kinder than us. At least, I hope so.'

'As do I.' I take one last glance at the Litanies. 'Did you know that Siegfried visited the Friant court? Aron mentioned it.'

'Siegfried?' Her hand drifts up to her neck. 'Lots of nobles spend time abroad.'

'A man came to see me this morning. A merchant from Atratys. He saw Siegfried in Vauban three weeks ago. The Creator only knows where Siegfried is now.' I pause, unwilling to share with Odette my fear that Siegfried is already back in Solanum. 'But Tallis – it has to be the Friants who are hiding her. Perhaps I should go there myself. Lure her out.' Odette starts to speak, but I don't wait to hear her objections. 'Or maybe . . . maybe we should invite Prince Eorman here, and then –' I shrug – 'keep him. Hold him hostage until he gives Tallis up.'

'Aderyn, you can't . . .'

'Why not? Secure the kingdom, bring the nobility in line behind me, get them to change the Decrees and then . . .' Freedom. To go home to Atratys, if I choose. To be with Lucien.

Footsteps ring on the marble floor. There's a large man close behind us, a noble by his clothes, though I don't recognise him. He bows. Hesitates, as though he's not sure whether to go past me to the altar or speak to me.

But I'm too anxious to discuss my plan with Aron to wait. I nod to the man and move towards the doors. 'Odette, will you –'

Her scream cuts across my words.

'A knife, Aderyn! He has a –'

69

Four

The blade flashes down and slices into my upflung arm; hot tendrils of pain bloom across my skin. The man deals Odette a blow that knocks her sideways as he raises the knife again, grabs hold of my gown and drags me closer. I twist away, barely aware of Odette's screams, trying to yank the fabric from his grasp. The shift of my weight knocks him off balance and I scramble backwards. But he recovers. Keeps coming. Keeps slashing the knife through the air until my shoulder blades slam into the wall. He crushes me against the stone and forces my chin up with the side of his blade. I try to push him away, but he's too heavy – I get no leverage.

He holds a small vial in front of my face. Flips up the stopper with his thumb and presses it to my mouth.

'Drink it. Or die.'

I clamp my lips shut, moaning my defiance. There are shouts in the distance and the sound of running feet. The bell of the Citadel clangs in alarm.

The man leans harder against my injured arm. The agony

of it blurs my vision and snatches what little breath I have left; if it goes on much longer, I'll have to open my mouth, I'll have to scream –

'Drink it, damn you, or I'll –' He looks around, swears, brings the knife up above his shoulder –

Hands seize him, pulling him away from me, and I can breathe again. But I can't move. I just stand there, watching as the Dark Guards force the stranger to his knees and pin him there, one axe blade against his throat, another at the nape of his neck. His hands are swiftly manacled behind his back.

Two of the Venerable Sisters, robes flapping, hurry towards me. 'Your Majesty, are you hurt?

I swallow. 'My arm. That's all.' I cradle the injured limb, clutching my upper arm and breathing hard, gritting my teeth against the pain. 'Where's the princess?'

'Safe, Your Majesty.' It's Hemeth, Aron's favourite captain. 'After she alerted us, she went to find the king, but I sent two guards with her.' He jerks his head at the kneeling noble. 'Orders?'

I gaze at my would-be assassin. Whatever his rank, he assaulted the crown. According to the Decrees, I could have him executed here and now, without trial. One word, and the two axes currently keeping him silent would lop off his head. I could order the guards to hang him in the arena and leave his body for the true crows to peck at. But I would not defile the Sanctuary. Nor would I willingly disregard the process of law.

Besides, I want to know who he is, and why he tried to kill me.

'Take him to the dungeons. Question him.' A door slams somewhere in the Sanctuary. 'Search the Citadel – all of it.

Make sure there is no one within our walls who does not have good reason to be here. And take that vial with you.' The small bottle the man had is lying on its side nearby. Some of the liquid is pooled on the floor around it, but it doesn't look empty. 'If we have an alchemist in the Citadel, or in Farne, see if someone can work out what it is.' I fear that I already know the answer.

Hemeth nods, orders the guards to lead the prisoner away and picks up the vial between gloved finger and thumb. One of the sisters comes closer. 'I've sent Sister Geanne to make sure the doctors are summoned, Your Majesty, but if you'll allow me . . .' She takes my arm carefully in her hands, and I realise I'm bleeding heavily. The dark blue of my sleeve is black with blood; it wells up through my fingers as I grip my arm. Drips onto the polished stone floor. The sister lifts the stole from her neck, carefully prises my fingers away, and ties the stole tightly around the wound. 'Now, lean on me, and we'll get you back to your apartments.'

I want to refuse her help, but a wave of dizziness makes me change my mind; I'm relieved when she takes some of my weight, and guides my steps out of the Sanctuary, Hemeth hovering next to us like an anxious parent.

Aron meets us in the courtyard, sword drawn, more guards and other members of our court at his heels.

'Aderyn! Where is he?'

'On his way to the dungeon. I've asked . . .' My head swims and I stumble. Beside me, the sister staggers as I pull her off-balance.

Aron swears, trying to steady me with his elbow without

losing his grip on his sword. 'Damn it! I can't . . . Will somebody not help me?'

Servants bearing a litter are already pushing their way through the crowd, but before they can reach us, Lucien steps forward.

Aron swears again, under his breath.

I get as far as forming the word *no*. Lucien gathers me into his arms and begins striding towards the stairs.

'Relax, Your Majesty. I've got you.'

There's no resisting it; I let my eyes close and allow my head to rest against his shoulder. Allow my mind to wander, away from the attack just made against me, to the other times he's held me in his arms like this. The first, after he rescued me from the rock dragon, on the beach at Merl. The second, when he was carrying me to his bed. I suppose I giggle, because he murmurs, 'What's funny?'

I don't know, and Lucien does not press me for an answer.

Before long we reach the receiving room. Odette and Letya are there, waiting with servants and doctors. Lucien carries me through into the audience chamber.

'Where –'

'Here. The . . . the sofa.' The thought of him taking me into my bedroom makes me want to laugh some more, and I wonder whether I'm becoming hysterical. He places me gently on the sofa. As the doctors swarm around me and begin to cut away my sleeve to get at the wound, I hear Odette ordering everyone to leave.

Luckily, despite my blood loss, the cut is clean and shallow. The doctors wash the wound and apply an aromatic ointment that numbs it a little. Still, I have to bite on a leather strap and cling to Odette as they stitch the cut closed. By the time it's over, and the doctors have gone, and I'm lying on the sofa in my dressing gown, I feel as if I could sleep for a month. Letya has gone to rest; she is planning to sit up with me during the night, in case I develop a fever. Odette is pouring us both a cup of chocolate as Aron comes in.

'How was it?' His face, scrunched into a sympathetic grimace, suggests he was hovering outside the door as the doctors worked.

'I've had worse.' It's true. I don't remember the particular shade of pain inflicted by the hawks that attacked my mother and me. Or the exact sensation of the needle over the days it took to sew my shredded skin together. But I recall the horror of my long recovery well enough. The sickening dread every time a doctor came near me. The way my hands would cramp after every examination because I was gripping the bedlinen below me so tightly.

Aron half-smiles and squeezes my uninjured shoulder. 'I'm sorry.'

'Don't be. It wasn't your fault.'

He drops his gaze. 'But what kind of a king am I, if I can't prevent my queen almost being assassinated in the very heart of the Citadel?'

'You're a good king,' Odette replies.

'She's right.' I smile at him. 'I always said you would be.'

'Others won't agree though. They'll say it's just another example of us being too weak to protect Solanum.' He sighs. 'You know they will.'

'That's why we have to act.' I wriggle against the silk cushions behind me, trying to find a more comfortable position. 'We know Siegfried was in Vauban. He might not be there now, but I'm sure Tallis is still in Frianland. Let's invite the Crown Prince here and compel him to give her up.'

As Odette murmurs my name in a tone of faint despair, Aron frowns. 'Compel?'

'Put him under house arrest.' He's already shaking his head, so I add, 'Despite Lord Pianet's panic about a flightless plot, the man who attacked me is a noble. We have to force Siegfried and Tallis into the open, Aron. We can't just sit here, waiting for someone to succeed in killing one of us –' I break off, flinching, as my attempt to sit upright sends pain spiralling up my arm.

'Right now,' Odette says, 'you're not going anywhere.' She pushes me back onto the sofa.

Aron nods agreement. 'Let's see first what information can be extracted from that creature they just took to the dungeons.' He uncrosses his long legs and stands. 'In the meantime, rest. Heal. I promise to tell you as soon as there's anything to tell. Would you like me to –' He's interrupted by a knock at the door and huffs in irritation. 'What now?'

The blue-robed servant bows. 'Lord Rookwood requests a brief audience, Your Majesties.' I can see Lucien lurking in the receiving room behind.

'Really, Rookwood?' Aron asks. 'You think this is the time for a social call?'

The servant hesitates until Aron flings up his arm. 'Oh, very well. Let him in.'

Lucien nods to Aron, but he talks to me. 'I'm sorry, I wouldn't have disturbed you if you'd been asleep. But I couldn't rest, just hearing it from the servants.' His dark eyes scan my face. 'I had to see for myself that you weren't seriously hurt, Aderyn.'

'Aderyn?' Aron snaps. 'You are my wife's subject, Rookwood, a fact you would do well to remember.' There's an unbecoming sneer twisting his mouth, reminding me of how he used to look at Lucien when we first arrived at the Citadel. 'You will address the queen as *Your Majesty* from now on. Do I make myself clear?'

'Abundantly so.' Lucien crosses his arms, reddening. '*Your Majesty*.'

'Why, you –' Aron's hand goes to his sword hilt as Odette jumps up and puts her own hand on his arm.

'Brother . . .'

Odette's tone is gentle, whereas I'd happily scream at both my husband and my former lover – I'm too tired to want to deal with this. But I understand how Aron must be feeling. To have had Lucien do what he could not, and in front of so many people. To be always aware that if I die – or if I lose my ability to fly, or if our marriage is dissolved – that he will be once more a mere flightless prince. A person of no consequence. An irrelevance.

'It's just a flesh wound, Lord Rookwood; my arm should heal in a few days. I am very tired, however. I thank you for your concern, and for your assistance earlier today.'

My formal tone has the effect I intended. Lucien lurches backwards, staring at me, executes a shaky bow and walks out, without another word.

The impulse to run after him is almost too strong to resist. Tears spring into my eyes. I can't look at my cousins.

'I want to go to sleep.'

Aron goes to summon Fris as Odette helps me up from the sofa.

'Oh, Aderyn . . .' She doesn't say any more, but the compassion in her voice is enough to make me cry.

I'm soon tucked up in bed. Aron comes into the bedroom, pats my hand and murmurs in my ear, 'I'm sorry I lost my temper. But thank you, my dear. What you said to Rookwood . . . I know what it must have cost you.'

I'm half asleep, so I don't reply. My last waking thought is of Lucien: whether I should send him away from court. I've never intended to hurt him. Yet all we seem to do now is plant barbs in each other's flesh.

The doctors are right. When the dressing on my arm is finally removed a few days later, the skin around the cut is pink and puckered, but not inflamed. I'm given a different type of ointment, to speed the healing, instructed not to transform for another week and advised not to over-tax my strength with work. But otherwise, I'm told, I have returned to perfect health. At least physically. The salves and bandages haven't helped with the hours of wakefulness, when I've been straining my ears to catch the slightest sound of movement nearby. Wakefulness that only ends when I finally fall, exhausted, into a deep, nightmare-ridden sleep. Letya and Fris have hardly been able to wake me some mornings. Still, despite Fris's timidly offered advice, despite Letya's more robust comments – delivered between sneezes, since she seems to be coming down with a cold – I don't say anything to my doctors. Instead, as soon as the doctors have left, I walk up to join the meeting in the council chamber.

Aron hurries forward. 'My lady, you need not be here – surely you should be resting.'

'The doctors have given me permission. And I want to be here; are you not planning to interview my would-be assassin today?'

He nods. 'The guards are fetching him now.' He bends closer to murmur in my ear, 'Are you sure, Aderyn? That you wish to see him?'

'I'm sure.' I walk to the windows at the far end of the room. Before I've done more than take in the view of the landing platform, jutting out into the fjord, the doors open to admit the prisoner. He's accompanied by four Dark Guards and his wrists are bound by heavy iron manacles, chained to an iron collar fastened round his neck. We gather in a loose semicircle as he is brought to stand before us.

The man is no longer wearing the rich clothes he had on in the Sanctuary. Instead he's in a robe. The dark fabric is stained with darker spots of fresh blood, from where the metal collar is chafing his neck. His lank hair is the colour of ash, his skin a darker grey; some branch of a corvid family, I would guess. He scowls at us.

'Who are you?'

'Tierce, Lord Hood.'

'From Celonia?'

The commander of the Dark Guards consults a scroll handed

to him by the council scribe. 'No, one of our own, Your Majesty. A junior branch of the House of Cornix Liath. He holds a small estate in the west of Olorys.'

'How did you gain entrance to the Citadel, Lord Hood?'

'It wasn't difficult.' His voice is rough, harsh as a crow's caw. 'I gave my credentials to the guest master and told him I had a petition to present to Your Majesties. He gave me a room.'

Lord Pianet clears his throat. 'The guest master followed correct protocol and informed me of Hood's arrival. But we had no reason to be suspicious. I have already suggested to Lady Finch –' he gestures to the Warden of the Citadel –'that our procedures may need to be re-examined.'

'And why, Lord Hood, did you want to kill me?'

He shrugs, shifting the iron collar against his neck despite the pain it must cause him. 'Two reasons. First, no good will come to Olorys from your monarchy. We've no Protector, and we all know you're going to annexe Olorys to the crown.'

'You're wrong. What is your second reason?'

'I like to be on the winning side, and Tallis will win. Sooner or later.' He gestures, as well as he is able, to Lady Yaffle, the most senior member of Convocation for Olorys. 'You ask her. She must know about the disappearances. People of my rank, small landholders from the empty marshes of Olorys – I've lost count of how many have vanished in the last two months. No one speaks of it, but we all know the truth. I volunteered, but Lord Siegfried has the means to bend others to his will. And Tallis . . . I've heard what she does to those who cross her. Spilling noble blood to her is of no more account than laying poison for rats. She wants the crown, and she doesn't care what she has to do to get it.'

'May the wings of the Firebird defend us,' Verginie of Lancorphys murmurs.

Hood turns his bloodshot gaze on her. 'Save your prayers. I won't be the last Siegfried and Tallis send against you.'

Aron turns to the commander of the Dark Guards. 'Who did Hood have dealings with?'

'He gave us a name –' the commander spreads his hands wide – 'but the woman turned out to be a go-between, as is the man who instructed her. We've not yet caught anyone with any real information.' He points to one of the guards, who opens his gauntleted hand to reveal the small vial Hood was carrying. 'We still don't know what this is. We've not been able to force it out of him either.'

I step closer to Hood. 'It's Siegfried's potion, isn't it? The one he was giving me in small amounts to make me transform. The one he was planning to give to Princess Odette, to turn her into a swan forever.'

Behind me, one of my councillors gasps. Another swears. But Hood only grins. 'If you say so.' His stinking breath makes my stomach heave.

Aron sighs. 'Well, if Lord Hood won't cooperate, I suggest we make him drink the potion so we can see what effect it has.'

Hood's grey skin takes on a waxy pallor. Still, he spits at Aron, 'I'll drink it. Better that than die at your hands, you crippled nothing.'

Aron's mouth tightens, but he merely says, 'As you wish. I'm not a cruel man, however.' He nods to the guards. 'Unchain him first. And undo the clasp of his robe.'

They obey, three drawing their axes while one removes the collar and manacles. Hood is breathing hard, but the guard with the vial doesn't hesitate. He flips up the bottle's hinged lid, holds it to Hood's lips and tips it into his mouth before backing quickly away.

The room is silent. Waiting.

Nothing happens. Hood begins to laugh, but the laugh changes into a panicked gasping as he clutches at his throat. Or tries to. His shoulders twist, and the skin on his arms begins to stretch and tear, and he throws his head back and screams as feathers push through his flesh and his legs buckle and his skull elongates –

I turn away, closing my eyes as bile rises, sour in my mouth. His screams go on and on, until they become the shrieks of a giant rook. When I look again, the man that was standing there is entirely gone.

Several of my councillors are murmuring prayers. Verginie holds her hands, crossed at the wrist, in front of her face: an ancient gesture to ward off evil. The commander of the Dark Guards has his hand to his mouth, as though he's about to vomit.

Lord Corvax is the first to speak. 'That did not look . . . normal.'

He's right. It was too slow. Too agonisingly violent.

Hood flaps his wings and pecks at the discarded robe.

Aron gestures to the flightless guards waiting at the edges of the room and they gradually move closer, until they are within a couple of wingspans of the huge bird. This close to a transformed noble, the guards should be writhing on the floor in agony. Aron frowns. 'Do you feel nothing?'

The nearest shakes his head. 'No, Majesty. Nothing.'

Pianet approaches the huge rook. Hood squawks and flaps his wings again, trying to get further away.

Pianet shakes his head. 'I think . . . I think he's gone. I can't sense any thoughts, or personality. Just confusion. And fear.'

One by one we close our eyes, feeling with our minds. While in flight, we can communicate with each other without speech. A noble in human form can still sense the thoughts of a noble who is transformed. But now, with Hood, there is nothing. No semblance of humanity.

His power to shift his shape has been stripped from him, it seems. So has his mind.

'Monstrous,' someone says. There are murmurs of agreement. I shudder as I realise exactly what my fate would have been if Hood had succeeded.

Abruptly, the bird begins to caw and flap its wings, twisting its head from side to side as if seeking a way out, snapping its beak at the guards nearby.

'Open the balcony doors!' Aron has to shout over the shrieks of the rook, but the guards hear him; another moment, and the huge bird is flapping across the fjord and out towards the sea.

I turn to the nearest servant. 'Fetch us some wine, please. And a doctor.' One of the guards is bleeding from a scratch inflicted by Hood's beak. I pause, waiting for my heart rate to slow. On the faces of my councillors I see the same mixture of shock and horror that is churning up my own stomach. Aron slips his hand into mine.

'Were we right to let him go?' I ask. 'What if he attacks someone?'

'True rooks feed on carrion. I suspect Hood will not find enough to keep him alive for long.'

Lady Yaffle, the Oloryan representative, is hovering nearby. I turn on her. 'How many, Lady Yaffle?'

Her eyes widen. 'Your Majesty?'

'Hood said you would know about the abductions, so I'm asking you. How many of my subjects have been seized by Tallis? How many have had their humanity torn away from them by Siegfried's potion?'

The woman's green-tinged skin flushes darker beneath my scrutiny as the other councillors gather closer, waiting for her answer. 'He . . . He must have been lying. I'm not aware of any abductions.'

'He had no reason to lie.' Aron's voice is cold. 'So shall we ask why?' He looks around at the council. 'Why one who claims to represent the Dominion of Olorys, who is lobbying to be awarded the title of Protector, is not aware of what is happening within that dominion? Unless, Lady Yaffle, you merely chose not to share the information . . .'

'Well . . .' Yaffle twists her hands together. 'The truth is, Your Majesty, I haven't been back to Olorys since the snowstorms. And what with the Solstice celebrations, and the demands of my own estates, I can hardly be expected to . . .'

Aron tuts, takes the pen out of the fingers of the scribe who is hovering nearby, and makes a note in the book the man holds.

The noblewoman bobs her head forward as she gulps. 'That is to say, I will meet with the other members for Olorys and begin investigations immediately, Your Majesties. I can only apologise for the lack of oversight . . .'

'I'd like daily reports on your progress.' Aron makes another note in the book, before adding, 'Starting this afternoon.'

Lady Yaffle dissolves into a morass of assurances and half-finished sentences, the servant returns with wine, and we soon resume the council meeting, beginning another circuit of the room. I'm certain, after the sighting of Siegfried and the attack by Hood, that my councillors must agree to begin preparing Solanum for war. But my certainty is misplaced. They are still driven by doubts, worries about the cost, assertions that Siegfried and Tallis don't have the power to attack an entire kingdom. Someone suggests that raising the congregations – the combined forces of flightless and nobles that comprise our army – when we have no obvious target, will make us look weak and paranoid. And then Patrus of Brithys bows to Aron and says, in his most unctuous voice, 'Of course, one might have expected such hasty and ill-timed action from the late king, your father. But despite your youth, Your Majesty has often displayed a wisdom that King Albaric sadly lacked.'

I wait for Aron to explode with wrath. Or to cut Patrus down to size with one of his acidic comments. But instead he opens his mouth, shuts it again, changes colour and finally looks at me.

'Perhaps it would be as well to be cautious, my queen. To conceal our preparations for as long as possible, while we gather more evidence. Let us agree to delay raising an army for now.'

Can Aron not recognise that Patrus is manipulating him?

Patrus coughs, covering his mouth with his hand, but I'm sure he's smirking. I want to scream at him, to order him out of the room. And perhaps I should. Perhaps I should defy my councillors and order an army to be raised in the teeth of their objections.

But my uncle Albaric spent enough time screaming at people. He still ended up dead.

'Lord Pianet.' The steadiness of my voice surprises me. 'Please write to Prince Eorman of Frianland and invite him to visit us.' I glance at Aron, daring him to interfere.

Pianet's eyes widen, but he nods. 'I will see to it, Your Majesty. Are you considering entering into an alliance with Frianland to invade Celonia?'

'No. I meant what I said at the Skein. We will continue to give aid to the Celonian nobles as we are doing, but that is all.' I look around the circle of councillors. 'I would suggest that we attempt to broker a peace treaty between Celonia's nobility and her flightless, but they've no reason to listen to us. Perhaps, if we'd implemented some of the reforms the king and I have proposed with regard to the flightless in Solanum, we might be able to speak to them with some authority. But, as it is . . .'

Lord Corvax and the other members of Convocation at least have the decency to look embarrassed.

'That is enough for today.'

Dismissed, the guards and councillors file out of the room. I notice Valentin hovering on the other side of the door. Waiting for Aron presumably. Before I can leave, Aron catches hold of my hand. 'Aderyn . . .'

'You should have supported me, husband.' I jerk my fingers from his grasp. 'Valentin said he likes building things. Perhaps

85

he can build you a spine.' I stride out of the council chamber without waiting to see his reaction.

Letya's cold gets worse. For the next few days she's confined to bed, waited on by one of the housemaids, while Fris and I manage as well as we can without her. I write again to Lancelin at Merl asking him to strengthen the castle's defences, and I order Lord Pianet to set the clerks to study the Decrees; the ancient laws of Solanum have frustrated enough of my plans, but I'm hoping that buried somewhere in their detail will be something that allows the monarchs to bypass the Skein and summon the congregations without its agreement. I also ask him to set one of his agents to investigate Patrus of Brithys. I've learned first-hand what a duplicitous bastard Patrus is, intent on securing power through any means: he tried to abduct me to force me to marry him, and there are the persistent rumours that he murdered his other wives. I'm sure he's working against our monarchy; I just need proof.

Winter still holds the kingdom in its grip, but at least there's no more snow. The nights are full of stars and frost, the days bright and clear, but with air so cold it claws at one's throat. The sunshine doesn't improve my mood. I can't transform due to my injured arm, and riding alone – I'm not speaking to Aron – is not particularly enjoyable. I go once to the training room but leave when I see Aron there, fencing – and laughing – with Valentin. Instead I make my way to the Citadel's walled gardens. As I walk I brood on Tallis, and Hood's description of her, until I almost expect to see her emerge from behind the leafless trees. But instead, I find Veron. He's crouched at the edge of a flower bed, examining the delicate silver fronds of a frostfeather flower. I turn quickly onto a different path.

But I suppose he must see me; he calls out to me soon after. 'Your Majesty . . .'

'My Lord Veron.' I wait for him to catch up with me, and the two Dark Guards who are trailing after me drop further back. 'I didn't mean to interrupt you.'

'You didn't. And I would enjoy some company. My thoughts . . .' He shrugs. 'They are not good companions.'

We continue wandering about the gardens for a while. He asks me the names of various plants, and I answer him as far as I am able. Eventually I feel obliged to invite him to accompany me to the royal apartments for some refreshment. The servants bring cakes and hot drinks; once they've left, I return to the subject we'd been discussing at Aron's dinner.

'So, my lord, now you've been in Solanum a little longer, do you still find it so different to Celonia?'

'Perhaps it is not as strange as I thought. I'm growing used to your customs, and your food no longer gives me the, um . . .' He presses a hand to his stomach.

'Stomach ache? Cramps?'

'Yes, that.' For the first time he laughs, and I notice the way dimples appear in his cheeks. 'And I see you Solanish are not so different from us.'

'But surely you've encountered nobles from Solanum before?' I remember Siegfried and his travels. 'Did you never visit here when you were younger?'

'Oh, well – I met the Solanish ambassador once, I believe.' He pauses for a moment and pours himself another cup of chocolate. 'I've been thinking about what you said – about improving things. Your mother, she was a Protector, was she not? And tried to improve many things, from what I've been told.'

The change of subject throws me, but I'm pleased by his interest. I begin to describe some of the improvements my mother made in Atratys. Schools and hospitals for the flightless. Charitable provision for those fallen on hard times. Local laws to protect those working in our growing tin-mining industry. He leads me on to describe more of the changes Aron and I want to introduce across the kingdom.

I stop talking when I realise I'm on the point of revealing my wish for a flightless assembly, a plan that no one apart from Aron yet knows of. Veron prompts me to continue, but I shake my head.

'No, I'm sure I'm boring you.' The Celonian noble seems decent enough, but I've made the mistake before of putting my trust in people who didn't deserve it. 'Forgive me.'

'There's nothing to forgive. You love your kingdom, and especially your Atratys. Your enthusiasm is –' he opens his hands, as if searching the air for the right word – 'charming.' He inclines his head. 'I honour you for it.' The smile fades from his eyes. 'I love Celonia in the same way. There is nothing I wouldn't do for the sake of my country. I hope you understand.'

I don't immediately reply; I'm not entirely sure *what* he wants me to understand. In any event, I won't be led into making a promise that may end up costing the lives of my subjects. But I have to say something. 'I trust you will be able to return to your home. But you and your people are welcome here, my lord, whether you stay for months, for years, or forever.'

He holds my gaze – was he hoping for more? – but then leans back in his chair and smiles again. 'My brother will be glad to hear that. I'm not convinced that I will be able to reclaim him for Celonia, even if I am able to reclaim some of Celonia from my flightless compatriots.'

'But surely, if you asked him to return with you, to help you rebuild –'

'Oh, he will join me, of course. Though I'm not sure that his heart will be in it.' He gives me that searching glance again, before standing. 'I'll trespass on your time no longer – in my flight from Celonia I regret that I neglected to bring any formal evening attire, so I must go to the tailor if I'm not to disgrace myself at the ball next week. I understand it is an important event?'

'Oh. Yes, it's held each year to celebrate the end of the Wars of the Raptors.' I'd almost succeeded in forgetting about it. I've no desire to dance with Aron at the moment, and I expect to spend most of the evening having to watch Lucien flirt outrageously with various beautiful noblewomen. But I can hardly explain that to Veron. 'You will attend then?'

'Of course. We may be in the middle of a crisis, but that is no reason to ignore the conventions of polite society.' He grins suddenly, and the dimples return. 'And I hope that you will do me the honour of dancing with me. I expect to find that you move with as much grace in the ballroom as you do with a sword in your hand.'

I feel my cheeks grow warm, and hope that Veron doesn't notice. 'Thank you, I'd like that.'

He takes my hand and, to my surprise, kisses it. 'Until then.'

89

Five

Two days before the ball, late one afternoon when I'm in my sitting room with Letya, Lord Pianet enters bearing Prince Eorman's reply to our invitation to him to visit. The prince declines the invitation – he offers his father's ill-health as an excuse – but he sends a gift: a jewelled brooch – with another, private letter addressed to me. With the brooch still in my hand I tear the second letter open and read it aloud.

'*My dear madam, I believe Frianland and Solanum could have a rewarding future together, one way or another. But I must build that future with someone. I hope it will be you. Contracts that are no longer fit for purpose may – should – be broken, and you may find that help with conditions attached is better than no help at all. This brooch is made in the form of a traditional Friant love knot, and may be separated into two pieces. Send me one half and I shall know what to think.*'

Pianet snorts. 'The prince must have been drunk when he wrote that.'

'I disagree. It's plain enough. He wants to unite the kingdoms by marrying the ruler of Solanum, and he doesn't care if that's me or Tallis. He doesn't care who knows of his ambitions either. The contract he refers to is my marriage contract with Aron. If I somehow sever my marriage bonds and agree to marry him, he'll help me catch Tallis. Or he'll hand her over. If I refuse . . .' I hand the letter to Pianet, who studies it, frowning. 'Show it to Convocation. See if they still think I'm being – what was Lord Patrus's word? – paranoid. Have you found anything of use in the Decrees yet?'

He shrugs slightly. 'Not so far, Your Majesty. But although the main clauses of the Decrees are well known, there are indeed many minor regulations which have not been in use for many years. I'm hopeful that we will discover something to serve our purpose.'

Pianet leaves, and I drop the love knot brooch into the wastepaper basket.

Letya exclaims. 'Aderyn!'

'What? I'll wear no gift from him.'

'But it could be sold, to help the poor.' She picks the brooch out of the basket and gazes at it, turning it so the multicoloured gemstones catch the light. 'It's ever so pretty.'

Her enchantment makes me smile, soothes the anger that's making me pace the carpet. 'It's yours then. Keep it.'

'Are you sure?'

'Of course.' But even Letya's happiness can't keep me from worrying over what I should do next. I wander across to the tall arched windows that look over the gardens, fiddling with the rings on my fingers. Eorman is too wily to come within my grasp, apparently. But there's nothing, theoretically, to stop me inviting myself to the Friant court. Or perhaps I should go to Vauban with a company of loyal nobles and try to draw Siegfried out. If he's still there.

I have to do something.

Lucien comes into view on the path between the knot gardens. He's pacing slowly, one hand clutching a letter, the other running repeatedly through his blue-black hair. He must have been at it for a while. As usual, when he's particularly worried or distracted, his hair is sticking up in tufts. I step back from the windows before he sees me. His anxiety is probably nothing to do with me. I've not seen or spoken to him since the day I was attacked. But guilt, for the way I dismissed him, crawls across the skin between my shoulder blades.

Letya is still examining the brooch, taking it apart and reassembling it. Before I ever came to the Silver Citadel, Lucien spent two years at the Friant court, attached to our diplomatic mission; I wonder whether he ever gave anyone a love knot. Whether there was anyone else before me.

Before I can change my mind, I hurry to my desk, write a note asking Lucien to come to my apartments before dinner and hand it to Letya.

'Would you give this to Lucien's servant?' She raises her eyebrows at me, so I add, 'I need to ask him something about his time in Frianland. And I can't to talk to him in public. I don't want to hurt Aron's feelings.'

True enough. But I'm also fed up with trying to do everything right. Trying to match up to everyone's expectations. With or without an excuse, I have to see Lucien.

When Letya returns she helps me dress for this evening's

banquet. I've selected a sleeveless gown of rose-pink watered silk with a draped neckline, and a silver belt, studded with dark pink dew crystals, that sits on my hips. Letya sets a narrow silver band with more dew crystals in my pinned-up hair. I tell myself I chose the gown because it is new and I want to see how it looks. I almost succeed in believing my own lie.

Lucien arrives punctually; his eyes widen when he sees me. He pauses on the threshold of my sitting room.

'Come in, my lord. Close the door behind you.'

He obeys.

'You sent for me, Your Majesty?'

'Yes, Lucien. Will you not be seated?'

'I prefer to stand, if Your Majesty has no objection.'

'As you wish.' I clear my throat. 'So . . . I've asked you here because I want you to tell me everything you remember from your time in Frianland.'

'Everything?'

'Everything as it relates to Siegfried. Who he met, where he went. How he behaved.'

Lucien shifts his gaze, staring straight ahead. 'There's not much to tell. During my time there he visited twice, that I was aware of, and stayed for some weeks. He attended court functions, but due to our inequality of rank, I was not seated anywhere near him. I don't know who he met, and I had little opportunity to observe his behaviour. I regret that I'm unable to provide more assistance. I trust Your Majesty will be able to obtain better information from another source.'

His cold politeness cuts me just as effectively as Lord Hood's blade. It stings all the more since I can't really blame him.

I chose Aron over him, again, and he clearly doesn't – or won't – understand why. 'Please, Lucien. There must be something that you remember . . .'

'I would help if I could, Your Majesty. But as I say, I know nothing of relevance.' An edge of disdain creeps into his voice. 'And to be sure, you are too well provided with loyal courtiers to want anything I might be able to offer.'

'Really?' Irritation drives away my guilt. 'Would you like me to drop to my knees and beg for your help? I'm sure that Tallis at least must be in Frianland. If I go there myself, lay a trap for her with me as the bait –'

He flings his hand up, exclaiming scornfully. 'Ridiculous.'

'Then what do you suggest I do? If my idea is ridiculous, help me. Tell me what you remember about your time there. Or suggest some other way that I can end this nightmare.' He doesn't answer. 'No. You'd rather spend your energies hurting me, when I'd have thought that you of all people should know what's at stake.'

'Of course I know.' Lucien's mouth twists into a scowl. 'Do you think Odette is the only one who dreads their return? Do you think I don't know what they cost me, that I wouldn't do anything in my power to stop them from –' He breaks off, breathing unevenly, and his eyes narrow. 'Someone else could be interrogating me about Frianland. Why did you really ask me to come here this evening, Your Majesty?'

My mouth is dry. I pour some water from the jug on one of the side tables and take a sip. Lucien is watching me, frowning.

'When I last saw your father, Lord Rookwood, he told me

that he expected you to return to Atratys. Why have you remained at court?'

'Why?' He shakes his head, turning away. 'Because, despite what you did, despite everything, I discovered that being away from you is torture. Worse torture than being near you but not being able to touch you.' He laughs. 'At least, I thought it was worse. But now I know that as well as watching you with Aron, I'm supposed to stand there while you insult me, just so he can feel better about his life –'

'By the Firebird, what did you expect me to do?' I fling away from him and begin striding up and down the room. 'You know how precarious his kingship is. You know how much he's had to suffer already because of his injury. And then you practically force your way into the audience chamber, just to remind him, apparently, that you were able to do something he wasn't.'

'I was worried about you!'

'Were you? Because ever since I married Aron – to save *your* life, by the way – you've acted like you can't stand to be around me. If you're so in love with me, Lucien, then why have you been trying so hard these past weeks to push me away?'

We're face to face, glaring at each other. My heart's thumping in my chest. I don't know whether I want to kiss him or punch him.

'You haven't answered my question.' Lucien's voice is husky. 'Why am I here?'

I could lie, but the blush I can feel rising across my chest and neck would give me away. 'Because I want you, damn you. Because I can't stop thinking about you. Because I keep reliving that one night we spent together, and –'

His arms are around me and he's kissing me: mouth, jawline,

neck, breastbone, over and over. He drags the pins from my hair, twists his fingers into the long tresses and fastens his mouth on mine, deepening the kiss. And I can't resist; I pull him hard against me and push my hands up beneath his tunic, digging my nails into the bare skin of his back, drowning in the wave of desire that floods my limbs, kissing him hungrily until I'm barely able to stand. 'Oh, Lucien . . .'

I rest against his shoulder and shut my eyes, and he holds me close, laying his cheek against the top of my head, encircling me. My blood pounds hot through my veins. Beneath my palm, I can feel the rapid answering beat of Lucien's heart. Almost – almost – the last months fall away, and we are back together in Lucien's room, knowing that we will have to face Siegfried and Tallis, but believing that we will at least be able to face them together.

'By the Firebird, Aderyn, please – tell me we can be together again. There must be a way. I love you – I need you – too much. I can't –' He puts his hands on my cheeks, raising my mouth so he can kiss me again, lingering over it. 'I don't want to live like this.'

Neither do I. I know what I promised Aron, but our marriage is not really a marriage. Instead it's fast become a prison. Although Aron is kind and generous, he doesn't love me as a husband. He never will. Surely – if Lucien and I are careful, if we keep it secret so Aron is not hurt or shamed by it – surely there is a way I can be with the one I love and not ruin everything.

The clock strikes the half-hour. I disengage Lucien's hands and step back, allowing my gaze to roam over his flushed skin, his burning black eyes, his lips. 'We'll find a way, Lucien. But we have to be careful – no one can know. And Aron –'

'I don't want to hurt him either. I'll think of somewhere we can meet, somewhere no one will be able to find us. Somewhere that's just for us.'

I go on tiptoe to kiss him, pressing my lips to his as though I can somehow absorb a part of him, carry it with me until we're next together. But time is ticking onwards. 'You have to leave. Aron and I will be meeting to go to the great hall soon, and you can't be here.'

He nods, lifting one hand to my face. 'I'll send a message through Letya.' He drags his fingers through his hair, shooting me a slightly rueful glance, as if he's aware that his attempt at tidiness hasn't really helped, straightens his tunic and leaves. I pick the hairpins off the floor, go to the large mirror hanging on the far side of the room and study my face. My hair is tangled into knots. Quickly I take off the silver band, run a comb through the top layer – it will have to stay loose around my shoulders – and clip the band back into place as well as I can, all the time hoping that the blush will have faded from my skin before Aron arrives. In the few minutes I have left, I pick up one of my books of astronomy and set myself to understanding a chapter on comets, trying to slow my pulse and calm the disorder of my thoughts. Trying, especially, not to think about Lucien.

I don't get beyond the second page before there's a knock at the door.

'The king is ready, Your Majesty.' The servant waits by the door, ready to close it after me.

'Thank you.' I put my book aside, stand and smooth my skirts. In the audience chamber Aron is waiting, studying one of the paintings that adorn the walls. He offers me his arm but says nothing as we descend to the great hall.

Aron's silence continues through dinner. He scowls at his plate, stabs at his food and barely says a word unless it's to call for more wine. My appetite fails. I force myself to consider the possibility that Aron saw Lucien leaving my apartments, that he has already guessed what is in my mind. Or perhaps he simply hasn't forgiven me for calling him spineless. However, as the meal progresses, I'm no longer sure that Aron's ill-humour is directed at me. I catch him staring at the table where Veron and Valentin usually sit, though they are not present this evening.

But Aron doesn't choose to explain his mood to me, and this time I don't ask. I get up from the table as soon as I can and escape to the long gallery, where I try to walk off the craving that has been thrumming through my body since Lucien kissed me. It doesn't help. When I find myself in the middle of a conversation with Lord Corvax, wondering how long I'll have to wait to be with Lucien again, I excuse myself and go to bed.

Still Lucien haunts me. Although I lie in the silent darkness of my room with my eyes closed, I can't sleep. My mind refuses to be silenced.

I sigh, fling off the bedclothes and get up again.

There's no moon tonight, and the sky above my private landing platform is a field of stars, fractured at one edge by the jagged black mass of the mountains. The air is cold enough to make me shiver, but I step out of my nightgown and into the chill water, gasping a little as it rises around my legs. Then every other sensation is overwhelmed by the familiar rush of transformation: the eruption of hair into feather; the lightening of bones as some shorten, some lengthen; the inevitable instant of pain as the scarred skin of my back stretches and re-forms. Now a swan, I glide for a moment across the lake before launching myself upwards.

The sky around the Citadel is quiet. I make a long, slow loop, out across the fjord, avoiding the city, before turning and following the foothills of the mountains back inland. Over the forest I breathe deeply, enjoying the mingled scents of pine resin and the night-blooming flowers of the winter rose. And in flight, I find peace. Each wingbeat seems to take me further from the problems I face as a human. I understand the stories now: the ones about nobles who become so addicted to the simple pleasures of the transformed state that they eventually abandon their humanity altogether.

I can almost hear the sea calling to me as I begin my descent.

But the exercise has served its purpose. Back in my human form, mind and body tired, I step out of the lake, put my nightgown on and go inside, not bothering to dry myself off. After the relative brightness of the starlit night, the vestibule that connects my room to the landing platform is dark. I'm groping my way when the sound of breathing makes me freeze.

'Aderyn.'

'Oh, Aron.' I press one hand to my pounding chest, trying to banish the images of Siegfried and Tallis – or some other faceless assassin – that had sprung from the shadows. 'You scared me.'

'I'm sorry.'

A sudden light makes me squint; Aron has turned up the

flame of the oil lamp that stands on my bedside table. He's barefoot, wearing only a shirt, untucked, and dark trousers.

'What are you doing here?'

'I couldn't sleep.'

'Neither could I.' I slip into bed and pull the covers up. 'That's why I went for a flight . . .' Even by lamplight, even though he tries to hide it, the flash of misery on Aron's face is too obvious for me to pretend not to notice. 'I'm sorry.' Apart from the night that Letya was arrested, he's hardly ever spoken to me about the accident that cost him his arm. I've never heard him complain about the ongoing discomfort. But I know he must miss being able to fly. I did, when I lost my ability to transform, even though I tried to convince everyone – myself included – that I didn't. 'Here.' I plump up the pillows and pat the bed next to me.

He hesitates for a moment, rubbing the back of his neck, shrugs, and sits on the bed, swinging his long legs up onto the counterpane.

'Do you want to talk?' I ask. A stupid question – why would he be here otherwise? – but I don't know how else to start the conversation.

'Yes.' I think he's about to mention Lucien, but instead he says, 'You were right, the other day. Pianet showed me the letter from Eorman. I should have supported you at the council meeting. Forgive me.'

'Of course. And I'm sorry about what I said to Valentin. About you having no backbone. It was . . . spiteful.'

He laughs. 'I deserved it.'

'But it's not true. You're one of the bravest people I know. Patrus was just manipulating you.'

100

'I know. I knew at the time, but –' He huffs and rubs his hand over his face. 'Before I lost my arm, before I was cut out of the succession, I used to go to meetings of the royal council and the Skein. I used to watch my father bully and belittle people, and I used think: I'll be different, when it's my turn. I'll show them a king can be strong without being cruel.' Aron's mouth curves into a slight smile. 'Unfortunately, it didn't quite work out as I planned.' He shifts his hand closer to mine, until the outside edges of our fingers are touching. 'I don't want to be like my father, Aderyn. But I'm scared. Of being thought weak. Of becoming irrelevant again. So I second-guess every decision I make, and it's exhausting. You must have noticed.'

'No. I haven't.' I shift position so I'm facing him. 'Honestly, Aron, you always seem so certain. So sure of yourself.' I shrug. 'Well, apart from when you gave into Patrus. But no one watching you could ever doubt that you were born to rule. Whereas I . . .' I sigh and pick up my luckstone from the bedside table. 'I'm so new to all of this. I'm still just feeling my way.'

'You're much better at it than you realise, Aderyn. And you should trust your instincts. They're good.' Aron takes the luckstone from my fingers and examines it. 'I've been talking to Valentin about things. Just to get another perspective, you understand. And he thinks you're right. That we should be taking action, raising an army. He suggested invading Frianland . . .'

'I hope we can find some middle way between doing nothing and invading an entire country.' Aron is still turning the luckstone over and over, so I add, 'And if you're worried about Eorman's letter, you needn't be. Even if it were possible to dissolve our marriage vows, I would never cast you off to marry him. I wouldn't do that to you.'

'I know you wouldn't. You're a decent person, Aderyn.' He smiles at me. 'But you're also possibly the most stubborn swan I've ever met, which is saying something, given our family. Just promise you're not going to fly off to Frianland to search for Tallis on your own. We'll figure a way out of this together. Agreed?'

I smile back at him and nod. 'Agreed.'

Aron drops the stone back into my palm. 'Get some sleep.'

It's only when he's gone that I realise what I said. I promised I wouldn't betray him with Eorman. But what about Lucien?

I put out the lamp, wondering just how decent I really am.

Aron isn't the only one who is worried about me dashing off to Frianland. The next morning, as she's brushing my hair, Letya suddenly introduces Fris's cousin into the middle of our debate over what dress I should wear for the ball tomorrow.

'Instead of rushing off on some mad scheme you should ask Fris about her cousin's baby's father,' she says. 'Actually, you should ask Fris to bring her cousin to the Citadel, then you can talk to her yourself.' She stares at me in the mirror and narrows her eyes. 'Have you forgotten what I told you? About the baby's father, and how he claims to be —'

'No, no, I haven't forgotten,' I interrupt hastily. 'He's not a noble and he's not like the ordinary flightless. He's a different kind of person, or so he says.' I sigh. 'I'd like to believe him. We could really do with some allies. And I did ask the merchant who was here from Atratys – he says he's heard a similar story up in Fenian, though he doesn't believe it. But I've not had time to find out anything else.'

'All the more reason to talk to her.' Letya scrunches up her face as she drags the hairbrush through a particularly recalcitrant tangle.

'Ow!'

'I'm sorry, but what in the Creator's name have you been doing to your hair? It wasn't like this when I dressed you for dinner last night.'

I remember Lucien's fingers twined in my hair, and drop my gaze. 'Nothing. Went for a flight, that's all. Will you ask Fris then? Arrange a time for her cousin to come and see me?' My request brings to mind another thing I haven't done. 'And I promise I'll start interviewing to find a clerk to take over my diary. It's been a month; you should have reminded me.'

'You've had enough to think of recently. But I'll go and talk to Fris now.' Letya finishes plaiting my hair and curls the whole into a bun. She leans close to my ear. 'And you can tell Lucien that if he tangles your hair up again, he can spend the hour it takes to untangle it.'

In the mirror, I watch my face flame red as Letya winks and laughs. She whisks out of the room before I can think of anything to say in reply.

Later in the day, Aron and I go for a ride. Tomorrow is a national holiday, and the Victory Ball is supposed to be one of the most important events of the year. The public rooms of the Citadel are thronged with servants putting the finishing touches to the preparations; I'm glad to escape the bustle. Aron is quiet, tilting his face up to catch the sun as we pick our way slowly along the lower slopes. But he seems happy at least. I assume that whatever had upset him – an argument with Valentin perhaps? – has been resolved. Our conversation is limited to observations of the beginnings of spring around us, until, as we reach the stables, he turns to me.

'In case I forget to mention it tomorrow, you shouldn't feel that you can't dance with Lucien. Because of me, I mean.'

'I hadn't really thought about it.' A lie; I've been thinking of little apart from Lucien ever since we kissed yesterday, and I'd almost decided that it would be safer if we didn't dance together at the ball. 'Thank you though. I'd like that.'

He dismounts, passes the reins to a waiting groom and pauses, watching as his horse is led back to its box. 'There's no reason not to. It's just a dance, after all.' It's not until he's gone that I realise he was talking more to himself than to me. Perhaps he's thinking about his own choice of dance partners. About Valentin? They've been spending a lot of time together. It might be only wishful thinking on my part, but maybe Aron and I will find a way we can both be happy. Even if it isn't with each other.

Aron's permission, and the fact that we're now on speaking terms again, mean that, when the hour comes for me to dress for the ball, I'm looking forward to it as much as I was dreading it a week earlier. Fris is gradually growing more confident in her own taste, and it takes a while for her and Letya to stop arguing about my outfit. But I'm ready with more time to spare than I expect: time enough for me to stand in front of the mirrors in my dressing room and admire myself.

The dress is in a new fashion from Ryska. A knee-length

blue silk gown, with diamond-set buttons down the front of the bodice, worn over a full-length, square-necked, silver satin underdress. The blue is exactly the same shade as the flash of bright colour on the wing of a jay. In my hair, Fris sets the diamond tiara Aron gave me to mark our marriage – it had belonged to his mother. The gift reminds me of our wedding vows, and the guilt I've so far succeeded in banishing rattles its chains. But Aron asked me to wear the tiara. I do want to please him, as far as I am able.

Aron is wearing a new tunic of silver satin slashed with green, set off by a silver crown studded with emeralds. He seems pleased when I compliment him. It's clear that we've both taken extra care with our appearance this evening, but any fleeting worry over whether we're too finely dressed is dispelled when I see the great hall. I'm dazzled by the huge display of silver-gilt plate, by the tall crystal vases filled with exotic flowers, by the jewel-encrusted costumes of my courtiers. Solanum's unbroken peace since the Wars of the Raptors has had its benefits.

If there are any enemies concealed within our ranks this evening, they must surely be overawed by this display of wealth and power. Either that, or they're more tempted than ever to take it for their own.

The orchestra in the gallery tunes up for the first dance, and Aron and I take our places. Lucien is there too, dancing with a noblewoman from Lancorphys, but when he smiles at me I know I've no need to be jealous.

The first half of the ball passes in a blaze of light and colour. I dance with Aron more than once, with Odette and with

Nyssa Swifting, who has returned from Zenaida castle and is no longer wearing deep black. I dance the lavolta with Lucien, savouring every lift into the air, every moment his hands are tight around my waist.

And then the master of revels calls out the next dance: a quadra, a dance for four people. Aron touches my shoulder. 'Shall we join with Veron and Valentin?'

Thane of Fenian and his son, Grayling Wren, are heading in our direction, so I quickly agree.

I don't know the quadra very well; for the first few minutes I have to concentrate on the relatively complicated sequence of steps and jumps and turns. But as I gain confidence I switch my attention to my dancing partners. I discover Veron dances the way he fights: vigorously, moving as if the music is always just a little too slow for his taste. Still, despite his energy, he doesn't seem to be enjoying himself. There's a tightness around his mouth and a slight crease between his eyes and his gaze is fixed downwards. I realise he's listening to Aron and Valentin's conversation.

'. . . but do you really think you could teach me?' Valentin asks, as the four of us come together in the centre of our square, touching our right hands together and walking clockwise in a circle.

'It will take time, and patience, from both you and the horse, but yes; I'm sure I could.' Aron smiles. 'Riding has given me a freedom I thought I'd lost. A completely different experience to flying, but one I'd like to share with you. I'll ask the stable master if . . .' I lose the end of his sentence as we separate again, and Veron and I face each other. We press our right palms together and step forward, twisting slightly and circling each other in a way that enables me to speak more softly.

'What's the matter, my lord?'

Veron glances at me, startled. 'Your Majesty?'

'You look disapproving.'

A faint flush colours his cheeks. 'In Celonia, men do not dance together.'

'But we are not in Celonia.'

'I'm aware. But it is true, is it not –'

He breaks off as the dance carries us back into formation with Aron and Valentin. Aron is laughing, his eyes sparkling.

'So you've learned how to build a boat, and you technically know how to sail, but you've still never been on the water?'

Valentin laughs too, even though he seems to be laughing at himself. 'Our father . . .' He pauses as the four of us bow to each other and change direction. 'Our father so thoroughly disapproved of nobles behaving like flightless that . . .'

We separate into pairs again. Veron grips my hand a little tighter than seems necessary.

'It is true, is it not,' he murmurs, 'that your marriage laws allow things that are not allowed in other jurisdictions?'

'Our marriage laws allow for the fact that people do not love according to rules and regulations. People are free to marry whomsoever they please.' Except for me, of course. I catch a glimpse of Lucien across the other side of the hall, and decide that I do not want this argument with Veron to spoil my evening. In any case, the quadra is ending. Returning to our original positions, the four of us make the final bow to each other. The music dies away. 'Come, Lord Veron. I'll not quarrel with you tonight. Instead, allow me to introduce to you to one Solanish custom I believe you will enjoy: flamed sugar cake.'

Aron and Valentin, still chatting, have already drifted towards the long gallery, where refreshments have been laid out. Veron hesitates, looking after them, but only for a moment.

'Of course.' He smiles and offers me his arm. 'I should be honoured.'

When I wake late next morning, my throat is sore from hours of too-loud conversation, and my feet ache. Still, I smile to myself as I stretch my limbs out, taking up as much space as possible in my comfortable, lavender-scented bed. Lucien danced the penultimate dance with me. He took the opportunity to tell me that he'd heard I was looking for a new clerk, and that he'd like the chance to apply for the position if it was still available. I can feel that we're on the cusp of falling back into the give and take of our former relationship, that brief but perfect moment after we stopped misunderstanding each other and before Siegfried and Tallis ruined everything.

I'm still thinking about Lucien – how handsome he was last night, the warmth of his gaze when our eyes met – when Fris and Letya enter my bedroom, bearing my breakfast and the news that Fris's cousin is waiting in my audience chamber.

She looks a little like Fris: the same wavy chestnut hair, the same slightly upturned nose, though she is delicate and pretty where my maidservant is strong and sharp-featured. Fris introduces her. 'This is Accris, Your Majesty. My first cousin once removed on my father's side.'

Accris pushes herself up from the chair and I realise that she's extremely pregnant.

'Please, stay where you are. Would you like some water, or a hot tisane?'

She shakes her head, glancing at Fris.

'You needn't worry, Accris. Just tell Her Majesty what you told me. About the baby's father.'

Accris shifts in her seat, placing one hand protectively on her swollen belly. 'Praeden, his name is. I thought he come from up Farne, being as he was so fine and handsome, and carried a sword. Though he weren't like the merchants. Even the rich ones are scared – scared of the nobles, and scared of the guards. But Praeden didn't seem to be scared of nobody.' Her voice has the same cadence as the people I encountered in Lower Farne last summer. She sighs. 'But he weren't from up Farne, cos if he was my pa would've found him by now. He told me he come from a place called Galen, and were visiting someone at the Citadel.'

'And did he tell you where this place is?'

'Fenian, he said. Told me it was the fifth Impenny island.'

'The fifth? You're quite sure?' She nods, so I go to the atlas that sits on a stand in the corner of the room and turn to the page showing the Dominion of Fenian. 'But there are only four Impenny islands.'

Accris juts out her jaw. 'Fifth, he said. And he told me that his people were called the Shriven, on account of them being given a special gift by the Creator, what meant that they couldn't be burned by no noble.' She draws breath and darts a glance at Fris. 'With all respect to Your Majesty, of course.'

I study the map. There is something beyond Sceada, the fourth of the Impenny islands, something right at the edge of the map. At the edge of the world. But it's not a place – it's a natural impenetrable barrier. The Pyre Flames. The idea that there's anything beyond it is absurd. Like the whole of Accris's tale. I drum my fingers on the atlas's thick parchment.

'He had a mark . . .'

Her voice rouses me from my brooding. 'What kind of mark?'

Accris slips a hand into the bag she carries and pulls out a piece of paper. 'I drew it, in case Your Majesty was wishful to see it. He said all his people were marked like this.'

Fris brings the paper to me. Accris has drawn on the back of what looks like a page torn from a book of Litanies – often the only book found in the homes of the very poor. The image she has sketched is a crest of sorts: a hand, palm out, with a pattern of dots above it. Crudely drawn, and I don't recognise it. Yet her story reminds me of something . . .

'Did he say who he was visiting in the Citadel?'

'No. Though he talked as if it were a man. Majesty . . .'

I tear my gaze from the paper.

'I ain't lying. I've no cause to lie.' Accris lifts her chin again. 'My family's going to take care of me and the baby. So I don't want nothing. But Fris said it might be important.'

'Thank you, Accris.' I frown at the symbol on the paper again. 'I hope Fris is right.'

'So do I,' Letya adds as she and Fris start to usher Accris out. 'I'd have liked to meet this Praeden. It must be nice, never to be scared . . .'

I lock Accris's sketch inside my desk, trying to ignore the

wistful note in Letya's voice. Not to think about how hard it must be for her to be friends with me, given everything I now represent.

I spend the next few hours scouring the books on my shelves, hoping to find some evidence – other than Accris's tale, and the stories heard by Pater Craxby – that this Praeden wasn't just a liar; strong, well-armed people who can't be harmed by us nobles might be just the allies we need. But pouring over page after page produces a headache instead of enlightenment. Either my sleep-starved brain is too dull, or I'm fooling myself because I want Accris's good-looking lover to be telling the truth. Eventually I swear, roll back my cramped shoulders, abandon the books now scattered across the carpet and go for a walk.

Perhaps because of the ball last night, or perhaps because of the misty rain, there are few people in the gardens. I wander the empty gravel paths, letting my mind drift, until I turn a corner and see Valentin, sitting on the same stone bench where I sat and talked with Siegfried last year.

He's weeping.

Six

I hesitate. But he looks so utterly miserable.

'Lord Valentin? What's the matter? Is there anything I can do?'

He jumps up, dashing a tear away from his face. 'Your Majesty, forgive me. I . . . I –'

The bench is damp, but so are my skirts. I take a seat. Valentin walks away; comes back; sits down again and drops his head into his hands.

I wait for a moment, gazing at his hunched back, trying to decide exactly what I ought to say. How much I should guess.

'Have you . . .' I clear my throat. 'Have you had an argument with Aron?'

He draws in his breath, but doesn't raise his head to look at me. 'No. Why would you think that? Why would you think that I –' He breaks off. But before I can explain myself, he adds, 'It's Veron. Veron, and other things.'

'Oh. I'm sorry. I've never had an actual brother or sister. But . . . siblings argue, don't they? Letya is just like a sister, and she and I argue. And Aron and Odette – they don't disagree often, but when they do . . . explosive is the word I'd use.'

He smiles. 'I'd like to see that.'

'It's quite entertaining.'

We both fall silent, Valentin staring down at a letter he's pulled out of his pocket.

'Please, Valentin. Tell me what's wrong. Have you had bad news?'

'This?' He turns the letter over in his fingers. 'No, this is a letter I'm supposed to send. Something Veron asked me to write. This is just the . . .' He mutters something in Celonian. 'I think you would say, the feather that tips the scales. I've been sitting here, feeling angry with my brother, and now I feel guilty too. Guilty that I am still alive to be angry, while others I grew up with are dead, or missing. Guilty that, despite my good fortune, I feel trapped. As if there is too much . . .' Valentin huffs. 'I can't think of the word. But it is as if I cannot breathe. Do you understand?'

'Yes.' I stare up at the grey granite mass of the Citadel. 'Yes, I understand.'

'My brother expects things of me. Demands sacrifices. But I'm not like him. He is obsessed.' He sighs and turns to me, frowning. 'He speaks of duty, but the truth is, Veron wants Celonia back the way it was. Sometimes I think he would sacrifice anything – or anyone – to get it.'

'I'm sure your brother loves you. He must want you to be happy, even if other considerations are currently distracting him.'

'Perhaps.' Valentin doesn't sound convinced. He goes back

113

to twirling the letter between his fingers, frowning. 'Why did you ask me about . . . about His Majesty, just now?'

'Well . . . I know you and Aron have become friends over the last few weeks. I just wondered whether you'd had a disagreement.' I smooth out my damp skirts. 'I know Aron can sometimes be a little . . . caustic.'

'No.' He shakes his head. 'His Majesty has been nothing but kind and generous. So very kind. And if it were possible that –'

I wait, but he doesn't complete the sentence.

'If what were possible?'

He smiles, though it looks like an effort. 'Nothing. A pleasant dream, that's all. From which –' he stands, holding up the letter – 'it may soon be time to awaken. Thank you for your patience, and your counsel, Majesty.' He blushes and tugs on one earlobe. 'If you would perhaps consent not to reveal our conversation to anyone . . .'

I lay my hand over his and squeeze it briefly. 'I won't breathe a word of it.' He looks relieved. I wonder if I should sit with him a while further but my stomach grumbles, reminding me that I'm supposed to be hosting a lunch for the Ryskan ambassador and her husband. 'I'm sorry, Valentin, I have a meeting. Will you be all right on your own?'

Valentin bows to me. 'Of course. But, please, allow me to escort you inside. Once I've taken this letter to Veron for his approval, I am planning to spend the afternoon in the library. You have a fine collection of books. And your chronicler has been most helpful . . .'

I don't pay attention to the end of his sentence, because I suddenly remember why Accris's story of a man who is neither flightless nor noble seemed familiar when Letya first mentioned it to me, back on that cold morning in early Thula.

It's because I'd read it in the library.

I've no time over the next few days to follow up my revelation. The body of a sea captain, matching Craxby's description of the man he saw talking to Siegfried, is found near Wyching, on the southern coast of Atratys. I fly to the area with Lord Pianet to meet the local nobility and encourage them to review their defences. On my return, Lord Pianet tells me his clerks have uncovered a five-hundred-year-old Decree that allows the monarchs to raise a direct tax on all nobles 'for defence'. It's clear from the context that the tax was intended to fund a network of fortresses, only one of which was ever built. But the letter of the Decrees is always more important than the spirit, and the wording is vague enough for us to twist it to our purpose. Aron and I summon the four Protectors and inform them that, if they refuse to instruct the nobles in their dominions to begin summoning the congregations and preparing for war, then we will bypass them and the Skein and impose a direct tax on all nobles, at a rate of our choosing. It doesn't take long for our threat to work. We meet with Convocation, and with the support of the Protectors, however unwillingly given, get their agreement to the funding of weapons and other supplies. We put Verginie of Lancorphys in charge of making sure summoning is carried out quickly; the kingdom has been at peace for so long I fear we have grown complacent.

In the midst of everything, I snatch a few moments alone with Lucien. He comes twice to my rooms, but when Lady Crump informs me that queens do not receive young, unattached noblemen late at night, I realise one of my guards or servants has been less than discreet. Or I am being spied on. Lucien tells me that he's found somewhere we can meet safely: an empty cottage at the far end of the fjord, where it flows into the sea. But we'd have to fly there, and I've no time to do that at the moment. We switch our brief meetings to the furthest corners of the gardens, and hope.

Finally, everything is set in train, as far as it can be. The first morning I have with no engagements, I head to the library with Accris's drawing tucked in my pocket.

The book of which her account reminded me is still there, chained into place in one of the tall oak bookcases: *Tales of the Flightless of Olorys*, by Gullwing Frant. I pull it out, sit at the desk below the shelves – the same desk I sat at last summer, the first time I consulted this book – and start skimming the pages. I'm about a third of the way through before I find the beginning of the story I only half remember. It isn't long, and the details, such as they are, do not exactly match Accris's tale. In Frant's version, the mystical flightless are called Gifens, not Shriven. Their hiding place is a land filled with treasure situated somewhere in 'the north', which Frant clearly takes to mean northern Olorys rather than northern Fenian. But, like Accris, Frant makes much of both their immunity to nobles' touch and their unusual strength. He describes the story as old: 'a myth that's been recounted for many hundreds of years, since before the War of the Raptors'. His tone of amusement makes it clear he thinks it is nothing more than myth. And I would almost certainly agree with him, if it wasn't for the illustration.

I spread out the scrap of paper bearing Accris's sketch next to the picture in the book. The printing is not good quality and I have to tilt the book to catch the light from the window, peering at the page. But within a few moments I'm certain. The two images are practically identical.

I examine the illustration again. Surely it must be more than a coincidence: an ancient mythical symbol, recorded fifty years ago in Olorys, now resurfaces again, carved into the flesh of a man from a completely different part of the country?

Perhaps there is something in Accris's story. Or perhaps the sense that Siegfried could be somewhere nearby is making me desperate. I summon the chronicler, have her unchain the book – there are some advantages to being queen – and return with it to my apartments.

There's no banquet this evening. I'm relieved; I'm worn out with debate and civility. Instead, I have supper with Aron and Odette. It's the first time the three of us have been alone together for a while. We avoid any mention of war or Siegfried or Tallis, and talk about more domestic matters. The school for the poorer flightless in Farne and the hospital that's still being built; the likelihood of Atratys finally winning a lance in the joust which is set to take place in a couple of days' time; Lord Blackbill's growing and obvious devotion to Odette. I start speculating on the heroic deeds Blackbill might undertake to finally win Odette's hand, and Aron unflatteringly compares him to one of the dogs that the flightless keep as pets. Odette makes a pointed reference to one of Aron's past love affairs, but otherwise she takes our teasing with good humour. She's too well-mannered to seek any revenge, despite the opportunities offered by the complicated nature of my relationship with Aron.

Discussion of that has to wait until Odette, yawning, has retired to her own rooms. Though even then, it comes up by accident. Aron and I are talking about the Eyria, an abandoned fortress in the mountains north of the Citadel, the only one built as a result of that ancient Decree Pianet found. I'm studying an old description Aron found in a book, wondering whether it would be advisable – or even possible – to reopen it, when Aron says, 'Valentin thinks there are abandoned tunnels underneath the Citadel.'

'What?' I laugh. 'Why?'

'You know he's interested in architecture. He found some old maps hidden away in the library, which were made after Cygnus I seized power. He thinks this palace was built on top of an older structure.'

I know there are lower levels of the Citadel that lie empty, filled with rotting treasures; Siegfried led me down there once. And our dungeons inhabit a network of long tunnels. 'It's possible, I suppose. Maybe the two of you should investigate.'

'We did. We took some of Hemeth's men and went as far as we could until it got dangerous. Collapsed ceilings, and so on.' He pauses, pouring out some more fennyflower cordial and wrapping his hand around the steaming cup, staring into the honey-coloured liquid. 'I know you know that I like him, Aderyn. Does it bother you?'

I pluck a petal from the flower arrangement in the middle of the table and hold it over the candle flame, trying to ignore the sudden churning in my stomach. 'No. Why should it? You're allowed to like people.'

We both watch as the petal curls and blackens and finally shrivels to no more than a wisp of ash.

'I think . . .' Aron props his chin in his hand, still staring at the flame. 'I think that perhaps it is becoming more than a liking, at least for me.' He sighs. 'Veron is angry with his brother. I suspect that he thinks our friendship might be developing into something more for Valentin too.'

'Is it forbidden then, in Celonia, to love one's own sex?'

'Not by law. Frowned upon. Discouraged. But more to the point, Valentin is betrothed.'

'Oh.' I remember the letter Valentin told me he'd been obliged to write. 'To a woman, I presume.'

Aron nods, lifting his eyes to mine. 'An arranged marriage: the lady is rich. Or was, before the revolution. No one knows now if she is alive or dead. They sent to Celonia for information, but have received no word. Still, Veron feels Valentin is bound by honour to return to Celonia, as long as there is any possibility that she might yet be living. And if she is alive, to marry her.'

'And Valentin doesn't want to. Especially since he's met you.' I sigh. Valentin's tears, the conflict with his brother which he mentioned but didn't explain – it all makes more sense now. Would things have been different if he and Aron had met a few months earlier?

Aron's next words make me blink.

'When we were exploring beneath the Citadel, Valentin and I were alone for a moment. We'd turned back, and the guards hadn't yet followed us. He kissed me.'

Just once? I can't count the number of kisses I've exchanged with Lucien recently. My buried guilt crawls onto my shoulder,

119

hissing at me in happy malice. Aron broods over his cup. But I can't leave it alone. 'And? Did you like it?'

He gives a snort of laughter. 'Of course I liked it. It was –' His breath catches. 'It was everything I've been imagining.' He rubs his eyes with finger and thumb. 'I'm going to tell Valentin he should go when his brother leaves.'

'But why? There may be nothing for him to go back to.'

'There is nothing for him in Solanum.' Aron extinguishes the flame in front of him. 'I have a wife and a kingdom to care for. I promised you I would not forget the vows we made. And Valentin will survive.'

I remember the young Celonian weeping in the rain and wonder how Aron can be so certain. 'Will he?'

'Of course. I got over Lucien, eventually. And over Lady Thressa Scopling too.' I suppose he sees my raised eyebrows, because he adds, 'I lost my arm and my place in the succession, and she suddenly lost her appetite for my company. She married Lord Arden's younger brother a little later, and now lives on a very comfortable estate in Dacia.'

'Detestable woman. If she ever comes back to court, perhaps we can find an excuse to banish her again.'

'I appreciate your desire to avenge my slighted honour. But my point is, Valentin will recover. Perhaps he'll find happiness with his betrothed, if she's still alive. And I'll recover too, in time.'

So he says. But all his rationalising can't disguise the misery in his eyes.

Sitting there, in the dim light of the remaining candles, I almost tell Aron about Lucien. Suggest that we should find a way that we can both be happy. Ask whether it would be the end of the world if it became known that the king and queen loved each other as cousins, as dear friends, and not as husband and wife. But Aron gets up and rings the bell for the servants to clear the table, and the moment passes. He wishes me goodnight and I am left to think about Lucien, and the promises I've made to both him and Aron.

I fall asleep wondering how I can possibly keep faith with both of these men that I love in such very different ways.

For the next couple of days, I am not good company. I find fault with everything, lose my temper and snap at everyone. Even Letya. I know why I'm doing it; alone at night, lying in bed, I think about Valentin, and Aron's plan to send him away, and compare it with my own plan of secretly spending as much time in Lucien's arms as possible. The comparison eats away at my peace, like a worm in an apple.

Still, I don't believe I can bear to give him up.

And then Aron gives me a present. It's waiting for me in my sitting room when I return from dinner: my mother's telescope. The one that Patrus broke last year when he attacked me in my chambers. Aron's had it repaired. Better than repaired; the note that accompanies the gift tells me that I should have had it at Solstice, but Aron sent the telescope to Ryska – where all the best telescopes are made – to have stronger, up-to-date lenses fitted, and the work took longer than expected. There's a custom-made brass stand and a green leather case too. Impatient to test it, I carry the telescope out onto my landing platform and point it at the moon.

It's all that I could have hoped for. The detail revealed by the new lenses – the valleys and plains – sends me hunting for a sketchbook in an attempt to capture everything I'm seeing.

It's not until over an hour later, when I go to put Aron's letter away, that I realise there's a second page.

I've been thinking about our discussion, and our future. Arranged marriages are not infrequent. Neither are marriages between cousins. Perhaps, once the immediate threat to our throne has been dealt with, we should consider whether, given time, our own marriage could become more than it currently is. For our own sakes, as well as for the good of the kingdom. Though you may doubt it sometimes, I do want you to be happy. Your affectionate husband, Aron.

The letter drops from my fingers to the floor, carrying my heart with it. Aron is thinking about me and the kingdom, while all I'm thinking about is Lucien . . .

My guilt has given up whispering. It roars in my ears like the midwinter sea.

Letya comes to help me undress, but I send her away. I throw open the interconnecting doors of my rooms and pace their length over and over as the moon rises higher, hoping that if I think hard enough, for long enough, I'll come up with a different solution to the one with which my conscience keeps presenting me.

I don't of course.

Aron has suffered enough over the last few years. Even if his reasoning is wrong, even if he cares too much what our nobility may think, eventually I acknowledge the truth. I can't be the one to make him suffer more.

I wait until the Citadel is quiet before leaving the royal apartments, dismissing the guards who are supposed to attend me. The last time I visited Lucien's room was when I had to tell him that Aron and I were married, that we couldn't be together. I can hardly believe I'm going there this evening to tell him the same thing again.

When I knock, gently, I'm almost hoping that he's already asleep. But the door opens and there's Lucien, his dark hair messy, wearing only his trousers – no shirt or shoes, wide-eyed with surprise. He grabs my hand and draws me inside.

'Aderyn.' He smiles at me. 'What are you doing here? Not that I'm not glad to see you, my lady –' he kisses my palm and the inside of my wrist, and my stomach flips – 'but I thought we were trying to keep this secret? I was about to leave for our cottage . . .'

That explains his minimal clothing. I guess he was planning to drop from the window of his room and transform as he fell; I've seen him do it once before, and I've no doubt of his skill.

He hands me a letter. 'I was going to have Cynsel deliver this to you in the morning.'

I scan the contents quickly – the note tells me he's gone ahead, and suggests I meet him at the cottage in two days' time – an Ember Day – and that we spend the afternoon together. My heart races as heat washes through me. I want so badly to say yes.

Lucien is moving about his room, rummaging through piles of books and clothes – he is definitely the untidiest person I know – throwing various items into a leather bag. 'I've already been to the cottage a few times and taken some supplies.

123

Tried to make it more comfortable.' He glances at me, and I'm surprised by the faint blush that's bloomed on his cheeks. 'There's a well and a hearth and a bed, of course, but not much else. I hope you won't be disappointed.'

His note crumples in my fist. I have to tell him. And it has to be now.

'Lucien . . .' I barely force the word out – my voice has sunk almost to a whisper. But something in my tone, I suppose, is enough. Lucien stops what he is doing and stares at me, the colour draining from his face. For a long moment, we are both silent.

'But you said – you said we'd find a way. You agreed that we could be together. That we should be together.'

'I know.' I want to hold him, to kiss away the agony in his eyes. But I can't move. 'I know what I said. And I meant it. But now it comes to it . . . I – I can't hurt Aron like this. I can't truly be happy with you if it means making him suffer. I'm sorry.'

At the mention of Aron's name, Lucien snarls and sweeps the leather bag and its contents off the bed. 'Aron be damned. He's done this to us. He cares nothing for the pain he's inflicted. And yet you talk about not wanting to hurt him?' He shakes his head. 'Think, Aderyn – we deserve to be happy. And Aron won't even know . . .'

'But I'll know. Even if he never finds out, how can I look him in the eye? How can I know that he is denying himself happiness because of the vows we took, while behind his back I'm making a mockery of those same vows?' I dash away a tear that is creeping down my cheek. 'It's wrong, Lucien. I love you. I'll always love you. But I can't live a lie. Don't you see? Eventually it would destroy us.'

124

There's a vein pulsing in Lucien's forehead. Through gritted teeth he hisses at me, 'You can't live a lie? And yet you can lie to me, over and over?' In a few strides he closes up the gap between us and seizes my upper arms, jerking me forward. 'Is this really about Aron? Or is the truth that you enjoy torturing me, Aderyn? That you enjoy seeing how far I'll bend to your will, how often you can change your mind before I break?'

'That's not true! You know it's not.' I press my hands to his chest, trying to push him away, but his grip is too tight. 'Lucien, you're hurting me –'

'No more than you're hurting me.' He pulls me closer, his tear-filled eyes searching my face. 'You love me, Aderyn, I know you do.' His voice breaks. 'You love *me* . . .'

He crushes his mouth against mine, kissing me savagely, one hand behind my head, the other pinning me against his chest.

And I'm frozen. Torn between desire – because I do love him, will love him, whatever he says or does – and revulsion at this unexpected violence.

Lucien begins kissing my neck and I gasp for breath. 'Please, stop –'

He freezes – looks at me, his eyes full of horror – begins to release me –

'Let her go.' Aron is standing on the far side of the room, his sword drawn and levelled at Lucien. 'I'm about to strike your head from your shoulders, and I would not have my *wife* witness it.'

Lucien backs away from me, breathing hard. He's trembling, staring at me, not Aron. 'I'm so sorry. I don't know what

I was – I didn't mean to –' Groaning, he drops to his knees. 'Please, Aderyn . . . Please forgive me.' He stays kneeling there, as if he's waiting for Aron to carry out his threat.

'Well?' Aron turns to me, one eyebrow raised. His voice is hard and cold. 'Shall I kill him?'

'Of course not.'

He sneers. 'As you wish, my lady. On your feet, Rookwood.' Lucien obeys, dragging one shaking hand through his hair. 'It may surprise you to know that I didn't come here this evening planning to interrupt –' Aron waves the point of his sword from Lucien to me and back again – 'whatever this started out as. Instead, as someone who used to count you as a friend, and in the clearly mistaken belief that I owed you something, I came to ask you about these.' He sheathes his sword, pulls a bundle of papers from his tunic and tosses it onto the bed.

Lucien gazes at the bundle, but makes no move to pick it up.

'Go on,' Aron nudges. 'Open it.'

Lucien reaches for the papers and undoes the outer wrapper. Slowly at first, but then with what looks like desperation, he scans sheet after densely written sheet. 'By the Creator . . . Where did you get these?'

Aron sits at Lucien's desk and crosses his legs. 'It hardly matters. It is not the source but the content of those letters that are important. Damning, are they not?' He glances at me. 'You remember the flightless plot Pianet uncovered? The one that mistakenly led him to accuse Letya? It turns out it didn't only involve flightless.'

I grip the back of the chair that stands next to me, leaning on it. What was it Pianet said? That the plot involved someone close to me, someone who would never be suspected, who could strike when least expected . . .

Aron is drumming his fingers on the desk, watching Lucien. 'When Aderyn told you she was to be queen, did it occur to you to tell her that you'd been planning a revolution?'

'But I wasn't – I sought reform, not bloodshed.' Lucien bites his lip as he goes through the letters again. 'I pulled back, when I realised what they were planning. I wrote, told them I'd have nothing more to do with it –' But whatever proof he's looking for isn't there. The loose sheets of paper flutter to the ground. 'You have to believe me. Aderyn, I would never hurt you.' He closes his eye, frowning as if in pain. 'I mean . . .'

I remember his words to me, when we first journeyed to the Silver Citadel all those months ago. His urging that I should trust no one, including him. And I remember discovering him dictating a letter in the gardens in the middle of the night. Doubt keeps me silent.

Aron clears his throat. 'At the risk of stating the obvious, Rookwood, you were hurting her when I walked in.'

Lucien swings away, staggers to the side table nearby where a decanter and glasses are set out. He pours himself a glass of wine, spilling half of it. Drains it in one go. 'What now?'

'I won't harm you. Or publicly expose you. But I am going to banish you.'

'From court?' Lucien asks. He's leaning on the table, head bowed.

'No. From Solanum. Forever.'

'What?' Horror loosens my tongue. 'No, Aron. Please . . .'

Aron turns to me, pity mingling with contempt in his

expression. 'My queen, all the evidence suggests that Lord Rookwood engaged in treason. If I take these letters to Convocation, you know what the result will be.'

Execution. Exile for Lucien's family. I cover my face with my hands, trying to think. Such a blow would kill Lord Lancelin.

'Even you, Aderyn, must agree that I'm being merciful.'

Lucien takes a step towards us. 'If I'm to be banished, so be it. But release Aderyn from her vows. Let her come with me.'

'Release her?' Aron stands. 'The monarchs of Solanum marry for life, Lucien, you know that. Only death can undo our vows. And as to her leaving with you while still pledged to me, it's out of the question –'

As Lucien and Aron begin to argue I focus on the wall hanging between the windows: the new royal crest of the House of Cygnus Atratys – of my house – gleams in silver thread against dark blue wool. And on my left hand, my rings – the coronation ring, the ring of Atratys, my wedding ring – weigh heavy on my fingers.

I can't abandon the future I've been fighting for. Not even for Lucien. Not for a man that I'm not entirely sure I know any more.

'Enough.' My voice surprises both men into silence. I stand up straighter, relinquishing my grip on the chair. 'I am your queen. I am not a possession to be fought over. And I do not need permission from anyone, not even from my husband, to come or go.'

Aron turns on his heel, striding to the window. But I can see his face – his anguish – reflected in the glass. 'You must do as you wish, of course.'

Lucien, smiling, is walking towards me.

'No, Lucien.'

'But . . .' He stops, frowning. His hand drops. 'Does it mean so much to you then? Being queen.'

'If there was another way, I would take it. But you know very well that Convocation will not allow Aron to rule without me.'

'Convocation will allow Aron to marry someone else, to rule with her. They'll not be so blind as to risk the throne being empty –'

'You're being blind, Lucien.' I clench my fists as frustration stiffens my spine. 'Deliberately so. Have Convocation shown any willingness to bend from the letter of the Decrees?'

He doesn't answer.

'No. The Skein will descend into fighting over who is to replace me, and either Tallis or Eorman will invade. Siegfried is likely already here. If I walk away, the kingdom will fall. The only question is when.'

His face hardens. 'So this is it? This is how it ends?'

I nod. 'Perhaps it is for the best.'

'Banished? Alone?'

I spread my hands, helpless. 'The Elders have spoken, and the Decrees are what they are.'

He shakes his head. 'I never thought I'd hear you quote that saying to me.'

'And I never thought to hear of your involvement in a plot against the crown. Against me, Lucien. How could you? How could you keep such secrets?'

Lucien opens his mouth as if he is about to say something

more. But instead he backs away until his legs hit the end of the bed, slumps down and drops his head into his hands.

The anger that has sustained me is dissolving into grief.

'Lucien . . .' I reach out for him. But there's nothing I can say, or do, that could possibly help. Aron walks past me and opens the door.

'We should leave him be, Aderyn. Rookwood, you have until sunrise the day after tomorrow to put your affairs in order. Come and see me at the seventh hour, so we can make arrangements for your maintenance.' He pauses, then adds, 'Whatever you might think of me, Lucien, I would not have you starve.'

Aron takes my hand and leads me from the room. He has to: I am blinded by tears.

I do not see Lucien again. By nightfall the next day, he is gone.

Seven

The next few days remind me of last year, when my father died. In some ways, they are worse. As Aron told me the first day I arrived, there are no secrets in the Silver Citadel. Everyone at court seems to know Lucien has been banished. They do not know why, but they try to guess, hoping for some hint of scandal; they watch me, and wait.

So I pretend. I pretend not to care. I pretend that everything is exactly the same as it was. If I talk a little too loudly, or too fast, or look a little paler than usual, I hope people will not notice. Or that if they do, they will put it down to the fact that the four Protectors have each received a letter from Tallis, offering them various incentives in return for placing Aron and me in the dungeons and publicly declaring their support for her. Of course, they all swear they are still loyal to us, but Aron's mood grows even bleaker.

I haven't told him why I went to Lucien's room that evening, and he hasn't asked. We don't speak to each other unless we have to. Odette knows the truth – I love her too well to have her think badly of me – but her kindness and her pity chafe me. Apart from Letya – who condemns both Aron and Lucien in strong language, but understands me well enough to realise that, after that, I'll not want to talk about it – the only person I can relax around is Veron. He doesn't know Lucien and he seems, despite my earlier suspicions, to know nothing of our history. When he says I look tired, I tell him the dark shadows beneath my eyes are due to affairs of state, and he takes my words at face value. Besides, I expect him to be gone soon. Lord Pianet informs me the Celonians have chartered a boat to take supplies to one of the islands off their coast; they are establishing a base from which to launch an attempt to retake their lands. In the meantime, walking or flying with Veron becomes a welcome distraction. He is too full of his own concerns to pry into mine.

Two weeks after Lucien's departure, another bad dream – I'm in the Citadel, but every doorway is blocked, and every inhabitant apart from me is dead – drives me from sleep before dawn. My windows are open, but despite the breeze fluttering my curtains, the bedroom seems airless. I get up and fasten a cloak around my shoulders.

As usual, two guards are on duty outside my rooms. I ask one of them to accompany me; together we head for the door that leads to the landward ramparts, the massive exterior walls that protect the Citadel complex from the mountains behind.

The path that runs along the top of the ramparts leads my guard and me away from the main bulk of the Citadel. I can breathe out here, but the wind is treacherous; it blows stronger, buffeting me, forcing me to clutch my cloak with one hand

and steady myself with the other against the rough-surfaced granite parapet to my right. The parapet reaches above my head, its top sections curved inward like the crest of a wave. To my left is a much lower parapet, and beyond that a sheer drop down to the arena, stables and tournament fields.

Occasionally, the solidity of the stone is broken by what the guards call gaze-gaps: narrow horizontal slits, wider on the external side. As the wall tracks south-west, between the palace and the lower slopes of the mountains, I stop to stare through the nearest of these openings. The mountains are fading from black to grey, but I'm not really seeing the forests and crags gradually being revealed by the dawn. In my head, I'm conjuring a map of the kingdom. Letya, with her gift for picking up gossip, gathered news yesterday from a Brithyan servant: Patrus has ordered the entire contents of one of his houses – one that sits along the Brithys–Atratys border – to be moved to another property deeper inside his dominion. It seems more likely than ever that southern Atratys is where the first attack will be made.

I catch the sound of geese, crying to each other as they fly above the banks of mist that cling to the mountaintops. Nobles tend to communicate silently during flight, calling from mind to mind, so these are probably true geese. Probably, but not definitely. I peer at the grey clouds, remembering Siegfried's potion and the horror of Lord Hood's forced transformation, and I wonder.

A gust of wind even stronger than the rest plucks at my clothes and threatens to unbalance me. I take pity on the young guard, shivering despite his heavy armour, and go back inside.

But there doesn't seem any point in going back to bed. Instead, I write to Lord Lancelin, passing on Letya's information and asking him to review again the defences in place around our southern coast, to hurry the fortification of port towns and the gathering of supplies and weapons. I write a note to Lord Pianet asking him to question Patrus, and I write out an order to the commander of the Dark Guards to have the houses of Tallis's nearest relatives searched for a second time.

The summoning of the congregations is progressing as fast as possible, but nothing Aron and I are doing seems like nearly enough. And all the time, Lucien haunts my steps.

As soon as the second hour has struck, I summon Fris and send one of my other maids to fetch the guest master. He is elderly and slow; I'm dressed and most of the way through my breakfast by the time he reaches the audience chamber.

'Your Majesty.' He bows deeply. 'My only wish is to serve.'

'Thank you, Guest Master. Tell me, is Lord Grayling Wren currently at the Citadel?'

'Lord Wren . . .' He closes his eyes in concentration. 'Why, yes, Your Majesty. His lordship returned from Fenian three days ago. But the Protector of Fenian –'

'Yes, I know Lord Thane is here.' The overbearing father will not likely be of any use, but the spineless son might. 'Send a note to Lord Wren.'

The guest master snaps his fingers at his attendant acolyte, who has pencil and paper at the ready.

'Her Majesty sends her compliments and requests his presence in the audience chamber –' I'm about to add *as soon as is convenient*, or some such pleasantry, but I'd rather have

Lord Wren nervous than comfortable. 'That's all.' The underling hurries to my desk, and seals the note; another moment sends him running out of the room to deliver it.

My phrasing has the desired effect. Lord Wren, a little out of breath, is shown into the audience chamber less than half an hour later.

'Majesty.' He gulps and bows. 'You sent for me.'

'Yes, I did.' I dismiss the servants. 'There. Now we may talk freely.'

At my invitation he falls into step next to me, and we pace the room silently for a few moments. There are beads of sweat clinging to Wren's hairline.

'So, my lord,' I begin eventually, 'you are well-versed, I assume, in the stories and folklore of Fenian?'

His eyes widen – he was not expecting this question, clearly – but he nods.

'What can you tell me of the Shriven?'

'The Shriven?' Wren darts me a look; he suspects that I'm making fun of him. 'They're a nursery tale, nothing more.'

I wait, hoping he will feel compelled to fill the silence.

He does. 'It's a story the flightless tell.' As he walks, he twists his hands together. 'A story about a people concealed in the far north, who are somehow neither flightless nor noble, but something in between. An abomination,' he adds hastily, 'if it were true.'

'And . . . ?' I prompt.

'And . . . the flightless speak of it as some sort of hallowed place. Full of wonders and riches. Though they won't tell where it is, even when you –' Wren makes a gesture, as if he is grabbing something. Or someone. A blush overlays his sallow features. 'I asked a servant about it, when I was a child. But he couldn't tell me anything. Because it's not real, obviously.'

Asked? My guess is that Wren tried to force an answer out of the unfortunate servant by touching them. I keep my expression neutral, masking my disgust.

'Interesting, the stories we tell ourselves.'

He bobs his head. 'Yes, Your Majesty.'

'Now, correct me if I'm wrong –' I wrinkle my brow, acting the part of someone trying to remember – 'but did not your father, at some point – oh, when was it . . .'

'Not my father –' Wren spits out the words, the colour disappearing from his face as rapidly as it had arisen. 'My grandmother, Grayla, mounted an expedition. Purely to demonstrate her loyalty to the Crown. She thought . . . she thought these Shriven might be a threat, if there was any truth in the stories. But she found nothing. No monstrous creatures. No sign of habitation.' He pauses. 'How did you know, Your Majesty?' The blush threatens to reappear. 'I mean . . .'

I didn't know, of course. The most powerful families have a way of keeping some of their doings – anything particularly treacherous, or ridiculous – out of the official chronicles. But the House of Cygnus Fenys has long had a reputation for being permanently impoverished. I remember my father's phrase quite clearly: '*the rulers of Fenian piss away their wealth like too much weak wine.*' It was not hard to imagine that one of the Protectors, desperate for money, might have sought out a fabled land of treasure that supposedly lies within their own dominion.

However, I'm not about to tell Grayling Wren that it was just a lucky guess. I stop walking and face him.

'Remind me, my lord, of the name of the area your grandmother searched?'

He stares back at me, one eyelid twitching. Trying to work out, no doubt, exactly what I know, and why I'm asking, and what he should tell me. Or what he should lie about.

Another moment and he sighs, drops his gaze and murmurs, 'The Impenny Islands, Your Majesty. All four of them.'

'Thank you, Lord Wren. That will be all.'

He bows and moves towards the doorway that leads back into the receiving room. 'Um, Your Majesty . . .'

'Yes?'

'My father – I'd prefer if . . . That is to say, if you'd be so good –'

His features twist in an agony of embarrassment and anxiety; I can't help feeling sorry for him.

'We've had a pleasant chat, Lord Wren, that's all. But if your father asks, you may tell him that I'm considering appointing an assistant to Lady Finch, a sort of deputy Warden of the Citadel.'

I haven't said that I am considering appointing him. But it is enough. Lord Wren changes colour again, utters a couple of inarticulate phrases of thanks, and backs himself out of the room.

Alone, I go back to pacing, trying to subdue the excitement that has sparked into existence in the pit of my stomach. Yes, Grayling Wren's information ties in with the tale that Fris's cousin shared. But it still could be nothing. Still likely is nothing. My mathematics is too rusty for me to attempt to calculate the odds of the existence of a hidden haven, occupied by some sort of . . . altered, enhanced flightless people. But the odds are irrelevant. Only the flightless have absolutely nothing to gain by Tallis and Siegfried seizing the throne. If there's any possibility at all that these Shriven exist, then it's among them I should look for allies.

Besides, as I've discovered before, stories sometimes turn out to be true.

Before dinner, I take Odette into my confidence. She doesn't actually laugh at me. Still, it's obvious she doesn't set much store by my evidence, consisting as it does of one old story, the testimony of a flightless woman from Farne – corroborated only in a general way by a flightless man from Atratys – and Grayla of Fenian's failed expedition. She suggests, as gently as possible, that Grayla would surely have found these Shriven, if they actually exist to be found. But when I mention Accris's insistence that her lover was not from one of the four known Impenny Islands but from a fifth, undiscovered land, Odette falls silent, pursing her lips and twirling one finger through a lock of white-blonde hair.

'Beyond the Pyre Flames?'

'That's what I wondered.'

'Impossible.' She shakes her head. 'You've not been there, Aderyn. I have. The Flames are beautiful, but they're terrible too. Dangerous. If you want stories, there are plenty built upon the power of the Pyre Flames.'

I lean forward in my chair. 'I need to do something, Odette. I can't just sit here and wait any longer, either for the war to start or for a second Lord Hood to try to kill me.' An image of Lucien stepping out of the shadows with a knife in his hand forces itself into my mind. I push it away. 'Besides, what if the Shriven do exist? If I could find them, persuade them to join us . . . You've flown to Fenian before. And your navigation skills are better than mine. Better than most. Would you come with me?'

My cousin hesitates.

'You're worried about Aron, aren't you?'

'I don't like to leave him alone here, without either of us.'

I understand why. Before Aron became king, he was a prince who could no longer fly and had been cut out of the succession, ignored or openly mocked by many of the nobles he now rules over.

'Aron won't be entirely alone. He has Hemeth, and his other friends in the Dark Guards. And Valentin of course.'

A faint blush tints Odette's skin. 'I wasn't sure whether you . . .' She smooths her skirts over her knees. 'Aron told me he's going to encourage Valentin to leave with the other Celonians.'

'I know. Aron isn't exactly my favourite person at the moment, but I still think Aron and Valentin should enjoy each other's company while they can. And if I invite Veron to fly north with me too . . .'

Odette smiles. 'You're a good person, Aderyn.'

I shrug. 'Will you come? We won't be away for long.'

'Yes. I'll be glad of an adventure and a change of scenery, even if we find nothing. Apart from me and Veron, who else are you considering?'

139

'Nyssa Swifting. She needs a distraction. One or two of Lord Pianet's agents. And perhaps, if you have no objections, Lord Blackbill, since I expect he might try to follow you whether he's invited or not. I've been watching him, and I've decided that he looks at you in exactly the same way that Thane of Fenian looks at his dinner.'

Odette raises an eyebrow at me. 'And how is that?'

'Why, cousin, as if he is completely and utterly besotted with you.'

Odette laughs, and for the first time since Lucien left, I do too.

Another few days, and my arrangements are complete. We are to fly by night to Rogallyn, a town in the borderlands between Lancorphys and Fenian, outside of which Nyssa's family has a manor house. From there another night flight will bring us by sea to the northern most tip of Fenian: the so-called Harrowed Lands. Veron seems happy to accompany me, Nyssa less so, but neither of them refuses. Apart from Odette, the only person who knows our destination is Verginie of Lancorphys, since I prefer to ask her permission before entering one of her manor houses.

I still haven't said anything to Aron. But I must.

I go to his rooms after lunch, the day before I'm hoping to fly north. My plan is to ask him to ride with me, and to tell him about Accris's story, and the expedition I've arranged, while we're outside the Citadel walls. He might be more reasonable while engaged in one of his favourite activities. If not, he'll at least have the relief of being as sarcastic to me as he likes, without the risk of anyone overhearing. But when I enter his sitting room, Aron is not alone. He's standing there with Lord Pianet, Lord Corvax, the commander of the Dark Guards and three nobles from my own Dominion of Atratys.

I look from one to the other. 'What's happened?'

'An . . . incident, at Hythe last night.' Aron glances at Pianet. 'I'm sorry, Aderyn.'

Hythe. A busy port within my dominion. I tighten my fingers around the luckstone in my pocket. 'How bad is it?'

'The shipyard's been burned down. Buildings, the ships under construction . . . Almost everything.'

'An accident?' I ask. Though I already know the answer.

Pianet shakes his head. 'It doesn't appear so, Your Majesty. Luckily the alarm was raised before any of those in the area came to harm. But, strategically and economically, it's a heavy blow.'

I take a breath to steady myself. Is it beginning? 'I should go to Merl immediately. We ought to –'

'No.' Aron steps forward, his hand held out. 'You can't. It's too dangerous.'

'I have to. I'm not staying here while my dominion's under threat. Merl is well defended; I'll be safe enough there.'

One of the Atratyan nobles turns to Aron. 'Please, Your Majesty . . .'

Aron pinches the bridge of his nose. 'I didn't want to tell you. You've been through enough recently. But Hythe wasn't the only place that was attacked last night.'

'Merl?' I whisper.

He nods, adding quickly, 'The attack was repelled. Lord

141

Lancelin is safe. But there were some casualties, and a lot of destruction.'

I stay perfectly still; there's a sharp edge inside me suddenly, as if something has broken. If I move too quickly, if I give in to my impulse to rage and scream, it might hurt too much to stop.

Aron takes my hand. 'I'm sorry. I'm just trying to protect you.' He peers into my face. 'Say something, Aderyn.'

'I'm still going.'

'But . . . don't you understand? It's dangerous. Others can go and report back to us.'

'I don't need protecting, Aron.' I pull my fingers from his grasp. 'What I need is . . . What I need is Tallis and Siegfried locked up in my dungeons. Or their heads upon spikes on my battlements.' I dig my nails into the palms of my hands. 'I'm going to Merl. Lord Pianet, you'll accompany me – you and whoever else you believe may be of assistance.'

Pianet glances at Aron, but he won't disobey. 'As you wish, Majesty. When do we leave?'

'As soon as possible. Within the hour.'

'This is a mistake,' Aron says. 'But by all means, do as you wish.' He swings away from me. I still hear him murmur, 'You always do.'

I send a note to Odette postponing our expedition north, but I've no time to see her before I meet those who are to accompany me on the Citadel's landing platform. Veron is there, and at first I think it's coincidental, that he's leaving for another destination – the island from which they are planning to reclaim Celonia perhaps. But he tells me he has volunteered as a way of making return for our hospitality. I thank him, automatically, but my thoughts are on my home. Every moment of delay is unbearable; I launch myself into the air with something like relief, dreading what I might find when I get there.

The grey afternoon fades quickly into dusk. Soon, we're flying by starlight filtering through fractured clouds. My wings beat away mile after mile as my kingdom – mountains, fields, forests, lakes, towns – slips past below. From the Crown Estates, through northern Brithys and then south-west across Atratys towards the coast.

The spaciousness of flight soothes my mind, numbs some of the fretful anxiety that I have worn like a second, too-tight skin for more weeks than I can remember. Moonrise finds us high above the town of Brindle Burn, a prosperous farming settlement on the Brindlefall Plain. I distract myself from the ache in my wings and lungs by trying to remember every fact I ever learned about the town: population, source of wealth, land ownership. It doesn't take long. My wings begin to slow and I start to drift lower as exhaustion creeps up on me.

Until the horizon shifts, and I see the ocean, glinting between drifting strands of fog, and my home on its rocky promontory.

Despite the hour, the grounds of the castle are full of activity. People repairing walls, boarding up windows and dragging things – bits of broken furniture, I guess – into a barrier that's taking shape across the spit of land that connects Merl to the rest of the kingdom. The gates that stood there appear to have been destroyed. As hard as I look, I can see no remnant of the limestone statue of swan and cygnet that stood next to them. There are armed guards on the battlements and transformed nobles circling above the castle and burning torches everywhere, fighting back the shadows. The nobles challenge us as we approach. One of them, a large brindled owl, I recognise as Pelias Feathershawl, a woman who leases one of my estates nearby.

Pelias, where is Lord Lancelin?

In the main hall, I believe, Your Majesty. But –

I make for the landing platform without waiting for the end of her thought. My companions follow me. I shift my shape, take a robe from the waiting servant and hurry inside. Here, at least, the damage doesn't seem too bad. There's a broken window, some missing tapestries, a couple of damaged paintings that have been stacked up against the wall. Nothing that can't be fixed.

But on the threshold of the great hall I stop short.

It's unrecognisable. A nightmare version of the place I grew up in. The walls and ceiling are black with smoke, the plasterwork and wood panelling cracked or burned away entirely. Tattered remnants of the long velvet curtains flutter from buckled iron poles. All that's left of the windows is twisted lead, fringed with a few jagged fragments of coloured glass. I press my hand to my mouth and try to hold back the tears that have sprung into my eyes.

Lancelin is sitting hunched on a half-charred oak chest with his back to me. As I get closer, I notice the pencil and notebook in his hands. But he's not writing. He's staring at the empty fireplace.

'My lord . . .'

144

He startles. Pushes himself up off the chest and bows. 'Your Majesty.' His skin and hair are smudged with ash and there's a bandage around his right hand. 'Forgive me.' He gestures to the devastation around us.

'My dear friend . . .' I put my arms around his neck and hug him, as I used to when I was child, not caring what my courtiers might think. 'As if I could blame you for any of this.' I dash away a tear that's creeping down my cheek. 'I'm just glad that you're safe. How many . . . ?'

'Twenty-two dead, eighty-five injured. Though not all of them are expected to survive. Still, it could have been worse; we had a little notice of the attack from someone who escaped the fires at Hythe. The long gallery is being used as an infirmary.' He drags a shaking hand over his face. 'Our attackers were mercenaries, both noble and flightless. Their ships arrived a little before dawn.' That explains the destruction at Hythe; they wanted to make sure we'd have no ships in which to pursue them. 'We drove them back, eventually. They fled to their ships and then into the fog banks. But we weren't quick enough.' Lancelin sighs and looks around the hall. 'Such wanton destruction. It's almost as if they knew where to strike at us to cause the most pain. The library. Your mother's sitting room. Your room . . .'

I grip his hand tighter, but I don't ask Lancelin exactly what's happened to my room. I don't think I can bear to know.

'What about the estates and villages around Merl? Were there any other attacks?'

'I've been sending out pages and riders. All but one have reported back. There's no sign of the enemy, though I've ordered all coastal estates and towns to summon reinforcements.'

145

'The page who hasn't reported back, where was he sent?'

Lancelin takes a deep, shuddering breath. 'Hatchlands.'

Lancelin's estate. Lucien's home.

I swallow hard. 'Who is there, Lancelin?'

He drops his gaze. 'My wife. My younger son, Xavier, of course.'

I wait, watching my steward struggle between guilt and fear. Until he adds, 'And Lucien. I know it was wrong, my lady. Treasonable. But whatever he did . . . he's still my child.'

I'm already backing away from him. 'But they know, Lancelin. Tallis and Siegfried, they know what he means to me. If they find him there . . .'

'Wait, Your Majesty –'

But I don't stop for Lancelin or for Lord Pianet. I have to get to Hatchlands.

Even from the air, I recognise the house from the painting that Lucien used to keep in his room at the Citadel. I've flown fast to get here, outpacing anyone who came after me, pushing myself to the point of exhaustion. But now I hesitate, circling the house and park, wondering whether I should go to the landing platform or choose a less obvious spot. Wondering why the house looks so . . . forlorn. There are no lights shining from the windows. No servants on the landing platform.

But perhaps it's not surprising. There's no sign of any attack, and there are hours still to go before dawn; the household could all be in bed, asleep. The page Lancelin sent out could have been delayed. I could just return to Merl. But Lancelin will want to know that his family are definitely safe.

And I can't be this close to Lucien and not try to see him.

146

I bank and spread my wings, catching the wind to slow my speed as I stretch towards the lake that takes up most of the platform. Settling my feathers, I glide through the water for a couple of minutes, but I can't rest. Along the wall that rises from the platform and curves towards the main first-floor entrance there are hooks with robes hanging from them; I transform, step out of the water and cover myself.

The door into the house is unattended and unlocked. I let myself into the hall and take in my surroundings: marble floor tiles, wood-panelled walls, a staircase rising to a galleried landing. No furniture apart from a round table, recently polished – the sweet scent of beeswax clings to the air – and a long case pendulum clock standing in one corner. Its steady tick barely disturbs the silence. Even my breathing seems too loud.

There's no sign of Lucien. Of anyone. There are rooms opening off the hallway; all are in darkness, but two have their doors ajar. I'm creeping towards the nearest of these when someone whispers my name.

'Aderyn.'

Lucien is standing on the second-floor gallery, illuminated by moonlight spilling through the large window above the front door. My pulse races. But before I can speak, he puts one finger to his lips and beckons me to follow him. As I begin to climb the stairs – flinching at every creak of the floorboards – Lucien goes up the next set of stairs, to the third floor. He waits for me to start climbing those stairs, then turns into a doorway to his left. By the time I gain the top of the second set of stairs he is at the end of a series of interconnected rooms; I see him silhouetted against another large window.

147

Why will he not allow me to catch him up?

Quickening my pace, I hurry through the rooms to reach the window. The room I've entered is empty, a dead end. I turn slowly, puzzled, wondering how Lucien has somehow evaporated. Until a tapestry hanging on one wall catches my attention; it's moving gently, as if caught by a draught. Sure enough, when I pull the tapestry back, there's a small door set into the wall. And beyond that, stone stairs spiralling upwards.

'Lucien?'

'Up here.'

He speaks louder now. I follow the sound of his voice and emerge into a circular room, the walls of which are almost entirely glass. The only solid section frames another small door, which I imagine will give access to steps leading to the roof. We're standing in a beacon tower – houses near the sea often have them. Taller than the buildings they mark, the windows of these towers have niches where oil lamps may be suspended, to guide transformed nobles home. No lamps are lit tonight, but the moonlight slanting through the glass is enough.

Lucien, finally, is waiting for me.

'Aderyn.' He inclines his head, but makes no other movement. 'What are you doing here?' There's a note of suppressed tension in his voice, but he doesn't smile, or glare. Doesn't seem anxious that I've discovered him somewhere he's not supposed to be. As far as I can tell, his expression is one of indifference.

'There's been an attack at Merl. And at Hythe. Your father –' I press a hand to my chest, a futile attempt to slow the rapid beating of my heart. 'He was worried about you. You, and your mother and brother.' Still Lucien says nothing. Just watches me, a faintly contemptuous lift to his eyebrows. My nails dig into my palms as I take a step forward. 'He sent a page, but received no reply . . .'

Finally, Lucien drops his gaze. 'I know about the attacks. And about the page.'

'You knew? Then why didn't you send him back to Merl?'

He moves away from me towards a large oak chest that stands back against the curved wall, lifts the lid of the chest and gestures inside.

Aron's voice, telling me I'm making a mistake, echoes in my mind. Lucien is leaning against the wall, his arms crossed. I walk to the open chest and look inside.

'Oh, by the Firebird . . .' A boy is curled up in the bottom of the chest. Dead: his eyes, unseeing, stare into nothingness, and his hands are already curled into claws. There's a leather cord around his neck. I try to get it free, but the touch of his skin – cold as meltwater – makes me flinch and draw back my hand. I force myself to try again. This time, the cord comes lose, revealing his badge of office: the Atratyan coat of arms.

Lucien hasn't moved.

'How?' I want to clamp my hands over my ears, to drown out the suspicion that is jeering inside my head. 'Please, tell me this wasn't you . . .'

'It wasn't.' The voice comes from behind me. 'It was me.'

There, at the top of the stairs, clad in the same sort of dark robe that I am wearing, standing where I was just a moment ago, is Tallis.

Eight

Only a few months have passed since I last saw her. Hardly enough time for me to forget the cold beauty of her features, or the way her silvery hair is broken up by a single streak of black. But still I doubt the evidence of my own eyes. How can she be here with Lucien?

Unless . . . unless she has Lucien's family somewhere. She came here after the attack on Merl, found Lucien, took his mother and brother hostage and killed the page. It's the only explanation for the empty house, for her presence, for Lucien's strange behaviour.

Tallis appears unarmed, as am I. But she is alone, and there are two of us, and Lucien has a dagger tucked into his belt.

I swing back to him.

'Quickly – stop her, before she . . .'

My words wither on my tongue.

Lucien has already drawn his dagger. He is pointing it at me.

'Lucien, I know she's threatening you.'

His gaze doesn't waver. Neither does his blade. I back away a little, palms raised. Try again.

'I know she must have your mother, or your brother. But together we can –'

'You're mistaken, Aderyn.' As Tallis walks to his side, Lucien shakes his head. 'My family are quite safe. You, on the other hand, are not.'

I can't breathe. This is impossible. And . . . and *ridiculous*. To think, even for one minute, that Lucien would ally himself with the woman who tried to torture him to death –

Mad theories spin out of control through my brain: this is an impostor, not Lucien at all – or Tallis is forcing him to pretend – or I am somehow hallucinating this entire scene . . .

I would gladly believe any or all of them. And yet Tallis is smiling at Lucien, quite naturally. Nodding her agreement. 'Very good, Lord Rookwood. I see you are a man of your word. Now, explain to her exactly how mistaken she is. Tell her why you're here.'

'I am here from choice, of my own free will. No pressure is being brought to bear upon me. I am here so that I may prove that my allegiance is now to Tallis.'

'To Tallis? I don't understand.'

'Ha.' He smiles at me. 'Who do you think told the mercenaries how to gain access to the shipyard at Hythe? Who do you think described the best way to attack Merl?'

'No. No, you couldn't have . . .'

He grits his teeth. 'Who do you think sketched for them the layout of the castle, who told them to be sure to destroy those parts that you love the most?'

I stare at him, numb, too shocked to move or speak, until a ripple of laughter from Tallis frees my tongue.

'You bastard.' I shake my head. 'Twenty-two people lie dead at Merl. And for what? Because Aron exposed you as a traitor? Because I wounded your pride?'

Lucien lunges forward, bringing the tip of his blade to within a feather's breadth of my neck.

'Wounded pride? Is that what you think this is? Aron tried to kill me. For what is banishment from my home and family but an endless, never-dying death? And you . . .' The dagger drops a little, and something that might be regret flickers across his features. But it is gone in an instant. And his voice, when he speaks, rakes me like a talon. 'You have made it abundantly clear, Aderyn, that I mean nothing to you. That my family, despite years of service to your house, means nothing to you. So I will return the compliment, and give my loyalty to one who will reward me and mine.' Before I can react, he seizes my hair with his free hand, forces my head back as I gasp with pain and places his blade across my throat. 'I told you once not to trust me. You should have listened. Shall I kill her, Tallis?'

'It is rather tempting, isn't it?' Tallis walks over to Lucien and rests one hand upon his arm, forcing him to lower his blade. She turns to me and I can see the gleam of triumph in her eyes. 'But killing her here and now, Lord Rookwood, would be rather more merciful than she deserves. Where would be the glory in it? Besides, cutting her throat just seems so . . . uninspired. Particularly as I have something much more elaborate planned for her.'

Lucien steps away from me and I stumble, catching myself on the window frame nearby, pressing one hand to my mouth as my stomach heaves.

'When then?' he questions.

'When we have taken everything from her. When she's watched everyone she cares for suffer and die. When I am sitting once more in my rightful place on the throne of Solanum, then . . . then we will chain her, and that crippled prince she's married to, in the arena, and every noble in the kingdom will witness their failure and execution.' She pauses. 'Look at me, Aderyn.'

I cannot find the will to disobey.

'Death is waiting for you. A public death, rich in pain and humiliation.' She gives me a friendly smile. 'You will try to evade it, but you will not succeed. Come, Lucien.'

Together, they move towards the small door that leads to the roof.

'You won't win.' My voice is weak, but loud enough to make them pause. 'Your evil is unmasked. Yours and Siegfried's. And if I die, if I and Aron fall, others will rise up in our place.'

She shrugs. 'Then they will die too. You see, Aderyn, that's the difference between me and you. Between me and pretty much . . . well, everyone actually. You're all so . . . anxious. Anxious to please, anxious to do the right thing. Or at least to appear as if you are. And so, when you should strike, you hesitate – even Siegfried. Alas, my brother is sometimes weaker than I would wish. But I know exactly what I want, and what I want is all that matters. The kingdom will be mine. I really don't care how many of my subjects I kill along the way.' Another bright smile. 'I can always get more.'

She turns away and they go through – no backwards glance from Lucien – and I hear a key turn in the lock.

Their precaution is unnecessary. My legs, that have been trembling since Lucien drew his knife against me, give way. I could not follow them even if I wished to.

A voice, somewhere nearby. I blink, and terror flares: I can't *see* –

My perspective shifts. I remember where I am, and realise that sea fog has rolled in off the water, surrounding the beacon tower in a carapace of mist, plunging the room into total darkness.

Someone is calling my name.

'Here . . .' My throat and mouth are parched; I swallow and lick my lips, and try again. 'I'm up here.'

A lamp emerges from the stairwell, its light painfully bright. Too bright for me to see who's holding it.

'Aderyn – you're injured . . .'

Veron. He's on his knees next to me, his arms are around me, and I'm sobbing, clutching at his robe, crying so hard that I can barely breathe. He pats my back, murmuring Celonian phrases, and lets me weep until I'm too exhausted to weep any longer.

'Are you hurt?'

I shake my head.

'What, then?'

I don't want to describe the agony of Lucien's betrayal, to try to compare the pain of his words piercing my heart to the pain inflicted by the hawks who tore open my back. So I turn

154

to the facts. 'Lucien was here. He was with Tallis. He is . . . It was him who led them to Hythe. And Merl.'

Veron swears softly. 'If only we'd got here sooner. We followed you almost immediately, but the fog delayed us. Thank the Creator you are unharmed. Come.'

'Wait – there's a body, in the chest over there. The page Lancelin sent . . .'

Veron's arm tightens around my shoulders. 'I'll tell Pianet, but we must get you out of here.' He hangs the oil lamp from the hook in front of the nearest window, so it casts its glow more widely, and looks at me. 'Can you walk?'

'Yes. Yes, of course.' I use the edge of my robe to dry my face, and tuck my damp hair back behind my ears.

'Better.' Veron smiles slightly and grips my shoulders. Standing, he holds out his hands to me and pulls me to my feet. 'Come. Let's find the others.'

Guiding me, letting me lean on him as much as possible, Veron takes me back to the Hatchlands landing platform. A couple of the torches have been lit, smudges of red in the dense fog; by their light we see two of Pianet's people, one of whom hurries to recall the others who are searching the house.

I wait, silent, listening to the mist-muffled rush of waves on the beach far below, dimly aware of Veron talking in a low voice to the others as they gather on the platform.

'Your Majesty . . .'

Lord Pianet is at my elbow.

'You know . . . ?'

'Yes. About Tallis, and Lord Rookwood, and the page. Hatchlands, as you may be aware, is entirely empty, the servants

155

and family all gone. I suggest, given the hour, and how far we've all flown, that we return to Merl and –'

'No. I want to go home.' And by home, I realise that I mean the Citadel. Lucien has desecrated – violated – the one place I thought I'd always be safe. I can't go back to Merl. Not now.

'Well . . .' Lord Pianet taps his toe on the flagstones. 'I must advise against a direct flight, Majesty. You're exhausted, and to fly so far in such a state . . . But I have a small house just across the border in southern Lancorphys. We could reach there without undue risk, rest for a few hours, then return to the Citadel.'

The scarred skin of my back is sore from having flown so far, so fast, and I'm in no state to argue. 'Very well.' I go back to listening to the sea while Pianet makes whatever arrangements he thinks necessary. When he tells me it's time, I transform and follow him into the air.

I don't remember the flight, or reaching Pianet's house. I don't remember anything of what I did for the few hours we spent there, though I suppose I must have slept, from physical exhaustion if nothing else. Still, despite my rest, my mind and senses remain dulled, and I'm aware of little until I'm standing on the landing platform of the Silver Citadel, squinting at the sun rising over the fjord.

Aron is waiting for me. As wrapped in sorrow as I am, even I can tell that he's furious. He keeps command over himself while we're in public, but as soon as we reach my rooms he orders my maids to leave my apartments. Letya stands her ground until I dismiss her; I'm too tired to take steps to avoid

Aron's wrath. She hesitates, tells me she'll be waiting in the next room, and closes the door behind her.

Aron turns on me. 'By the Firebird, Aderyn, what were you thinking? Are you so lost to all sense of propriety, of reason, of . . . of risk, as to fly to a house where you know that Lucien has been concealed?' He paces rapidly up and down, as if his anger is driving him. 'You're aware of the treason he's already been involved in. You know he has little cause to love me, whatever his feelings about you. It's bad enough that this *obsession* with Lucien has so overset your mind that you rush to his side without any thought for the consequences. But then to find that you put yourself in the power of Tallis . . .' He shakes his head and swears and kicks a chair that happens to be standing too close. 'They could have killed you, Aderyn. And then what would become of this kingdom you've sworn to protect?'

He reminds me of Lucien, after I told him how I'd become entangled with Siegfried. The lump in my throat swells painfully. 'I'm sorry.'

He glares at me.

'It was Lucien, Aron. I thought he was in danger. How could I have known that he, of all people, would lead me into a trap? That Lucien would . . .' I raise my fingers to my neck, feeling the welt left by the edge of his blade against my skin. 'But I understand now. That he no longer loves me. That he hates me, I mean.' I shiver beneath the thin robe I'm still wearing and sink onto the nearby sofa. 'You don't need to worry about my feelings for Lucien any more.'

Aron's pacing slows, stops, and he comes to sit next to me.

'I'm sorry he hurt you, Aderyn. More sorry than you realise.' He takes my hand. 'But at least we know now that Atratys is to be the first battleground. We'll send reinforcements from other dominions: flightless congregations and noble companies and ships from other dockyards. I've had the Eyria fortress reopened, and it's being repaired and restocked. There's no need for you to return to Merl.' At his mention of my childhood home my vision blurs. In my head, I'm back in the ruined hall. 'Please promise me you'll stay within the Citadel from now on, until this is all over.' His voice is softer, gentler. 'Please, Aderyn, I don't know how else to protect you.'

I want to promise what he's asking. To stay where it's safe, to allow others to direct our efforts so I don't have to think, or feel, any more than is absolutely necessary. But despite everything that has happened, I am still the Queen of Solanum. And I can't hide in the shadows while the flames of Tallis and Siegfried's treachery grow ever brighter. Besides, I've not forgotten my plan to fly north. We need allies more than ever, and if the Shriven do exist, then I mean to find them.

'I can't promise that, Aron. There are things I have to do . . .'

He straightens up. Releases my hand. 'I see. You're determined, then, to get yourself killed?'

'No, I –'

'We'll discuss this again later.' He stalks to the door. 'Perhaps Letya will be able to talk some sense into you.'

Letya comes in as soon as Aron has gone. She takes the throw from the back of the sofa, wraps it around my shoulders and passes me a handkerchief.

I realise I'm crying again. 'Merl, Letya. I can't believe what they did to our home. What Lucien allowed them to do.'

'My poor Aderyn,' my friend murmurs. 'If I had Lucien Rookwood here now . . .' She brings her lips close to my forehead, almost kissing me. 'I'll get the maids to draw a bath for you. Then food, and bed. And maybe tomorrow will be better.'

Tomorrow isn't better. Nor is the day after, nor the day after that. I go through the motions, attending meetings with Lord Pianet and my other counsellors as normal, but my resolve to do something meaningful to counter the threat of Tallis and Siegfried falters. My plans to find the Shriven do not progress. Instead, I hoard my grief, forcing myself to think about Lucien, to remember every interaction I had with him, to relive over and over the moment he asked Tallis whether he should kill me. And this Lucien, constructed out of my memories: I talk to him. Rage at him. Clutch him to me as if I can somehow forge a different reality out of something as insubstantial as mist.

Until, the fourth morning after my return, Fris brings me my breakfast as usual, and I notice her eyes are red and puffy and realise she's been crying.

'Fris? What's the matter?'

'Nothing, my lady.' The shortness of her answer surprises me. She turns away and begins tidying the bedroom, yanking the curtains open so hard that one of the hooks is torn from the heavy fabric.

'Please. Tell me what's wrong.'

159

She takes a deep breath and pulls a handkerchief from her pocket, twisting it in her hands. 'I just heard yesterday, Majesty. My brother Crael was injured in the attack on Merl. He's died.'

My stomach lurches; I push the plate of food to one side. 'Oh, Fris. I'm so sorry. Is there anything I can do? Would you like to return to Atratys for a while?'

'No, thank you, my lady. Crael is beyond my help now.' She dabs at her eyes with the handkerchief, sniffing. 'And my duty lies here. Is there anything else you need?'

I can feel the blush creeping up my neck. Maybe Fris blames me for the attack on Merl, maybe she doesn't, but as she watches me it seems that she must know that truth: that since I got back to the Citadel, I've done nothing other than think of Lucien. Of his betrayal. Of how much I miss him still. The possibility that there could be others grieving as much as myself had not occurred to me.

I'm ashamed of myself.

'Lay out some clothes for me, please, Fris. And send one of the maids to find Odette.'

Mourning Lucien will achieve nothing. I'll not continue to weep over him while my people suffer.

He isn't worth my tears.

Odette is still willing to fly north with me in search of the Shriven, and she agrees to talk to the others who were going to join us. I ask Lord Pianet to nominate two agents to accompany us, though I don't tell him where we're going. And I don't say anything at all to Aron. Given the promise he tried to extract from me before, I can't imagine he's going to be supportive of a plan that involves leaving the Citadel to search for a mythical people who supposedly live on an island that doesn't appear to exist.

I should have known that he'd find out anyway.

Odette and I are in my sitting room, poring over maps and discussing landing sites, when Aron walks into the room.

'When exactly were you planning to tell me about this little expedition, wife? Or was I just going to wake up one morning to discover you and my sister had disappeared?' He stares at us, eyebrows raised, a red flush across his cheeks.

Odette and I glance at each other. 'Aron,' she begins. But he ignores her and waves his hand at me.

'Atratys has been attacked. And now we have reports that Eorman of Frianland is busy building a fleet of ships in the harbours nearest our own coastline. We're at war, Aderyn, in case it's escaped your notice. A queen does not abandon her throne to go off on some –'

'Stop telling me what a queen does or doesn't do! I've had enough of you and Lady Crump lecturing me. Searching for potential allies is the only thing I can actually do right now.' I met with the royal council yesterday; the congregations are gathering, defences are being strengthened, but we still haven't discovered the hiding place of the mercenaries who attacked Atratys. 'I'll be gone for a few days, Aron, that's all. And as crazy as you think my plan is, if there's any chance that these Shriven are out there –'

He flings his hand into the air, exclaiming contemptuously. 'Ridiculous. Though you seem not to have considered the possibility that, if these creatures do exist, they might prefer

161

to kill you than help you. You, and my sister.' He glares at Odette. 'Send Pianet's gentlemen out on this wild dragon hunt. Let them take the risk.'

Aron means the nobles secretly employed by Pianet, nobles who have to work for the crown because they no longer have the land or income to support themselves, and we can afford to pay them.

'But which one of the gentlemen would be able to negotiate an alliance? If these people do exist, I doubt they will consider themselves bound to us by any ties of loyalty. We'll have to persuade them to trust us. And how better to do that than for me to go to them myself?'

Aron's jaw tightens. 'Odette, please – for my sake, stay here. This adventure will accomplish nothing and could cost everything.' He draws himself up. 'I forbid you to go.'

'Forbid me?' Odette's hands go to her hips. 'You're not my parent, Aron. And in case you hadn't realised, we're not going alone, and we're flying to the opposite end of the kingdom to where the danger is.' She crosses her arms and juts out her chin. 'If Aderyn goes, so do I.'

Aron is trembling. 'Fine. As you've pointed out before, Aderyn, you are the queen. Your time is yours to waste as you wish. But if anything happens to my sister, I'm holding you –' he jabs his finger at me – 'responsible.'

He turns on his heel.

But I can't restrain my tongue any more. 'You told me I always do what I want, Aron. But that's not true. If I'd done what I wanted, neither of us would be on the throne. We wouldn't be married either. I'd be at Merl, with Lucien –'

I gasp as soon as the words leave my mouth, remembering the letters Aron found, the proof that Lucien was considering rebellion even while he was taking me to his bed.

Aron flinches, but he leaves the room without looking back.

Aron doesn't mention the expedition again, either to me or to Odette, but he is hardly speaking to me at all. Our arrangements are almost complete. The only thing I'm waiting for, impatiently, is the arrival of Lancelin from Atratys. After Lucien's treachery, leaving Lancelin in charge of the kingdom's wealthiest dominion, even as my steward, was impossible. He's being placed under informal house arrest at the Citadel; the only compensation for the humiliation this will cause him is the hope that at least here he will be safe. Despite the sense of urgency that is eating at me, I can't leave without seeing him.

Two days after my fight with Aron, Lancelin reaches the Citadel, though I don't know how he managed the flight. As soon as I enter his room, I realise that my steward is a shadow of the man I saw at Merl after the attack. His stoop is more pronounced, his dark skin has an ashen tinge, and his eyes . . . He's looking at me, but he doesn't see me. Not really.

'Lancelin . . . I'm so sorry. About Lucien. About everything. There's been no news as to the whereabouts of your wife or your other son?'

He shakes his head and pushes the candle that's burning on the table a little further away from him. 'Lucien must be concealing them somewhere. Whether they are with him by force or by choice . . .' He gropes for the seal of the House

163

of Cygnus Atratys, which he has worn for so long around his neck. 'I must return this to you.'

I take it from him, staring down at the familiar outline.

'I know what you might have to do,' he murmurs. 'I understand that you might have to kill him.'

His comment silences me. I've thought about capturing Tallis and Siegfried. About ordering their executions. But I've not yet been able to bring myself to consider doing the same to Lucien.

Perhaps Lancelin senses my discomfort.

'He's chosen his side, Aderyn. Lucien will be a dangerous opponent. You shouldn't take the risk of showing him mercy.' My steward clears his throat and turns away from me a little. 'If he is truly capable of betraying his dominion and his people to side with a woman who would destroy them, then he doesn't deserve mercy.'

'But . . . he's still your son, Lancelin.'

'Not any more. After what he's done . . .' He hunches further over in his chair. The grief he radiates is infectious. Despair settles on my skin like snow, chilling me more effectively than any real frost.

'I have to go, my lord, but I'll be back in a few days. Letya will come to see you, so if there is anything you need . . .'

'Thank you, Your Majesty.' He takes a book from the table and begins turning the pages. But when I glance back, just before closing the door, the book is on his lap, and he's once again staring at nothing.

The first stars are showing themselves against the eastern sky, and my six companions are waiting on the landing platform.

Letya is there too. She is wearing gloves, so I take her hands in mine for just a moment.

'Be safe, Your Majesty. I hope you find what you're looking for.'

'So do I, my dear friend.' I drop the luckstone into her hand. 'Until I return.'

She retreats into the safety of the Citadel. I linger for another minute, wondering whether Aron will come to bid us farewell. But he doesn't. And I won't delay any further.

It's time.

We've not flown far before Veron speaks a question into my mind.

Is this the right way? You said we were going to Olorys.

Somehow the silence shifts – I sense the curiosity of the rest of my companions. Apart from Odette, they are all waiting for my answer.

I'm afraid I lied, my lord. We fly north.

The first night's flight brings us to Rogallyn Manor a couple of hours before dawn. Lamps are lit on the landing platform, and I can just make out two heavily clothed flightless waiting at the far end next to a pile of robes. Lady Verginie sent a note preparing her servants for the arrival of a party of her friends; they know we are nobles, but nothing more. We will use no indicators of rank or family on this journey. Each of us carries a waterproof package containing a fur-lined robe, a pair of light boots and a dagger for our exploration of the Harrowed Lands. Lords Lien and Pyr, Pianet's two gentlemen, have bulkier parcels, which I suspect conceal additional weapons. We land, shift to our human shapes and remove the packages from around our necks as the servants hurry forward with robes. I'm not used to flying with a burden; the muscles at the base of my skull send prickles of pain down my spine and across my shoulders. We follow the robe-bearers into the tapestry-hung entrance hall and find another servant waiting for us, clad in the gold-and-green livery of the House of Cygnus Lancorphys.

'Lady Nyssa.' He bows. 'Welcome back to Rogallyn. Your room has been prepared for you, and the guest rooms on the second and third floor for your friends. A selection of clothing has been made available in each room.' His gaze flickers swiftly across us, lingering for a moment on the bundles we clutch in our hands. 'If three of the gentlemen would like to accompany me to the third floor . . .'

'Thank you, Glisk. Ladies, and Veron, will you follow me?'

We proceed in silence up the carpeted staircase to the next landing. From here, Nyssa leads Odette, Veron and me along a narrow corridor, while Glisk and the others continue upwards. She points to a door.

'This is my room. The guest rooms are those three doors at the end.'

'Thank you, Nyssa. Go and rest. We can ring if we need anything.'

She nods and disappears into her room as the rest of us walk on. Odette says goodnight at the next doorway. The other two rooms are opposite each other, divided by a window set into the end wall of the corridor. I pause briefly, trying to make out what might lie in the darkness beyond the house, but there's nearly an hour to go before dawn. All I can see is my own reflection, broken up into fragments by the leaded panes. My neck still aches; as I turn away from the window, a sudden stab of pain makes me flinch.

'By the Firebird, I need to get stronger. Goodnight, Veron.'

'Wait —' Still behind me, he sets down his bundle and rests his hands on my shoulders. 'I believe I can ease your discomfort. May I?'

'If you think it will help.'

He begins kneading my muscles, touching me firmly through the thin fabric of my robe, applying just enough pressure with his fingertips to loosen the knots of tension without hurting me. My shoulders sag as the pain eases. The sensation is so pleasurable that I force myself to place my hand over his to stop him.

'Thank you, Veron. That was most . . . helpful. How did you learn to do that?'

'Our father used to make Valentin and me practise carrying heavy loads while we flew. We learned to tend to each other's aches and injuries.'

I stare up at him.

He laughs, his dark eyes crinkling. 'It wasn't as bad as it sounds. And knowing how to dress wounds, or merely how to make another person more physically comfortable, is a useful skill.'

'Indeed.' Silence falls between us. Lengthens. 'Well, goodnight.'

Veron takes my hand in his. 'I felt your sorrow, when we were flying. Your mind felt —' he pulls a face — 'grey.'

I don't know what to say. It's a risk we take when flying with others. The power that enables us to speak from mind to mind also lays open our feelings for others to read. I'd hoped that I'd buried my grief deep enough to conceal it. But apparently not.

'Veron, I –'

'I'd like to help you feel better again, Aderyn. If there's anything I can do, to soothe your pain, or help you forget your sadness, even for a little while, I hope you'll tell me.' He raises my hand to his lips and kisses my fingers.

I swallow hard. 'Goodnight, Veron. And . . . thank you.' Pulling my hand away, I hurry into my room. Hurry into bed, trying to ignore the loneliness, the sudden longing for physical comfort that stirs – unexpected and unwanted – in the pit of my stomach.

Nine

I wake late in the day, but there are still many hours left until sunset and our second flight. Everyone seems on edge; Lien and Pyr are bickering over something, and even Odette speaks sharply – for her – to Lord Blackbill. I seek solitude in the gardens, but staring at the sky doesn't make the light fade any quicker. Driven back inside by a burst of squally rain, I take shelter in a room that seems to be furnished for reading and music; it smells of lavender and old books. But I'm not alone: Veron is seated at a harpsichord, studying the music on the stand in front of him, slowly running his hands over the keys. There's a familiarity to the plaintive melody, as if it might be a memory, if I could just catch hold of it.

Veron notices me hovering by the door. I turn to go, but he calls after me.

'Stay, please – I've found something that might interest you.'

He hands me the music book from which he was playing: a collection of songs bound together with a jewel-studded gold clasp. There's an inscription in the top right corner of the first page.

For Verginie of Lancorphys from Rothbart and Diandra of Atratys, with joyful wishes on this Feast of the Firebird. A date follows: the summer Solstice, a year before my mother died. I run my fingers across the ink, brown with age. The handwriting is Lancelin's; he must have organised the gift. With the music still in my right hand I try to pick out the tune.

I haven't the skill to go beyond the first few bars. But as the last note fades, I suddenly remember my father, sitting playing this exact piece while my mother sang. The image in my mind is definitely a room at Merl. The west drawing room, I think, though we have no instrument there now, nor anywhere in the castle. Perhaps my father had it removed after my mother's death. It would have been like him, to shut away or destroy what he could no longer bear to see.

Veron has moved away from the instrument and is strolling around the room.

'This reminds me of my home. We have a room like this, a room for reading and music and pleasant conversation. Or had, at least. Who knows what is left of it now?' He runs one finger across the strings of a gilded harp standing in the corner. 'I used to enjoy days spent like that.'

'I enjoyed hearing you play. You're very accomplished.'

He laughs and shakes his head. 'I'm out of practice. But it helped me pretend for a little while.'

'Pretend?'

'That the revolution hadn't happened.' He walks back to where I'm standing. Comes close to me. 'That I was back home with my music and my books, and a beautiful woman to talk to.'

170

Blood flares in my cheeks beneath the intensity of his gaze. 'Veron . . .'

'If I'd met you – or someone like you – someone to inspire me to do what is right, to strengthen my will, then perhaps things would have been different. I could have been happy.' He takes the music book gently from my fingers, and I realise I've been holding it like a shield between us.

'I hope you still will be happy. Surely, it's not impossible.'

'So much of what I want is impossible.' He lifts one hand almost to my face, as if he's about to caress me. My heart beats faster, and all I can think of is Lucien, and how he kissed me, and how I've promised to spend the rest of my life with Aron, without being kissed or held by anyone ever again –

Veron sighs and turns to the keyboard and plays a few notes. 'Still, I have my duty to my people. That will have to be enough.'

I nod, both relieved and disappointed. 'Yes.' I echo his words, applying them to myself. 'Duty will have to be enough.'

'Where are we going, by the way? Further north?'

'Yes. The most northerly tip of Fenian. The Harrowed Lands.' He frowns, so I add, 'It means tormented. Wounded. There was a great war in Solanum, long ago, when the kingdom was invaded and overcome by Vilm the Bastard. The nobles and flightless of northern Fenian refused to submit, even after Vilm was crowned at the Silver Citadel. In retribution, he ploughed the ground with salt and slaughtered the entire population. The rivers ran red with blood. Or so the story goes.' I shiver, remembering Tallis's words to me at Hatchlands, her willingness to kill no matter what the cost. 'There are other stories of course. That the land is empty because it's too close to the

Pyre Flames. That the Flames drove the people mad, until they plunged into the sea . . .'

'And once we're there?'

'It depends on what we find.'

He raises an eyebrow, waiting. Shakes his head and sighs when it becomes clear I'm not about to tell him anything more.

'You don't trust me.'

'It's not you, Veron.' I lay my hand on his shoulder, remember the words Lucien spoke to me last summer. 'Someone told me once to trust no one. The longer I live, the better advice it seems. I think, if I want to stay alive, I need to follow it.'

'If being alive is all you wish, then yes, perhaps. But to fully trust no one . . . it is to live alone, even if you are surrounded by people.' He runs one hand through his silver hair, in a gesture that reminds me of Lucien. 'I know what that feels like.' A pause. 'Aderyn . . .'

'Yes?'

Veron smiles suddenly – but the smile is too bright, too forced. 'If only we had someone else to play for us. I enjoyed our dance at the ball very much. Come –' he bows and holds out one hand – 'will you not dance with me now, though we have no music? Who knows if we will have the chance again.'

Veron's rapidly shifting mood confuses me. Alarms me, a little. I wonder what he was actually about to say to me, before he changed his mind. 'I'm not really in the mood to dance, Veron. And I'm sure there will be other occasions –'

'Please?' He stares at me, his arm still extended. There's a sort of desperation in his voice.

So I nod. 'Very well.' Sweeping a formal curtsy, I take his hand. 'What shall we have?'

'A chaconné, I think. Something in a minor key, to suit the times.' Veron starts humming quietly, a slow, sad melody, and we move through the steps of the dance.

But my mind is occupied by something different: by thoughts of my future, if I survive. I think about the letter Aron left me with the telescope, his suggestion about what we might become to each other, and whether he would still even want that, given the way we've been fighting. About Letya and Odette and whether they will marry and leave the Citadel.

Perhaps Veron is right. Perhaps my future is to be alone.

Our dance ends. Ignoring the imaginary Lucien who haunts me, I go on tiptoe and kiss Veron gently on his lips, escaping before he can react.

I don't see Veron again until we are assembled on the landing platform a couple of hours later, our bundles once again around our necks. Odette and Pyr – a native of Fenian and a member of a cormorant family – are standing slightly apart, discussing the route. I approach my cousin and squeeze her hand.

'Ready?'

'Yes.' She raises her voice to address the others. 'Pyr and I have agreed that we'll keep just west of the coast as much as possible, avoiding the lands held by the Protector, turning slightly inland once we're past Dyrg. Keep close. The storms off the northern coast of Fenian are frequent and deadly.'

We hand our robes to the heavily clad attendant and shift

our shapes. Rogallyn Manor is soon lost in the darkness behind us.

Odette was right to warn us. Over the next few hours the wind strengthens to a gale, and we are forced to alter our course more than once. The storm we flee from is transforming the sea into a mass of towering, white-crested waves. Waves that claw and smash their way over cliffs and harbour walls and leave destruction behind.

I pity the people caught in the storm's path, but we can't turn aside and help them; it's enough of a struggle to make headway through the buffeting wind. We fly in silent formation, listening for Odette's instructions, taking turns at the front so that everyone gets a chance to rest, at least a little, in the updraught of air that comes with following behind. By the time we reach the moors marking the southern boundary of the Harrowed Lands, my entire body aches; every muscle, every bone, every feather.

But gradually the sky lightens, revealing the landscape below us: a mess of boulders and stunted trees and broken slabs of limestone criss-crossed by streams that run in and out of rocky crevices. I start to look for the coastline, beyond which lie the four Impenny Islands. And beyond the furthest of them, the Pyre Flames.

Odette told me I would know the Pyre as soon as I saw it. She is right.

The flickering light breaks across the horizon ahead of me, filling my vision. All my companions, even Odette and Pyr, who have seen it before, exclaim in wonder. Odette leads us down towards a cove where a spit of rock has created a lagoon. She banks and loses height, skimming across the cliffs, slowing as she descends, turning sharply at the last minute into the shadow behind a tall outcrop. We land on or near the small body of water. Transform. But despite our exhaustion, no one lies down. We hurry into our robes and down to the beach.

Veron, standing next to me, murmurs something in Celonian. 'What does that mean?'

'It means . . . beautiful. Magnificent, I suppose. I know the story, of course – the funeral pyre of the Firebird, burning at the end of the earth, until the end of time. I've seen paintings, even. But the reality . . .'

'Quite.' I can't tear my gaze away from the view. Strands of brilliant blue and green flame blaze up from the sea, fading eventually into space. They stretch from left to right as far as I can see. The four islands are dark silhouettes against a jewel-coloured backdrop.

'Dangerous though,' says Pyr. 'Can you feel it? The flames call to our blood. Like a magnet; if you get too close, you can't escape. And then . . .' He opens his hands and makes a whooshing sound. 'Incineration.' His orange-tinted face breaks into a smile.

Pyr is right; there's a sort of prickling sensation beneath my skin that wasn't there before. 'What lies on the other side?'

'Nobody knows. You can't go through it, as I said. The Flames extend far below the waterline, and they're too high to fly over. And there's no gap. An unbroken circle of fire . . .'

We all stare at the Flames, mesmerised. Until Nyssa sags and stumbles against Lien.

'Sorry – I'm just so tired . . .'

'We should rest, at least for a little. It must be nearly dawn.' Even as I speak, the sun rises and bleeds the colour from the Pyre flames, turning them into something more like a wall of shifting light. Harder to see. But what does that matter, when we can feel their presence? We troop back into the darkness of the cove, each claim a space on the sand and lie down. Sleep comes quickly.

I wake to bright daylight and a clear blue sky above. The tops of the cliffs that surround us are sunlit, though down here at their base we are still in shadow. Waves rush against the beach, punctuating the constant murmur of the waterfall that tumbles into the lagoon, and there are true gulls screeching and circling above the lagoon. They flap off when I push myself up. I stretch – my body is stiff from flying and from lying on the hard, damp sand – take a deep breath, wrinkling my nose; the air stinks of seaweed. Most of the others are still asleep, but Odette is sitting wrapped in her robe and clutching her knees, staring out to sea. I pull on my robe and join her.

'Did you sleep?'

She nods. 'I've not been awake long. What's our plan?'

'Find something to eat. Then start searching the islands for signs of habitation. Maybe search the coastline of the mainland too, if we have time. Accris claims her lover spoke of a fifth island, but . . .' I gesture towards the impenetrable barrier of the Pyre Flames.

Odette picks up a shell and turns it over in her fingers. 'Have you thought about how long we should search for?'

'Two days. Three at most. We're cut off up here, and if there's another attack on Atratys, I want to know. Besides, we've no real shelter, and I don't know how easy it will be to find food. I won't risk anyone's life on the basis of hearsay and mythology, but perhaps we'll spot something that Grayla and her people missed. The symbol, for example; the crest, or whatever it is, that Accris's lover had on his arm.' Accris's drawing, and the page from Frant's book, are tucked into the small leather pouch hanging from my neck; I grip it in my hand like a talisman. 'We'll cover as much as we can in three days, then return.'

'And if we find nothing?'

'Then we're no worse off than before.' I stand up and brush some of the sand from my robe. 'Would you wake the others? I'm going to the waterfall to bathe.'

Two days come and go. We fly over all four islands and across every wingspan of the coast that forms the northern boundary of the Harrowed Lands. But we find nothing. No houses, no crops, no fishing nets. No symbol helpfully carved into the top of a cliff. Not so much as a footprint, however low we swoop. I know the others sense my growing desperation. I can't stop my thoughts swinging like a pendulum back south, towards the Citadel, and beyond to Atratys, worrying about what might be happening. When we return to the cove at the end of the second day of searching, I wrap myself in my robe and sit alone and brood.

Odette settles on the sand next to me.

'You should eat something. Pyr's cooking fish.'

'I'm not hungry.'

My cousin sighs, but doesn't press me. We sit in silence for a few minutes, watching the Flames and listening to the soft rush of the tide.

'Aderyn,' she murmurs, 'let me see Accris's drawing again.' I pull the folded pages from the pouch and pass them to Odette. She tilts them so the light falls on them. 'These dots above the hand . . . Could they be a constellation?'

I take the pieces of paper back from her and squint at them. There's a difference I hadn't noticed before between Accris's sketch and the page I tore from Frant's book. The dots that Accris has drawn above the hand look random, whereas those in the illustration . . . I gasp. 'I think you're right. It's the Wishbone. Accris didn't know what she was looking at, so she didn't copy it correctly.' I jump up, grab Odette's hand and pull her up next to me. 'It's the most northerly constellation. It circles the Pyre Flames so it's very dim – you can only see it if you know where to look.' Together we crane our heads back, scanning the sky. But now I know what I'm searching for, it only takes me moments to spot the faint arc of stars that make up the constellation. 'There . . .'

My excitement fades, even as I point out the Wishbone to my cousin. 'It doesn't make any difference though. We've found nothing.'

Odette and I both stare out at the dark bulk of Sceada, the fourth island and the most distant, that seems to lie almost beneath the Wishbone constellation.

'Maybe they've died out,' Odette says. 'Perhaps that's why we can't find them.'

178

I shake my head, remembering Accris's swollen belly. 'At least one of them is very much alive.' I fold up the drawings and put them back in the pouch. 'We've one more day. Perhaps we can't find them because we're looking in the right place, but in the wrong way. We'll go back to Sceada tomorrow and search it on foot.'

'On foot?'

Odette sounds dismayed, but I nod. 'Whatever else they may be able to do, no one claims these Shriven can fly.'

I barely sleep that night. We've only a few hours before we have to fly south again, so I wake my companions as soon as the sky begins to lighten and we fly to Sceada. We land at the water's edge on the north side of the island, close to the flickering barrier of the Pyre Flames, and put on robes and boots.

'Can you feel it?' Odette shivers. 'It's even worse, out here. It hurts.'

We all nod, and rub our arms or faces, because it does hurt, a little. It's as if the Flames are burrowing beneath our skin, trying to draw something out of us. I wonder for a moment if our power to transform came from the Pyre Flames; if the Flames are trying to reclaim it. Clutching my robe tighter about me I grab Odette's hand, but she resists, still staring ahead.

'My mother told me it was a bad omen, to see the Pyre Flames. She said that was why Fenian is so poor and sickly – the people are cursed, because they live too close.' Looking at me over her shoulder she asks, 'Do you think it's true, Aderyn?'

'I think it's just a story. A story someone made up to feel better about their life. A way of explaining misfortune, or giving hope that misfortune might be avoided. A way of . . . taking back some control, I suppose.' I sigh. 'Just like the story about the Shriven in Gullwing Frant's book. Doesn't mean either of them are true. Come on.' I point to a peak that sits above a dark cave opening into the hillside. 'We'll get a good view of the land from up there.'

We set off briskly and begin to climb; the landscape is rocky and uneven, full of unexpected pits half concealed by the scrubby, sharp-needled bushes that spread everywhere. My hands and arms are soon covered with scratches. Our boots slip on the lichen-covered rocks. We take them off. Before we've reached the peak, Veron nudges me and points to the eastern sky.

'Look.'

Storm clouds are gathering on the horizon.

'Pyr, how long do we have?'

Pyr squints, trying to judge the distance between the storm and the island. 'It's moving quickly. Perhaps we should fly the rest of the way up.'

Lien shakes his head. 'We won't be able to land if the ground's covered in more of this this damn stuff.' He grunts and swears as he rips his robe away from the grip of one of the spiny shrubs. 'No one could live here. This is –' He breaks off, glancing at me, his tawny skin flushing darker.

Hopeless? Pointless? Everyone's watching me. The first spots of rain hit us as the edge of the storm arrives, and I turn away. This desolation of rock and thorn offers nowhere to hide from the truth: I'll find no allies here.

The hope I'd been clinging to dissolves. My jaw aches as

180

I grit my teeth, trying to hold back the tears of frustration that are blinding me, trying to swallow the curses that I want to scream into the teeth of the rising wind.

'Aderyn?' My cousin's voice.

But I can't answer. I can't let them hear the desperation and fear and grief that I thought I'd buried –

Odette grips my shoulder.

And her touch is enough. It reminds me of who I am. Of my responsibilities. I can't break down. Not here, not now.

My pulse slows. I take a deep breath, wipe the tears from my face and turn back to the others. 'Let's wait in the cave for the rain to pass. Then we'll fly home.' No one replies, but they follow me all the same.

We make the shelter of the cavern just in time, chased inside by a rumble of thunder. At least there's plenty of space; the cave runs straight back into the hillside, and its roof disappears into shadows above.

'Lien, you brought some candles, didn't you?' My voice echoes, unexpectedly loud.

Lien brings out a tinderbox and a few candles from the bag around his neck and lights the wicks, but they do little more than deepen the darkness. The rain has begun to fall heavily, obscuring the sea beyond, splashing loud against the rock floor. Together, we make our way further in. Far enough to see that, although the cave narrows towards a sort of natural arch, there's no obvious end.

'A tunnel?'

'Could be,' Lien replies. He tests the floor with his foot. 'Slope's not too steep. We could go a little further, if you wish.'

As the others try to make themselves more comfortable, collecting moss and ferns from the rock crevices to make a fire, Lien and I walk slowly forward. Our candle flames flicker; there's a breeze coming from somewhere.

The walls in this part of the cave are flatter, and free of vegetation. I run my fingertips across the surface of the rock, discovering long, regular gashes that might have been made by the blade of a chisel. A projecting rectangle that might almost be a pillar. Perhaps the arch is not so natural after all. I lift my candle higher and something catches my eye. 'Lien . . .' He comes to stand next to me. 'What does that look like to you?'

'Hard to say . . . A shield, maybe?' He tilts his head, squinting, then walks to the opposite wall. 'Um . . . That might be another one, up there. Strange . . .'

I strain my eyes to make out the details of the carving – if that's what it is. It might be nothing to do with the Shriven. And even if it is, a remnant of whatever lost society once lived on this barren rock is of no use to me. We've flown over Sceada; the whole island is boulders and brambles. If this tunnel once led to somewhere more hospitable, that landscape is long since gone.

Still, I wish I had more light. I edge my way forward, drawn by the tunnel . . .

A scream echoes through the cave. I turn back, but something – someone – falls on top of me, knocking me to the ground, dashing the candle from my hand.

'Ambush!' Lien roars, dropping his own candle and heaving my attacker away from me. But there are more figures – more than I can count in the dim light – leaping from ropes somehow

182

secured above. I can just make out Lien and Pyr, swords drawn, hacking and slashing their way closer to the cave mouth, trying to forge a path for the rest of us. Pyr turns, wrenching his blade out of someone's leg, and bellows at me to transform, to escape.

But I'm not leaving alone.

Blackbill's nearby, yelling for Odette – or at her, I can't tell – grappling with one of our assailants until a second attacker fells him with a blow to the head. Fumbling for my small knife in the pouch that hangs round my neck, I clamber onto an outcrop of rock and scan the cave.

'Odette?' I can't see my cousin anywhere. 'Odette –'

A hooded man lunges at me with a sword. I leap off the rock and grab the exposed skin of his wrist, expecting him to scream as my touch incinerates his skin.

But he doesn't. Just seizes my other arm with his free hand, gripping so hard it hurts. We struggle together as his blade gets closer to my face, until I land a kick between his legs and he staggers back. A shriek rings out: Nyssa, blood gushing from her nose, has been pinned against the wall by one of our enemies, but before I can reach her someone is slashing a sword through the air in front of me, and Pyr is yelling at me again to shift my shape, and Veron –

Without warning, Veron transforms.

It doesn't seem to hurt our attackers – if they're flightless, they should be writhing on the floor screaming, this close to a transformed noble – but it shocks them. Their attention is focused on Veron's beating wings and viciously hooked beak. Only for a moment, but it's enough. I charge into the man nearest to me, sending his blade flying and leaving him sprawled on the ground. Grab the sword. Hurry to put my foot on his chest and the point of the sword against his neck.

'Surrender, or he dies!'

The masked figures nearest me step back. Finally I see Odette. But there's a knife at her throat, and her hands are bound. There's nothing I can do. I drop my stolen sword. Lien and Pyr lay down their weapons and raise their hands, while Veron transforms back into human form and picks his robe off the floor. Blackbill is supporting Nyssa; she's pinching her nose, blood still welling through her fingers. Our attackers herd us together at sword point.

'Lights.' The voice of someone used to command.

Some of the masked people pull out tinderboxes and candles. I blink in the sudden brightness, shielding my eyes from the flames. When I look back, a copper-haired woman is standing opposite me. She's wearing armour of a sort I've never seen before; the candlelight glints off a breastplate and arm guards that seem to be made from overlapping, iridescent scales. The others drag off their masks, revealing a mixture of men and women, older and younger. But all of them, apart from the woman who seems to lead them, have the stars of the Wishbone constellation painted across their cheeks, and their skin shimmers in the dim light.

'Who's your leader?' the copper-haired woman growls. No one replies, and Odette cries out as the one holding her yanks her head further back. 'Answer me.'

'You traitorous scum,' Lien snarls. 'If you think Tallis is going to save you from –'

184

'You think we're nobles?' The woman spits on the floor. 'For the last time: who is your leader?'

Fear brushes my skin into toad warts, but I've come this far, and – if this woman is what I believe her to be – I've come for this. And I won't risk Odette. I edge around Veron's tall form. 'I am their leader. Who are you?'

'You may call me Damarin. I'm going to take one of you for interrogation. It can be you, or her.'

'Interrogation followed by what?'

'Depends on what we find out.' She shrugs. 'I make no promises. We may bring you back here and allow you to leave. Or we may not.'

We're outnumbered and surrounded. There's not really any choice.

'Very well.' I step forward, and Odette is released.

'Your Majesty, no –' Lien moves towards me, only to be brought up short by two swords levelled at his chest.

'Oh . . .' Damarin walks around me. 'A queen, is it? Bind her. And the rest of you, I'll leave you here under guard while we decide what to do with you. If you value this woman's life, and your own, don't try to escape. And don't try to follow; you'll be lost in moments. There's a maze of tunnels and chasms down there in the darkness.' She grins. 'And then there are the things that live in the tunnels and chasms. Rash –' she nods at one of the older women – 'bind their legs, but don't harm them, as long as they cooperate.'

One of Damarin's people jerks my wrists forward and ties them tightly together with a length of rope. Another gags me; the rough, sour-tasting fabric forced into my mouth makes my stomach heave. At least my robe hides the fact that my knees are shaking. Damarin takes hold of the other end of the rope and starts walking. I half turn, trying for one last look at my friends, but she's too fast. Unless I follow her, I'll fall.

'Aderyn,' Veron calls, 'don't let them –' His shout ends in a grunt of pain, as if he's been punched. Have Damarin's guards already disobeyed her orders? I look over my shoulder, pulling back on the rope.

But it's too late. We've passed through the arch at the end of the cave. The curve of the tunnel has hidden Veron and the others from my sight.

Damarin swears and yanks on the rope, dragging me forward again. I have to hurry to keep up, and as the light fades my feet find enough sharp-edged stones in the sandy floor to make me regret discarding my boots. For a few more minutes we walk through a sort of twilight. But then the path twists further to the left.

Darkness swallows us.

Ten

My eyes are useless.

This is not the darkness of night, lit by some faint shimmer from the stars even when they are veiled in cloud. This is an absence of light such as I've never experienced. A heavy, suffocating blankness. Sightless, I listen instead. To Damarin's footsteps. To the plink of liquid dripping onto rock. To distant grumblings that might be the sea crashing against the island or might be something else entirely. To my own uneven breath.

Our journey in the dark goes on and on.

We're heading down, I think. At least initially. Then the floor levels out and Damarin speeds up again. Sceada isn't so big that it should take us more than three or four hours to walk the whole length of the island. Still, trying to keep count of my steps proves futile. Blind as I am, I soon lose track – of time, direction, distance, everything. My legs tire. I start to stumble against unseen obstacles: I trip over rocks, or lose my balance in some water-filled rut. Each time, Damarin curses my clumsiness. Each time, she jerks on the rope to pull me upright, over and over, until my wrists are chaffed sore. The cold air, laced with sulphur and the stink of seaweed, burns my throat, and I'm terrified that I'm going to choke on the gag in my mouth. And what if Aron was right, and the Shriven – if that is what they are – just want to kill me? Maybe Damarin is waiting for the right moment to let go of the rope, to vanish and leave me alone down here. Perhaps that has been her plan all along. That I should wander in the darkness, until I fall and break my neck or die from dehydration and hunger.

The whispers start softly at first. The faintest of murmurs, just on the edge of hearing. But as they grow louder, more persistent, I realise they're calling to me – even though they speak in no tongue that I recognise. Calling to me, summoning me into the shadows.

I slow down. The rope goes slack and for an instant I panic that Damarin's left me, until I feel her fingers against my face. She pulls the gag loose.

'Drink.' Water gushes into my mouth and over my chin and I gulp down as much as I can.

'Please, where –'

'No questions.' The gag is wedged back into my mouth. Damarin tugs on the rope and forces me forward again. 'If you hear voices, ignore them.'

I try. I try to concentrate on the thud of my captor's boots against the rock floor. On the rapid thump of my heart. But it's hard. Twice more, at least, we stop for water. Each time we start walking again, it gets harder. The whispers return, louder than before, and panic clouds my mind. Ahead of me, images from the past rear up in my vision. My uncle, King Albaric, his skin rotting from the effects of the poison created by my father and administered by Siegfried and Tallis. My father himself, ordering me with his dying breath to stay at Merl. In my hallucination he is alive again, his voice frail and quavering as he scolds me.

You see what has happened, Aderyn, what you have lost, and all because you wouldn't listen . . .

But then my perspective shifts, and my father becomes Aron, and he's holding Odette's hand while he spits his anger at me.

You're reckless, Aderyn, reckless and selfish! I begged you not to go, but you wouldn't listen, and now it's too late . . .

And to my horror, I realise that Aron and Odette are no more than pale, blood-smeared corpses, lying in the ruined throne room of the Citadel, sprawled across the marble floor together with Letya and Lancelin and everyone else I've ever cared for. They are all dead, and I am to blame. And there, on the throne itself, amidst the desecration, Tallis and Siegfried sit and smile, mocking me for my guilt and my helpless grief.

What have I done? Coming to this place, risking my entire kingdom on the basis of hearsay and wishful thinking . . . The voices behind me are still whispering. But now, compared to the nightmares ahead of me, they seem soft and comforting, promising easy oblivion. One desire consumes me: to yank the rope from Damarin's grasp and run towards the voices. To run into the darkness, to embrace whatever fate awaits me, because I can't resist for a second longer –

The light comes back. Just a faint glimmer of daylight, illuminating the far end of the tunnel but bright enough to hurt my eyes. The voices shrivel and disappear, and so does my need to follow them. Damarin allows me to stop walking. I sag against the wall, out of breath, trembling, clammy with sweat. She unties the gag from my mouth and places the water bottle in my bound hands. I drain it quickly and look back down the tunnel from which we've just emerged.

'What . . . what was that?'

Damarin smiles grimly. 'You heard them then?'

'Voices – yes. Who do they belong to?' I peer into the darkness, half expecting something monstrous to be lurking in the shadows.

'The ghosts of those who've died down here, supposedly, calling others to share their fate. Myself, I think it's just the darkness and lack of air playing tricks on you.' Her glance falls on my bloodied wrists. 'Come on, we've still a way to go. I'll unbind you once we're above ground. Not before.'

'Surely, we can't still be under Sceada,' I say. 'It's not that big . . .'

'We're not.' She turns away, and I realise that the other end of the rope is tied around her waist.

'Are we going back towards the mainland?'

'No more questions!' She waves the gag in my face, threatening. We keep going for maybe another half an hour, in silence, until the tunnel rises steeply and opens out into a cave full of cool air and daylight. It seems enormous compared to the narrow confines in which we've been walking. The sandy floor gives way to grass as we emerge onto a hillside.

Far below, the sea glitters and shifts in the sunlight.

'Where are we?'

'Beyond the Pyre Flames.'

190

'Impossible.'

Damarin points, directing my gaze to the line of distorted space further across the sea. She's not lying: I can feel the subtle tug of the Flames beneath my skin. And as I watch, golden afternoon sunshine floods through the fracturing cloudbank and lights up faint, shadowy shapes on the far side of the Flames. Sceada, and the other islands. We've been walking for most of the day, and we've walked right under the sea.

'Welcome to Galen, the fifth of the Impenny Islands.'

Damarin pulls me away from the sea, towards a low turf-roofed building partially concealed by a stand of trees. There are two guards on duty outside; another two are already approaching us, spears at the ready. Damarin greets them in a language I don't understand. 'Well,' she switches back into the tongue of Solanum, pulling the pins from the coil of coppery hair on top of her head and shaking it out into heavy waves, 'for tonight, you'll be kept here. The one who must decide your fate will not reach us until tomorrow –'

'Tomorrow?'

Damarin's hazel eyes widen. 'You're disappointed? Are you so eager for death, if that is what awaits you?'

I'm exhausted, and my feet and wrists are bleeding, but to wait another day, not knowing whether my friends on Sceada are safe, not knowing what's happening at the Citadel . . . I'm sure Damarin won't allow me to fly to wherever their ruler is. But there are horses grazing in a paddock on the far side of the hut. 'Can't we ride?'

My captor gapes at me. 'So it's true then? I read the reports: a flightless king, and a queen who tames horses, but I didn't believe them . . .' She draws her dagger and aims it at my throat. 'If you're not some whelp of the House of Cygnus Fenys, hunting for treasure, then who exactly are you? The truth, mind. We know you've been camped for two days on the mainland, and we know you've been searching for something.'

I take a deep breath. 'My companion wasn't lying. I am Queen of Solanum. And Protector of Atratys. My name is Aderyn. And if you are who I hope you are, I've been searching for you. I'm here to ask for your help.'

For the first time, Damarin laughs.

Less than an hour later – I've taken some food and water, but refused every suggestion that I should rest – Damarin and I and two of the guards are riding into the heart of Galen. My hands are untied, my wrists washed and bandaged, and there's nothing – in theory – stopping me from transforming and flying away. But, as Damarin points out, there's nowhere for me to fly to.

Plenty of places to run to though. Galen is no Sceada, no barren rock. It's immense. From my mount's back I can see farms, villages and clusters of buildings in the distance that might be large towns or even cities. The road snakes down from the hill into a broad valley, passing from there through villages and towns. Everywhere I look, the land is busy with people: bent over in the fields, pulling up weeds; driving sheep through pastures; selling wares from market stalls; repairing thatched roofs; scrubbing steps; chatting in groups outside taverns. Children play among the trees and on the village greens. So far, Galen reminds me of the fertile uplands of central Atratys.

But this is an Atratys of the past. The Atratys of history books. Apart from blacksmiths' forges, there's no industry that I can see. No waterwheels. No engine houses. There are no dome-roofed Sanctuaries either. Instead, each settlement seems to have a narrow stone building topped with a tower and bearing a depiction of the Firebird. As we pass, some of the people call out to Damarin, exchanging snippets of news, perhaps, or asking about me. I'm fairly sure I hear the word *eorldryt* more than once. Their tongue sounds tantalisingly close to the local dialect of Solanish that's spoken in Fenian, but not close enough for me to understand. When I ask Damarin what *eorldryt* means, she tells me it's a word for nobles and a useful insult, but won't explain further.

As the shadows lengthen, we ride as fast as Damarin will allow along the cartwheel-rutted main road. So far, we seem to have been making for a large walled town on the far side of the valley. But it's still some distance away when Damarin changes direction. We turn off the main road and ride along a grassy track through a narrow patch of woodland, until we emerge in front of a castle built partly into the side of a hill.

Guards – liveried, but bearing no crest that I recognise – bar our way. We rein in the horses and come to a halt. As Damarin greets a man who appears to be the captain – they grip each other's forearms in some sort of salute – I look about me. There are targets set up nearby; a group of guards, men and women, are practising with longbows, bending the heavy wooden limbs with ease, sending arrow after arrow thudding home. I stare, fascinated; I've never seen archery before. Bows are banned in Solanum. According to the Decrees, even owning one is punishable by death. The whole place has an air of efficient organisation, from the people at work in the gardens and smithies around the castle, to the teams unloading supplies from the small boats drawn up on the river that skirts the edge of the hill. Does this place consider itself a separate kingdom? Could it perhaps become the seventh dominion of Solanum, if its people were willing?

Damarin interrupts my musing. 'Our ruler's within; she's been told of our arrival.'

We cross the drawbridge into the castle keep. Servants take the horses, and I follow Damarin inside, through a series of connected towers and up two flights of stairs. I try to brush some of the dirt off my robe as we walk, and imagine how horrified Letya would be if she could see my appearance right now. The thought makes me smile a little, and steadies my breathing.

This castle is nothing like the Silver Citadel, or Merl. There are guards, but no uniformed servants. The furniture in the rooms through which we pass is plain wood – well made, but basic. There are rushes strewn on the floor. No curtains, no carpets, no upholstered sofas. It's like stepping back in time.

Damarin opens a door and shows me into a small whitewashed room. There's a low bed against one wall and a narrow wooden stand with one drawer, on top of which has been placed a large bowl and a pitcher full of water. Hot – there's steam rising from it.

'You may wash here, and change into fresh clothing, if you

wish.' She points to a tall cupboard in the corner of the room. 'A servant will fetch you shortly.'

I glance out of the small barred window; the afternoon is fading into a rainbow-tinted dusk.

Damarin must sense my impatience. 'My mother doesn't like to be rushed, Aderyn of Solanum. You'd do well to remember it when you meet her.'

Her mother? But Damarin is gone before I can question her; on the other side of the door, a bolt scrapes home. I'm trapped. And even though I chose to be here, even though I flew here in the very teeth of Aron's advice, I'm scared.

Automatically, my mind running upon my friends held hostage on Sceada, I slip off my robe, wash, tidy my hair with an ivory comb I find in the drawer and examine the contents of the wardrobe. It doesn't take long. I pick the shorter of the two long-sleeved linen chemises, add the green sleeveless gown and secure both around my waist with the rope belt. The leather pouch containing Accris's sketch and the page from Frant's book is still hanging around my neck. Then I sit on the bed, trying to ignore the prickle of the rough linen against my skin, planning what I might say to Damarin's mother. Two armed guards unlock the door before I've arrived at anything especially persuasive.

They lead me into what appears to be the main hall. A hammer-beam ceiling made of some dark wood sits above whitewashed walls almost entirely covered by large tapestries. I recognise the image depicted on one of these tapestries, which hangs by itself on the furthest wall: a hand, palm out, with the Wishbone constellation above it. The sign of the Shriven. Most of the floor space is taken up by four long oak tables, one set widthways across the top end, three others running the length of the room. A woman is seated in a large chair – almost, but not quite, a throne – in the centre of the top table. There are piles of paperwork spread out before her, and what looks like a map. Damarin is there. She's swapped her scale-like armour, tunic and breeches for a russet silk gown, cut to the ankle, that brings out the copper in her hair, and she's decked with gold chains and bracelets. She's talking to the woman in the chair; as I enter the room, she leans across the table and taps her finger on the map. Both look up as my guard beats the end of his spear against the flagstones.

'My lady mother –' Damarin gestures at me – 'this is Aderyn, who claims sovereignty over Solanum. Aderyn, this is Jaqueth, my mother and ruler of Galen.'

I immediately see how alike Damarin and her mother are. The same hazel eyes, the same high forehead, the same red hair, though Jaqueth's tresses are streaked with grey. In the dimly lit hall – the windows are small for a room of this size, and the tapestries seem to soak up what light there is – their skin shimmers in the same way I observed in the cave on Sceada. So, now I come to look at him, does the skin of my guard. Some side effect of living this close to the Pyre Flames, perhaps?

My speculation is cut short. Jaqueth stands, in a rustle of silk skirts, and guards I had not noticed step out of the shadows.

'You bring a noble before me, daughter. And yet her hands are not bound.'

'I led her bound through the tunnel, but I thought, given

the identity she claims . . . I apologise if I have done wrong, my lady.'

Jaqueth walks around the table and comes to a halt in front of me. She's about my height, more delicately built than her tall, broad-shouldered daughter.

'Is this how you greet a ruler in her own hall?'

I'm not sure what to do. The correct way to greet a noble ruler is to bow with arms stretched back in imitation of wings – but Jaqueth does not fly. Instead, I sink to my knees and drop my gaze.

'Hmm. Lift your head a little, that I may see your face.' I obey, still staring at the floor. 'You are young, to be a queen. Barely out of childhood.'

'I am of age, Lady Jaqueth. I was next in line, and I claimed the throne rather than risk having the kingdom fall into civil war.'

'You are married then? I assume the old Decrees still apply – all that nonsense about ruling in mated pairs.'

'Yes.' I try to swallow, though my throat has become so dry it hurts. 'Yes, I am married.'

'But not, perhaps, willingly?'

I don't answer. It seems safest.

Jaqueth walks around me, inspecting me. I follow her movement as well as I'm able from the corner of my eye, recognising her attempt to make me uncomfortable. I did it to Lucien once. My left kneecap begins to ache from the sharp edge of the paving stone.

'Give me your hand.' Jaqueth runs her fingers across my palm. 'How did you find out about us? One of the Fenian nobles, I assume.'

'No. That is, I did ask a Fenian noble, but I read about you first in a book, last year. And then my best friend told me about a flightless woman in Farne who claims that one of your kind is the father of her child.'

'I see.' Her tone is one of displeasure. 'And how does your noble friend come to be concerned with a flightless woman's plight?'

'My friend isn't a noble. She's flightless too.'

Jaqueth laughs. 'You're lying.'

For the first time, I look up at her. 'I am not.'

Damarin steps forward. 'She can ride, Mother. She doesn't seem . . . typical.'

Jaqueth hesitates.

'Please, I'm not here to spy on you or steal from you. I'm asking for your help. My kingdom is in danger.'

'What is that to us?' Jaqueth shrugs. 'We owe you no allegiance. War and famine could claim every single noble in Solanum and beyond, and still we would not care.'

'But what of the flightless? What of those who still tell stories of you, believing you will come to their aid? What of the baby shortly to be born in Farne, a child of Galen as well as Solanum?' I drag the leather pouch from around my neck, pull out Accris's sketch and offer it to Jaqueth. 'What of the child's mother, and others like her, who have no hope of real freedom? With your help, I could do more than defeat those who threaten our peace. With your help, I could change everything –'

Nausea, sudden and sharp, pitches me forward onto all fours. I clutch my stomach with one arm, screwing my eyes shut and gritting my teeth against the urge to vomit.

'When did she last eat something?' Jaqueth asks.

'I offered her food at the guardhouse,' Damarin replies, 'but she ate little.'

A sigh. 'Guards . . .' Hands on my arms, pulling me upright. Jaqueth stares at me. Shakes her head. 'Get her a chair, and bring refreshments. Well, Aderyn of Solanum, I suppose we will hear what you have to say.'

I eat, and we talk. Jaqueth wants to know everything, from the beginning. I have to tell her all the details of my mother's death, my uncle the king's treachery, my father's alliance with Siegfried. I have to explain how Letya and I became friends – sisters really – during the years when I was not able to transform. How I grew fond of my cousins and wished to help them, about the plans Aron and I have to help the flightless, about Tallis, about Siegfried's potion, about the attack on Merl and the threat from Frianland.

The only person I don't mention at all is Lucien.

Still, I have no sense of whether or not Jaqueth will be willing to help me. I manage to contain my impatience, just about. But when she returns, for the third time, to Siegfried's attempt to seize the crown, I can't prevent my gaze drifting towards the dark windows of the hall. The candles in the iron sconces are already burning low. There are no clocks here, but in the back of my mind I still hear the time ticking relentlessly away.

'Am I keeping you from something?' Jaqueth's tart tone recalls me to my surroundings.

'I apologise, Lady Jaqueth. But I'm worried about my

friends still waiting for me on Sceada. And about what may be happening in Solanum, in Atratys especially. I fear some terrible blow will befall us soon.'

Jaqueth drums her fingers on the arm of her chair and murmurs something to one of her advisers. 'So, you are looking for allies, and you ask us to risk our lives in support of your monarchy. What do you offer in return?'

'Friendship. Assistance – we have technology which may be of use to you. Medicines, perhaps, which you do not have here. Markets for your goods: if, as you say, the Pyre Flames do not harm you, then you can sail through them to the mainland, I assume, to trade with us.' I think of the archers I saw practising outside. 'Even your existence – it changes the balance of power. If our monarchy has the support of a people who, though flightless, are well armed, and immune to our touch, I believe the nobles of Solanum may finally be convinced to accept the creation of a more equal society. That won't benefit you directly, but it will help our flightless population; those who tell stories about you, who have kept your memory alive. Surely that is worth something.'

Jaqueth does not answer. She sits, elbows resting on the arms of her chair, hands clasped in her lap, gazing out of the nearest window. Eventually she shifts in her seat and looks at me.

'Do you know what our fabled treasure consists of?'

I've seen little evidence of huge wealth – no gold or jewels such as those that adorn the Silver Citadel and its occupants. So I shake my head.

'Our treasure is the gift given to us by the Creator: the Pyre

Flames, that protect us from the outside world and grant us our immunity to the touch of those such as you. The young people, like Damarin here –' she nods at her daughter – 'will tell you it is to do with the soil or the air or some such. But however they do it, the Flames keep us safe. And we have our own stories. Stories of great suffering, of devastating battles, in the time before our foremothers retreated behind the Flames. Our isolation protects us.'

'But your isolation is not complete. You speak our language. You worship the same Creator we do. Some of you, at least, journey through my lands. Surely you can see that there might be benefits to both our peoples, if we can agree to –'

'No.' Jaqueth lifts her chin and stares at me. 'Our isolation keeps us safe and must be preserved. I would not willingly risk our people in a war that cannot affect us. You are a queen – you must understand.'

The hope that had been building within me collapses. But we refused to give more help to the Celonians for very similar reasons. 'Yes,' I sigh. 'I understand.'

Damarin clears her throat. 'Do you know the name of the man who got the flightless woman pregnant?'

'Yes. It was . . . Praeden. I think that's what she said.'

Jaqueth's nostrils flare as she turns towards her daughter. Damarin says something in her own language, something placating, I guess.

'And do you know anything apart from his name?'

'He told the woman, Accris, that he lived on the fifth Impenny island, and that he was visiting someone who lives in the Citadel . . .' The realisation hits me. Now I know these people are real, I can search for more of them. It would be possible, if unpopular, to have everyone in the Citadel examined, to see who bears the Shriven's mark. For the first time since I arrived, I wonder if I have something more concrete to bargain with. 'May I ask how many of your people are currently residing in my lands?'

Jaqueth glares at me and launches into a long discussion with Damarin. I don't understand anything, although it's clear they're both angry, and I catch the name Praeden more than once. It occurs to me that perhaps this Praeden is important to either Damarin or Jaqueth. Him, or the person he was visiting.

Eventually Damarin crosses her arms and clamps her mouth shut. Her mother summons the advisers around her, and for a few moments I have nothing to do but wait. The exhaustion I've been staving off creeps up on me; I lean back in my chair, and my eyelids have begun to droop when Jaqueth stands. I get quickly to my feet.

'Aderyn of Solanum, you should know that by our law your life is forfeit. We do not welcome strangers into our lands; of the few we've caught attempting to breach our borders, none has ever been allowed to leave.' My heart beats faster and I glance at the windows, wondering if – transformed – I could smash my way through the leaded panes. 'However,' Jaqueth continues, 'in your case, we are willing to make an exception. You and your companions on Sceada are free to go. I will consult further with my advisers, and send to our agents on the mainland for more information. It may be that we decide to give aid to Solanum, eventually. She shoots a glance at Damarin. 'But it will not be soon.'

I bow. 'Thank you for listening to me, Jaqueth. For considering my request. But if you do not come soon, it will be safer for you to not come at all. If Tallis wins, if the House of Cygnus falls, I fear there will be nothing left of Solanum worth saving.'

Damarin is to escort me back below the Pyre Flames. The ride across Galen is painfully slow, the night too dark for speed. Despite the late hour, there are groups of people dotted along the road. Apparently, word of my visit has spread, and some are curious to see me. Damarin pays them no attention, but then she's hardly said a word to me since we took leave of Jaqueth. It's a relief when we reach the small guard house outside the cave in the hillside.

I go into the guard house to change back into my robe. When I emerge, Damarin is waiting with a rope.

'I have to bind you again: my mother won't allow any more exceptions to our rules.' She ties the rope around my wrists, loosely enough that it doesn't hurt. 'But we'll take a torch this time.'

'Is that allowed?' I ask.

'It'll make our journey quicker.' She grins. 'And I'm confident you won't be able to find your way back through the tunnel alone, even if you are insane enough to try. Ready?'

I can't help shivering as I peer into the sullen darkness of the cave. But for me, this is the only way home. 'Ready.'

As we descend from the cave into the depths of the tunnel I cling as close to Damarin as I can, staying inside our small circle of light. The torch reveals countless other tunnels, branching from the main route, and unexpected shafts dropping into the gaping darkness. There are rustlings and skitterings and the slither of unseen things in the shadows that surround us. My throat starts to sting from the sulphurous fumes, but at least the whispering voices stay silent. On and on we walk, weariness enveloping me like soft down, until, half asleep, I stumble and lose my balance.

'Careful –' Damarin crouches down and passes me the water bottle.

'I'm sorry. I'm so tired . . .' I frown, studying my companion's face. 'Strange, that you are not.'

'The people of Galen may not be able to fly, but we're strong.' She hesitates. Leans in closer. 'I'm going to try. To persuade my mother to send help, I mean. Or to come myself if she still refuses. She'd be furious if she knew I'd told you, but we have problems on Galen just the same as other places. Our population grows too large, and there's nowhere else for us to go. No other lands, as far as we've discovered, that lie within the circle of the Pyre Flames. Too many people and not enough work. Some are growing restless. They want more . . . opportunity. People like my brother.'

'Praeden?' I whisper.

'Praeden is one of my brother's more disreputable acquaintances. My brother left Galen secretly nearly three years ago. My mother knows he is alive, but did not, until today, know where he was.' She hisses slightly. 'I pity Praeden if she decides to try to force the truth out of him.'

'I don't suppose you're going to tell me your brother's name?'

She pulls back a bit and grins at me. 'You suppose right.' The grin fades. 'We have agents on the mainland – if I can get word to you at the Silver Citadel, I will. But I can promise nothing. Look to your own defence, and don't rely on us.'

'I understand. But, thank you, Damarin. For at least thinking about helping us.'

'Come. A little further and you'll feel the air change.' She pulls me to my feet and we trudge on. And she's right; the air grows fresher, and the flames of the torch flicker and dance in the growing breeze. The floor begins to slope upwards, and the tunnel curves to the right, and we emerge into the cave on Sceada.

Not a moment too soon: Lien, feet still bound, bellows and kicks over one of the Shriven guards as the others draw their swords.

'Lien – enough.'

The moment passes. Damarin orders her people to release my companions as she cuts the rope from my wrists. 'You are all free to go.'

'Aderyn!' Odette runs towards me. 'We've been so worried . . .' She hugs me, then grips my shoulders. 'You look terrible. What did they do to you?'

I return her hug. 'I'm well. They've been talking to me, not torturing me. It's just been a long day . . .'

'Aderyn, I must return.' Damarin has already sent the others back into the tunnel. She grips my arm just below the elbow, the same gesture I saw her use earlier. 'If I don't see you again, may the Firebird keep you safe in the shelter of her wings.'

She stubs the torch out on the floor. When my eyes adjust to the darkness, all I can see is the mouth of the cave, illuminated by the night sky and the glow of the Pyre Flames, and my companions, silhouetted against it. Damarin has gone.

Veron is next to me. 'Who exactly are those people? Odette tried to explain, but it doesn't make any sense. And are they nobles who have lost their power to transform? Do they live in these tunnels, or –?'

'I'll give you answers, as far as I'm able. But can we return to the mainland? I don't think it's safe to linger here. And I'm exhausted, Veron . . .'

He doesn't reply. I can see he's frowning, but I can barely make out his eyes in the darkness; they are pools of shadow. Lien and Pyr hustle him out of the way. 'Come, Your Majesty,' Lien says. 'Back to the mainland. I for one have had enough of this place.' We leave the cave, tie our robes back into bundles and climb down to the beach and the sea to transform. The Pyre Flames call to me, plucking at my skin and my blood even as I fly away from them.

Eleven

When I next awake, the sun is already well risen above our campsite on the Fenian coast, and someone nearby is roasting fish. I rub the sleep out of my eyes and walk over to where my companions are seated around a fire.

'Aderyn, you're awake.' Odette holds out a large leaf. 'I saved you some.'

'Thank you, cousin.'

I'm starving after yesterday. For a while I concentrate on eating – there are gorse flowers, roasted bloodthorn root and stellaria leaves too, thanks to Pyr's skill at foraging. But eventually the others' desultory conversation dries up; they are waiting for me to finish, so I can tell them why we came here, and what I discovered.

I explain, as well as I am able. There is general disbelief; Lien and Blackbill both wade knee deep into the waves and peer out across the sea, hoping to catch some shadowy glimpse of Galen through the barrier of the Pyre Flames. I think they would doubt my sanity if they hadn't seen the Shriven for themselves. Nyssa and Odette ask lots of questions about the people and how they live. I can't give them many answers. Various suggestions are made as to ways of forcing the Shriven to cooperate with us. All of which I reject as both dishonourable and impractical: there's no way for nobles to reach Galen apart from the tunnel, which is easily defensible. And I don't know what the Pyre Flames might do to ordinary flightless. After we've been talking for about an hour – and Lien has reverted for the fifth time to the impossibility of flightless being able to effectively rule themselves – I end the discussion.

'We need to get back to the Citadel. And now we've discovered what we set out to find, I don't suppose there's so much need for secrecy. We could fly straight back . . .'

'But you need to rest properly, Your Majesty.' Lien is shaking his head. 'Pyr and I are supposed to keep you safe. Bad enough you went alone into that nest of treacherous, witch-whelped Shriven, or whatever they call themselves.' His mouth twists into a grimace. 'It's a long flight to the Citadel. Why not return to Rogallyn, spend a night there first?' He jerks his head towards Pyr. 'He does his best, but I for one could do with some decent food. And at Rogallyn we could gather news –'

'I disagree,' Veron interrupts. 'Surely it would be better to fly straight back to the Silver Citadel? The distance can't be much further.' The urgency in his voice surprises me.

'With respect, my lord –' Lien's tone makes it clear he views Celonians as little better than the Shriven – 'it's not up to you.'

I hold up my hand. 'Lien, please . . . Veron, is there some reason you wish to reach the Citadel sooner?'

He hesitates, picking up a broken seashell and turning it

over in his fingers. 'No, no reason. I'll fly wherever you wish me to.' The words are accompanied by a smile, but it seems a little forced. Perhaps he's worried about his brother.

'It might not be so much longer,' Odette observes, 'if we take the Ash Pass and approach the Citadel from the south. Much safer than flying across the mountains at this time of year. We'll avoid the coastal storms on the route to Rogallyn, and from this direction the wind will be at our backs.' She squeezes my hand. 'I already feel guilty about leaving Aron. If we can get home a little earlier . . .'

'Then it's settled: we'll return straight home. If we leave soon, we may even be able to sleep in our own beds tonight.'

Within half an hour we've cleared away the evidence of our fire, wrapped our robes and knives back into bundles, and transformed.

As we fly over the cliffs, I take a last look at the endless flickering dance of the Pyre Flames, twisting the sunlight and casting faint rainbows across the waves.

Odette is right: riding on the wind instead of fighting it, our return journey is easier. We pass over Tarsig Castle, the stronghold of the Protectors of Fenian, as the late-afternoon sun casts long, slanting shadows across the pink heather that carpets the Tarsig Downs. I allow my mind to wander, to relax into the rhythm of flight, to rest in simple physical sensations: the rush of air across my feathers, the emptyness around me. We approach the pass through the mountains, and I can feel the cold air rolling down from their peaks. The wind gets faster as it's funnelled through the pass, and so do we; the rush of speed is intoxicating, and the exhilaration of my companions fills my mind as Odette banks and leads us in a wide sweep around the western foothills of the Silver Mountains, back into the Crown Estates. The moon begins to rise. The slender crescent gradually breaches the horizon, until it lies before us like a beacon.

We're nearly home.

I recognise the lakes and towns below us now. We cross the River Argent and begin to turn north. Once we reach the River Farne, the Silver Citadel is visible directly ahead.

Strange, it is not as brightly lit as I would expect. But perhaps it is later than I think.

Odette, how long have we been flying?

My cousin, at the front of the formation, does not answer.

Odette?

Something's wrong.

I push myself faster so that I'm flying next to Blackbill and directly behind Odette. For an instant I'm caught in the downdraught of her powerful wings; I quickly adjust my own wingbeats so we are out of phase, evening out the air current. But Blackbill takes the hint and drops back, allowing me to drift left and take his position at Odette's shoulder.

Cousin, are you sure? I try to calculate days and hours, wondering if I've somehow lost track of the calendar, if we've arrived at the end of an Ember Day or some more solemn occasion.

Trust me, Aderyn. I've lived here all my life. Something's wrong —

There's a note of panic in Odette's voice. And as we get closer, and I realise that the landing platform is in darkness, I begin to catch the same sense of unease. Something *is* wrong.

The flag bearing the crest of Cygnus Atratys still flutters from the top of the upper south tower. But the wind carries the sound of raised voices . . .

What about the private landing platform? Veron asks. *The one behind the royal apartments?*

Odette begins to alter course, to lead us around the Citadel to my rooms.

I stop her.

Odette, change places with me.

But, Aderyn, we have to get inside quickly and find Aron –

Please. I have an idea.

I feel the conflict in her mind, but she slows, allowing me to overtake her, and drifts back into the updraught created by my wingbeats. I give myself a moment to become accustomed to the strength of the wind in this position, to the absence of any support from another noble ahead of me, then I alter our course again, taking us out across the grounds of the Citadel, heading for the lake at the far side of the gardens. The same lake where Siegfried first gave me the potion that allowed me to fly again. It's usually deserted; I hope it still will be.

I touch down on the surface of the lake, wings spread, using wind and water to come to a halt. The others land, in the lake or beside it, and we transform. Robe ourselves. I look around the circle of expectant faces. We all have knives, but a sword in my hand would help steady the panicky rhythm of my pulse.

'There's a doorway in the kitchen gardens that leads into the lower levels of the castle. I suggest we enter there and make our way into the Dark Guard quarters. We may get information there, and we can definitely pick up more weapons.'

211

Lien nods. 'I know the doorway. But if there's danger, Pyr and I should go first. Allow us to make a circuit of the Citadel on the wing and report back to you.'

'But if there's been an attack – if you're followed –'

'We both have practice in disappearing and evading pursuit. Forgive me, my queen, but you've taken enough risks in the last few days. You're too important for me to allow you to enter the Citadel with no knowledge of what lies within the walls. His Majesty and Master Secretary Pianet would say the same.'

I sigh. 'Very well. And I suppose it would be useful if one of you can find a way to land without being seen, gather some news and meet us in the Dark Guard quarters.'

'Aderyn . . .' Odette's voice is desperate.

'The rest of us will wait until the moon has risen clear above the mountains. After that, we'll make our way inside. With or without you.'

Lien and Pyr bow, transform again and swoop off towards the Citadel.

I fall to pacing the lakeshore, straining my ears for the sound of approaching footsteps, checking the progress of the rising moon every few steps. Odette is gazing up at the sky; at some point, I notice, Blackbill has put his arm around her shoulder. Nyssa is pacing too, wringing her hands. Her mother is inside the Citadel. Or was, when we left. Veron sits apart, hunched inside his robe, head bowed. It almost looks as if he's praying.

Neither Letya nor Aron can fly. Neither has an easy means of escape. But they're both clever. Resourceful. They'll have found a way out, if it came to it. Both of them will be fine.

That's what I keep telling myself. My mind slides away from the possibility that it might not be true.

I glance at the mountains again. The moon is floating above them, clear black space around it. Odette turns to me.

'Can we go?'

I nod. But before we get any further Lien approaches – from the opposite direction to the Citadel – lands and transforms.

'Pyr?'

'He's inside. There's been an attempt to seize the throne; I fear the Dark Guards have been overwhelmed. There are many dead and wounded in the entrance hall and throne room – nobles as well as flightless – and I saw guards wearing the colours of the House of Cygnus Brithys.'

'Patrus.' I grip my knife tightly. 'By the Firebird, I wish the knitting needles I stuck in his eye had killed him. Did you see the king? Are any still resisting?'

'I saw skirmishes around the Sanctuary – Dark Guards battling some others who wore no insignia – and it sounded as if there's fighting in the east towers. I don't know where His Majesty is, but Pyr will search for him.'

'Let's go.' I glance behind me. 'Veron?'

He is still sitting by the lake, but when I call, he stands up and joins us. His face is pinched – worry about his brother, I suppose – but we've no time to spare for words of comfort.

At least the gardens are empty. Our arms tucked inside our dark robes, and our hoods raised, we pass as quietly as possible between hedges and borders, keeping to the shadows of the trees. Closer to the centre of the Citadel I can hear shouts, screams, the shattering of glass as someone – a swan, but I don't know who – smashes through one of the windows of the great hall and escapes into the darkness. Odette slips her hand into mine and grips it tightly.

As we walk, I turn the possibilities over in my mind. Is Patrus acting alone? Did he decide the throne was ripe for the plucking, and seize the moment of my absence? Had he planned to attack? Or is he working with someone else? Tallis and Siegfried, or Prince Eorman? That would explain those fighting with no visible allegiance. Or could Patrus and another Protector have united against us? Could the flightless of Farne finally have risen up in rebellion?

Unless . . . unless this is Lucien's doing.

The windows of the east towers explode and fire flames into the night. I gasp, covering my mouth with my hand as bile rises in my throat. There are apartments there for courtiers and visiting nobles. Lancelin is there . . .

Someone jumps from a window – screaming, burning, shifting erratically from human to bird and back again. The scream is silenced as they plunge into the fjord.

Odette and I begin to run.

We reach the kitchen gardens. There's no choice here but to follow the gravel paths between the raised beds; each footstep echoes around the walled space. We make it to the door at the far side, pause – no sound of pursuit – open the door, hurry into the small vestibule and along the corridor – lit only by small, high windows – that leads to the ground floor of the Citadel. At the far end the corridor splits into three.

I hesitate. I've only been here once, and that was when Aron and I were racing to stop Lucien's execution. One path leads up to the entrance hall, one to the kitchens, one to the guard room. 'Which way?'

A shriek of pain slices through the silence, making me jump, and the clash of metal on metal reverberates down the central corridor. That must be the way to the first floor.

Lien gestures. 'This way, I think.'

We hurry along the right-hand corridor, keeping close to the doors that lead to storage rooms in case we need somewhere to hide, trying to combine speed with secrecy.

The armoury has already been ransacked. My stomach heaves, and I hear Nyssa retching; the room stinks of blood and smoke and excrement. Most of the weapons are gone, and there are corpses lying across the flagstones. Two Dark Guards, three others, one of whom is wearing the colours of Cygnus Brithys. I ask Veron and Blackbill to cover the bodies of the Dark Guards with their cloaks, and to search the others for any information that might be useful. At least Pyr is waiting for us. He's injured: blood from a head wound is tracking its way down the side of his face.

'What news?'

'I found a Dark Guard captain. He'd been left for dead, but he wasn't – not quite.' He pauses to drain a cup of water Lien has found from somewhere. 'The attack began during the evening banquet. Patrus and his followers took the guards by surprise and opened the Citadel gates to a force that was waiting outside.'

'Led by whom?'

'Tallis is here, and Siegfried.' Beside me, I hear Odette's

sharp intake of breath. But at least he hasn't mentioned Lucien.

'And Aron? Where's the king?'

'He didn't know. Earlier on, His Majesty had ordered everyone to fall back to the Eyria. But the last time the captain saw him, he –' Pyr swears and wipes away the blood that has trickled into his eye. 'He was fighting just outside the royal apartments.'

'We have to find him.' Odette is already moving towards the door, Blackbill following her. I make a grab for her arm.

'We will. But Aron's sensible, and Pianet would have found a way to get him out – he's probably already at the Eyria. Why don't you and Blackbill go straight there, and the rest of us will search in the Citadel.'

Odette is no fighter, and I'm worried that fear will paralyse her if she's actually confronted by Siegfried.

She shakes her head. 'No. I'm staying with you.'

'But, Odette, please –'

Her mouth sets into the same stubborn line that I'm more used to seeing on Aron's face. 'You know how he is – he won't leave until there's no hope the Citadel can be held. He couldn't bear to have people think he wasn't . . .' she breaks off, breathing unevenly, 'that he isn't strong enough. I'm not leaving unless I'm certain he's safe.'

'Very well. But stay back. And if we run into trouble, promise me you'll transform and get away.'

A sort of a nod. As much of a promise as I'm going to get, clearly.

'Pyr, are you well enough to come with us?'

'Yes. It's just a flesh wound.'

I glance at Nyssa. She's standing with her back against the wall, her arms clutched around her body, staring at the corpses on the other side of the room. 'I'm sure your mother's not here, Nyssa. She'll have escaped to the Eyria or to Lancorphys. You should go and find her.'

She looks up at me, uncertain. 'But . . . I should stay and help –'

'Fly to the Eyria. If the other Protectors are there, ask them to send word to their dominions if they haven't already, to the leaders of their congregations. Those who have been sent to Atratys need to turn back – we have to gather a force to retake the Citadel. Then go and rouse what support you can in Lancorphys. Veron, will you go with her?'

'I need to find my brother. If Aron is still here, then . . .'

I understand him. 'Blackbill, then?'

The young lord looks to Odette.

'Go,' she says. 'I'll join you once I'm sure Aron's safe. And Blackbill –' Odette takes his face in her hands and kisses him, as he lifts his arms to embrace her – 'fly swift, fly straight, my love, and may the Creator guide you.'

Blackbill kisses her in reply, bows to me and holds out a hand to Nyssa. 'Come, my lady.'

They leave, hurrying back the way we came.

Odette stares after them as the rest of us begin searching the room for whatever weapons haven't been taken. I find a sword; it's not particularly well balanced, but the blade is sharp. I grip it tightly and wish for my mother's sword instead. But that is in my rooms. Or was.

I wonder whether I'll ever see it again.

Everyone is ready. We make for the nearest menial staircase, as Letya calls them; from there we can access the second floor directly, without risking the entrance hall or the main staircases. Of course, Tallis might know of the existence of these routes, but I'm not sure she would have spent much time wondering how the servants got around the Citadel.

Lien edges the door open and peers upwards. Like the ground-floor corridors, the towers containing the menial staircases have small windows at regular intervals. Enough to provide light to see by, too high to allow any pleasant view.

He looks back at us over his shoulder. 'Clear, I think. Although –' he frowns, and drops his voice to a whisper – 'someone's crying . . .'

We begin the trek upwards. I try to visualise where we are. The tower we're in, I think, links to the long gallery on the first floor; I remember seeing servants passing in and out of a doorway concealed in the wood panelling. But I'm not sure exactly where we will come out on the second floor. Somewhere quiet, I hope.

The source of the crying is close by. Just past the first-floor doorway a girl – a housemaid, judging by her grey uniform – is sitting on the stairs, hugging her knees and weeping and rocking back and forth. When she sees Lien she opens her mouth to scream, but he brings his sword up against her neck.

'Be silent!' he hisses.

I crouch down in front of her. 'We won't hurt you, but you must be quiet. Do you understand?'

Her eyes widen as she recognises me. She nods.

Lien lowers his sword.

'Good. Have you seen the king?'

She shakes her head. Stifles a sob.

'What about Mistress Letya, my waiting woman?'

'Yes, Majesty. She were with a Dark Guard in the kitchens. They were telling people to go to the dungeons. But when the invaders broke through the doors I . . . I ran away –' She gives in to tears.

'Did you see what happened to Letya? Did she escape?'

'I don't know . . . I don't –' She starts sobbing again, and it's all I can do not to grab her, to try to shake her into remembering.

Odette lays a hand on my arm. I force myself to take a deep breath. To focus on the fact that Letya was not alone.

'You should get out of here. Go straight down – the armoury is empty. From there you can get into the kitchen gardens. The back gates past the stable yards might still be unguarded.' It doesn't seem much of a plan, but I don't know what else to suggest. Unlike the nobles, the flightless inhabitants of the castle can't transform and fly over the high walls. This girl is trapped here just as Letya might be; I've read enough history to know what invading armies do to those left behind. I hold out the hilt of my knife. 'Take it. And hurry.'

She grabs the knife from my hand and runs down the stairs.

We continue our climb.

Before long, we're at the door that opens onto the second floor. Lien motions us to stand back and presses his ear to the dark wood. Turns the handle, pulls the door open a fraction and peers through the gap. Closes it again.

'The corridor leading to the royal apartments. All's quiet.

219

There are bodies, but none living as far as I can see. I suggest we return the way we came and –'

Odette pushes past me. 'I won't leave my brother.' Her voice is almost a sob. Before Lien can stop her, she's through the door and in the wide carpeted corridor.

The torches along the walls are still burning. As Lien and Veron stand guard in the corridor, and Pyr watches the staircase up which we came, Odette and I start looking for Aron. The dead have been there for a while – the blood staining the carpet is dark – and come from both sides. Dark Guards, members of my court, some of Tallis's unbadged mercenaries. But Aron, thankfully, is not among them.

'He must have escaped, Odette. We should have checked the stables for his horse.'

'But he could be within.' She gestures to the double doors at the end of the corridor that lead to the receiving room.

'He wouldn't allow himself to get trapped like that –'

Lien interrupts. 'It's too quiet – I don't like it. We should get out of here.'

'Odette –'

'We can check the other apartments, then fly from the landing platform behind your room. It won't take long.' She clasps her hands together. 'I beg you, Aderyn. Even if he's dead, we can't leave him here.'

'Lien,' Pyr calls softly, 'someone's coming down the stairs.'

We've no choice. Stepping over bodies, Veron opens the doors to the receiving room. Once we're all inside, Lien and Pyr lock the doors and shove a chest of drawers in front of them. The room is in darkness. Still, there's enough light coming through the windows to reveal more death: two grey-clad housemaids and a third woman in a dark-coloured gown, brown hair escaping from beneath a linen cap.

As the others move to check the audience chamber, I drop to my knees beside her. Move her gently onto her back, to confirm what I already fear.

Fris.

There are burns blistering and disfiguring her forehead. Her throat has been slit. The wound, crusted with dried blood, gapes at me.

She was unarmed, and had in any case no skill with a weapon. She posed no risk to anyone. Why would someone do this to her?

I've no gloves on, but she is beyond being harmed by my touch. I close her eyes as carefully as I can, given my trembling hands. Whisper my sorrow. Murmur what lines I can remember of the Benediction of the Dead.

But she cannot hear me, and I have no time to mourn.

Pyr crouches next to me. 'I've been through His Majesty's rooms. They've been ransacked, but there's no one there.' He glances up at Odette. 'Dead or alive.'

I touch Fris's face in farewell, and stand. 'What about Letya? And Lancelin?' I glance at Veron. 'What about Valentin?'

Lien shakes his head. 'We've been fortunate so far. The chances of us searching the Citadel, and finding them, and not getting caught, are virtually non-existent. You have to think of what's best for the kingdom, Your Majesty. We need to leave while we still can. Those who haven't already escaped . . .' He shrugs and spreads his hands in a gesture of regret.

I know he's right. But to turn my back on those I love, to abandon them . . .

Veron takes my hand. 'Come,' he murmurs. 'There's still hope.'

All I can do is nod my acquiescence.

Lien hurries us through the open door into the audience chamber; only my sitting room and bedroom now lie between us and the landing platform. Still no sign of pursuit, no sound of battle. I start to wonder whether Tallis and Siegfried have lost too many followers, whether they've withdrawn, abandoned the Citadel. Lien raises a hand, makes us wait while he checks the door to the sitting room, beckons us forward again.

The sitting-room curtains are flapping in the breeze from one of the tall windows; the glass has been smashed. There's more mess here. My books are scattered across the floor, pages ripped out. Broken furniture litters the floor, and the painting of Merl Castle that hangs on one wall has been slashed into ribbons.

I can think of only three people who would hate me enough to do that: Tallis, Siegfried and Patrus. One of them must have been here.

I ignore the tiny voice at the back of my mind that whispers Lucien's name.

Lien is at the last door, the one that leads into my bedroom. He listens, opens it a crack, beckons us forward as before. He enters, followed by Veron and Odette. Relief bubbles through my veins, making me light-headed. Odette turns to me.

'Aron – do you think they've captured him, Aderyn? Or do you honestly think he's escaped?'

I open my mouth to reply.

But it isn't my voice that answers her.

'Oh, he tried to escape.' Candlelight – bright enough to blind us after the darkness – flares from a lantern, as the door slams shut behind us. I spin round, raising my sword, shielding my eyes with my free hand, squinting to make out the figure behind the light. 'Tried desperately, poor, flightless prince.' The voice slithers across my skin like ice. 'But he was trapped in the end. As you have been.'

The figure comes nearer. Golden-blond hair, blue eyes, the same charming smile as I remember.

Siegfried.

Twelve

Pyr leaps in front of me as Lien, sword in one hand, dagger in the other, bellows and darts at Siegfried. But he doesn't get far: more nobles rush out of the shadows and overpower him, seizing his weapons and pinning his arms behind his back. Veron is quickly disarmed. I grab my cousin's hand and pull her close as the room grows lighter and others – at least ten men and women, bearing swords and dark lanterns – become visible.

Odette's rapid, gasping breaths fill the silence.

Siegfried hands his lantern to someone else and moves closer. Close enough for me to see the puckered scar left by Tallis's ring when it sliced open his cheek. It must have become infected, I suppose, and is now a permanent reminder of her fury at his failure to kill Odette before they fled the Citadel last autumn. Apart from his head, he is fully clad in plate armour.

'You –' he points with a dagger at Pyr, still standing in front of us with his sword held ready – 'get out of my way.'

Pyr doesn't move.

Siegfried sighs. 'Really?' He gestures, and three of his followers approach Pyr, weapons raised. Lien cries out as one of the men holding him presses the point of a dagger into his neck. 'You can't win, Aderyn. But if you're happy to see your people die . . .'

'Pyr,' I order, 'lower your sword.'

He obeys. Two men move in to seize him. Another steps into my line of vision.

Lucien.

Siegfried laughs as I gasp and flinch away, unable to disguise my dismay. I search Lucien's face, desperately hoping for some sign that he's not really part of what's happening here, for some hint of regret for the path on which he's embarked. But his expression is just as impassive as it was at Hatchlands, when he stood next to Tallis and offered to kill me.

'Disarm her, Rookwood.'

His eyes fixed on mine, Lucien holds out his palm for my sword. Anger flares in my belly, twisting the ache in my chest into something sharper. I don't see how I can fight my way out of this. Lucien's in armour, and as close to me as he is, there are too many blades pointed at me for me to have a hope of stabbing him. But I'll be damned if I'm going to make it easy for him. I spit in his face – another soft laugh from Siegfried, though Lucien barely reacts – and throw my weapon onto the floor at my feet. Lucien has to stoop to pick it up.

'Good.' Siegfried removes his gauntlets. 'Rookwood, go and find my sister and Lord Patrus. Tell them we have them. And invite them to join me here. We'll be on the queen's landing platform, I think.'

'As you wish, Lord Siegfried.' Lucien bows and strides out of the room without another glance at me.

Siegfried looks around the room. 'Such a pleasant space. My sister always liked this room. I'm sure she and Lord Rookwood will be very comfortable here.' He smiles at me. 'Lucien and my sister have become close in the last few weeks. She's had many lovers, but he might actually be her favourite.' He waits, watching greedily for my reaction. But I don't believe him. Either that, or I've spent so long dwelling on Lucien's betrayal that nothing he is accused of can surprise me any more. Siegfried's smile slips away, replaced by a scowl. 'Bring them outside. It won't do to get blood on the carpet.' As his people move to obey, he grabs my wrist. 'And don't try to transform. Not unless you want Aron to suffer even more than he already is.'

Odette groans and covers her face with her hands, but I'm not allowed to help her; she and I are separated as we're seized and herded outside at knifepoint. I try to look around and see who our attackers are: there are a couple of lords from Brithys, another three from Olorys. The rest I don't know. But it gives me some hope that the other dominions are still loyal to Aron and me.

Loyal for the time being at least. For as long as we're alive.

Once we reach the landing platform behind my apartments the five of us are placed in a line, surrounded by our enemies. All of them have weapons drawn, the closest blades almost touching our skin, and most are wearing armour of some sort. A couple bear torches. The wind flutters cloaks and hair and churns up the surface of the artificially created lake until its waters, crimsoned by the fire still blazing in the east towers, look almost like flames.

Could I escape, if I transformed? Possibly. Surprise might give me enough of an advantage to avoid the swords levelled at me. But that would mean leaving Odette behind. She won't follow me, even if she can. She won't leave without Aron.

Siegfried paces slowly in front of us. He stops in front of Veron.

'You must be the leader of what remains of Celonia. We will deal with you later.' He waves a hand, and two of his followers pull Veron out of line and hold him separately. 'Now, the rest of you, take off your robes.'

'You wouldn't dare.' I clutch my robe tightly. For a noble to force another noble to disrobe is not against the Decrees, but – even more than touching a flightless person without consent – it is held to be an act only committed in defiance of ancient custom: immoral, uncivilised, something that only one who possessed an ignoble and corrupted mind would even consider.

'Oh, but I would,' Siegfried replies. 'Remove them, or I will have someone else do it.'

'I'm not going to let you –' Veron's interference is rewarded by one of his captors driving a fist into his stomach. He doubles over, grunting in pain.

Siegfried laughs. 'How very chivalrous. But I'd keep silent if I were you, Lord Veron.'

A few of those in the circle around us shift uncomfortably, looking away or down at the ground. A small white-haired man murmurs, 'My lord, is it really –'

'I said *silence*!' Siegfried barks out the word, his voice cold with fury. He seizes the man – a member of a gull family,

I think – and jerks him forward. 'Unless you want to join them?' The man shakes his head and mutters an apology and Siegfried shoves him away. He turns back to me. 'Do as you are bid.' The woman nearest me presses the point of her blade against my back.

'Will you let Lien and Pyr go? They're only here because of me. They've done nothing to you.'

'You're in no position to bargain, Aderyn. I won't ask again.'

I reach up and undo the three fastenings, as slowly as I can. Slide the robe off my shoulders. Allow it to drop to the floor, grateful for the relative shelter of night. My instinct is to try to cover myself, but I refuse to give Siegfried the satisfaction of seeing the humiliation that is making my blood burn. Instead, I stand up straight, lift my chin and glare at him.

He takes a moment to walk around me in a circle, slowly, before coming to face me again. 'I'd forgotten how handsome you are, Aderyn. Except for those hideous scars on your back, of course. It's a pity the hawks failed to finish you off when they killed your mother. Given what lies ahead, it would have been much better for you if they had.'

I dig my fingernails into the palms of my hands, willing myself not to react to his taunts.

Still, bastard that he is, he smiles. 'And the rest of you. Your robes. Now.'

My three companions follow my example. Siegfried resumes his pacing, until he stops in front of Odette.

'My beautiful betrothed.' He wipes away one of the tears tracking down her face. 'We have unfinished business, do we not?'

I see Odette swallow. 'I'm never going to marry you, Siegfried.' Her voice quivers, but she speaks clearly.

'Oh, I'm not talking about marriage.' Siegfried brushes his fingers across Odette's neck, then points to the scar on his cheek. 'You remember how I ended up with this? I disappointed my sister. It's not a mistake I'm planning to make again.'

Too late, I understand. I shout a warning to Odette, try to push her out of the way before the woman behind me seizes my hair and yanks me backwards.

It happens almost in slow motion. I see realisation bloom in Odette's eyes as Siegfried snatches the sword from his belt and grabs her arm. Hear her desperate cries as she tries to pull away from him. She starts to transform into a swan, and for an instant I hope –

But she's not quick enough. He drives the blade up beneath her ribs and clasps his free arm around her as she struggles against it, gasping in pain. Until, eventually, she stops struggling. Siegfried yanks the blade out, breathing hard, and lets her go.

For a moment Odette stands, shaking, clutching the wound, blood flowing black in the darkness across her hands and stomach and legs. But as she staggers forward and mouths my name, she drops to her knees. Her eyes turn up, almost as if she is looking to the high peaks of the mountains, and the wind catches her hair – turned silver-gold by the light of the burning Citadel – and flutters it around her shoulders like feathers. Or like a shroud. More blood trickles from the corner of her mouth and she stretches her arms wide, as if trying to take flight one last time –

She falls to the floor, and is still.

229

'Odette? Odette –' I scream her name over and over, fighting to get away from the woman holding me. She can't be dead. She can't be . . .

But my cousin doesn't move. Doesn't blink. Only the Last Flight is left for her now.

I can't tear my gaze away from Odette's body. Dimly I'm aware of Lien and Pyr yelling at Siegfried, struggling to reach him. But I don't want to scream at him. Not yet. I just want to hold my cousin in my arms, straighten her splayed limbs.

'Please –' I try to turn my head towards Siegfried, despite the woman's grip on my hair. 'Please, let me go to her.'

He laughs. 'You're asking me for a favour?'

'Yes. For the Creator's sake, Siegfried, in the name of all that we hold sacred, I'm begging you: let me attend to her.'

The laughter fades. He glances briefly at his followers, then nods. 'Quickly then.'

The woman releases me, though she keeps the point of her sword hovering near my back. I drop to my knees next to Odette's body. Her robe is still on the floor nearby; I spread it out, as far as I'm able, and drag her body onto it. Straighten out her legs. Slide her arms through the slits in the side. There's nothing I can do about the still-bleeding wound in her torso, so I fasten the robe instead. There's blood on my hands, my knees, everywhere. I try to wipe the worst of it off my fingers before I comb out her hair. Finally I lift her head, arrange the hood of the robe beneath it like a pillow, and close her eyes. And all the time I'm talking to her gently, apologies mingled with useless declarations of love.

I'm so sorry, my darling Odette, I'm so . . . There, that's better, you'll be warmer now, and your hair, your beautiful hair . . .

Forgive me, I beg you . . . Oh, Creator, please, make this not true, make it . . . My dearest Odette, I'm so sorry . . .

A cold, steady rain has begun to fall. It mingles with my tears.

'My lord –' Lucien has returned. He stops short, his dark eyes wide, staring at Odette and me.

'Where is my sister?' Siegfried asks. 'Rookwood?'

Lucien drags his attention back to Siegfried. 'In the great hall, with Lord Patrus. She asks that you bring the queen – I mean, the prisoner – to her there.'

Siegfried sighs. 'Very well.' He jerks his head in the direction of Lien and Pyr. 'They're irrelevant. Dispatch them.'

'No –' My shout is drowned out by Lien's groans as the man behind him runs a sword through his abdomen. He clutches the protruding blade, staring down at it in seeming disbelief before collapsing, moaning in pain as it's withdrawn. Pyr has seized a sword from one of our captors. He falls dead, hacked by multiple blades, before he can use it.

I screw my eyes shut, and in my head it's this morning, and I'm on the beach in Fenian watching Pyr cook fish while Lien argues with him about some point of military history, and Odette is smiling, holding out a leaf that she's using as a plate –

I saved you some . . .

But I couldn't save her. I couldn't save any of them.

Someone – Siegfried? – grabs my arm and tries to jerk me upright. I resist – I don't want to leave Odette, not here, not like this – but he brings the flat of his blade down across my back, making me cry out with pain and shock.

'That was a warning, Aderyn. Next time I'll use the edge. Now get to your feet and follow me.'

231

As we start to make our way back inside, Lucien snatches my robe from the ground and drapes it over my shoulders. Either Siegfried doesn't see, or he doesn't want to pick a fight with his sister's favourite.

I clutch the robe around me. Though if I was braver, I would throw it back in Lucien's face. His pity sickens me.

What am I going to do?

I try to think, though my mind keeps swinging back to the three bodies on the landing platform, like a compass to a magnet. If Aron is alive – *if* – he won't be for much longer. As soon as Tallis has me, she'll kill him. She told me she would. She'll make me watch him die; him, and Lancelin and Letya too. If she's caught them.

I have to stay alive. To stand a chance of saving any of those I love, I have to escape.

But how can I leave Odette behind?

We're back in my bedroom, Veron temporarily walking next to me. He looks as if he's going to be sick; his skin is pale as bone, even in the red of the flickering lamplight. As I watch, he retches, stumbles towards me and steadies himself on my shoulders. His mouth is close to my ear. He whispers something that might be *window* . . .

One of our captors curses him and drags him upright again.

I keep my eyes straight ahead, not looking at him. Trying to decide whether Veron has just given me a warning, or suggested a plan.

Window . . . Does he mean for us to jump?

We reach the door that leads to the sitting room. There are people with swords ahead of me and behind me, but – for a wingbeat of time, as we move through the narrow space of the doorway itself – no one apart from Veron is next to me.

It's now or not at all.

So I start to sprint, dodging past furniture, my heart beating so hard I can barely breathe. I head for one of the big, broken windows of my sitting room. I don't think I can do this. I don't want to leave Odette. But I have to try.

Someone is at my heels; Veron, I hope. I speed up, blinking away my tears, ignoring the pain that flares through my left foot, the sword that clatters to the ground nearby and the shouted orders behind me. The only thing that matters now is the open night sky beyond the empty frame.

Veron draws level with me, rips away his robe and vaults over the windowsill.

I don't want to leave Odette. But if I hesitate, I'm lost. So I leap –

The remnants of the window scrape my skin, but I'm through. Falling. Tumbling towards the rocky margins of the fjord until the transformation takes me and the wind catches my wings and carries me up and out towards the mountains.

I'm not alone.

A large silver-and-fawn gyrfalcon is matching my speed and direction: Veron.

You understood. I wasn't sure. And then I thought, at the last moment, that you wouldn't jump.

I almost didn't.

Where shall we go? They're bound to pursue us . . .

The private landing platform is almost below us. Could we carry Odette's body, between the two of us?

233

Veron must sense my hesitation. *We'd be too slow to escape, Aderyn. I'm sorry.*

He's right. Looking back, I can already see Siegfried, standing by another open window. It looks as if he's pulling off his armour. Not everyone has the skill of transforming as they fall, but it seems like something Siegfried would have taken care to master.

We need to get to the Eyria. Fly fast.

As if the eight-winged eagles of hell were behind me.

We speed up. Racing towards the mountains, hoping to lose Siegfried and anyone else who hunts us as we enter the narrow passes that lie between the needle-like peaks. In the east the sky is growing light; sunrise approaches. But the shadow in these ravines is too deep to be dissolved. Veron follows me as I twist and dive and skim over rocky pinnacles and beneath overhanging cliffs of ice. We fly on, higher and higher into the mountains, through air that smells of winter and forgotten places, racing against the dawn. Until Veron banks too slowly. He yelps with pain as his wing strikes a stone outcrop.

That was definitely too close.

We've still some way to go; we have to cross the peaks and come down towards Dacia. Can you see anyone following us?

He swoops below me, flips and flies back a little way before repeating the manoeuvre to return to his position in the updraught from my wings.

Siegfried and one other are still tracking us.

Damn —

I try to force my wings to beat faster. The entrance to the

Eyria lies on the far side of the mountains; if there's any chance that Siegfried hasn't yet discovered where it is, I cannot be the one to guide him there. But my shoulders are burning and I can hear the rasp in my lungs as they labour in the thin, frost-laden air, can sense my altitude falling . . .

The crows explode upwards out of the darkness of the gorge that lies below us. Four of them, their wide black wings above me like slices of deep night against the twilight sky.

Name and family! Name and family! Their voices in my head deafen me.

Aderyn, Cygnus Atratys . . .

I hear Veron identify himself.

Your Majesty, one of the crows replies, *we thought you were lost. We're being pursued –*

I don't need to say any more. The crows leave me and bear down on Siegfried and whoever the owl is who's accompanying him. Veron and I reverse course to offer help, but we aren't needed. The skirmish is short. Our hunters become the hunted; they try to resist, but with the odds against them, injured, they soon turn tail and flee. The crows chase them far enough back towards the Citadel to ensure they don't try to return.

We regroup and fly in exhausted silence on towards the Eyria. The crows lead us further through the heart of the mountains; I'm relieved to be able to follow them without concentrating on my surroundings. I don't want to think about what I've left behind. Or what's to come. For the time our journey lasts, I withdraw into my body, try to feel nothing but the movement of my wings and the ice crystals blowing off the mountainside and across my feathers.

But this moment of calm and isolation can't last forever. The crows climb higher, winding their way between the jagged spires of rock that form the summits of the two highest mountains.

The plains of Dacia lie before us, swathed in trailing tendrils of mist.

We begin descending, traversing slopes and gullies until we reach the lower foothills of the Silver Mountains. There are huge crevasses here, mostly filled with boulders. The crows fly lower, leading us into one of these, slightly wider than the rest. I can hear the rush and gurgle of the river that runs along the bottom of the crevasse.

But I don't see the gateway, hidden as it is in the deep shadow of the high walls, until it's right in front of me.

The river has been dammed to form a pond of half-frozen water – deep and black and cold enough to make me gasp – to one side of the gate. While the others drop onto the stony ground beside the water, I land there, transform carefully and swim to the side. There are no flightless here yet – I don't know how many hours it might take until the first of them arrive – so other nobles hurry forward from the gateway with fresh robes.

I take one gratefully. Wrap myself in its warmth. My rescuers are standing nearby, examining the gashes and bruises inflicted by Siegfried and his follower.

'You're Lord Corvax's sons, aren't you?' I hold out my hands to them. 'I don't know how to thank you; we might not have made it here without you. Please, tell me you're not seriously injured?'

They all bow, and one – Lord Bran Shadowshaft, the eldest of the four, I think – says, 'Just a few scratches, Your Majesty.

We're glad we could be of assistance. The king ordered a watch set in case you –'

'The king?' I swallow hard. 'Aron is here? But how? Siegfried told us he'd been captured.'

Shadowshaft shakes his head. 'He stayed fighting at the Citadel, directing the resistance for as long as he could, until my father and Lord Pianet begged him to leave. They and some others brought him here.'

'Thank the Creator.' The flood of relief is intense enough to make me want to cry. I press the heels of my hands to my eyes, realising in my next breath that I'm going to have to tell Aron what happened to his sister.

I remember our last conversation, before I flew north. He warned me that I was putting Odette at risk.

I've almost forgotten about Veron's presence until I hear his voice.

'Do you know what happened to my brother –Valentin of Falco Gyr? He should have been with the other Celonians . . .'

'I heard my father speaking of them,' Shadowshaft replies. 'Those who haven't yet left the kingdom were gathered at the house in Farne when that traitor Patrus opened the gates to the Citadel. His Majesty seems to have had some warning of the attack. I'm sure he would have put them on their guard.'

'We should go to Aron.' I take a step forward and flinch as the injury to my left foot, no longer numb from the cold, sends a spike of pain up my leg. Veron offers me his arm – he seems to have managed to avoid the scattered glass during our escape – and I limp slowly within the gates of the Eyria.

In the torchlight, my surroundings remind me of the tunnel that leads to Galen, but the Eyria, although based on a network of caverns, is so much more than that. Passages and caves in the sheer mountain face were linked and expanded, widened in some places and covered over in others, to provide an enormous protected fortress that is almost imperceptible from the air, a refuge built into the mountain itself.

Beyond the first gate is a narrow passage that leads to a second gate. Behind this, the tunnel widens into a huge cavern. Here there are passages lined with storage rooms, hewn out of the rock. Shafts driven upwards towards the mountain face provide ventilation and some small amount of natural light. A spring bubbles from a fissure on the far side of the room; it tumbles into a wide marble basin before being channelled into a gulley that bisects the floor. It's obvious that Aron's preparations have been thorough. Some of the storage rooms are filled with barrels of food and drink, others packed with weapons and armour, wood, candles, robes and clothing. One larger room appears to be set aside for healing; I glimpse beds set up within, while nobles wait in a line outside for treatment. There are people everywhere, gathered in small groups, some standing, some lying on the floor sleeping. As I hobble past, I'm recognised. There are murmurs of surprise and relief, and my progress slows; some of my courtiers want to talk to me, to ask me questions or tell me of their narrow escapes or share their grief. But I can't linger. The more I hear, the more desperate I am to reach Aron and find out exactly how bad our situation is.

We pass through another tunnel and emerge into a large, echoing space, also lit partially with lanterns, supplementing the narrow shafts of light coming from the ventilation holes high above us. From here, other tunnels radiate out. There's what looks like a stone table at the far end of the cavern, around which a group of people are talking. They turn as we enter. I recognise some of my councillors, members of Convocation, Arden of Dacia and Verginie of Lancorphys. Valentin too. Veron murmurs something under his breath. At that moment they begin to hurry towards us, Aron leading the way.

'Aderyn, by the Firebird . . .'

He sees my face. Stops. His smile melts away. 'Where's Odette? Where's my sister?'

I can't find my voice.

Aron grips my shoulder. Shakes me. 'Where is she?'

'. . . I'm so sorry, Aron. Siegfried –'

His hand drops.

'Captured? Or . . . or dead?'

'Dead.'

He just gapes at me.

'I'm sorry. If I could have saved her, if I could have stopped him – I didn't want to leave her there, Aron. I'm so sorry . . .' I repeat my apology, knowing full well that my words are useless. But I don't know what else to do. Aron is still staring, as if he hasn't understood what I've told him. 'Please, Aron,' I lift my hand to his face, 'say something . . .'

He takes a long, shuddering breath. 'What happened?'

'We were searching for you. We thought you might be trapped in the royal apartments, or injured. But we didn't find you, and we were just about to leave when . . .' I frown and press my fingers to my temples. 'They were waiting for us.

Someone must have told them I wasn't in the Citadel. Patrus, or – or . . .' I can't bring myself to say Lucien's name. 'They took us to the landing platform behind my apartments and then –' My stomach churns. 'I'm sorry –'

'Why didn't you send her away? You sent Nyssa here, and Blackbill. Why didn't you make her leave?'

'I tried to, but she refused. She wouldn't leave the Citadel until she was certain you weren't there. And then Siegfried told us you'd been captured, and he threatened to hurt you . . .'

He groans as he turns away, dropping his head into his hand. 'No. No!' There are swords and shields carefully piled against the wall nearby. Aron bellows, seizes a sword and starts swinging the blade wildly, sending the other weapons clattering onto the stone floor, slicing through the rope from which a nearby lantern is suspended. It crashes down and a pool of blazing oil floods across the ground.

I make a grab for Aron's arm and pull him back, away from the flames. 'Please, stop –'

He yanks his arm free and turns on me.

'This is all your fault!' His face is twisted with rage and he flings the sword away. 'She was kind and she loved you, and you used that. You encouraged her to leave the Citadel. To go off with you on your pointless expedition, even though I begged her to stay. She should have been with me, Aderyn.' He thumps his fist against his chest. 'I'd have sent her away as soon as the attack started. Siegfried would never have touched her. She'd still be alive –'

'Odette chose to go with me because she was brave and adventurous. And if she'd stayed, she would have stayed with you, and faced the same risks. You know she'd never have retreated to safety without you.'

Aron glares at me, breathing hard, his green eyes glassy with unshed tears. 'We argued, the last time I saw her. I stormed off. I didn't even get to say goodbye . . .'

My heart aches for him, aches as if it's being crushed inside a mail gauntlet. I reach out and brush my fingers across the back of his hand.

He jerks away from me. 'Don't touch me.'

Veron pushes between us. 'This is not Aderyn's fault, Your Majesty. I was there: she did everything she could to save Odette. If you're looking for someone to blame, blame Siegfried. Not your wife.'

Aron shoves the Celonian in the chest. 'Stay out of this! You're a guest in our country, nothing more.'

Veron's hands clench into fists. Before he can respond, Valentin puts his arm around Aron's shoulders. 'Enough, Veron. Can't you see he's distraught?' He steers Aron away and starts to guide him out of the cavern.

'But, Aron –' I start to limp after him – 'please . . .'

He doesn't look back, but I feel everyone else's gaze upon me. Hear the unspoken questions: what of Letya, of Lancelin, of Fris? What of Lien and Pyr?

Did you really do everything you could?

How many more will have to follow you to their deaths?

I don't know how to answer.

Thirteen

Verginie of Lancorphys puts her arm around my shoulders.
'Come along, Your Majesty . . .'

I shake myself out of my stupor. 'No. I need to talk to
everyone. Understand what happened.'

'Indeed. But first you have to eat.'

Perhaps something in her voice reminds me of my mother.
Or perhaps I'm just too exhausted, too overcome with grief
to argue.

The next few hours are a blur. Food and water are brought,
and a hot tisane, but as soon as I've eaten, despite Verginie's
urging that I should rest, I insist on meeting my councillors
to receive a report on the attack and its aftermath. I'm still
the queen, for now, at least, so I must act like one. Even if it is
just that – an act. The members of the Skein who are present
describe the shock of betrayal, panic, desperate last stands. No
one has emerged unscathed. It's clear many more lives would
have been lost if Aron hadn't received information suggesting
an assault on the Citadel was imminent. But not even Lord

Pianet seems to know where the intelligence came from. The kingdom is divided in half: Brithys and most of Olorys have come out in support of Tallis and Siegfried, while Fenian, Dacia and Lancorphys remain loyal to us. Atratys, *my* Atratys, leaderless as it is, has been claimed by Tallis. We have no information yet as to whether it's come under fresh attack. I try to imagine the wreck that is now Merl Castle, my childhood home, being handed over to one of her supporters. To Lucien, perhaps. But no matter how much I prod, I can't seem to feel anything about it. I am already overwhelmed by loss.

Lancelin did not escape the Citadel. Thane of Fenian is dead.

I explain, for the second time, my meeting with the Shriven. There is more scepticism about their existence, so I'm relieved that Veron at least has survived to confirm their immunity to our touch. But, given the doubtful outcome of my meeting with Jaqueth, the whole seems more like an interesting story than something of concrete use.

Besides, how will Damarin find us, even if she does persuade her mother to send help?

Nyssa is shaking my shoulder.

'Aderyn? You fell asleep . . .'

I rub my face and glance around. I'm still seated at the stone table in the main hall, but the others who were with me have dispersed. Only Veron remains.

Everything aches, apart from my foot, which is throbbing.

Blinking, I look up at Nyssa. 'You got back safely. You and Blackbill.'

'Yes.' She hesitates. 'I'm so sorry, Aderyn. Perhaps if we'd stayed –'

'It wouldn't have made any difference. He'd have killed you too. Blackbill, at least. He might have kept you alive to bargain with.' I reach up and try to massage away some of the pain in my shoulders. 'How is he? Does he know?'

Nyssa understands that I'm talking about Blackbill, and Odette's death. 'He knows. Lord Corvax told him. I sat with him for a while, but he's bewildered. He doesn't want to believe it's true.' She shakes her head. 'Time will help, a little.'

She should know, of course.

'Come, you should have that foot seen to.'

I glance down. My left foot is red and swollen, but between them Veron and Nyssa get me to a small room high up in the complex, high enough that there's a shuttered opening in the rock that passes for a window. The room contains nothing but a straw-stuffed mattress and a lantern, but at least it's private. Nyssa goes to fetch one of the Venerable Sisters who are serving as healers in the absence of our flightless doctors. Despite the pain in my foot, the mattress is soft enough, especially since I've not slept at all since the few hours snatched on the beach in Fenian, that I struggle to keep my eyes open. Veron sits cross-legged on the floor next to me.

'Would you rather I go?'

I shake my head. Realistically, the chances of Letya and Lancelin both surviving and escaping the Citadel are slender. Almost everyone I care about is either dead or missing. And I remember Tallis's promise to me that night at Hatchlands: that she would kill me, but only after she'd taken everything from me, after she'd forced me to watch those I love suffer and die . . . Despite the constant hum of voices I can hear drifting up from the main caverns, I've never felt more alone. 'Stay with me, for a little . . .' I rub my eyes. 'Have you spoken to your brother?'

'Yes. He is still with Aron. We believe the rest of my people have escaped to the base we've established on Thesalis.'

'You and Valentin should join them. Get out while there's still time. Perhaps you'll be able to return one day.' I try to imagine a future for Veron in which he forges a peace within Celonia and becomes a better king than those who preceded him. I can't imagine any future for myself.

A howl of agony rings through the Eyria – one of the injured being operated on, I guess – and I'm back on the landing platform, listening to the screams of Odette and Lien and Pyr as they die, unable to help them. A spike of grief punches through my numbness. I roll onto my side, curl my legs up against my stomach and hug them tightly as tears spill across my cheek.

Veron says something in Celonian, then adds, 'I am sorry. We've both of us seen too much death.' He brushes the tear away and smooths my hair back. Kisses my cheek.

I turn my head to look up at him. Hesitate. But the pain of everything that's happened is too much for me to bear alone. I lift my mouth, and he presses his lips against mine. Kisses me deeply as my body begins to relax.

'Rest now, Aderyn.'

I stop fighting my exhaustion and close my eyes. Hear him sigh, I think. Feel his fingers brush against my cheek and his hand come to rest on top of mine.

'I'm not going to Thesalis,' he murmurs, just on the edge of hearing. 'I'll stay here. I have to see it through . . .'

I start to wonder what he means, but the end of my thought dissolves into sleep.

In the dream, I'm at Merl. My home is undamaged, and Letya and Lancelin are there. My parents too, which is how I know it's not real. I find my mother in her rose garden, and I'm able to sit next to her and tell her about Odette, and Lucien, and she puts her arms around me and tells me all will be well . . .

I don't want to let go.

For a while, I lie still with my eyes closed, trying to cling to the sensation of my mother's embrace.

It doesn't last. The lumpy straw mattress beneath me, the wind moaning outside the Eyria, force me fully awake.

I'm alone in the small, lamp-lit room. My foot is bandaged, and there's a crutch leaning against the rock wall; I suppose someone dealt with my wound, though I have no memory of it. The cracks in the window shutter reveal a dark night sky beyond.

I stare at the rocky ceiling and pick Veron as the least horrible thing to think about. His invitation to me at Rogallyn was clear enough. I like him. Desire him, even. For a while I consider the possibility of taking him to my bed. There would be a certain satisfaction in it. A feeling of somehow taking revenge, against both Lucien and Aron. The thought of being able to lose myself in his arms – to forget about Tallis, about Odette, about everything – is even more of a temptation. And what does it matter if people gossip? We might all be dead in a few days' time.

But despite all my arguments and justifications, something holds me back. Shame, perhaps. Or not wanting to use him.

Or the fact that, despite everything Lucien's done, despite the fact that it's pathetic, and demeaning, and absurd – I still love him.

I can't take things any further with Veron. I suppose I should tell him so, sometime soon.

I turn on my side and try to get back to sleep.

The next morning I go in search of Aron. Nyssa takes me to his room. I stand outside the door and plead with him to talk to me. Beg him to say something, even if all he can manage are words of blame.

He doesn't reply.

I summon my surviving councillors and try, since I have to do something, to work out what to do next.

Over the following few days we send messengers to the loyal dominions to carry news of the assault and hurry the sending of aid. We listen to reports from the scouts sent to observe the Citadel, and start to make plans for various possibilities. For launching an attack on the Citadel, if things go well; for being under siege in the Eyria, if things go badly. Patrus, I'm sure, knows where the Eyria is located. It can't be long before he shares that information with Tallis. The chant of the Venerable Sisters, reciting the Litanies and singing the Benediction of the Dead, forms a constant background to every activity. Too many who escaped the Citadel have since died of their wounds.

Aron begins attending our meetings, though he speaks to

me as little as possible. His cheeks are hollow, his pallor even more pronounced than usual. I ask Valentin to make sure he takes at least a little food each day. Sometimes, in the deeper darkness of the night, I think I hear him weeping.

Three days more, and small groups of flightless begin to arrive: Dark Guards and servants who escaped the Citadel. Fewer than I had hoped, though some have apparently fled elsewhere, to towns and villages in the Crown Estates, and some are attempting to join the flightless companies that have been raised in the dominions. Aron searches in vain for any sign of Hemeth, his best friend in the Dark Guards. I haunt the main cavern too, holding my breath every time I catch a glimpse of ash-blonde hair, praying that it might be Letya.

It never is.

I try to stop hoping, because the disappointment hurts more each time.

But one evening, eleven days since I escaped from Siegfried, one of the young maidservants who used to assist Fris and Letya does arrive, and is brought to my room.

'Cora!' I almost forget myself and take her hands. 'I'm so glad to see you. You're unharmed?'

'Yes, Majesty.' She bobs her head and glances around my room, pursing her lips at the general disorder. 'And as I can see Your Majesty has no one waiting on you, I'd be pleased to do so.' A fierce light comes into her hazel eyes. 'That Tallis is a wicked woman. Her and her followers.' She sniffs and blinks away tears. 'I saw what they did to Fris. She was trying to stop them from going into your rooms. They had no call to kill her.'

'Tallis *is* wicked, Cora. But I hope we'll have revenge one day. For Fris, and for all who died.' I push down the grief that's always waiting to overwhelm me. 'Did you see anything of Letya, at the Citadel or on your way here?'

'Not since the attack. I was airing your bed when the bell started tolling. Letya ran in and shoved a bag into my arms and told me that if anything really bad was happening, I was to go straight to the dungeons. But why would I go to the dungeons? There's no way out down there.'

She's right, but she's also the second person to tell me that Letya was encouraging others to go there. I wonder what knowledge my friend picked up while I was in Fenian. Whether it might have saved her.

'How did you escape?'

'I was hiding in the audience chamber. There's a blocked-up window behind one of the tapestries. That's how I saw, when Fris was . . .' Her hand flutters to her throat. 'And then I ran, as soon as I could. I got out past the stables.' She lifts the bag that's hanging across her body and offers it to me. 'I still brung it though.'

'Thank you, Cora.' I recognise the bag; Letya made it one winter from an old yellow gown that had become too faded and out of fashion to wear. She embroidered the straw-coloured satin with pink roses, because she wanted to hurry the arrival of spring. I grip the bag tightly. 'Thank you. Please, go and get some food, and rest. I don't need anything this evening.'

When Cora's gone, I shut my door and tip the contents of the bag out on my bed.

Letya has saved some of our treasures. I turn them over,

examining them through the tears that have clouded my vision. Her favourite knitting needles. A novel her brother sent her for the Firebird feast one year. The diptych Lancelin gave me for my eighteenth birthday, with a painting of Merl Castle on one side and a portrait of me and my parents on the other. The gaudy Friant brooch Letya was so taken with a few weeks ago. And a small leather pouch. Inside are two rings. The ring belonging to the Protector of Atrratys, that had been my mother's, and my coronation ring. I weigh them in the palm of my hand for a moment, before tipping them back into the pouch. I failed to protect my dominion, and I've lost my throne. I don't deserve to wear either of them.

Maybe I never did.

I wake early the next morning. My head is aching, so I dress myself and go down through the Eyria to where the medical supplies are stored. Apart from those on guard, no one is awake, but I'm able to find a vial of tincture of willow on one of the shelves. I slip it into my pocket and walk through to the main cavern where the spring rises, to get something to drink. I stay there once I've taken my medicine, leaning on the marble basin, listening to the water gurgling against the stone.

Until I'm distracted by voices coming from a corridor nearby. The voices are speaking Celonian, I think. But even though I don't understand the words, I can tell the speakers are angry. Curious, I tiptoe closer, ducking into one of the shallow storage alcoves that line this corridor.

The voices belong to Veron and his brother. I've hardly seen Veron since we kissed. I suppose I've been avoiding him, or perhaps we've been avoiding each other. Perhaps he's thought better of his decision not to leave, but hasn't wanted to tell me. It would make sense, if that's what he and Valentin are arguing about: Veron's expectations about Valentin's future, and Valentin's affection for Aron.

I'm sure that's it. I'm about to return to the main cavern, when Valentin breaks into my own language.

'I do reject it, Veron. I reject all of it.' His voice is low, but so raw with fury I catch my breath. 'After what you've told me, I would rather stay here as one of them. I'll speak their tongue, and offer them my allegiance, and if necessary I'll die with them. Better death than having to live knowing my own brother is a murderer!'

A pause; all I can hear is the sound of Valentin's agitated breathing.

'Will you betray me then?' Veron asks.

'What do you think?'

Footsteps, receding. One of the brothers has gone further into the Eyria. A moment later I hear Veron swear. He calls after Valentin, swears again, then strides in my direction. I flatten myself against the wall, hoping the shadows and his own distraction will be enough concealment.

Veron passes me and carries on towards the main cavern.

I hesitate, but not for long. Some of the alcoves here contain weapons. I swap the vial in my pocket for a dagger and hurry after Veron.

He's crossing the cavern, making, apparently, for the main exit. I run to catch up, slowing before I reach him, trying to make our meeting look accidental.

251

'My Lord Veron . . .'

He turns, blinking in surprise. 'Your Majesty. I . . . I couldn't sleep. I thought some fresh air might help.'

'May I join you? We can walk up the ravine a little.'

He draws breath before answering. 'Of course.' There is wariness in his eyes. Still, he offers me his arm. Once outside, I lead the way further up the gorge. This early in the day, the tall rocky walls allow only a little dim light to filter down this far. I have to pick a route among the boulders that line the edge of the foaming, rushing river.

When we're are out of sight of the Eyria, I turn to face Veron.

'Aderyn . . .' He puts his hands on my upper arms. He thinks I've brought him here to kiss him.

'Why did Valentin call you a murderer? What's going on?'

He recoils at my words, snatching his hands away before catching himself and curving his lips up into something that's almost a smile.

'You heard that?' Veron laughs unsteadily. 'My brother is angry with me. And perhaps . . .' he shrugs, 'perhaps he is right.'

'Is this to do with Aron? Does Valentin blame you for what happened to Odette and the others? Or has Tallis captured some of your people?'

Another shrug. And I notice for the first time the dark shadows beneath his eyes. 'Valentin blames me for many things.'

'But you're not a murderer –'

He stoops to pick up a stone. Hurls it into the river. 'Are you absolutely sure about that?'

Doubt, cold and sudden, slithers down my spine.

'You don't know me at all, Aderyn. You don't know what I'm capable of.' Veron shakes his head and turns away. 'Even though I tried to tell you.' He looks back at me. 'I will do anything – *anything* – to give my people back their home.'

My heart beats so fast it sickens me. 'What have you done?'

'What I had to do!' he snaps, his sudden anger forcing me back. 'Frianland threatens invasion, and you refuse to do anything more than give us sanctuary, and meanwhile my people have nothing. No home, no means of support, no future. Nothing.' He takes a deep breath. 'I heard you talk about your love for Atratys. You're the same as me. Valentin calls it betrayal, but you would do the same, if it came to it.'

It's like a candle being lit. Or the pieces of a puzzle fitting together. Inside my head, small things that must have been burrowing into my brain suddenly snap into place. The way Veron attempted to persuade us to go to the landing platform behind my apartments, even though I have no recollection of ever telling him that such a place existed. The fact that Siegfried recognised him, and told him to keep quiet. The words of Craxby come back to me: his comment that the Friant side of Vauban was full of Celonians since the revolution.

Eorman hadn't been sheltering Tallis. She and her brother had been at the Celonian court . . .

I swallow down the bile rising in my throat. 'That was why you didn't want us to spend a night at Rogallyn, why you were so anxious for us to fly straight back to the Citadel: in case Lady Verginie's people had received news of the invasion. You didn't want them to warn us. You were supposed to deliver us straight to Siegfried.' Veron isn't looking at me. 'What did they promise you?' He doesn't answer, so I shove him. 'Tell me!'

'Once they have the throne, they'll help me recover Celonia. And then we'll form an alliance against Frianland. They promised me I could have you too.'

'You –' I raise my hand to strike him, but he seizes my wrists.

'Listen to me, Aderyn: you cannot win. Tallis is too strong. Too . . . mad. If you want to end this bloodshed, if you want to save yourself and Aron, you have to give up the crown and submit to her –'

'Submit? Have you lost your mind?' I try in vain to free myself from his grip. 'You want me to betray my own people? To submit to someone who will destroy the kingdom, who's already vowed to kill me?'

'I can protect you.'

The idea is so ridiculous I laugh. 'You saw what Siegfried did. How, exactly, are you planning to protect me?'

'But I didn't know Siegfried was going to kill Odette and the others.' His voice rises. 'I swear. Once this is over, I'll take you to Celonia. You'll be safe there.' He pulls me closer. 'I'll look after you. And maybe, in time –'

'What? You think if I'm given to you as a spoil of war, as a possession, that eventually I'll love you? Your brother's right: you are a murderer. And you're as mad as Tallis. I could never love someone like you. You disgust me.'

Veron's eyes narrow. 'You liked me well enough to kiss me.' His hold on my wrists tightens and he's breathing hard, his mouth twisted in anguish and fury. For a moment – long enough for fear to snake through my veins and freeze my blood – I wonder if I'm going to survive this.

The river is loud. Would anyone hear if I screamed?

I kick him in the shin. The surprise is enough to loosen his grip, giving me the chance to yank my left hand free and snatch Veron's dagger from the belt at his waist.

But I don't point it at him. On instinct, I turn the blade on myself, digging into the soft flesh of my breast. 'You'd better kill me then. Because that's the only way you'll take me to Celonia: as a corpse. I'll never submit to Tallis. And I'll never submit to you. Kill me now, and maybe you'll have time to escape. Your brother might already have told Aron what you've done.'

A bead of sweat trickles down one side of Veron's face as he stares at me. His grip on my other wrist slackens. I pull away and shove him as hard as I can, sending him stumbling backwards. He loses his footing on the loose scree of stones, and slips and slides until he's half in the river, half on the bank. But he doesn't try to get up. Just lies there, leaning on one elbow, his head in his hands.

I draw my own dagger out of my pocket and stand over him. 'You're wrong, Veron. I'm not like you. I'd die for Atratys, but I wouldn't make a pact with hell itself in order to save it. And as for Aron and me – we took you in. We offered you a home, we gave you the possibility of a different future. True, we didn't help you fight for your beloved Celonia. But did it ever occur to you that the Celonia that you and your fellow nobles had created might not be worth saving?'

He doesn't answer. Doesn't look at me.

'Get to your feet. I ought to kill you where you lie, but we're going to see Aron. He's the one who's lost his sister to your treachery. If he wants to claim your life in return, I won't stop him.'

Veron crawls to the river's edge, splashes some water on his face and scrambles upright. 'I'm ready.'

I walk him at knifepoint back along the gorge, but once we approach the Eyria, I conceal the weapons in my pockets. There's the outline of a plan forming in my mind, and I don't want to draw any attention to myself or to Veron. Hemeth, if he's alive, has still not reached the Eyria, but his lieutenant, Danby, is among the Dark Guards on duty near the gates.

'Where is the king?'

'In his chamber, I believe, Your Majesty.'

'Send one of your men to him, to ask him to come to the tower room. Tell him . . . tell him I've something important to show him. A message we've received.' Hopefully I've been cryptic enough to confuse anyone who is listening but not so cryptic that Aron will ignore my request. 'And I'd like you to accompany us.'

Danby issues an order to one of the other guards, who hurries away. He falls into step behind me.

The tower room – reached by a sloping passage that leads up and back towards the gate it overlooks – is sparsely furnished, but it's private. I tell Veron to sit in one of the two available chairs. Once Danby has lit the lamp and barred the shutters across the roughly hewn window, I ask him to bind Veron's wrists to the arms of the chair. The lieutenant opens his eyes wide in surprise, but he doesn't question my order, and Veron doesn't resist. Finally, I send Danby to fetch some wine, bread and cheese, and ask him to wait outside.

Aron enters the room not long after. His eyes slide from me to Veron and back again.

'Aderyn? What is going on?'

'Have you seen Valentin yet this morning?'

'No.' The blood drains from his face. 'Though he slid a note beneath my door asking to speak with me. He wrote that there was a confession he had to make . . .' He leans back against the door, gripping the handle as if it's the only thing keeping him upright. 'What's happened? What have they done?'

'Not Valentin.' Veron leans forward, his voice urgent. 'My brother didn't know anything until last night. I decided it was time to reveal my plans, but his reaction was . . .' He laughs a little, though his voice cracks. 'So honourable, my little brother. He'd have woken you last night and told you everything, if I hadn't used what little love he retains for me to force him to delay.' He closes his eyes as if in pain. 'Please, whatever you do to me, spare my brother.'

Aron doesn't reply. He comes to stand next to me. Reaches out to take my hand without saying another word. Keeps hold as Veron outlines for us the exact extent of his treachery, from the point where he first met Tallis and Siegfried at the royal court in Celonia, to today.

At the end, Veron slumps back in his chair.

Aron releases my hand and begins pacing the narrow confines of the room. His voice, when he finally speaks, vibrates with anger.

'You came to us begging for sanctuary, and all the time . . . I wish I'd turned you away. I wish I'd never seen you.' A guttural sound, the mockery of a laugh, escapes his throat. 'And to think we believed that Frianland was harbouring them.' He crouches down in front of Veron. 'Look at me.'

Veron doesn't respond quickly enough; Aron deals him a backhanded blow across his face. 'I said look at me, damn you!'

Veron slowly raises his eyes to meet Aron's gaze, as a trickle of blood escapes from his bottom lip.

'Siegfried may have killed my sister, but you helped him. And if it's the last thing I do as king, I'm going to make you pay.' Aron straightens up and goes to the door to summon the guards.

'Wait –'

He glances back at me. 'Aderyn, if you're about to ask for mercy –'

'I'm not. I'd have him killed here and now, if it would serve our purpose.' I bring the daggers out of my pockets. 'After what happened to Odette and the others, I want to plunge these knives into his chest –'

Veron tenses, bracing himself.

'And I would, without a second thought.' My hands are shaking. I lay the daggers carefully on the table. 'But what if there's a way to use him? A way to use his relationship with Siegfried for our own ends?'

Aron lets go of the door handle. 'Go on.'

'Veron, will Siegfried still trust you, even though you escaped with me?'

He nods. 'I believe so. Tallis has the bloodlust, the burning, consuming hunger for power, the ability to sway men's minds through desire and fear. Siegfried seeks power no less, but he is more considered in his approach. He plans – every detail, every possible outcome. It was he who stationed Tallis and her mercenaries in the entrance hall, and the Brithyans on the tower tops, in case you decided to land there instead of the private landing platform. He told me, if anything should go wrong, and you were to escape, that I should follow you and pretend to escape with you, unless there was a certain way of capturing you myself. Of course, I wasn't supposed to suggest to you a way of escape, but I felt guilty, after seeing what Siegfried did to Odette and the others . . .' He turns his head away from me. 'Still, I regretted my moment of weakness before long. When I accidently hurt myself during our flight here, it wasn't an accident. When the crows arrived, I was about to slow down. To tell you I had to stop flying. I was fairly certain that you wouldn't leave me to face Siegfried on my own.'

My stomach turns as I realise how close I'd come to disaster. 'You bastard.' I feel Aron's hand on my back, steadying me.

Veron doesn't look at me. 'I'm sorry. All I've ever wanted was to do the best for my people.'

I take a deep breath, trying to focus. 'So what now? Is Siegfried waiting to hear from you?'

'Yes. I'm to gather information on your plans, then return to the Citadel before they besiege the Eyria.'

I turn my back on him. 'What if we let him go? He could feed Siegfried some false information.'

'Such as?' Aron asks.

'Well . . . Supposing he says we've arranged a meeting somewhere nearby, with Eorman of Frianland? To persuade him to join with us against Tallis. If Siegfried believes there's an opportunity to ambush us, he'd take it, don't you think?'

Aron runs his fingers along his jawline. 'Perhaps. We'd have to make it convincing. What would we be able to offer Eorman, in return for his assistance?'

'Marriage,' Veron murmurs.

A spasm of irritation flickers across Aron's face. 'What?'

'Eorman wants another kingdom. Cheaper to get it by marriage than invasion.'

'But he can't marry Aderyn.'

Veron sighs. 'Tallis and Siegfried know that your marriage is . . . unusual.'

Aron grits his teeth and glances at me. 'I suppose we can thank Lucien for that?' Fortunately – the last thing I want to do is discuss Lucien – he doesn't wait for my answer. 'Continue.'

'They might well believe that Aderyn, following Lucien's defection, would look for someone to provide her with children. A way of securing the succession. And I think I could convince them it's true if I go to them in anger.'

'I don't understand.' Aron looks back at me. 'Why would Veron be angry?'

'He'd be angry because Siegfried and Tallis have already promised me to him, after they've killed you, as some sort of –' I raise an eyebrow – 'reward.'

'What? Help take my throne then make my wife into your concubine?' Aron bares his teeth and takes a step nearer Veron, reaching for one of the daggers. 'Just let me kill him now –'

'Wait, Aron, please.' I catch hold of his arm. 'You can do what you like to him after he's helped us.' I turn to Veron. 'You do know that they were never going to keep their promise to you, don't you? If they get the chance, they'll kill me. And you, I should imagine. No matter how loyal you think you've been. And they'll probably invade Celonia for good measure.'

He drops his head further. 'I was desperate, Aderyn. What else was I supposed to do?'

'Talk to the flightless people in Celonia perhaps? Maybe not yet, but in a year's time – when they've grown sick of the bloodshed. There are things you could offer them – your experience in government. Your knowledge of the wider world. You could have tried to address some of the inequalities in your society, the things that pushed your flightless into rebellion in the first place. Or did it never occur to you that your king met the end he did because he was simply not fit to rule?'

Veron says nothing.

'What do you think, Aron? If we can lure Siegfried, or Tallis, or both of them even, to a place of our choosing, perhaps we can stop the evil at its source.'

'Cut off the head, and the body will wither?'

'That's the idea. I don't think Brithys or Olorys would keep fighting without them.'

We both look at Veron.

'If we do this,' Aron says, 'and you betray us, then I will kill Valentin myself.'

Veron's head jerks up. 'But . . . you love him, I thought.'

'I do love him.' Aron's voice is both soft and sharp, like a flint knife wrapped in silk. 'But I love my country too. And I love my wife, whatever you may think of the nature of our relationship. So trust me: if you bring further harm to my kingdom or those I care for, your brother will be the one who suffers the consequences.'

Fourteen

Veron slumps in the chair again. 'I understand. I will offer Tallis and Siegfried no further information on your activities here, and I will tell them only what you wish me to. I swear by the Firebird, and on my brother's life.'

Raised voices come from the passage beyond. Aron opens the door as I snatch up a dagger.

'Majesty,' Danby says, 'Lord Valentin here is insisting he be allowed to see you.' The Dark Guard has his hand on the hilt of his axe.

'Let him in.'

Danby stands aside and Valentin ducks into the room, closing the door behind him.

He takes in the scene. Blanches.

'You're going to kill him . . .'

'No.' I replace the dagger on the table. 'Not that he doesn't deserve it.'

Valentin swallows hard and turns to Aron. 'Forgive me. I would have come to you last night, but . . .'

Aron clasps Valentin's shoulder. 'You love your brother. There's no crime in that.'

'But what he's done . . .' Valentin sighs and runs both hands through his hair. 'What are you going to do with him?'

'He's going to help us.'

'You trust him?' Valentin's tone is incredulous.

'He won't betray us further. He's sworn on your life.'

Aron holds Valentin's gaze, until the Celonian looks away and murmurs, 'So be it.'

Aron summons Danby. 'Lord Veron is to be kept under arrest, but I don't want it to be obvious to anyone else. Valentin, will you go with him? The queen and I have some things to discuss.'

Another moment, and Aron and I are alone. He goes to the small table and pours two glasses of water. He passes me one, takes the other and sits in the chair Veron has vacated.

'Will you sit and talk with me, Aderyn?'

I nod and pull the other chair closer, studying his face. He's grown gaunt over the last few days. If Odette could see his bloodshot, dark-shadowed eyes, his unshaven jaw, she'd barely recognise her handsome, fastidious brother; another life Siegfried and Tallis have wrecked. 'I'm so sorry, Aron. If I could have forced Odette to leave, to fly to the Eyria, I would have done. I know I'm responsible. I know she was only there because of me. I should have found a way to save her –'

'No,' he interrupts, 'I'm the one who should be apologising. It was Siegfried who murdered my sister. Him and Tallis between them. I should never have blamed you. But I was angry. So angry I couldn't control it. I didn't want to control it. Losing my sister . . . it was – is – an agony such as I've never known.

Nothing compares to it. Not even the day of my accident, when my arm was ripped away –'

Tears silence him, running unchecked across his cheeks. I wait until he recovers a little.

'I don't know how to go on without her, Aderyn. She's always been next to me. Standing up for me. Consoling me. I thought she always would be. I feel . . .' he stares up at the flickering lamp, 'untethered. Adrift in a world that I no longer recognise.'

I reach across the small space that separates us and grip his shoulder, but I don't say anything. Aside from platitudes, what words could I possibly utter that would be of any use right now?

Aron sniffs and passes his cup to me while he wipes the tears from his face. As he takes the cup back his glance falls on my wrist, on the bruises that are beginning to blossom there.

'Veron?' he asks.

I nod.

'Bastard.'

I smile slightly. 'But a bastard who loves his brother, apparently. And I suppose he has shown some sense of responsibility towards his people.' I take a sip of water. 'Maybe he isn't entirely rotten. Perhaps he just made bad choices.'

'Perhaps.'

We both fall silent. I wonder if Aron is also thinking about Lucien. About the choices we've all made.

'I wasn't . . .' I search for the words. 'I wasn't in my right mind, when I came back home after finding Lucien with Tallis at Hatchlands. I was already grieving his loss before I went there. And then, after I realised what he'd done . . . I think I blamed you, though I shouldn't have. Perhaps grief and anger did make me reckless.' I consider my determination to make the journey north regardless of what Aron or any of my advisers said. Did I just want to have my own way? To prove to everyone that I *was* queen, whatever Tallis threatened, and that – being queen – I was entitled to do whatever I pleased? I remember my uncle, Aron's father, and his insistence that he was above both law and custom, and it makes me feel sick. 'I know I said some things that hurt you, Aron. And I'm sorry.'

'I think we can both agree,' he replies, 'that neither of us has exactly been at our best over the last few weeks.'

I nod. 'That much is true.'

'Will you tell me everything that happened? I still haven't heard all the details about these Shriven, or whatever they call themselves. And I want to know . . . I want to know about my sister.' His fingers tighten around the cup until it trembles in his hand. 'How she died. Everything.'

'I'll tell you anything you like. But may I ask you something?'

'Of course.'

'Will you really kill Valentin, if Veron betrays us?'

'If he is as innocent as Veron claims?' He shakes his head. 'No. I am not Siegfried. Or my father. But hopefully Veron doesn't know that.' His gaze drifts to my wrists again. 'You spoke of bad choices just now. Was this all a mistake, Aderyn? Our marriage? You and me trying to rule Solanum together? Would it have been better for the kingdom if we'd allowed Arden of Dacia and Thane of Fenian to claim the throne, and fight it out between them?'

'No. We'd have had civil war earlier, that's all. And it would have only made things easier for Tallis. Besides, you're a far better king than either of them would have been. You've at least tried to help the flightless, to start some sort of reform.'

'The flightless might not agree.' The corner of his mouth turns up, ever so slightly. 'But you can't deny it might have been better for us. If I'd helped you free Lucien, and then let you go . . .'

'What's done is done, Aron.' I don't want to think about Lucien. Even hearing his name is like . . . like driving a sharpened quill into a barely healed wound. 'For better or worse, we're in this together. Lord Rookwood has made his choices. And we all have to live with them.' I put down my cup and look at my hands. Since my father died, this is the longest I've gone without wearing a ring to signify my status. The Protector's ring, that belonged to my mother, and the Monarch's ring, that I received at my coronation, are in my room, but I cannot bring myself to put them on. The ring Aron gave me to mark our wedding is somewhere in the Citadel.

One way or another, all are lost to me.

But perhaps, sometimes, a loss can also be a gain. There are no rings on my fingers, defining who I'm supposed to be: Queen, Protector, daughter, wife.

For the first time since I saw my mother die, and my father locked me up at Merl, I'm free to define myself.

Aron and I don't tell anyone else about the deception we're planning. Veron may be the only spy in our midst, but we can't be certain. So our schemes evolve in secret. It takes three days of not much sleep, but eventually we hammer out a ploy that we hope might pass undetected.

We decide that Tallis and Siegfried will more easily believe that I have betrayed Aron than that Aron is willing to step aside. Obsessed with power themselves, will they not assume that both Aron and I are similarly determined to cling to the throne? So, Veron will return to Siegfried and try to lure him out by telling of his 'discovery': that I plan to abandon Aron in order to form an alliance with Eorman of Frianland. I find myself hoping that Lucien will have repeated to Tallis what he said to my face: that I wanted the crown more than I wanted him.

It's possible, of course, that Eorman has already offered to support Tallis. However, Eorman's only loyalty is to himself; if I had, in fact, offered him a better deal, he would take it. I know it, and so does Tallis.

We consider forging a letter from Eorman to support our deceit, but since we've no examples of his handwriting to copy we have to give up the idea. Hope instead that Veron is convincing. And that Siegfried and Tallis are easily convinced.

For about an hour after the scheme is finalised, confidence makes me feel a wingspan taller than I am. But it doesn't last. The closer we get to Veron's departure, the more difficulties I foresee. What if Siegfried doesn't believe him? What if he does believe him, but sends others to attack us, while he and Tallis stay safe at the Citadel? The day Veron is due to leave, I spend most of my waking hours stalking the caverns and corridors of the Eyria. I cannot wrench my mind away from the ever-growing list of things that might go wrong. By evening, I'm exhausted. I go to my room, sit on my mattress and brood. Cora comes in a little later, wearing fine leather gloves. She brushes and plaits my hair, then sits cross-legged next to the lamp and begins mending a tear in the dress I've just taken off. I know she likes to be busy; she says it stops her worrying so much about the future.

But it's late, and I want to be left alone.

'Don't worry about making it neat, Cora. It's not as if any of us are looking our best at the moment.' The clothes stored at the Eyria are plain, basic, one-size-fits-all, adjustable by drawstrings. Since I'm short and slightly built, the drawstrings have a lot of work to do.

I think with regret of my clothes at the Citadel – no doubt plundered by Tallis for her own use by now. My clothes, and my jewels.

Oh.

'Cora, pass me Letya's bag, will you?'

She obeys. I slip my hand inside and bring out Eorman's brooch, the Friant love knot. It glints in the lamplight. I sigh, as some of the tension I've been carrying around drains from my muscles.

There's a candle burning on the floor next to me; I bring it closer to examine the jewels in my palm. At the centre of the brooch sits a cluster of Friant sunstones, the colour of dressed flax. They're surrounded and divided by loops of emeralds and rubies, with an outer rim of amethysts. The whole thing is set in gold. I turn it over, trying to see the mechanism by which the brooch can be split into two. I smile as I remember Letya playing with it while she was sitting on the sofa, taking it apart and putting it back together again like a puzzle . . .

Pressing two of the rubies at the same time turns out to be the trick. The central section with the sunstones and emeralds drops into my lap, leaving the outer portion of amethysts and rubies. I return that to the bag. Picking up my candle, I clutch the remainder of the brooch in my hand and hurry along the passageways to the room Veron is sharing with Valentin.

I raise my hand to knock, but Veron – wearing a dark robe – opens the door as I do so. His brother's tear-stained face is just visible for a moment before Veron steps into the corridor and closes the door behind him.

I stiffen. Step back a little. It's the first time I've been alone with Veron since he followed me to the river.

He sighs. 'I'm not going to hurt you, Aderyn. I gave you my word.' He glances back at the door. 'I just bid my brother farewell.'

That explains Valentin's tears, and the anguish etched deep in Veron's face. To allay suspicion, Veron won't return to the Eyria after speaking to Siegfried and Tallis. We won't see him again until the date set for the ambush.

Opening my hand, I show him the brooch. 'I brought something that might help with your journey.' At the end of this passage is a large space where lots of people are sleeping. I can't hear anything but the odd snore. Still, I lower my voice and beckon Veron close, just in case. 'Eorman gave it to me. It's part of a type of brooch called a Friant love knot. He said if I ever sent it back to him, he'd know I wanted his help.'

Veron picks up the brooch and holds it between his finger and thumb. Even in the dim light of a single candle, it's beautiful. 'I presume he wanted something in return?'

'For me to get rid of Aron and marry him. Make him King of Solanum. I told you: the line you're going to feed to Siegfried isn't remotely far-fetched. Tell him you're carrying this as a sign: that I'm ready to marry Eorman, and that Eorman should launch those ships he's been building to support me.'

Veron smiles a little. 'I will. But how did you –'

'Letya – my friend – sent it for me.' I touch the brooch gently with my forefinger, hoping she knows that I'm thinking of her, refusing to accept the possibility that she's dead. 'She knew I'd need it, somehow. Perhaps the tide of fortune is finally turning in our favour.'

'Perhaps.' He unties the bundle he's carrying and puts the brooch inside it. 'Will you walk a little further with me? Aron suggested I leave via the lower entrance; Danby and others of his company are guarding it tonight.'

Together, we wind our way down through the caverns and tunnels of the Eyria. Although he asked for my company, Veron doesn't attempt to talk. He stares straight ahead, frowning, absorbed by whatever's going on inside his head. In the silence, my mind wanders. I'm thinking about Damarin, worrying over whether she's persuaded her mother to aid us, when I find we've reached the lower entrance.

Danby and another guard are standing by the doors, ready to slide back the bolts and lower the drawbridge. We're down in the foothills of the mountains now, and the river that travels through the gorge past the upper entrance has widened here into a natural barrier, flowing deep and fast just the other side of the lower gate.

I'm about to wish Veron luck when he says, 'May I ask something of you?'

'You may *ask* . . .'

'Will you keep an eye on Valentin, when I'm gone? We seem

to have done nothing but argue since we escaped Celonia. But everything I've done – everything I've said – I thought it was for the best. I only ever wanted to protect him. Once I've delivered Siegfried to you, please, send him away. Send him to the safety of our base on Thesalis. And make sure . . .' With one finger he traces a vein of copper that runs through the wall next to us. 'Make sure he remembers that I care for him.'

Something in Veron's voice makes me shiver. 'You can remind him yourself, when you're back with us.'

He smiles a little and shakes his head. 'I don't know. I feel as if I won't be here again. I read today's verse from the Litanies and . . .'

'And what?'

'It doesn't matter.' He straightens up and hangs the pouch around his neck. 'I expect I mistranslated it. I don't read your language as well as I speak it.'

I suppose my doubt and confusion show on my face. He takes my hand, kisses it and smiles again – but a proper smile this time, the smile that first forced me to like him: wide and dimpled and full of life. 'Whatever happens, I swear that you can trust me with this mission.'

The oiled bolts are drawn back. The doors open and the cold night air flows inside, carrying the sound of the river and the scent of some sweet night-blooming herb. Veron hands his robe to Danby, flexes his shoulder muscles and steps onto the drawbridge.

I've not often stood and observed someone transform at night. Perhaps that's why the beauty of it still entrances me. The soft glow that envelops the skin. The liquid flow from one shape to the other. The way the arms unfurl suddenly into feathers. I watch Veron change from a man into a handsome silver-and-fawn gyrfalcon.

He twists his head back to look at me, briefly, before spreading his wings and taking off into the darkness.

I bid Danby goodnight and trudge back to my room. There's a piece of paper tucked into my palm; at least that's what it feels like. It was put there by Veron when he kissed my hand. I wait until I'm alone, behind a closed door, before I examine it.

A handwritten message. Copied from the Litanies, judging by the stanza and verse reference at the beginning of the line. I read it. Take off my outer garments, get into bed and read it again.

The spring returns, but the swallow does not. He has been taken by winter, and his journey ends in cold starlight.

Does Veron truly fear that he won't be able to return? Or does he mean not to? I feed the paper into the flame of my lamp, and watch his words burn.

The date of my supposed wedding to Eorman is five days away. Enough of a gap for Veron to reach the Citadel and spin his tale to Siegfried and Tallis, but not long enough for them to send anyone to Frianland to confirm his story. Still, it seems too much time to kill. Too much time to worry about being killed, certainly. Now Veron's left, I decide to take more people into our confidence. The surviving Protectors and members of the royal council approve the plan, with one exception: they want me to stay safe at the Eyria while others risk their lives. I can tell Aron would prefer that too. But I refuse. I'm certain that

Siegfried, if he comes, will be searching for me. My presence may be the only thing that convinces him it is not a trap. I point out that we have only one chance at this. Remind them of what it says in the Decrees: the monarch must be first in flight, and last in retreat. Ask them what kind of queen I would be if I refused to risk my life for my kingdom.

What I don't tell them is how much I want to be the one to strike Siegfried down. I doubt his death will bring me peace. But peace is no longer what I'm hoping for.

My advisers give in, and my plan is approved without alteration.

From that point, I leave most of the details to Aron. The fact that he can't be present at the ambush infuriates him. He channels his irritation into preparation, making sure everyone is drilled in the details, trying to ensure we are all ready – as far as we can be – for whatever Siegfried and Tallis might throw at us.

I spend hours practising my sword fighting, honing my technique while imagining various ways I might kill Siegfried. But otherwise, my role does not require much planning.

I am to be the bait. I just have to stay alive.

I've not forgotten Veron's request. The day after he leaves, when I have a moment to myself, I go to find Valentin. He's not in the tiny room he was sharing with his brother. I wander around the various caverns, watching for a glimpse of silver-gold hair, until I run across him in one of the caves used for storage, down near the lower gate. He's standing at the far end of the cave with his back to me. There's a lantern on the floor next to him, and he seems to be touching the wall of the cave, but at the sound of my approach he turns. There's a knife in his hand.

'Your Majesty –' He lowers the blade and straightens up. 'You startled me.'

'I'm sorry.' I smile. 'I've been looking for you. I promised your brother I would keep an eye on you. And Aron is so busy at the moment. I thought you might be lonely.'

He clears his throat, and even in the lamplight I can see that he's blushing. 'I've spoken to Aron – I mean, His Majesty – already, but want to say this to you also: if it would make you feel safer, for me to be in custody . . .' He shrugs. 'I would understand it. In Celonia – Celonia as it was – both Veron and I would probably have been executed by now.'

'I don't want to lock you up, Valentin. You've done nothing wrong. Just being related to Veron isn't a crime.' He's looking at me as if he's not sure whether to believe me, so I change the topic. 'What are you doing?'

'I was wondering what is behind this wall.'

'Isn't it just the end of the cave?'

'No. Look here.' He lifts the lantern.

If I peer closely, I can just about make out what look like shallow cracks running across the rock face. Then I realise I'm looking not at cracks, but at joins – as if pieces of rock have been fitted together with some sort of cement between them. A built wall, not a natural one. I run my fingertips over the surface, feeling the slight difference in textures between rock and mortar. 'How strange. I wonder why someone would block this off.'

'Perhaps for safety. Maybe the floor beyond has fallen away. Although there's a definite draught. Here – feel.' He guides my hand to a place where the mortar has crumbled – helped, I suspect, by the point of his knife.

'There's a breeze.'

'Yes. I wonder if it's another tunnel. And if so, where it goes. Somewhere under the mountains, I'm guessing, from the direction.'

'Here be serpents,' I murmur.

'What?'

'It's the type of thing they used to write on old maps – a way of labelling the unknown. I used to spend a lot of time studying maps, before I left Merl.'

He glances at me out of the corner of his eye. 'Do you think there's something down there?'

The trace of anxiety in his voice makes me laugh. 'No. The monsters are all out in the open, and they look like us.' I flatten my hand against the mysterious wall. 'Let's get it taken down. I'll ask for some volunteers to help you. It'll be good for people to have something to distract them while we wait.'

I don't bother to specify what we're waiting for. There are only two paths before us now: death or victory. Cooped up in the shadowy confines of the Eyria, I'm beginning to think the end can't come quickly enough, whichever of the two it happens to be.

Claustrophobia, uncertainty and fear are a potent mix. Over the next few days arguments and fights begin to break out, among the nobles and the flightless. Most people in the Eyria don't know what Aron and I have been planning. But somehow, everyone seems to sense that some crisis is approaching. I spend much of my time walking through the caverns talking to people, trying to give them the reassurance I'm far from feeling myself.

We summon the council and order those in authority to make sure that everyone has some task they can apply themselves to, some distraction from the limited rations and lack of daylight and space. It helps, a little. Still, I find myself standing outside the gate on the afternoon of the day appointed for the ambush with a sense of relief – to be getting away from the simmering cauldron of the Eyria, to finally be doing something, even if I'm risking my life in the process.

There are thirty of us waiting to transform. A small group, easily hidden in the location we've chosen, but enough – we hope – to deal with our opponents. Aron selected those most skilled with a sword, young nobles on the whole, men and women of a similar age to ourselves. Blackbill is there, seeking revenge for Odette's death. Some of the others lost parents in the attack on the Citadel and have just inherited their estates. I wonder if I might be looking at the seeds of a new court: a group of nobles loyal to me, and to Aron, not given power by Aron's father. But you have to be a queen to have a court. At the moment the likelihood of Aron and me sitting once more on the throne of Solanum is too remote to be worth thinking about.

Aron himself is standing next to me, issuing last-minute instructions.

'. . . so just stay with Lord Corvax's sons, and if it looks as if it's going badly, then you have to promise me that you'll –'

'– transform and get away and leave everyone else to it.' I take his hand. 'Yes, yes. I know.'

He gazes down at me, faint amusement in his green eyes. 'No heroics, Aderyn. Please?'

276

'I'll try to be good. If you promise the same.'

The amusement fades. 'I've no opportunity to be heroic. Stuck here as I am . . .'

'Afterwards, I mean. If I'm captured . . .' I squeeze his hand tighter. 'Don't take any risks. And whatever they threaten to do to me, don't give in. Keep fighting as long as you can.'

'I will.'

I'm about to say goodbye, to tell him I'll see him again in a few hours. But instead, I do something I've never yet done. I step forward and slip my arms around him, hugging him, closing my eyes and resting my head against his chest. His body stiffens in surprise. Then his arm goes around me, and I feel the brief pressure of his lips on the top of my head.

'You're the only family I have left, Aron. Stay safe.' I loosen my hold and look up at him. 'I'll be back. I promise.'

'I'll be waiting.' He glances up at the sky; the sun is beginning to sink towards the mountains. 'It's time.'

I take off my robe and hand it to Aron; a bundle containing another robe is already hanging from my neck. Around me, the others are disrobing too, taking positions in or next to the river. The water foams cold around my legs as I wade out, testing the soles of my feet against the stony riverbed.

Deep enough. I spread my arms, lift my head and close my eyes –

Wind-borne, almost weightless, I circle once around the Eyria. Aron is standing with his arm raised in farewell. I swoop low above him in a final silent leave-taking, then journey out towards the plains of Dacia.

Fifteen

The flight seems to take less time than when we tested the route two nights ago. The sun is still visible, bleeding into the horizon, as we arrive at the small wooded valley Aron and I chose as the place for my fictitious rendezvous with Eorman. It's west and a little south of the Eyria, where the Silver Mountains have shrunk into rounded hills. I land on a small, weed-choked pond, shift my shape and step out. Aside from a tunic and another robe, my bundle contains an ancient, rather dented, but very ornate crown; Aron found it among the other bits of detritus with which the Eyria was stuffed, and had it polished. Its purpose is to make me obvious. To draw the eyes of our attackers towards me, to make them think that they see what we want them to see. For the same reason, Lord Shrike, who is the closest in build and colouring to Eorman, has placed a polished-up silver circlet on his dark hair, and Lady Finch has a fat book – an abandoned and worm-eaten collection of verse that is posing this evening as a Book of Rites.

It must look as if I am in the process of being married.

Our weapons are already here, transported last night, hidden in the undergrowth. I can't risk a sword belt – it will be unpleasant enough ripping through the loosely sewn seams of my tunic if I have to transform in a hurry – so I drive my blade into the ground in front of me and draw my robe around it.

Bran Shadowshaft, the eldest of Lord Corvax's sons, approaches me.

'Are you ready, Your Majesty?'

'I think so.' I scrunch my toes through the cool grass. This low valley is sheltered; we're surrounded by the ripe buds of starflowers swaying on green tendrils, early signs of summer that are still absent from the higher ground. 'I hope they're on time.'

He smiles. 'When they arrive, we'll be waiting for them. My brothers are all nearby.'

'Thank you.'

As Shadowshaft conceals himself among the trees, Lord Shrike takes up position opposite me, and Lady Finch comes to stand between us. Four other nobles hover just behind us, acting the part of witnesses and guards. We all try not to scan the sky, try not to look as if we are expecting an attack.

Lord Shrike scowls at the overhanging branches. 'We'd get more warning in a clearer space.'

I stifle an urge to roll my eyes; Aron and I have already had this discussion with Shrike more than once. 'But we want to force them to transform, my lord. To fall upon them as soon as they've shifted their shape.' I hold out my hand. He takes it, and Lady Finch opens the book as if reading from it.

Not long now.

What will I do if Lucien comes? If I'm forced to watch as one of my people strikes him down? If I have to attack him, to defend myself or another from his blade? I think I'll be able to do it. But it's easier to dwell on Siegfried. To imagine him with my sword at his neck. Or buried in what passes for his heart.

Somewhere in the shadows a true woodpecker begins drilling into a tree trunk, the rapid hammer-beat of its beak a counterpoint to the thud of my pulse. I try to slow my breathing. Relax my muscles. But at the same time I'm straining my ears, listening for the *whoomph* of displaced air that signals the approach of a transformed noble.

It must be nearly time.

I watch the tops of the trees fade into darkness as the daylight drains away.

It must be time.

Unless they're not coming. Unless Veron failed, or betrayed us, or –

Wide wings beat in the air above us, circling, looking for a way to reach us or a place to land. We crouch, throw our arms up, act surprised. Keep our swords concealed. The nobles touch down at the outer rim of the valley, where the ground is clear of trees, forming a rough circle around us. They hurry to pull robes and weapons from the bundles they're bearing. Start sprinting towards us.

Not more than twenty of them. I can't see Tallis, but Siegfried is there. Siegfried, and next to him, Veron.

Wait, Aron told me. Wait until you can see the expressions on their faces –

At the last minute I yank my sword out of the soil and bring it round in a wide arc until the blade bites into the shoulder of the man running at me.

He screams, and the valley erupts.

The nobles hidden among the trees charge forward, falling upon our attackers from the rear. They in turn panic, realising they've been caught in a trap, torn between fighting and fleeing. Some immediately attempt to regain the open ground where they can transform. My people let them go – our target is Siegfried.

He must not be allowed to escape.

I watch the battle from a short distance away, protected by Bran and Fane Shadowshaft. My non-participation was agreed – logically, I am too important to risk. Unfortunately, logic doesn't stop me feeling useless. I grip my sword hilt, peering into the gathering dark, trying to work out what is going on. It's hard to tell friend from foe. The screams of those injured or dying sound the same whatever side they're on. I've lost track of Siegfried; I think he must have concealed his blond hair beneath the hood of his robe. But we have them surrounded. And there are too many of us; the invaders from the Citadel cannot fight their way out. One by one, they either fall beneath our swords or turn and run.

The other two Shadowshaft brothers are in the midst of the skirmish. I can feel the tension rolling off my companions like steam from a cauldron. They're leaning forward, intent on what is happening ahead of us.

Siegfried springs from the shadow of the trees beside us and drives his sword into Fane's side.

281

Fane cries out and stumbles. Still, he brings his sword up in time to block Siegfried's next blow. I raise my own blade and run forward but Bran gets in front of me, pushes me out of the way and charges at Siegfried. He doesn't reach him: Siegfried drags Fane up and throws him into his brother's path, forcing Bran to drop his weapon to catch him. Without pausing, Siegfried stabs Bran in the leg, snatches up his sword and hurls it away.

Then he stalks towards me, sword raised. Smiles. The same way he smiled at me when he stepped out of the darkness in the Citadel, when he locked Letya and me into the tower on the lake, when he told me how Lucien was going to die. The smile of a predator, assuming in his arrogance that he always has the upper hand.

I swallow and shift my feet, bracing myself to meet his attack. Bran is struggling to get to his feet, shouting at me to run. I ignore him. Siegfried has cost me too much. And now he's going to pay.

Siegfried lunges. A flicker of surprise crosses his face – that I've resisted his opening move, that he wasn't able to disarm me instantly? We trade a flurry of blows. He begins to frown.

I remember that he has never seen me fight, and I break into a grin.

'I told you I was going to kill you, Siegfried.'

'I think not. You . . .' he grunts as my blade splits the skin of his upper arm, 'you need to learn your place.'

'My place –' I nick him again, and he clutches his free hand to his side – 'is standing over your dead body, you bastard.'

Siegfried is stronger and heavier, but I'm quicker. Better.

And I've been waiting for this moment for months. Lord Pianet and the others notice what is happening and run towards us, shouting, and Siegfried's sword strokes become wilder and more desperate. He's moving position too, edging around so as to be nearer to the open ground at the edge of the valley.

But I'm not about to let him escape.

I fight faster, forcing him to give ground, to concentrate entirely on defending himself. He falls back again and again until I twist my blade and wrench his sword from his hand.

He drops to his knees and I think he's about to surrender, to beg for mercy.

But it's a feint. As I approach him, he dives beneath my blade, slashes his hand across my thigh and rolls back onto his feet. I think he's punched me, or tried to – there's no pain. Until I realise my robe has been torn, and I see the narrow blade of a dagger, its hilt concealed in Siegfried's hand. Feel the trickle of warm blood across my skin. Shock slows me down. Before I can react, Siegfried's foot connects with my chest and I fly backwards, losing my grip on my own sword as I hit the ground.

I scramble onto my hands and knees, and start searching the undergrowth, feeling for my blade. But Siegfried already has his sword in his hand and is turning back to me when Bran limps forward and swipes at Siegfried's legs.

Not close enough. Siegfried doesn't fall. He starts attacking Bran, raining down blow after blow, and I still can't find my sword –

But there's a big stone right in front of me. I pick it up in both hands, straining against the weight, stagger closer to

Siegfried and hurl it against his back. He pitches forward and lands on his sword arm – the crack of bone sets my teeth on edge – and screams.

Bran pins him to the ground and kneels there, gripping his injured leg, gasping for breath.

Another instant and Pianet and the others reach us. Bran stands and limps back towards his brother and Pianet drags my attacker to his feet. Siegfried's right arm is dangling at an odd angle, as if the shoulder is broken or dislocated. He yelps with pain as Pianet tears a strip of fabric from his robe and binds his hands behind his back.

'Don't worry, Your Grace,' Pianet murmurs, 'we'll put an end to your agony soon enough.'

I hurry to where Bran is now tending to his brother.

'How bad is it?'

'I'm not sure yet . . .'

Fane is conscious, but he's clutching his side and taking tight, shallow breaths as if trying to avoid expanding his chest.

Bran rips Fane's robe in half and begins fashioning a makeshift bandage.

'Your Majesty.' It's Lord Shrike, bleeding from a cut to his head but otherwise apparently uninjured. 'Victory is ours. There are none left to fight.'

I drag the back of my hand across my forehead, letting my shoulders relax and my breath slow. 'Thanks be to the Firebird. Take some of our people up, and make sure no one is hovering nearby in an attempt to follow us. But don't go too far. We need to –' I wince as the cut on my thigh begins to sting – 'we need to deal with Siegfried and get out of here.'

284

'You're injured, my lady?'

'Just a scratch.' I hope – I've not yet examined the wound, but it doesn't feel as if it's bleeding any more.

Shrike bows. As he goes to transform, I take a moment to look around the battlefield. Here and there, members of our company are putting an end to those of the enemy too badly injured to survive; a mercy, really. We cannot carry them, and I will not leave them here to die slowly. The last agonised voice falls silent. A sort of peace returns to the valley. I make my way back to where Siegfried is being guarded. It's unlikely he would be able to fly with his shoulder as it is, but Pianet is taking no chances; there are four blades levelled at Siegfried's neck, poised to strike should he try to transform.

'Report?'

'Eight dead among our enemies, plus the poor wretches who have just been dispatched. We're making a pyre of the bodies and all the weapons.' He points back towards the top end of the valley where the bedrock is exposed; I can just make out a couple of robed figures piling up branches over a large heap. 'No deaths among our people. Some injuries. Lord Fane Shadowshaft needs medical attention quickly.'

'Can he fly?'

Pianet nods. 'His brothers think so, with their help.'

I scan those gathered around me. 'Where is Lord Veron?'

'Missing, my lady. I assume he returned to the Citadel with those who fled.'

Siegfried, bloodied, teeth bared, hisses at me, 'My sister will realise that he has betrayed us. She'll make him suffer for his –' A jab from one of the swords quiets him.

Why would Veron risk going back to the Citadel? I need quiet and safety and space to think about it. But I have a job to do before I can return to the Eyria.

'Veron has chosen his own path. And we've no time to lose. I won't have any more lives sacrificed to this . . . creature.' There's a fallen tree trunk nearby. 'Bring him.'

Siegfried struggles, cursing and spitting as he's dragged to the tree trunk and forced onto his knees.

Everyone knows what's coming. Aron and I discussed it in advance with all the members of the Skein at the Eyria. We all agreed upon it.

Still, my mouth is dry. I run my tongue over my lips. Clear my throat, and summon the correct form of words to my mind.

'Siegfried Redwing, of the House of Cygnus Olorys, sometime Protector of Olorys, you have been found guilty of treason against the kingdom and the crown by a court of your peers. The crest of your house will be struck out. The name of your house will be dishonoured. And you yourself,' I take a deep breath, determined not to allow my voice to falter. 'And you yourself will be executed immediately, in accordance with the Decrees. The Elders have spoken.'

Voices around me echo my last words.

Siegfried laughs and twists his head to stare up at me. 'Do what you will, Aderyn. You think you've won, but you haven't. Death is coming for you.' He spits at me. 'You'll soon be reunited with your precious Odette. And with Letya, that flightless pet of yours.' He grins at the shock on my face. 'Did you not know that I tortured her to death, after you abandoned her at the Citadel?'

Letya –

I grab his hair, jamming my knee into his damaged shoulder, forcing his head up as he moans in pain, as fury and grief ignite in my core and I feel my features twist into a mask of rage. 'If I had more time, I'd cut out your tongue for daring to speak their names. I'd flay off a wingspan of your skin for every life that you've destroyed. All the tortures of hell that await you will never, *never* be as much as you deserve.' I step back and wipe my hand on my robe. 'Cut off his head.'

Lord Pianet rips away Siegfried's robe. Lady Finch puts one foot on his back and leans there, so his neck is pressed against the tree trunk. Shrike, who has just returned, hands Pianet the axe that was brought here yesterday.

Pianet lifts the axe high above his head. Siegfried rattles out oaths, cursing the kingdom, Aron, me –

A thud. Blood spurts, splashing across everyone who is standing close, tainting the air with a metallic tang. More blood trails as the head rolls across the grass.

My stomach heaves. But it is done. Siegfried has finally been silenced.

I spit on the ground to get the taste of death out of my mouth. 'Bring the head. Aron deserves to see it.'

'Shall we add the body to the pyre?' Pianet asks.

I want to say no. To tell them that Siegfried deserves no such consideration. That it would be more fitting to let the wolves eat him. But, if Tallis comes looking for him – and I'm sure she will – better to leave her in doubt. To have her wonder, even for a short space of time, whether we are holding Siegfried to bargain with. 'Yes. He can be a sacrifice to the shades of those we've lost. Let him burn.'

Shrike and another man take the axe and drag the body to the pyre. Pianet wraps the head in a robe. The Shadowshaft brothers check to see that Fane is able to transform, then the pyre is set ablaze. The rest of us shift our shapes and take to the sky.

Below us, the flames catch, and the dead begin to turn to ash.

Our return is slow: Lord Fane is struggling, and even those who aren't hurt are exhausted. The knowledge of Letya's murder is like a dense mist waiting to swallow me; if I allow myself to think about it, I'll be utterly lost. Instead, I shut my grief away and cling, while I can, to the revenge I extracted in return. At least there's no sign of anyone trying to follow us. As we get further from the valley I start to relax, despite the irritation from my injury. Still, in my mind I can hear everyone's murmurs of relief as the gates of the Eyria come into sight.

They are watching for us. Even before we've landed, the gates open and other nobles run out with torches and robes and pitchers of water. I spot two Venerable Sisters waiting to assist the injured; they take Lord Fane straight into their care.

I land on the river and shift back to my human form.

'Here.' It's Aron, standing on the riverbank, holding out a robe. I wrap myself in it. Then he's hugging me – no awkwardness now – and telling me how relieved he is that I've returned. Someone passes me a cup of water; I drain it, and lean against Aron as we walk into the Eyria.

'Everyone's gathered in the main cavern,' he says, 'but before we get there, tell me: are you injured? Did we lose anyone? And did Siegfried and Tallis –'

I laugh. Despite the confirmation of Letya's death, despite our failure to capture Tallis, the realisation of our victory against her half-brother sweeps through my veins in a flood of fierce delight.

'Questions later. I have something to show you first.' The crowd parts, waiting, as we walk through the cavern. 'Help me onto the table.'

Aron, catching my mood and grinning, swings himself up onto the stone table and pulls me up after him.

Pain flares through my injured leg and makes me stumble a little.

Aron steadies me. 'You're injured?'

'A scratch, that's all.'

Pianet passes me the bundle he's been carrying.

'People of Solanum.' The hum of voices quiets as I begin to speak. 'This night, we struck our first blow in the battle to regain our kingdom. Those who volunteered to defend you fought bravely, and none have been lost.' A cheer goes up. 'Our enemies were defeated. Many have been consigned to the flames. And the one who led them –' I reach into the bundle, stifling my disgust, grasping Siegfried's head by his hair and raising my voice – 'is dead.' As I lift the severed head high in the air, the cavern erupts into roars of approval from nobles and flightless alike.

'Wine,' Aron orders. 'Wine for everyone. Tonight, we celebrate!'

I wrap Siegfried's head back in the robe and return it to Pianet.

289

'What shall I do with it, Majesties?' He has to shout over the noise of people cheering and congratulating each other.

I glance at Aron, my eyebrows raised.

He hesitates for a moment, then says, 'Let everyone see it who wishes to – many others here have lost friends and family to Siegfried's cruelty. Then drop it from somewhere high and rocky. The birds may peck him clean at last.'

'As you wish, my liege.' Pianet bows and moves away.

Aron grips my shoulder, leaning close so I can hear him over the singing that has broken out. 'I can't believe you did it.'

'All those hours of fencing lessons finally proved useful.' My grin fades. 'But I have to tell you about . . . about Letya –' I press my fingers to my forehead as another wave of pain makes me dizzy.

Aron puts his arm around me. 'Aderyn?'

'It's nothing – Siegfried slashed my leg, but –' Another agonising surge, bad enough to make me gasp and clutch my injured thigh, but this time the pain doesn't ebb. And Aron is struggling to support me. I hear him shouting for assistance as I slip from his grasp and fall –

I wake up in my room to the muted sounds of ongoing celebration. A chair's been placed in the corner. Aron is sitting in it, reading. He closes his book as I sigh and turn onto my side to look at him.

'Do you feel better?'

'I think so.' My leg is bandaged, but it still aches. 'What happened?'

290

'Blood loss and exhaustion, the healers say. You've been asleep for most of the day, but they've promised me there's nothing to worry about.'

'Good.' I sit up, pulling the blankets around my shoulders.

'Lord Bran described to me what happened. He claims he was yelling at you to transform and escape, but apparently you had a sudden fit of deafness.' He raises his eyebrow, though there's still a smile playing on his lips. 'I'm so glad I made a point of asking you not to engage in any heroics.'

'I didn't plan to fight Siegfried, Aron. But I had to. I've never wanted to hurt anyone so much in my life. And after what he said about Letya . . .'

'Pianet told me. I'm sorry.'

I sniff and wipe away a tear. 'I can't believe she's gone. We've barely spent a day apart since I was twelve –' For a moment I hold my breath, pulling back from the pit of grief that's yawning in front of me. 'Let's talk about something else. Please.'

'Of course. I was thinking about the dominions. We'll have two to resettle once all this is over. Brithys, as well as Olorys.'

'I'll be glad to be rid of Patrus. Doesn't Lord Corvax have an estate in Brithys? Perhaps we can give that dominion to his family.'

Aron nods. 'They're certainly proving themselves deserving. And Lord Bran is Patrus's superior in every way. Intelligent, brave, handsome . . .' He gives me a rueful smile. 'I'd be tempted to fall in love with him, but I think that between you and Valentin my life is already complicated enough.'

'Does Valentin know that his brother hasn't come back?'

Aron crosses his legs and taps his fingers on the cover of his book. 'I spoke to him briefly. He doesn't know why Veron's gone, or where he is. Though I think we can assume he's returned to the Citadel.' He looks at me. 'Do you trust him?'

I shrug. 'Maybe Tallis has some additional hold over him; I suppose she could have taken some of his people into custody. But he did keep his word. He got Siegfried to the valley.' The last thing Veron asked me to do before he left here was to trust him. Despite his disappearance, part of me still wants to.

Aron stands. 'Do you feel well enough to join the party?'

'Yes. Let me get dressed, and I'll follow you.'

The celebrations run on into the night; everyone needs the release after so many days of uncertainty and anxiety, after so much suffering. I'm asked to retell the story of my fight with Siegfried over and over. But my injury and my grief catch up with me. I leave Aron enjoying an impromptu dance and go to bed.

But not to rest. My dreams are haunted by Siegfried's execution. Or not Siegfried: half the time the head that comes to rest at my feet is dark-haired instead of blond.

I pick it up and Lucien's dead eyes stare back at me.

I'm not surprised that I don't feel particularly refreshed the next morning, but I had expected that my leg would be better. Instead, if anything, it's worse. I send for the doctors again. A different ointment is prescribed, together with an elixir, and the wound is rebandaged.

The new medicine brings some relief. I try to go back to normal. Aron and I and our councillors begin planning for an assault on the Citadel once more strength has been gathered from Lancorphys and Dacia. It seems the obvious next step, though we all shrink at the thought of the amount of blood that will inevitably be spilled. Aron offers Valentin the chance to leave, to join the rest of his compatriots on the island they've taken for their base. I'm not surprised that Valentin declines. He looks at Aron with such warmth in his eyes that Aron glances at me anxiously; wondering, I suppose, whether the obvious affection that has sprung up between them makes me unhappy. He assures me when we're alone that our marriage vows are still sacred, that – since the kiss they exchanged in the lower levels of the Citadel – his relationship with Valentin has gone no further than the bounds of friendship allow. But I tell him that I wouldn't care if it had. I'm happy for them both. Glad that they've found some comfort in these comfortless days.

But my own comfort is short-lived. Four days after my return to the Eyria, four restless nights later, the inflammation has not only returned but has spread further. I can't bend my knee properly. More doctors are called in. They purse their lips and speak cheerfully enough to me.

It's only when I hear Aron questioning them outside my room that I hear the words *poison*.

A poisoned blade.

Now I understand Siegfried's last words to me before we executed him. *You think you've won, but you haven't. Death is coming for you . . .*

I have a few more lucid hours. By that evening, fever takes hold of me. I start to lose track of time, drifting on a sea of potions and bad dreams. Some days I shake with cold, feet frozen and teeth chattering so hard I can't speak. Some days

I burn, running with sweat, lips cracked and dry. They move me to a larger room high up in the Eyria, with a wide window to catch the breeze off the mountains. But I'm never comfortable. Never still. The pain in my leg grows so bad I want to dig my nails into my skin, to gouge away the wound that tortures me, if only I could get at it through the bandages.

There's always someone with me. Some of my visitors are alive. Nyssa, or Cora, or Valentin, or Aron.

Some of them are dead. Odette. Letya. My mother.

Whoever is with me, I ask them to promise that they won't let the doctors cut off my leg – despite the torment. Our monarchy stands or falls on my ability to transform, and I'm frightened that I won't be able to fly with only one leg. Everyone promises. But I'm not sure if I can trust them. I don't know if they're real.

Siegfried comes to gloat, sitting in the corner of the room and grinning at me like a death's head.

My brain unravels as my body fails. I catch snippets of conversation. Occasionally I understand, though I can no longer formulate the words to respond. One day, or night – I don't know which – Aron is sitting with me, holding my hand, when a guard brings him a report: ships, sailing down the Dacris River, approaching the Silver Mountains.

The Shriven. That's what I want to say. *Maybe the Shriven are coming to aid us at last. Send someone to find out.* But my mouth won't shape the words.

Siegfried's poison has taken my tongue. All I can do is moan.

Aron sends the guard away, finds a cool, damp cloth from somewhere and lays it on my forehead.

'My poor Aderyn. The doctors are concocting a new tincture, based on some different herbs, which they hope will provide some relief. Do you understand?' As I gaze up at him, he shakes his head and looks away. 'I wish I knew how to help you.'

The light in the room is fading, and the shadows scare me, but I can't ask Aron to light more candles.

I want my Letya. I want to see her again, just one last time before the darkness takes me. I want to tell her how much I love her.

But I think it's too late for that.

Sixteen

Candlelight. I can sense it through my eyelids. Candlelight, and a cool breeze that caresses my shoulder and makes me shiver just a little. I shift position and become aware of a weight across my body.

Blankets?

Or grave clothes? A winding sheet wrapped around me because they've placed me on a pyre in a funeral boat. Because they think I'm already dead. Perhaps the light I sense is the flame that's been lit to consume my body –

I gasp and push myself up onto my elbow, nausea twisting my guts, too scared to look.

'Aderyn . . .' Someone is with me. I feel a hand gripping my shoulder. 'Aderyn, be easy.'

Perhaps I am dead.

Or hallucinating.

Because it's impossible, but the man who's speaking to me – he sounds almost exactly like . . .

Lucien.

I open my eyes. And Lucien is there in the room, leaning over me. I try to scramble away from him, to yell for help, but I'm too weak – he clamps his hand over my mouth before I can make a sound.

Cora is sleeping in a chair in the corner, but she doesn't even stir as I wrap my hands around his arm and try to prise his fingers away.

For all the good it does, my limbs might as well be stuffed with down.

'Please, Aderyn, I swear I'm not going to hurt you. I promise . . .' His voice is low, pleading.

I stop struggling, too exhausted to resist.

He lifts his hand away from my mouth – slowly, in case I try to scream, watching me the whole time – and slips one arm around my shoulders. Cradles me against him as he places another pillow at my back. The sudden proximity – him holding me again, in gentleness – makes me catch my breath. But still Cora doesn't wake. Having settled me against the pillows, Lucien picks up a cup from the table next to the bed. 'Here. I've brought you an elixir. Drink it, quickly now.' He offers the bitter-scented liquid to my lips.

Does he not know Siegfried's poison has rendered me mute? I shake my head.

Lucien lowers the cup. 'Listen: I've done what I can for the wound to your leg, but you must drink this. It will take away the pain. And I promise, then you'll be able to rest.'

The rest of sleep, or death? Is he here to put me out of my misery? I keep my lips clamped shut.

Lucien sighs. 'You've no reason to trust me – I understand

that. Every reason to hate me, after what happened at Merl, and the Citadel. But I'm trying to save you.' A tiny shake of his head. 'I could tell you the truth, but you wouldn't believe me. And I don't have much time. *You* don't have much time.' He pinches the bridge of his nose and sighs again. 'You feel better, don't you?'

I mentally survey my body, considering. My leg still hurts. A lot. But it's a dull ache compared to the agony I was experiencing before. I'm tired, but I'm aware. I can think. So maybe the fever has gone too? Unless this is all a dream. Some partially lucid prelude to death, in which my brain and my senses conspire to tell me the story I want to hear.

That Lucien didn't betray me. That he still cares about me. That he loves me.

'Come.' Lucien brings the cup closer again, his dark eyes full of pleading. 'If not for your own sake, then for the kingdom. There's still hope.'

If this is a dream, it is preferable to reality. I open my mouth and Lucien – illusion or not – helps me drink from the cup. Drain it. When it's done, when he's given me some water to cleanse my mouth of the taste, he takes away the extra pillow and straightens my covers. Smooths my hair away from my head, smiling at me a little. His fingertips are cool and soft against my skin. I manage to lift my hand towards him. He takes it. Closes his eyes and presses it against the dark stubble of his cheek. Bends over to kiss me on the forehead.

I take a deep breath. He smells just as I remember: of living green things, and wide open spaces, and snow on the mountains.

'Go back to sleep now, my dearest Aderyn.'

I try to raise my hand again, but what little strength I have seems to be waning. All I can do is flex my fingers. A feeble movement. But Lucien – the Lucien of my fevered imagination, for surely this weakness must mean that my life is ebbing away – still understands. He lays my hand upon my belly, but he doesn't release it.

'Don't be afraid. I won't leave you. Not until you're asleep.'

A small mercy, given I am young and not ready to die.

But better than none.

Two things bring me to consciousness: a bright light, and the sound of singing. But this time, I'm not afraid. I open my eyes . . .

I'm still alive. Unless the afterlife is very like the Eyria. Alive, and staring at sunbeams filtering round the edge of the ill-fitting shutters. Cora is here, moving quietly about the room, singing beneath her breath as she dusts. Another sign, I think, that I'm not dreaming: none of the hallucinations so far has involved housework. I wiggle my toes beneath the blankets. Find, with relief, that I still have both my legs. My injured thigh is sore, but all my muscles feel as if they ought to work. In theory, at least. Cora starts strewing the floor with sweet fennel. Its fragrance rises and mingles with those of the lavender and the pale blue river roses that droop in a jug on the table next to me. She turns towards my bed. Gasps and drops the basket she's holding.

'My lady – may the Firebird bless me! I'll fetch His Majesty . . .'

'Wait –' A croak, but still, my own voice. 'Wait, Cora.' I start coughing; my throat is so dry it hurts. 'Water . . .'

Cora blinks, shakes herself and pulls a pair of gloves from her pockets. Once she has them on, she pours me a cup of water. I'm able to push myself up into a sitting position to drink it.

'Thank you. More?' I hold out the cup in shaking hands and she refills it. I quickly drain it again. 'How . . . how long?'

'Well . . .' She looks up at the ceiling and begins counting on her fingers. 'It's the twelfth of Laurus today, and it's been nearly a sennight since the fever broke. And you were ailing a fortnight before that . . .'

Nearly three weeks. I gesture to the shutters. 'Open them, please?'

She bites her bottom lip and stares at the floor.

'Cora?'

'We're not supposed to open the shutters at the moment, my lady. Why don't I fetch you a tisane? Or some soup?'

Something's happened. Though clearly Cora doesn't want to tell me what it is.

I shake my head. Rest for a moment against the pillows. 'Just . . . help me dress.'

It takes me a while. My limbs feel like wisps of feather, and I've no energy; being washed and dressed and having my hair brushed is so exhausting I have to sit down afterwards. Cora chatters away the whole time, telling me how relieved the doctors are, and how I've been muttering in my sleep but never properly woken until today. Eventually I'm ready, and once I've eaten a little, I feel stronger. Cora finds me a walking stick from somewhere and insists on following me as I make my slow progress down to the main cavern.

I hear the voices first: the counterpoint of Lord Corvax's ponderous tones against the background hum. The Skein, or what's left of it, appears to be in session, and most of the rest of the Eyria's inhabitants – noble and flightless – have gathered to watch. As I come down the stairs, peering over the sea of heads, I spot Valentin standing close to the central circle, leaning forward slightly, intent on what's being said. Everyone is so focused that, at first, I have to tap the shoulder of one of the nobles at the edge of the room to get him to move. But the rumour of my sudden arrival runs ahead of me. The crowd shuffles back to give me space. Nobles greet me, flightless call out blessings; if surprise is the most obvious emotion in their voices, I also hear relief.

The circle of the Skein parts, and Aron strides forward. 'Aderyn, you're awake –' He takes my hand and kisses it. 'But why wasn't I summoned?' He frowns over my shoulder at Cora. 'And the doctors, surely –'

'I'm well enough, Aron. I can speak to my doctors later. The Skein is gathered. There are clearly urgent matters to attend to.'

Aron sighs. 'I suppose, since you've already left your room . . .' He takes my hand and leads me forward, and for the first time I see the stranger standing on the far side of the circle. Clad in armour of strange, translucent scales over a leather tunic, trousers and boots, with her copper hair pinned into a bun, she looks just the same as when I first saw her.

'Damarin!' I break into a broad grin. It probably isn't very regal, but Lady Crump is not here to chide me, and I really don't care. 'When did you get here? And how? And why –' I glance at Aron – 'did nobody tell me?'

'You've only just woken up. When exactly was I supposed to tell you?' He's smiling, but there are fresh lines of anxiety on his face. 'I don't suppose there's any point suggesting that you should return to your room, my queen?'

'Absolutely none.' I hold out my hand; Damarin crosses the circle and we grip each other's forearms, the same gesture of greeting she showed me on Galen.

'I have come, Aderyn, as I hoped. And with me I've brought a company of my people, though there may not be enough of us to aid you as things stand.' She gestures over her shoulder. Forty or so men and women, all tall, all dressed as Damarin is, and armed with swords and longbows, stand at the far side of the cavern.

'Welcome, all of you. I'm glad to see you here. Though I regret not being able to welcome you to the Silver Citadel, as I'd wished.'

'We had news of the Citadel's fall from our agents.' Damarin grips my shoulder. 'I'm sorry for your sufferings. Three of those who were with you on Galen were lost, I understand.'

'Murdered.' I shudder, the bodies of Odette, Lien and Pyr appearing in front of my eyes even as I stand in the crowded cavern. My illness has not dimmed the clarity of that memory. 'We took some measure of revenge, at least.'

'And nearly paid for it with your life,' Aron interjects. 'Perhaps we should reconvene the Skein later . . .'

'No. Who knows how much time we have left? The shutters not to be opened, and Damarin talking about not being able to aid us as things stand . . . What's happened, Aron?'

Lord Corvax edges forward. 'If I may, Your Majesties?' Aron

waves his hand and Corvax clears his throat. 'Lady Damarin and her people –' Damarin rolls her eyes at his addition of a title – 'arrived approximately ten days ago, having sailed from northern Fenian, at which point we had within the Eyria one congregation from Fenian, three from Lancorphys and two from Dacia. Then, without wishing to alarm Your Majesty, approximately eight days ago –

'She doesn't need to be mollycoddled, Corvax.' Aron cuts across him. 'We're besieged. Tallis has mercenaries camped outside the lower gate and nobles patrolling above the main gate. That's why we dare not open the shutters. We've no way of bringing in any more soldiers, or any more food. Supplies are running low. Oh, and Arden of Dacia has fled.'

'He's joined Tallis?'

'Not according to the rather badly spelled note he was kind enough to leave. He's withdrawn to Guelph Castle and is recalling the Dacian congregations that are still in the field. Apparently his first consideration has to be the welfare of his own people.'

I sigh. 'He's waiting to see who wins.'

Aron nods. Takes my hand in his. 'There's more.'

'By more, I assume you mean worse?'

'The nobles above the main gates have been dropping . . . missiles.' His mouth twists in disgust. 'Severed heads. Tallis obviously realised we'd put Siegfried to death. She's been executing captives in retaliation.'

I hold Aron's hand tightly, grateful for the support of my walking stick. 'Who?'

'The few we've recovered had been mutilated beyond

303

recognition.' A rumble of displeasure from the onlookers fills the cavern. 'But they had messages in their mouths. Strips of paper.' He frowns and gives a tiny shake of his head, as if trying to dismiss whatever image is haunting him. 'Threatening more executions if you're not handed over.'

Is this how it will end? My life for those of my subjects? I take a deep breath. 'Perhaps –'

'Absolutely not.' Aron's grip strengthens. 'Don't even think about it. You were the one who came up with a plan to catch Siegfried. You'll lead us out of this too.'

Lord Corvax steps forward. 'You have the Skein's full support, Your Majesty.'

I nod, grateful to set that particular choice aside, at least for the time being. 'Then let us continue. What were you discussing?' I take Pianet's chair – my leg is beginning to throb – while another is found for him.

Our hope, Corvax explains, lies in the tunnel Valentin discovered lying concealed beneath the caves of the Eyria. It's now certain that the tunnel continues beneath the mountains towards the Citadel. But two questions remain: where exactly it will end, and whether we can clear it before our supplies run out or Tallis's forces attempt to break the siege. The alternative, a two-pronged attack on those besieging us, would result inevitably in much loss of life.

'And we do not have the numbers to make victory by any means certain,' Pianet adds. 'Even with the help of Damarin's company.'

'Our help is offered, but not yet promised,' Damarin interjects. 'Sufficient recompense has not yet been agreed.

That's what we were about to discuss, Aderyn, when you joined us.'

Lord Corvax almost flinches at Damarin's second use of my given name. 'The lady is correct. We were just about to open negotiations regarding the assistance they are offering, and what might be reasonably expected in return.' He puts an emphasis on the word *reasonably* that seems to chill the cool air of the cavern even further.

I glance at Aron. His jaw is clenched, as if he's anticipating a fight. I settle myself more comfortably in my chair.

'Very well. Then let us begin.'

The Skein debates for two more hours without reaching any agreement, and there's no end in sight. I'm trying to mediate what is turning out to be a particularly acrimonious row between Bran Shadowshaft, Grayling of Fenian and Vergenie of Lancorphys when Aron finally loses his temper, uttering oaths and threatening to invoke ancient powers given to the monarch in the Decrees to pass legislation during a crisis without the consent of Convocation or the Protectors. The three disputants look awkward – Bran especially so, as his father rebukes him – and beg his pardon.

'What shall we do?' Aron asks, dragging his hand through his thick blond hair. 'I can't take much more of this. Shall we reconvene tomorrow?'

I sip the water that's been set at my elbow, glancing around the cavern. It's still full of the Eyria's inhabitants, though they're mostly sitting on the floor now. Without their rich clothes and jewels, it's hard to tell the nobles from the flightless. Not that the two groups are exactly mingling. But everyone, for once, has the same aim: survival, for themselves, and for Solanum. A Solanum that they still recognise, that they can still defend with honour. There might never be a better moment to push for what I really want. I can almost see a different future, hovering tantalisingly just out of my reach, ready to become reality if I can carry enough minds with me. I utter a silent plea to my mother for inspiration, grip my walking stick and push myself to my feet.

'Members of the Skein. Friends. Nobles of Solanum. Look around you. Look at your flightless neighbours, observing our discussions, as concerned with their outcome as you are. And those from Galen, who have come here willingly, offering us their strength. Come from a place we didn't even know existed a few short weeks ago. The world has changed, whether we like it or not, in Solanum not less than Celonia. We cannot go back to how things were. I, for one, do not wish to.' I turn slowly, facing all those watching me, making eye contact with as many as I can. 'I'm willing to risk my life for you and for our kingdom. In return, I call upon the Skein to take a binding oath: that the king and I will be free to negotiate a treaty with Galen as we see fit, that the flightless will be given their own Convocation, with equal representation within the Skein, and that all of the Decrees will be considered for review.' As a riot of voices breaks out around me, I hold up my hand and wait for silence to return. 'Is the kingdom to be like a tree, that grows and lives? Or is it to be like an insect trapped in that tree's resin? Perfectly preserved, unchanging, dead. That is the choice before us. Life, or death.' Valentin nods slightly. My hand finds

Aron's and I lace my fingers between his. 'Celonia chose death. I would not have Solanum make the same mistake. Two days from now we celebrate the Solemnity of the Fledglings. You have until dawn that day to make your choice. Come, husband. Damarin. We will await the Skein's decision.'

As the noise level rises again, Aron and I leave the cavern.

The three of us make our way up to the tower room. Aron seems to have adopted this room as his personal space; there's more comfort here than I remember. Such comfort as is available in the Eyria: three lamps instead of one, herbs strewn on the floor, wine and food laid out on the table and woollen blankets padding the hard chairs. I sink down onto one of these, unable to suppress a groan as I rub the still-healing wound in my leg.

'I've no sympathy for you,' Aron murmurs, even as he pours me a cup of wine. 'You're supposed to be in bed.'

'I'm also supposed to be queen. That's more important right now.'

He rolls his eyes. 'Wine, Damarin?'

'Yes, I thank you.'

Once all three of us are seated, Aron raises his cup. 'A toast: to the stiff-necked nobles of Solanum, who would rather lose their heads than change their minds.'

Damarin smiles grimly. 'I heard what happened in Celonia.'

'You knew before I arrived on Galen, didn't you?' I can tell from her expression that I'm right. 'How? And how did you know to come here? How did you even find us?'

'I told you we have agents on the mainland. A network of

307

families among your flightless population who can be trusted to hold their tongues, who carry our trust from one generation to the next. There are a few among your Dark Guards; they sent word north after the Citadel fell to Tallis.'

I swirl the ruby liquid around the cup. 'Your brother. The one who ran away from home, the one Praeden was visiting . . . He's a Dark Guard, is he not?'

Damarin's face flushes darker. 'How did you find out?'

'A guess, that's all. You're all good fighters. And the guards have a special position at court. More ability to move around the Citadel and the kingdom.'

She raises her cup to me and grins. 'A good guess. But I'm still not going to tell you his name.' And – without checking for the mark they all bear – I won't be able to tell just from looking; Damarin's skin still has a very faint sheen, but nothing like the shimmer I observed on Galen. Nothing I'd notice if I wasn't expecting to see it. Some side effect of her distance from the Pyre Flames, perhaps.

Aron's expression has hardened. 'The Dark Guards' loyalty is divided then; they claim to serve you as well as us?'

Damarin takes a sip of wine before she answers. 'Say, rather, that their love for Solanum encompasses both you and their own kind. They have spoken highly of you as a wise king, and someone who wishes to improve the lot of all Solanum's citizens.' She inclines her head. 'And they like you, Your Majesty.'

Aron raises an eyebrow. 'I'm flattered.'

'You should be,' I add. 'We need them.' I keep massaging my leg as I think back over the arguments during the Skein. 'Damarin, how much do we have to promise for you to agree to help us in battle? Aron and I can grant permission to Galen to trade with the mainland. And we can offer you land for a settlement within either the Crown Estates or Atratys.' Damarin had asked for land within the sparsely occupied area of northern Fenian, which Grayling – the new Protector since the death of his father – flatly refused. 'But we'll need the Skein to agree to anything more than that.'

'Written commitment to land and trade will be enough for now,' Damarin replies. 'But we will hold you to your promises.'

I yawn and slump in the chair as exhaustion weighs down my eyelids. 'We're not aiming to deceive you. It's all theoretical at the moment, in any case.' I don't need to explain further; Aron and Damarin know as well as I do that we can do nothing without defeating Tallis first.

But if we do defeat her, what then? Once peace is restored, and Aron and I are back in the Silver Citadel . . . I study the flickering flame of the lamp on the table nearby. In noble families, especially when there's a large inheritance at stake, it's not uncommon for cousins to marry. So I try to imagine being with Aron as his wife – in truth, not just in name. To imagine taking him to my bed. For the sake of the kingdom, since we need an heir. For my own sake, since I know myself well enough by now to know that I cannot live out my life alone. But even if Aron was willing, I can't hold the image in my mind. My cousin turns into Lucien, however hard I try.

Aron is watching me; a blush rises and spreads its warmth across my neck and cheeks.

'Come.' He puts my cup on the table and holds out his hand. 'You nearly fell asleep.'

'Where's Damarin?'

'Gone to bed. Which is where you should be.'

I allow Aron to pull me up out of the chair, but I shake my head. 'In a moment. I've spent enough time in my room recently.' I look down at Aron's fingers entwined in mine, and make a decision. 'Afterwards – if there is an afterwards – I want you and Valentin to be together. Whether we get to change the Decrees or not.'

Aron drops his gaze. 'But how? Without changing the Decrees, we're married as long as we're both alive. And as long as we *are* married . . .' He shakes his head. 'I won't abandon the vows I took. I won't abandon you. Even if Valentin would consent to be with me on those terms –'

'We promised to love each other. I do love you, Aron. That's why I want you to be happy.'

'But think, Aderyn: you know it would be different for you. It always is for women. Our nobles might be willing to overlook me openly taking Valentin as my lover, even though he is a foreign prince, even though they might resent his influence. But as queen . . .' Aron sighs. 'I don't know. The monarchs of Solanum rule as mated pairs. Even if the Decrees were changed, where would that leave us as rulers? Would you expect me to give up the crown?'

'Of course not.' I raise my free hand and rest it on his cheek. 'We may not survive what's to come, and if we do I'm not sure what our future will look like. But I want you to be happy. I want you to have the man you love *and* the crown. You don't deserve anything less.'

Aron is silent for a time. Then asks me, 'But what about you?'

'I'll be fine.' My claim sounds unconvincing, even in my own ears.

Aron brings his arm around my shoulders, drawing me in so I can rest my head on his chest. I wonder what is happening in the cavern below. 'I hope I said enough to convince them.'

'It was a good speech; Letya would have been proud of you. To refuse your appeal, in front of the flightless and the Shriven . . . they'd have to be mad.'

'I've been wanting to ask you . . .' I pull back so I can look up at his face. 'How am I still alive?'

I know what I want him to say: that it's a mystery. That I was on the brink of death when I suddenly – miraculously – recovered. Because then there's a chance that Lucien really did come to me in the darkness. That he saved me.

'Oh.' Aron's eyebrows lift. 'Well, I sent two of Pianet's agents to the healers in Ryska as soon as the fever overwhelmed you. They returned with herbs and a new treatment regime for our doctors to follow. You improved soon after. I think, if we survive, we should found a medical school. More than one perhaps, a centre in each dominion where . . .'

Aron continues describing his plan, but I'm not paying attention. All I can think of is Lucien, and how he felt so real: the pressure of his lips against my forehead, the weight of his hand on top of mine. But if Aron's telling the truth – and why wouldn't he be? – then Lucien was just another of the dreams that have haunted me over the last few weeks. I can't stop the tears that spill across my cheeks.

'Aderyn, why are you weeping? Are you in pain? Shall I summon the doctors?' Aron is staring at me anxiously.

'No. It's just . . .'

He sighs. 'Is it still Lucien? I was sitting with you, when the fever broke. You were talking to him . . .'

What can I tell him? That it feels as if I've just lost Lucien all over again? I shake my head. 'Please, just hold me.'

As Aron tightens his arm around me again, I bury my face in his tunic and give in to my grief.

I wake the next morning feeling a little refreshed, grateful for the rapid healing our kind enjoys. But my injured leg is still stiff; on the advice of the doctor who attends me, I spend most of the day walking the staircases and caves of the Eyria. There are small knots of people everywhere. Nobles, discussing the demand I've placed before them. Flightless wondering what the Skein will decide. The skin between my shoulder blades prickles from my subjects' stares as I pass them by. The clammy air of the Eyria grows heavier still with the weight of expectation.

When I spot Valentin, in the corner of one of the caverns, I seize the chance for a distraction. He is sitting cross-legged on the floor with his fingers stuffed in his ears – the murmur of conversation echoes around the high stone ceiling – poring over what looks like an old map. When I stop in front of him, he looks up and smiles, a little uncertainly.

'Would you care to walk with me, my lord? I'd like to see how your tunnel is progressing.'

'Of course.' He gathers up the bundle of papers by his feet and we make our way down to the lower levels. Two Dark Guards are playing cards by candlelight; they jump up and salute as we enter the cavern beyond the lower gate. The wall at the end is gone. Instead, there's a black space, and a breeze that makes the guards' lamps flicker, despite the glass protecting the flames. Half of the cavern is filled with mining equipment: pickaxes, wooden props, coils of rope, buckets and more lamps. Valentin lights one of these and leads me forward into the darkness.

The lamplight reveals a wide, level road bored through the rock, winding back from the lower gate and into the mountain. The air is dry and cold and full of dust; its earthiness fills my nostrils and coats my tongue. The depth of the silence makes me shiver. I edge closer to Valentin.

'Is no one working on the tunnel today?' I strain my ears, expecting to catch faint echoes of metal on rock.

'People are working all the time, in shifts, but they're too far off for you to hear them. Five hours' brisk walk away, at least.' He sighs. 'And we've not yet connected this tunnel with any of those that run beneath the Citadel.'

I think about the distance between the Citadel and the Eyria, and the immense weight of the mountains above. 'I can't believe someone was able to construct such a thing.'

Valentin presses his palm against the smooth rock wall; there's something almost reverential in the gesture. 'I don't understand it either. No one in Celonia has the skill to make a tunnel like this. Aron tells me the technology doesn't exist in Solanum either. But clearly it did once. And yet, this space isn't on any of the maps I've found. Its construction, its purpose – both were forgotten, many centuries ago.'

'Have you come across anything dangerous?' I peer into

the darkness as a line from the Litanies rises to the surface of my memory. *From wind and water you are formed, and fire is in your blood, but earth has secrets you may not fathom.*

Valentin shakes his head, smiling. 'No one has been eaten. Not yet, at any rate.' Voices behind us draw my attention: a group of men with lanterns and pickaxes walk past, greeting Valentin and bowing to me. 'The next shift,' Valentin comments as they disappear further down the tunnel. 'It's hoped we might clear the current section of fallen roof today. I found a map of the dungeons in your library, before the attack, and Aron says –' He breaks off and drops his gaze.

'I don't mind, you know.'

He looks back up at me, but his expression is sceptical.

'Honestly.' I brush my hand against his arm. 'I know how Aron feels about you. I imagine – I hope – that you return his affection.'

'I do.' He swallows hard. 'But I understand there can be nothing more between us. Aron holds to his marriage vows. He gives me what he can, and I . . . I am content.'

The sorrow and longing in his eyes betray the lie in his words, though I've no doubt he believes he speaks the truth.

'I love Aron, Valentin. I want him to be happy. So please, don't despair. Many things may be about to change.'

'Perhaps.' He smiles slightly. 'And in the meantime, I have my tunnel.' He offers me the bundle of maps he's holding. 'Can you see, on that top sheet? It seems to show a shaft leading down from the dungeons.'

I take the maps and peer at the sheet Valentin indicated. It's much folded, and the lines of ink are little more than

314

shadowy tracings. Too faded for me to be certain what I'm seeing. And yet, my poor Letya had planned to head for the dungeons . . .

But if she reached them, she didn't find a way out. I hand the maps back to Valentin and rub my eyes, trying to dislodge the memory of that night in the tower in the fjord, the smell of Letya's skin burning as Siegfried gripped her neck. 'Thank you. I think I'd like to return to the upper levels now.'

'Of course.' There's concern in Valentin's eyes, but he doesn't question me.

We've only walked a few paces when I hear footsteps behind us.

'The returning shift?' I ask.

'Too soon for that. Perhaps one of the others forgot something.'

The footsteps get louder. Catching us up. Whoever it is, they're running. I look over my shoulder and shiver.

Valentin has raised the lamp higher, frowning.

'Valentin,' I whisper, 'your sword.' With our enemies just beyond the walls of the Eyria, everyone is under orders to carry a weapon at all times. I draw my own blade as Valentin places the maps and the lamp on the floor at the edge of the tunnel, and we conceal ourselves within the shadows.

The glow of another lamp illuminates a bend of the tunnel a little way back. The glow becomes a point of light as whoever is holding the lamp turns the corner. There are two figures, I think. Though it's hard to be sure who might be following them through the darkness.

I grip the hilt of my sword tighter as the footsteps slow down.

'Look,' one of the figures says, and I have to bite my lip to stop from gasping. 'Someone's been here . . .'

A woman's voice. One I know almost as well as my own.

But it's impossible. I must be hallucinating. Perhaps the whole of the last two days have been no more than the fever-induced delirium of a disordered mind –

The woman comes closer. Steps into the circle of light cast by Valentin's lamp, as she stoops to examine the bundle of maps.

If shock hadn't taken my voice, I'd scream out her name.

Letya.

Seventeen

I can't speak. But I can move: I step out of the shadows, and Letya sees me –

'Aderyn . . .' She presses her hands to her mouth as her eyes fill with tears. 'Is that really you? We'd heard a rumour that Siegfried had killed you . . .'

'I thought you were missing. And then Siegfried told me –' my breath shudders in my chest – 'he told me he'd tortured you to death. In the Creator's name, tell me you're not a ghost . . .'

'She's no ghost, Majesty.' The second figure lowers his lamp so I can see him clearly: Hemeth, Aron's friend and favourite guard captain. He puts an arm around Letya's shoulder. 'She's flesh and blood.'

'Oh, my dear sister –'

I drop my sword as Letya and I run towards each other. Grip each other's shoulders for the briefest of moments, laughing and crying at the same time. Valentin and Hemeth are both grinning at our delight.

'How did this happen?' I ask through my tears.

'We'll explain everything,' Letya replies. 'But I'm so hungry, Aderyn. We've been walking for hours – days – and we've been on short rations since the Citadel was taken.'

That explains her hollow cheeks, and why her dress is hanging on her so loosely. I glance at Hemeth. He's grown thinner too. But what really strikes me, for the first time, is the bright copper of his hair, and the colour of his eyes, and the very faint sheen that the lamplight brings out in his skin.

'Of course – we'll go upstairs and you'll have food and everything you need, and then you can answer all the questions Lord Valentin must have. But first . . . Hemeth, I would like to shake your hand, if I may. Please, will you take off your gauntlet?'

Hemeth's hazel eyes widen, but he does as I ask, removes the gauntlet and holds out his hand.

I place my hand in his, and he closes his fingers around it.

Nothing happens. No burning, no screaming. As I'd guessed, he is one of the Shriven.

'Did my sister give me away?' Hemeth asks.

'No. But I realised just now how like her you are.'

Letya's mouth has fallen open as she stares at our hands. 'But – but –'

'Come.' I smile at her. 'We have lots to talk about.' I lead the way out of the tunnel. Silent. My Letya has returned from death to life, and my joy is so deep that if I speak, I think it might drown me.

There are six of us in the tower room; enough that it feels a little crowded. Letya and Hemeth are still picking at the dishes – as much variety as the Eryia's storerooms can offer – that have been crammed onto the long table. Damarin sits on the arm of her brother's chair, one hand resting on his shoulder. Letya is next to me. Every so often we look at each other and laugh and I know she's feeling the same excess of happiness as I am. Aron and Valentin, having questioned Hemeth about his sudden appearance, are studying their maps again.

Valentin was right. The dungeon I walked through last year, the dungeon where Lucien was confined, forms part of a much older structure. But only a part. Hemeth has assured us that *that* dungeon, as large as I thought it was, is nothing in comparison to the area below, long concealed from the nobles in the upper levels of the Citadel. It seems that the Dark Guards, at least since news broke of the rebellion in Celonia, have been preparing this lower level as a refuge. Aron did not take this revelation well, until Hemeth pointed out that the guards had also reminded Aron of the existence of the Eyria. When Patrus of Brithys opened the Citadel's doors to Tallis's mercenaries, it was to this lower level that the Dark Guards tried to guide the Citadel's flightless servants, saving as many as they could. When it became clear that there could be no immediate attempt to drive Tallis out, they began looking for an alternative exit, and found the top end of the tunnel, the other end of which had been discovered by Valentin.

'So –' Aron taps his finger on the map – 'is this entire top section now clear?'

'Unfortunately not,' Hemeth replies. 'There's been much damage to the roof of the tunnel. But we've opened up a narrow passage, just wide enough for a person to crawl through. From that point we walked for the best part of a day before we found your miners – yesterday, it would have been. It seemed more sensible for them to go on working and for me to bring the news to you.' He gives Letya a warm smile. 'And Letya was desperate to find the queen.'

'Brother,' Damarin asks, 'how many are gathered in this refuge of yours?'

'About two hundred all together. Maybe more. But of those, most are servants, untrained in the use of weapons. There are twelve of our people, and another sixty-seven guards.' He glances at Aron. 'We've suffered heavy losses, Majesty.'

'I'm sorry, my friend. But now, with the element of surprise, and the addition of the guards and nobles we have here, and Damarin's people –' Aron breaks off. 'Your people, I suppose.' He sits back in his chair and leans his chin on his hand. 'I still wish you'd trusted me enough to tell me the truth.'

'But what could I have said, my lord?' Hemeth replies. 'Anything I told you would have betrayed the existence not only of Galen, but of others like me living in Solanum. I trust you, but I did not trust your father. If you'd accidently let something slip . . .'

'Understandable. My father did not die a good man, whatever he may have been earlier in his reign.' Aron pulls at a loose thread on his tunic. 'Valentin told me the royal guards in Celonia started the revolution there. I know there were at least the beginnings of a plot here, involving nobles and flightless, and perhaps some guards too.' He glances at me, and I remember Lucien, and the letters he'd written, the letters that led to his banishment. 'Were we ever in any real danger?'

'I can only speak based on the information I received, my lord.' Hemeth blushes slightly and purses his lips, as if considering what – how much, perhaps – to reveal. 'Many guards were unhappy with the treatment of the flightless during your father's reign. Including me. But when you and Lady Aderyn claimed the throne . . .' He shrugs. 'You know the guards respect you, and many hold you in affection. Besides, two of my countrymen were at the Celonian court. What they told me of the bloodshed there made me determined to prevent such violence erupting here, if I could.'

Valentin stiffens. 'Your friends helped the rebels in Celonia?'

'They didn't try to stop them, my lord.' Hemeth's eyes narrow. 'But why would they? What they saw there – the way the flightless were treated . . . the jousting horses kept in the stables at the Citadel are better used.' His face softens. 'We are on the same side, fighting a common enemy. And thanks to Their Majesties, Solanum at least has a chance of avoiding Celonia's fate.'

'Come –' Aron stands – 'I love you both, and want you to be friends.' As Valentin and Hemeth clasp hands he adds, 'Between the special gifts of the people of Galen and Valentin's talent for engineering, I hope we will overcome Tallis and build a new Solanum together. May the Firebird grant us luck, and a little time.'

'We add our prayers to yours,' Damarin says. 'May I steal my brother away? He's not yet greeted his comrades from Galen.'

'Of course.' Aron claps Hemeth on the shoulder. 'I'm glad

to have you at my side again, Hemeth.' He grins. 'And glad I no longer have to worry about hurting you.'

As Hemeth and Damarin leave, Letya yawns widely.

'You must be exhausted.' There's a blanket across the back of the chair; I tug it forward, around her shoulders. 'Do you want to go to bed?'

'In a moment, maybe.' She yawns again. 'But there was something else I wanted to tell you. And Lord Valentin . . .'

I turn in my chair to face my friend, tucking my legs beneath me. 'What is it, Letya?'

'Some of the guards have been sneaking out at night to gather news. Tallis is going to be crowned in the Sanctuary, at the next new moon.'

'And?'

'Well . . .' Letya has a plate on her lap; she picks at the bread, reducing it to crumbs. 'It's the Decrees, Aderyn. She has to be married before she can be queen, just as you and His Majesty had to be married.'

My heart begins to beat harder. I tense; if she tells me Tallis is going to marry Lucien, I cannot allow myself to react.

But Letya's not looking at me. She's turned towards Valentin. 'I'm sorry, my lord, but she's going to marry your brother.'

The colour fades from Valentin's cheeks. He strides to the shuttered window and stands with his back to us. 'I can't believe it. For my own brother to stoop to such a thing.' He drops his head into his hands. 'I do not know him at all.'

None of us speaks. Watching Valentin struggle raises an echo in my body; the shadow of Lucien's betrayal sweeps across my skin like a flame. And yet, for Veron to risk us finding out, and taking revenge – to play fast and loose with his brother's life . . .

'Perhaps there is more to this than we know. Perhaps some pressure was brought to bear on him. Perhaps he is being compelled.'

Valentin gives a bitter laugh. 'Perhaps. Or he thought I would be gone from here. Maybe he seeks to be a . . . a –' He spits a phrase in Celonian that I don't know. I look to Aron for a translation.

'He means that Veron seeks his own advantage,' Aron explains. He moves to where Valentin is standing and rests his hand on the Celonian's shoulder. 'He helped us, and now he is helping Tallis again, as a way of . . . manipulating the situation. Gaining his own ends. That is the sense, as near as I can render it.'

I think back over everything Veron said to me about his aims, about his duty to the surviving Celonian nobles. And of course, he probably didn't expect us ever to find out about his wedding plans.

Valentin has dropped to one knee in front of Aron. He draws the sword from the scabbard at his side and offers it to him. 'My life is forfeit. I will not do either of us the dishonour of pleading for clemency. I merely ask for your forgiveness, and offer you my own in return.'

'Valentin, my love . . .' Aron sighs and pushes the hilt of the sword away. 'Need you be so very dramatic?'

I almost laugh at the mixture of shock and relief on Valentin's face. 'But . . . but you said –'

Aron has walked back to the table and is pouring himself some wine. I'm not sure whether he's hiding his amusement, or whether he is hurt by Valentin's conviction that he would willingly sacrifice him. I beckon the kneeling Celonian.

'Get up, Valentin. No one is about to kill you. Why should you be punished for your brother's crimes? Do you really believe Solanum to be so . . . uncivilised?'

'But, after everything Veron has done . . .' He gets to his feet. 'I do not believe Celonia's last king would have been so understanding. In fact, I know he would not have been.'

'That is one of the many reasons I do not want Solanum to end up like Celonia.' The sky beyond the shutters – what little I can see of it through the cracks – is darkening. 'How long now do you think, Aron?'

'I would say the Skein has another ten hours or so to reach a decision by the deadline you gave them.'

Ten hours to change the course of history.

Letya has fallen asleep. I send for Cora, who takes her to my room, where a second mattress has been wedged into the small space; there aren't enough rooms in the Eyria, but even if there were, I want to spend as much time with her as I can.

Eventually Valentin goes back to the tunnel. Aron and I are left to wait alone.

He drops a kiss on the top of my head. 'What do you want to do? Read? Eat some of Hemeth and Letya's leftovers.' He turns up the flames of the oil lamps. 'Or we could play Battle.'

'We've no set.'

'Wrong, my dear. Lady Finch discovered one in a storage room, stuffed into the bottom of a barrel of rusted mail gauntlets.' He goes to the chest that stands in the corner of the room. 'Here. Shall we play?'

The wooden box he hands me is old – the lid is warped and doesn't fit well – but when I check inside, all the pieces are there, and the incised board is still clear enough. I lift out one of the eagles and smile at him. 'I'm going to win. You know that, right?'

Aron returns my smile. 'Don't be so sure. Valentin has been teaching me some moves. I might surprise you in the end . . .'

The game passes the time pleasantly enough, and if either of us thinks about Tallis or the Skein, neither of us mentions it. At some point we must both fall asleep, wrapped in blankets and curled up uncomfortably on the hard-backed chairs, because I'm dreaming when a servant comes to wake me. Dreaming of Lucien, of his hands caressing my skin, of his lips moving softly against mine. I sit up and push the image away and force myself to remember the reality: Lucien's blade sharp and cold against my neck, as he asks Tallis whether he should kill me.

Lord Pianet is waiting just outside the door.

'Well?'

'The Skein has made a decision, Your Majesty.'

I send a servant to fetch Letya before I wake Aron; after the promises I made her, that I would change things, I want her to witness this moment. Even if my hopes come to nothing. Aron blinks at me, fuddled with sleep, but I make him understand what has happened and we follow Pianet back down to the main cavern. It's still dark outside, but the space is once again packed with people. Letya is there, waiting with Cora just outside the circle of the Skein. Lord Corvax, leaning on one of his sons' arms as well as his staff, steps forward.

'The Skein has debated, Your Majesties. And we have come to the conclusion that you are right: if we do not change, we might lose everything. Therefore, as authorised by yourselves, by the Protectors and by Convocation, we will swear a binding oath to the Firebird in the presence of this assembly that, upon the defeat of Tallis, we will consent to the creation of an assembly of the flightless, of equal standing with Convocation, and that we will review the Decrees and make what changes are necessary to reflect the . . .' He hesitates, just for a moment. 'To reflect this new reality in which we find ourselves.'

Lord Pianet points to a large square of parchment which has been set upon the stone table. Lord Corvax hobbles forward, picks up the quill next to the parchment and signs his name. One by one, all the other members of the Skein do the same, until it is only the Venerable Mother, Aron and I who still have to sign. We add our names – and only our names, since the royal seal is back in the Citadel – and Pianet holds up the paper for everyone to see. Applause breaks out. It's sporadic at first but quickly grows in volume, echoing around the high cave.

I've struck my bargain with the people of Solanum. The future I've hoped for, since I agreed to marry Aron and claim the throne, is within my grasp.

But Tallis still stands.

A storm breaks over the Eyria not long after our meeting has concluded. The thunder echoing through the caverns keeps me awake, but at least it's not likely that Tallis will launch her attack in such weather. Eventually the wind falls and I snatch a few hours' sleep. But our situation is too urgent to allow me to rest for long. Besides, confined by my illness and now by the siege, it's been nearly a month since I've transformed and flown. My power swarms beneath my skin, itching to be used. I'm sure many of the nobles feel the same; as early as I rise, the Eyria is busy with people.

As soon as I've received the reports of the guard captains on the status of the siege, Letya and I make our way down to the lower gate and the tunnel entrance. There are more people gathered here than anywhere else. Whether by breaking up debris, mixing mortar or carrying supplies to the miners, everyone wants to help speed our access to the Citadel. Valentin tells me they have more volunteers than they know what to do with.

He and Aron, together with Hemeth, Damarin, Pianet and Lady Finch, are standing around a makeshift table littered with maps and lists.

'My lady.' Aron kisses my cheek. 'How are you feeling?'

'Well enough. What is our status?'

'To completely clear the tunnel?' Valentin asks. 'Five days. Perhaps six.'

'As long as that? I thought, now a connection with the Citadel has been made . . .'

Valentin spreads his hands wide. 'There is still at least ten wingspans of rock to clear, and –' he leans closer, raising his voice as some men nearby begin pounding rocks into powder – 'the tunnel roof to be made secure. Our people are working as hard as they can.'

'I know. But the people trapped below the Citadel are starving. And then there's Tallis's coronation. I'm sure she'll try to capture the Eyria beforehand.' I glance at Aron. 'Better to start her reign with us dead, if she can.'

'Aderyn . . .' Letya murmurs.

'It's true.' My advisers look away, or fiddle with the papers scattered across the table, but no one contradicts me. 'We need to redouble our vigilance. Can we increase the number of guards? Find some way of strengthening the defences around the lower gate?'

It's agreed that the number of guards on each watch will be increased by the addition of Shriven warriors, and a wall will be constructed from rubble brought out of the tunnel to divide the cavern behind the lower gate and give us an extra line of defence. The lower gate is the weakest point of the Eyria. The gates themselves are ancient and massive, but there are no outlooks above them – no windows anywhere that give a view of the ground directly in front of the gates – and no additional gates behind them.

As Letya reminds me, it is what it is, and there's no evidence of any surge in activity from our besiegers. But I'm still worried. Before I go to bed that night, I whet the blade of my knife, and I sleep with it beneath my pillow.

The noise wakes me: a boom, reverberating through the hollowed-out rocks of the Eyria. I push myself up on my elbow as Letya fumbles with the tinderbox. In the darkness I can hear her rapid, panicked breathing.

The candle flares just as another crash sends a drift of dust down from the ceiling above.

'Thunder?' Letya asks.

I shake my head, drag my night gown off and pull on my tunic and leggings. 'The lower gate. A battering ram or –'

Another barrage of noise, augmented now by faint shouting, screams. Letya clamps her hands over her ears.

A hammering on my door. 'Majesty –' Fane Shadowshaft is in the doorway. 'My father sent me. It's begun.'

The Eyria is in chaos. As Letya and Cora help guide those who can't fight away from the gates, a council of war is gathered around the stone table in the main cavern: most of the nobles, some of the captains of the Dark Guards and Damarin with her company. Hemeth is already at the lower gate, directing the defence.

'Whatever they were throwing at the gates,' Pianet says, 'they seem to have stopped. Could they have given up?'

'Unlikely. What did you see, Lord Shadowshaft?' Aron asks.

Bran, Corvax's eldest son, offered to run the risk of making a flight outside, and was injured in the attempt. He clutches a blood-soaked rag to his side. 'They've built some sort of device on the far side of the river, opposite the lower gates.'

'A catapult?'

'Something like that, but instead of rocks, it's firing large bolts into the doors. Iron, I'd guess. The army of mercenaries beyond stands ready.'

'And the main gate?'

'It looked as if most of the nobles who've been patrolling the area have drawn off to the lower gate.' He frowns. 'I don't know why . . .'

'Thank you, my lord, for risking yourself.' I hold out my

hand to him. 'If we survive, the Dominion of Brithys is yours, Protector.' Bran gasps and drops to one knee as Lord Corvax begins to thank me.

I cut him off. 'If we survive, Lord Corvax. Shadowshaft, can you describe the bolts?'

'They looked like . . . needles.' He sketches a shape with his finger. 'With an eye at one end.'

My stomach turns. 'They're not going to batter the gates down. They're going to attach ropes and wrench them from their hinges. Use them to bridge the river.'

Pianet has turned pale. 'We need a bigger force at the lower gate –' A new sound drowns out his words: the horrible, tortured squeal of wood against metal. I cover my ears with my hands as Pianet raises his voice to make himself heard. 'Your Majesties, you should get to safety while there's still –'

The end of his sentence is lost as the biggest crash yet fills the air with dust. We all draw our weapons and begin to run for the lower gate. Yells, screams, the clang of blades get louder and louder until the passage widens and the cavern is before us.

One gate is already down, bridging the river. Across it pour Tallis's mercenaries, all swaddled in heavy leather armour.

'Damarin!' I have to shout to attract her attention. 'Can your archers help?'

She nods. Shouts a command to her people in their own language. The Shriven spread out, seeking vantage points, pulling themselves up onto natural ledges in the cavern walls, and begin shooting into the ranks of the mercenaries. I wait long enough to see the first arrows find their marks before going in search of Hemeth.

'What's happening? Can we push them back and raise the gate?'

He takes a breath, wiping a trickle of blood from his forehead. 'We can't get outside, Majesty. There are nobles flying low above the gates. The flightless guards aren't heavily clothed enough to resist their power. We can't . . .' He winces. 'We can't get close enough for axes to be any good.'

Now I understand the mercenaries' clothing. It slows them down, but it also protects them from the nobles patrolling the skies above them.

'Arrows? Your people aren't affected by the nobles. Could they provide cover for the guards?'

He shrugs. 'Maybe.' We both survey the mass of bodies in the cave. A mercenary lunges between the nearest guards – I bring my sword up and brace my feet in time for him to run himself onto my blade. 'We need to get to the gate . . .'

Aron is fighting nearby, back-to-back with Valentin. I make a decision. 'If you can get to Aron, tell him I'm going outside.'

Hemeth nods his understanding and throws himself back into the fray. I turn, scanning for any other nobles nearby.

'Blackbill – gather who you can and meet me at the upper gate. We need to go after the nobles . . .'

A few minutes later, ten of us are gathered at the main gates. The noise of battle is muted here to a dull roar. It doesn't take me long to explain what's happening.

'Questions?'

Nyssa raises her hand. 'If the Shriven are shooting at Tallis's supporters, how will they know not to shoot at us?'

'We don't know yet if the arrows will have any effect on a transformed noble – there may be a reason bows are banned by the Decrees, but it may be just another law that serves no real purpose.' I pause, remembering the flightless man I saw burned to death last summer for owning a bow and arrows. 'Just . . . don't get too close. Our aim is to scatter the nobles, to keep them from coordinating attacks on the people below. To drive them back to the Citadel if we can.'

Everyone nods. We pull off our clothes, the guards open the gates a little and we slip outside.

An enormous, one-eyed swan swoops down, almost catching Blackbill with the leading edge of its wing.

Patrus. Even in my human form, I can sense the hatred and fear vying for dominance within him.

We hurry to transform and take to the air.

Go – Blackbill's voice sounds in my head – *I'll take care of him and join you.*

Now in the shape of a huge magpie, Blackbill dives at Patrus, wings spread wide, claws outstretched, screeching his defiance. The rest of us fly towards the lower gate.

The nobles there aren't expecting an attack from above. We fall on them, scattering them, and a ragged cheer goes up from the Dark Guards as they are able, for the first time, to push some of the mercenaries back across the makeshift bridge. But our enemies quickly regroup. I realise we are going to have to fight at close quarters, and a flicker of panic ignites in my belly. I've never done this before, never used my beak and wings and weight as weapons against another noble –

But you have, you know.

The voice doesn't belong to one of my companions. It's my mother's voice, speaking out of my memory, across the years.

332

Think . . .

When we were attacked by the hawks. The hawks that killed her. Even then, I tried to fight back. I can do it again.

A cormorant is pursuing Nyssa. Gaining on her. Blackbill is back with us – I wonder for a moment what happened to Patrus – but he is too far away to help her. I climb, bank, gather speed. Soar back down until I slam my left wing into the cormorant's neck. The impact leaves me stunned for an instant, but I recover in time to see the cormorant tumbling out of control through the sky. To see the Shriven archer below take aim and loose an arrow upwards –

The arrow slows as it approaches the noble. The tip begins to glow red as it punches its way through the power enveloping the noble's transformed body; some sort of friction, I suppose, heating the metal. I hold my breath, waiting, willing the arrow onwards –

The arrowhead pierces the cormorant's wing. He screams in pain, drops from the air and disappears into the battle raging below.

My elation evaporates as the next arrow, aimed at a grey heron, bursts into flame and disintegrates before it reaches its target. But at least now we know: the Shriven can injure and kill transformed nobles. If they can get close enough. And we know why the Elders banned bows in the first place: when they saw what they could do, the fact that they helped the flightless hunt for food would have become utterly irrelevant.

I sense the ripples of disbelief and confusion spreading through our enemies. Forced higher by the archers who are pushing through the broken gate, they're too far off now to prevent the Dark Guards driving a wedge through the mercenaries stumbling in their unwieldy armour. My companions and I harry them across the sky.

The grey heron seems to linger at the edge of our skirmish, flying slowly, avoiding any direct engagement.

I watch more closely. As soon as any of us gets close to the heron, a raven, a dark shadow against the night sky, swoops down to chase the attacker away. I make two feints towards the heron myself, banking and changing course at the last minute. Both times the raven intercepts my path. Forces me back.

He's flying silently, but I get close enough to pick up the shape of his thoughts. The tint of desperation.

It's Lucien. Which means the heron he is protecting must be Tallis.

This is my chance. If I can bring her down, or at least drive her low enough for one of Damarin's archers to put an arrow through her heart –

This could all be over.

I have to try to get to her. And if that means going through Lucien Rookwood, so be it.

I can't risk telling my companions my plan, in case one of our opponents overhears. Instead, I wait. Stay close by until I see Blackbill fly too close to the heron. On cue, Lucien drops from above to attack. I change course, flying below Lucien and climbing rapidly until I catch the underside of his wing with my own. He screeches as he loses control, but I don't wait to see what happens.

I turn and fling myself towards Tallis.

She flees.

I know she's heading for the Citadel, but I can't allow her to reach it. I push myself harder, slicing away the distance between us with each wingbeat, using every breath of wind.

And at first, it works. I gain on her. I begin to sense her rage. Hope flames brighter in my chest.

But I can't close the gap. My illness has weakened me. The ache in my wings becomes a constant burning that I can't ignore. I gasp for breath, struggling to get enough air into my lungs.

And we're almost at the Citadel.

I have to let her go. I begin to slow and turn . . .

The silver gyrfalcon appears from nowhere, swooping across me with talons outstretched, pushing me back towards the Citadel.

Don't fight me, Aderyn, I don't want to hurt you –

Veron.

I try to climb, to dive upon him as I did the cormorant, but I'm too tired to gain any height. I turn and turn again. Now there's a second noble, an owl, supporting him; every time I try to escape, they force me back onto my original course.

My altitude drops further.

Give up, Aderyn. Land in the Citadel, before it's too late –

The dark waters of the fjord are not far now. But if I land there, I know I'll drown. I'm too tired to save myself.

Exhausted, I drop from the sky and plunge towards one of the ornamental lakes in the Citadel's grounds. Hit the water. Slam into the stone edge of the lake. Transform. But I've not enough strength left in my arms to drag myself out. My fingers slip from the wet marble, and the water closes over my head . . .

Eighteen

'Come on – breathe –'

My throat is lined with fire.

'Breathe –'

Someone slaps me between my shoulder blades, once – twice – over and over until I'm coughing, dragging air into my lungs as I vomit water.

I push myself up to sitting. Shiver. Rub the water from my eyes, sweep the wet hair from my face and try to focus, despite the ringing pain in my head.

'Aderyn . . .' Veron is slumped on the ground next to me, breathing heavily. And around us –

Guards, some bearing torches. The ruddy light reveals the insignia of Cygnus Olorys. Their swords are drawn. One of them hands Veron a robe.

'Give her one too.'

'I only brought one, lord.'

'Then give her your cloak.'

The guard hesitates.

'Do it, damn you.'

The man unclasps the cloak from his shoulders and throws it towards me. The fabric is dirty and smells of sweat and woodsmoke. Still, I pull the cloak on, clutching it around my damp skin.

Veron – standing, robed – gestures at me. 'Bring her.' He begins striding towards the Citadel.

The nearest guard levels the tip of his sword at my throat. 'Get up. Hold out your hands.'

Even if I transform, I don't have the energy to escape. I obey, and he secures my wrists with iron manacles.

We start walking.

My captors lead me past the darkened Sanctuary up into the main entrance hall. Candles are burning in the crystal chandeliers, but there are few people around at this hour of the night to witness my degradation. The guards herd me into the throne room. As I walk barefoot across the black-and-white marble floor, I remember the first time I entered this room: the murmurs of the brightly dressed courtiers, the thump of the guest master's staff, Lucien at my shoulder as I made my way towards the dais and the huge swan, depicted in stained glass, in the window above.

But now, many of the windows are broken and boarded up, the room is empty apart from guards, and instead of my uncle, Tallis sits alone on the dark, gilt-burnished throne.

Veron is standing next to her.

My guards stop moving and withdraw a little, leaving me alone in front of my enemy.

'Well done, Lord Veron.' Tallis steps off the dais and strolls towards me. Her hair is tied back and she's changed from a robe into a dress of dark green silk with a plunging neckline. My mother's emerald earrings hang from her earlobes. I bite the inside of my cheek, trying not to show my distress; the delight in Tallis's eyes as she reaches up and touches one of the earrings tells me I've failed. 'Well, Aderyn. It's over. Your friends at the Eyria may survive this night, but they cannot win. And now we have you . . .'

'You have nothing. They won't surrender.'

'Oh, I'm relying on them not surrendering. I have no intention of giving you up. And no intention of letting them live.' She smiles at me. 'A public death, rich in humiliation – wasn't that what I promised you? And you've delivered yourself to me in time for my coronation.' The smile fades, replaced by a sneer. 'I'm going to make you regret what you did to my brother.'

Behind me, footsteps ring out across the marble floor. Three nobles approach the throne. One of them is Lucien. He's clutching his right arm.

Good. I hope I broke it.

'My lady, the attempt to end the siege has failed. The mercenaries have fled or been killed –'

'Enough!' Tallis snaps, glaring at him. She steps back onto the dais and begins to pace back and forth across it. 'You do not perceive who is standing before me, Lord Rookwood. The usurper, and murderer, Aderyn of Atratys. Captured by Lord Veron after you allowed her to evade you.'

'I was injured, my lady,' Lucien murmurs. 'But I sent another after her in pursuit. I thought it better to stay and observe the result of the battle, under the circumstances.'

'Yes, yes. Your excuses are all very reasonable, but they irritate me. It's fortunate for you that your service has so far been –' she shrugs – 'adequate.' Her gaze drifts to me. 'Aren't you going to pay her back?'

'My lady?'

'She hurt you, Rookwood. Shamed you in front of everyone. You must want revenge.'

Lucien turns slowly, looking at me for the first time. His face is etched with pain and exhaustion, but I've no pity to spare for him. I'm trembling, but I try to hide it, lifting my chin and clinging onto the news Lucien let slip: the Eyria did not fall. Aron and the others are safe, for now. Work on the tunnel can continue.

He comes to stand in front of me. Raises his hand and slaps me across the face hard enough to make me stumble. The unbalancing weight of the manacles sends me sprawling to the floor.

Tallis laughs.

My nose is bleeding. Blood splashes onto the white tile beneath me.

'That will do for now,' Tallis says. 'I'm tired. Veron, you may escort me to my apartments. Rookwood, put her in the dungeons.'

The guards encircle me again.

Tallis pauses. 'What happened to Patrus? He was supposed to give us warning if they attempted to leave by the upper gate . . .'

'Dead,' Lucien replies. 'He tried to flee with the rest of us when we realised the night was lost. But I suppose he was already injured. He wasn't fast enough, at any rate. The last I saw, he was being ripped apart by a magpie and a skua . . .' Lord Blackbill and one of Lord Lien's relatives, I guess. I almost smile.

'Pity,' Tallis observes, as she and Veron leave the hall.

Lucien grabs my arm and drags me upright, turning me so I'm facing the main doors. The prick of a blade against my back forces me forward.

Locked into a small, unlit cell, I lose track of time. Every few hours – I think – a guard brings bread and water, and for a few minutes the grate set into the door is opened to allow a little torchlight to fall into my cell. Other than that, the darkness is complete.

But though I'm blind, I can still hear things. Weeping, mostly, from the inhabitants of other cells. Shrieks of pain from those being tortured, loud enough – despite the thick stone walls – to make me retch and cover my ears. Water dripping from the damp ceiling. I know logically that the rats that would normally be here are absent, driven away by my power, but my mind conjures terrors from the darkness. I seem to hear them rustling through the dirty straw that lines the floor of my cell. To feel their teeth nipping at my feet, their tails whipping against my legs.

I huddle in the corner of the room and try to pray, but the words I've known all my life escape me.

At least exhaustion means that I sleep, some of the time. Or I think I do.

I know I must have been asleep when the door opens and someone comes in with a torch and sets it in a bracket on the wall. The light is painfully bright; I shield my eyes and squint, but I still can't see who it is.

'Aderyn . . .'

Veron.

He's crouching down in front of me. I'm chained by the ankle, but my hands are free. I punch him in the face.

He grunts in pain, but doesn't move away or attempt to retaliate.

'Leave me alone.'

'I can't. I'm supposed to cut off your hair.'

My hand goes to my long, tangled locks. 'Why?'

'I don't know. Why does Tallis do anything?'

'You're going to marry her. Surely you should know.'

He falls silent. Sighs. 'Come.' He holds out his hand to me. 'You have to stand up. Please, don't make this more difficult than it has to be, Aderyn.'

I hesitate. Think about fighting him: scratching his eyes out, or seizing the scissors he has in his hand and stabbing them through his heart.

But what good would it do? Even if he lies dead on the floor of the cell, I'll still be locked up in here. I push myself to my feet.

Veron lifts my hair back from my shoulders, takes the first few strands in his fingers and cuts them level with my jaw. As he works, the room is silent apart from the soft snip of the scissors.

It's only hair. But I can't stop the tears that are rolling down my cheeks.

'There . . . You can sit down again.'

341

As I return to my corner, Veron begins gathering the wisps of dark hair into a bag. I suppose he has to give her proof that it's been done. When it's finished, he stares down at me.

'You should have agreed to come with me, Aderyn. I could have protected you. You'd be safely concealed on Thesalis by now. Once I was married, once all this was over, and I had my homeland again, I would have taken you to Celonia and given you a house there. I could have come to visit you . . .' He crouches, tilting his head to look into my face. 'It breaks my heart to see you like this.'

'I understand. You'd come to visit me, and expect me to show you how grateful I am that you saved my life.' I pull my legs closer to my body, hugging them to me. 'You have no heart. You told us we could trust you.'

'You don't understand.' He lowers his voice. 'I did what I could. Concealed what I could. But after you killed Siegfried . . . It was hard, to persuade Tallis that I hadn't betrayed them. I have to protect my people. She has too many of my kinsmen locked up in the towers here. And she's sworn to help me regain Celonia, once we are crowned . . .'

'She's using you, Veron. As soon as she's taken everything she can from you, she'll kill you. And if she helps you reclaim Celonia, it will only be so that she can take that too.' I close my eyes and turn away from him. 'Get out.'

He stands up. 'I'll leave you in a moment. But please, tell me where my brother is. Did you send him to Thesalis after Siegfried's death?'

'First tell me how long I've been here, and how long it is until Tallis's coronation.'

He doesn't answer straight away. I wait.

'Rookwood brought you down here nearly three days ago. My wedding to Tallis will be celebrated at dawn in four days' time. Our coronation will take place straight after.'

Three days. And what did Valentin say? A minimum of five days to clear the tunnel. And then more time to get people in position, ready to attack.

'My brother?' Veron nudges.

'He's at the Eyria, with Aron. Or he was, at least. I saw them both fighting by the lower gate. I don't know if they survived.'

Veron utters something in Celonian – a curse, I guess – and swings away to slam his fist against the cell wall. 'You would not allow him to leave?'

'He refused to leave. He and Aron love each other. Valentin was there when we found out about your planned marriage. He told us that he doesn't know you.'

Veron curses again, spitting his rage at me, raising his fist, and I bring up my arm to ward off the blow –

But it doesn't fall. When I look again, Veron is standing with his head down, one hand covering his face. He sniffs and lets his hand drop.

'I've no choice, Aderyn. I can't change course. Not now.'

'Then we have nothing more to say to each other.'

Veron lingers for a moment, picking at a patch of moss growing on the wall. Seizes the torch and leaves.

Darkness, soft and suffocating as earth, buries me again.

Veron does not visit me again, but Tallis does. She has a maid with her, a flightless girl, who's carrying a large tub full of dried leaves. Agarica; I recognise the scent, and I know exactly what it can do. I watched Siegfried use the leaves' tiny barbs, full of acidic poison, to kill the assassin who murdered my mother. I saw the damage inflicted on Lucien's skin when he was imprisoned down here. I draw back into the corner of my cell.

When the maid has set the tub down and unfastened the shackle around my ankle, Tallis smiles at me. 'Take off that cloak, Aderyn, and lie on the floor here.'

I clutch the cloak tighter around me. 'No.'

She sighs. 'You're so predictable.' Without warning, she twists round and clamps her hands either side of the maid's head. The girl gasps with shock. 'Shall I burn her ears off?'

The smell of singed hair fills the cell. I hurry to obey Tallis's command as the girl begins to shriek. 'Please, let her go!'

Tallis releases the maid, who sinks to the floor, rocking back and forth and weeping quietly. 'Good. Offer me any resistance, Aderyn, and I'll hurt her again.' She pulls on a pair of heavy leather gauntlets, scoops up a handful of the agarica leaves and scatters them across me. My skin begins to itch, then to sting, as the tiny barbs of agarica release their acid. 'Now, tell me exactly what you did to my brother.'

I grit my teeth. 'We cut his head off.'

'No, no. Start earlier.' She adds more leaves to the drift across my torso. 'Start with when he landed.'

The pain is growing, but I try to focus, hoping that the quicker I respond, the quicker this will be over. 'He landed, and transformed, and they ran towards us, and – and –' I gulp down some air and jam my fingernails into the cracks between the paving stones – 'he was fighting the others first, and then – and

344

then –' But even as I gabble out my story, Tallis keeps tipping more leaves on top of me, until my skin burns and I'm writhing with the agony of it and she has to threaten the maid again to keep me still. Until I can't bear it any longer. I tip my head back and scream.

Tallis laughs. 'You may get up now.'

I scramble back into the corner of the cell, grab the filthy cloak and drag it round my shoulders. 'Why . . . ?' The torment takes my breath away.

'Because I can. I told you I'd make you pay, Aderyn. But you only got part way through your description of my brother's death. We'll continue this in a little while. I wonder if it will hurt more, or less, on the scarred skin of your back?' She jerks her head towards the maid. 'Come. Unless you wish to remain here.'

I'm left alone, cowering and weeping and unable to do anything to help myself. The pain fades, gradually, but Tallis is true to her word. She returns, again and again, and each time she has a flightless person with her to force me to obey, and each time she makes me start the story of the ambush and her brother's death, and I never finish. I am covered in tiny red welts and blisters that burn my skin like hot ashes. I'm no longer chained, but it doesn't help. I can't think, I can't sleep, I can't rest at all.

When the door to my cell opens again, I'm frightened. Is this fear what the flightless feel all the time when they're around us? I wonder how many times I'll be able to endure Tallis's punishment before I beg for death.

But the figure who sets the torch into its bracket isn't Tallis.

As my eyes adjust to the light, I realise it's Lucien. He carries a bucket and a bundle into the cell, and closes the door behind him.

My chest and stomach constrict at the prospect of some fresh torture inflicted by one I used to love. I run my tongue over my cracked lips. 'Has she sent you to persecute me now?'

'No. No, my darling, Aderyn.'

'Don't call me that. Don't you dare.'

'Please, I've come to help you.' He holds out his hands to me. I smack them away. 'Liar. Don't touch me.'

He shrinks back. 'But, don't you remember? I came to the Eyria, after Siegfried poisoned you –'

'Liar! That was a dream. I was talking in my sleep, and someone told you. You're just trying to trick me. Leave me alone.'

'No, Aderyn. It was real. The only moment of reality in this whole, long nightmare. Ever since I was banished, I've been walking through shadows, only half-awake. Only half-alive.' He drags his fingers through his hair in the gesture I remember so well.

But it's an act. It must be. After everything he's done, does he seriously expect me to believe him? 'I know I've made mistakes. But I'm not an idiot. The first piece of advice you ever gave me was to trust no one. In what possible world would I trust you now?' I kick out, forcing him further away from me. 'By the Firebird, Lucien . . . Do you think I've forgotten what happened at Hatchlands, when you held your knife to my throat? Or up in the throne room only a few days ago, when you hit me hard enough to –'

'Because I couldn't risk Tallis discovering the truth!' He groans, and clutches at his head. 'Please, Aderyn –' he lowers his voice again – 'you have to believe me. Up there in the throne room . . . I couldn't help you. She's growing suspicious.' Stooping, he begins to undo the bundle. 'Here, let me prove it to you. I've brought water for you to wash in, and a robe, and some of the lotion the healers gave me last year –' Sniffing, he sweeps a hand across his face. 'I should have got you out sooner, but I didn't know that she was using agarica –' His voice breaks. 'I swear, I didn't know. Not until Veron told me. I'll never forgive myself for everything you've suffered. Never.'

Veron? Why would he tell Lucien what was happening to me? Why would he care? Lucien is offering me a clean robe. I don't take it.

'What about the people who died at Merl, Lucien? What about the people who are still dying here? What of Lien, and Pyr, and Odette?'

He flinches at the mention of my cousin. 'I had no choice –'

'That's what Veron keeps telling me, dishonourable piece of filth that he is. And you're no better.'

Lucien grabs my wrist as I try to strike him. 'But I can explain everything! It was Aron's idea –'

I stop trying to pull away from him. 'Aron?'

'Yes.' He lets go of me. Holds his hands up, palms out, placating. 'I swear, I *can* explain. The morning after I was banished, before I left the Citadel, Aron offered me a choice: to endure permanent banishment from the kingdom, or to become a spy. To pledge allegiance to Tallis and risk everything to supply him with information about her plans. A chance to prove my loyalty, and clear my name.'

'Aron was behind this?' I shift position so I'm facing Lucien, despite a flare of pain from my tortured skin. 'He knew, and he didn't say anything? Why would he let me go on thinking that –'

'Because I made him swear that he wouldn't reveal the truth to another living soul. It was hard enough to convince Tallis to accept me. If she ever saw us together, she had to believe you hated me. It was my idea for him to tell you that you'd been talking to me in your sleep, when you were ill, and –'

'No.' I shake my head, thinking of myriad objections. 'How could you know about the poison? How could you even find me? You didn't know about the Eyria –'

'But I did!' He leans forward, pleading. 'Before the Citadel fell, I was in touch with Aron through Pianet's network of agents. And we'd arranged a place to leave messages, if all else failed; Aron thought of everything. When you didn't recover, he left word asking for my help. I was able to discover the type of poison that had been used, and the antidote.'

I hesitate, studying his face. 'Then why not give Aron the antidote?'

Lucien drops his gaze. 'He wanted me to. But . . . if it was too late to save you – if you were dying –' He breaks off, covering his face with his hands. When he looks back at me, there's a tear tracking down his cheek. 'I had to try to see you one last time. So Aron gave in. Though we knew we had to make you believe it was dream.'

I want to believe him. But still, there is so much death that might be laid to his account. 'The attacks at Hythe and Merl –'

'Were already planned. I did what I could to warn people. I was at least able to tell Aron that an assault on the Citadel was imminent, though I didn't know about Patrus's role. I'll always regret that I couldn't do more.' He edges closer, one hand out, slowly, as if I'm a wild animal that might flee at any sudden movement. 'If we survive this, I don't expect forgiveness. Or mercy.'

My words to him, more or less, after I confessed that I'd trusted Siegfried, and had placed myself – and my dominion – in that monster's power.

'Please,' he adds, 'let me help you.'

It's too dim for me to clearly read the expression in Lucien's eyes. I think I'd rather be tortured to death by Tallis than go through another betrayal at his hands. But I'm alone here. With no one else to turn to. And I so badly want for him to be telling the truth . . .

Perhaps the pain is making me delirious. I stretch out my fingers, half-expecting Lucien to vanish, to find myself once again in the blank darkness of the cell.

But I touch him, and he's real, and he smiles at me. A small, tentative smile. Enough, though, to remind me of the Lucien I fell in love with. I grip his hand, and he sighs with relief.

'We haven't much time. Quickly – wash the residue of the agarica from your skin . . .'

I pull off the guard's stinking cloak, crouch next to the bucket and begin splashing water over my lacerated skin. The relief almost makes me cry. In the end I pick the bucket up and tip the rest of the water over my head. Lucien hands me a towel, though anything but the slightest pressure against my skin makes me flinch.

'The lotion works quickly.' Lucien lifts a small earthenware jar from the bundle. 'Shall I . . .' He breaks off, dropping his gaze. 'Shall I put some on your back?'

I'm not sure I want him to touch me like that. After everything that's happened, everything he's said and done, it feels too . . . intimate. But I'm desperate. So I nod and scoop some of the lotion into my own hands. 'Very well, but talk to me at the same time. Where's Lancelin? Is he still alive?'

'Yes.' Lucien begins to smooth the lotion across my shoulders and down over my back. 'My father is alive, for now. But his spirit is broken. His belief in my treason, both real and falsified, has sunk him into despair. He won't speak to me. He won't even look at me.' His voice is raw with pain.

'I'm sorry, Lucien.'

'I brought it on myself. I chose to become involved in the plot against King Albaric, even though I knew it would lead to bloodshed. I could see that things in the kingdom had to change. I just didn't know what else to do.'

I understand. It's why I claimed the crown in the first place: because I thought I could change things.

Lucien passes me a clean robe from the bundle at his feet. 'We should go.'

'But what about the guards?'

'I drugged their ale.' He passes me the torch and picks up a sword, the last thing in the bundle. 'I'm not going to ask for your trust, Aderyn. I'm going to try to earn it.' Opening the door, Lucien checks the corridor is clear and leads me out of the cell.

We hurry through the long corridors of the dungeons, past cell after cell. Lucien tells me every space is full of people – nobles and flightless – who have offered real or imagined resistance to Tallis's regime change. Too many for us to try to free them all. I wonder whether we are near the entrance to Hemeth's secret refuge, but I don't know how to find it, and even if I did, I'm not about to take Lucien there. He's right: I don't trust him. Not yet.

At the gates to the dungeons, we edge past the sprawled bodies of snoring guards and abandon the torch. We're not making for the landing platform – there's too much risk of detection, even though Lucien tells me it's the middle of the night. Instead, we walk up to the ground floor and pass through the service areas: kitchens, pantries, linen stores, and so on. At least, Lucien walks, trying to look as if he is meant to be there. I, with my ragged haircut and overlong robe (one of Lucien's own, I guess) keep my head down and cling to his shadow. We see only a handful of servants. They stop and bow. Lucien and I ignore them, as they would expect.

By the time we reach the heavy oak door that leads to the kitchen gardens, and freedom, my heart is thumping so hard it almost takes my breath away.

Lucien turns the handle. Frowns. Tugs the door back and forth.

It doesn't open.

'It's locked.' He runs his hand over the keyhole and along the top of the door frame and stoops to scan the floor. 'I don't understand. I checked three times – the key was always here . . .'

There's no other exit to the gardens on this level. There

are windows, set high in the walls, but even if we could reach them, they're barred.

'Can we force the door?' I whisper. 'Or go back past the dungeons and through the Dark Guards' quarters?'

Lucien rams his shoulder against the door. The impact sends echoes along the stone corridors, but the door doesn't budge. 'It's too heavy . . .' He taps his fingers against his leg. 'Tallis has mercenaries quartered where the Dark Guards used to be. And I don't know exactly how long the sleeping potion will last; the guards in the dungeons might wake soon, and discover you're gone.'

'The entrance hall, then. The stairway to the courtyards . . .'

He nods and takes my hand. We hurry up one of the menial staircases. When we reach the door that opens into the entrance hall, Lucien checks again that our path is clear.

'There's no one around, that I can see.' He's right. Though the chandeliers blaze as usual, the huge space is empty of people. From the corner where we're standing, slightly shielded by a pillar, I can see the ornate gates that control the main route up to the landing platform and one of the doors leading to the great hall. The doors to the throne room are to our right. Together with the long gallery, these spaces that radiate off the entrance hall are the hub of the Citadel. But there's utter silence: no footsteps, no murmured conversation. Not even the crackle of logs burning in a fireplace. It feels almost abandoned.

The steps that lead to the stables and courtyards are on the opposite side of the entrance hall to where we're standing. Only twelve wingspans away, though the distance yawns before me like an abyss.

Lucien grips my hand more tightly and we begin to cross the hall – hurrying, but trying not to look as if we're hurrying. Though we're both barefoot, each step seems to ring on the marble floor.

Still, I think we're going to make it. There might be flightless in the courtyards – grooms, or night porters – but they won't be able to stop us transforming. And then we can escape to the Eyria. Join Aron and the others.

Lucien speeds up. We're nearly at the top of the stairs –

A peal of laughter, cold and high-pitched, splits the silence.

Behind us, on the second-floor balcony that runs across the entrance hall above the doors to the throne room, is Tallis. And not only Tallis: she's surrounded by her guards and courtiers.

We start running for the stairs, but before we've reached the third step armed guards charge us from below. Lucien raises his sword and drags me up the stairs and back into the entrance hall just as more guards burst through the gates that lead to the landing platform.

We're trapped.

'There's nowhere for you to go,' Tallis observes. 'I'd advise you to give up your sword, Rookwood. My mercenaries may lack the discipline of the Dark Guards, but they have a certain expertise when it comes to hacking people to death.'

The guards surrounding us edge closer. Lucien turns slowly, as if he's looking for a weakness he can exploit.

But it's hopeless. There are too many of them.

'Lucien . . .' I shake my head.

He looks at me – one long, agonised glance – and throws down his sword.

'Bring them closer,' Tallis orders. Sword points prod our backs. 'Really, Rookwood, I'm so . . .' She shakes her head and sighs. 'So disappointed in you. After everything I promised you. Were you not to have Atratys, and the head of the one who banished you to stick on a spike above the walls of Merl Castle? And now you have nothing. Fool. Traitor.'

'You're the fool, Tallis, for believing that you could ever have tempted me to betray my country and my friends to follow you. You are the traitor here. You, and everyone who stands by your side.'

Tallis laughs again. 'I've known for a while someone was supplying information to the enemy. I even suspected my betrothed.' She gestures to Veron, who is standing slightly behind her, staring at the floor. 'But he betrayed you, even while you thought he was helping you to betray me. Now, I suppose I have to decide what to do with you both . . .'

Lady Crump pushes her way forward. 'Execution, my lady. A blood sacrifice in the arena, to cleanse the Citadel of their treachery and inaugurate your reign.' She doesn't look at me, but her voice is gloating. 'To celebrate the crowning of a true queen.'

'An excellent idea. My betrothed had asked me to give him Aderyn as a wedding present, but much as I'd love to see her reduced to the status of a slave, this is better. Is everyone in agreement?'

The nobles around her, with varying degrees of enthusiasm, give their assent.

'Very well.' Tallis straightens up. 'Aderyn of the House of Cygnus Atratys, formally Protector of Atratys, and Lucien, of the House of Corax Anserys, you are hereby convicted of treason against me, the rightful queen, by a court of your peers, and are sentenced to death. The crests of your houses will be struck out. The names of your houses will be dishonoured.' She leans over the balcony, gritting her teeth. 'Your reign, Aderyn, such as it was, will be expunged from the records. It will be as if you never existed. As if you had died in the attack that killed your mother, as you should have.' Pausing, she takes a breath. 'At dawn, Veron and I will be wed. You will therefore be executed tomorrow morning, in preparation for our coronation. Get them out of my sight.'

Lucien and I are marched back down to the dungeons. Within minutes, I'm imprisoned in the darkness he helped me escape from only a short while ago.

At least, since every other cell is full, Lucien is with me. He rests his hands on my shoulders, trembling.

'I'm so sorry,' he murmurs. 'I've failed you.'

'No. It's my fault. I was supposed to stop her. I was supposed to save the kingdom. But I gave up almost everything I really cared about, and I watched those I love die, and I've still lost. Perhaps Lady Crump was right. I never was a true queen.'

'You're wrong, Aderyn.' The fierceness in Lucien's voice surprises me. 'You need to see yourself as others see you: brave, intelligent, kind . . . a born leader. My life doesn't matter. But I should – I should have been able to save yours. You're the queen Solanum needs. You always have been. After you and Aron married, I should never have got in the way . . .'

I feel something like a spot of rain on my arm and lift my

hand carefully so I can brush away his tears. 'Don't weep, Lucien. There's still hope. Aron will save us, if he can.'

'No. An assault on the Citadel will fail. The walls are too strongly defended.'

'There's still hope,' I repeat, trying to make myself believe what sounds like a lie, an easy platitude to dull the fear that threatens to paralyse me. Trying to instil some hope in Lucien without giving away Aron's plan. He and Valentin know the planned date of Tallis's coronation. Surely, the tunnel must be nearly ready. Surely, our forces must be nearly in place . . .

'I wonder how much time we have,' Lucien murmurs.

'I don't know. But if I have only a few hours left, I'm glad I'm spending them with you.'

His grip on my shoulders tightens. 'You still . . . Is it possible you still care for me, after everything I've put you through?'

I flatten my hand against his heart, feeling the rapid rhythm of his blood. 'I tried to hate you. I forced myself to dwell on what you said, on what you did – the pressure of your knife against my throat.' He groans, and I slide both hands up until they are resting on his face. 'But it didn't help. All this time . . . I've never stopped loving you. I never will.'

'Oh, Aderyn . . .' His pulls me into his arms, hugging me tightly, murmuring my name and covering my face with kisses. 'I'd allowed myself to hope a little, when you wanted to hold my hand that night in the Eyria. But it seemed so impossible . . . You haunted my dreams and my waking hours, but I thought I'd lost you.'

I put my arms around his neck, clinging to him. 'I dreamed

of you too. I dreamed of the night we spent together. When Siegfried suggested that you and Tallis had become lovers –'

'Never. I couldn't have done that. Not even to save my own skin.'

I pull away from him a little, hesitating.

But my future contains horror, and little else. I'm almost certainly going to die in a few hours. There's no time left for doubt. Or regret.

'Take off your robe and lay it on the floor.' I hear Lucien's faint intake of breath, but he releases me, and I feel the movement of the air as he spreads the fabric over the dirty straw of the cell. His hand finds mine. Guides me downwards until I'm on my knees. I unclasp my own robe, place it across us as a blanket and lie next to him.

'Aderyn . . . my only love.' As he slides his hand down the curve of my waist and around my back, I lift my mouth to his and lose myself – my dread, my pain – in his arms.

Nineteen

'On yer feet.' A guard wearing heavy gauntlets seizes Lucien's arm and hauls him upright. Another levels a spear at his chest, while a third holds the tip of his sword against my breastbone.

'Aderyn –' Lucien tries to turn towards me as his hands are manacled roughly behind his back, but the guard holding him jerks him forward, and the two of them drive him out of the cell.

'Wait –' A jab from the third guard silences me.

Lucien is gone. And I don't know if I'll ever see him again.

Another guard enters. 'Bring her.' I draw my robe around myself and get to my feet before the guard can manhandle me. He grunts, gesturing to the door.

I walk between my captors through the long passageways of the dungeons. The floor beneath me seems to be gradually sloping upwards, but I have no idea where in this maze of tunnels and rooms I am, until we emerge in an area with windows and I'm blinking in the strong daylight. We're near the arena.

The guards stop and one of them opens a door. I take a deep

breath and clench my fists – trying to stop my legs shaking, to prepare myself for whatever tortures might lie before me – and step through.

A cloud of rose-scented steam billows around me. It's rising from a bath that stands in the centre of the room. There are two grey-clad housemaids, both wearing gloves, waiting beside it.

The guard shoves me forward. 'Get on with it.'

One of the housemaids advances and jerks her head at the guard. 'You're not to be in here.' She puts her hands on her hips. ''Tisn't right. You'd better leave now or I'll tell Mistress Petry.'

Mistress Petry was – is, I suppose – the Citadel's housekeeper. I met her only once: a stern woman who doesn't tolerate any deviation from her rules. I'm not entirely surprised that the maid's threat works. The guard grumbles and swears, but he goes to wait outside with his colleague. As soon as the door is closed one of the maids curtsies to me.

'Your Majesty . . . we didn't want to. But they've threatened us, and – and . . .' She casts a glance at the other, younger girl – she can barely be more than fifteen – who is sniffing and rubbing her eyes. There's a large patch of burnt, blistered skin on her arm. Someone – a noble – has grabbed her.

'It's all right; please, don't cry.' I look around the room, but see nothing apart from the bath, a stack of towels and what looks like a dress over the back of a chair. The windows, as with all the spaces designed for the flightless, are small and barred, and too high to offer any view. 'What must I do?'

'You're to take a bath, Majesty. And then you're to get dressed, and then –'

The younger maid begins sobbing.

'Look after her. I can bathe myself.'

Taking off my robe, I lower myself into the hot water, wincing as it stings my still-sore skin. The bath is small, and the water only comes up to my waist – to make it harder for me, should I attempt to drown myself, I suppose – but there is soap, and a jug to rinse my hair. What's left of it. I take my time. But the maids are waiting with the towels, glancing every so often at the door, and eventually I can't draw it out any longer. I take a towel and step out.

'What am I to wear?'

The older maid takes the dress from the chair.

It's red. Like the dress I had on when my father died, like the dress Siegfried made me wear to the groomsday banquet. I swore then I'd never wear red again.

The gown is made of fine silk. Sleeveless, with a draped neckline that exposes my entire back, and the scars that I've always tried – when not transforming – to conceal. The skirt is full, but is slit to the thigh on both sides, so that my legs are revealed as I walk.

I understand. I am dressed like this for the same reason my hair was cut off. It is not enough that I am to be sacrificed. Tallis wishes to strip away as much of my dignity as possible.

All too soon, the door is opened and I am returned to my guards.

They leer at me. The one who is wearing heavy gauntlets yanks my hands behind my back and binds them there. They lead me out into the sunlit arena.

The first thing I notice is the net of cables strung between the Citadel and the sheer wall of the battlements opposite, and between the tall fences that form the other two boundaries of the arena, creating a lattice that effectively seals us in. Even if I could somehow free myself of the manacles around my wrists and transform, I could not escape. And if anyone tries to help us from outside, they will not be able to reach us. The sky is roped off.

The flightless inhabitants of the Citadel are crowded, silent, along the outside of the fences. Guards, with their swords drawn, are stationed behind them. I see the two stone pillars, sets of manacles and chains hanging from them as usual, only now there are piles of kindling at the base of each pillar.

We are to burn, then.

There's a platform at the edge of the arena that wasn't there before. My guards drive me round to the front of the platform; from here I can see that most of Tallis's courtiers are standing on the balcony that runs above the arena. Tallis herself is seated in a chair on the platform. I suppose she was worried about the rope net affecting her view of our suffering. She's wearing a dress of silver satin with a long train that puddles around her feet, and on her head – even though the coronation has not yet taken place – is the ancient Crown of Talons, its circle of sharp stone claws glinting in the sunlight. There are a dozen or so guards around her – all wearing the heavy leather gauntlets that allow them to touch us, at least briefly, all armed with either swords or axes – together with a few nobles. Veron, also clad in silver satin, is one of them.

Lucien is kneeling on the grass in front of the platform. He's wearing nothing but a pair of dark red trousers, and his hands are tied behind his back as mine are. He glances across as the guard pushes me to my knees next to him.

'Aderyn –'

'Silence,' Tallis snaps. One of the guards standing nearby unfurls a whip and lashes Lucien across the back. Lucien grunts with the force of it, but doesn't cry out.

Tallis stands. 'The sacrifice of a traitor to consecrate a new reign is an ancient tradition, sadly discontinued in recent times. Today sees the start not only of a new reign, but the ascendency of a new house. It is only fitting that the end of the House of Cygnus should be marked by the deaths of two who share its tainted and corrupted bloodline.'

The nobles begin to applaud. So, eventually, do the flightless.

'And yet –' Tallis waves a hand for silence – 'I am merciful. So I offer you a choice, traitors.' She sits down again and waves a hand towards the two stone pillars. 'You see the torment that is prepared for you. To be burned alive, fully aware of the other's suffering. But there is an alternative. I know that some nobles – including my dear brother, before he was murdered – feel it necessary to carry a sword as an alternative to the more honourable, pure form of defence that we carry within our own bodies.' Her voice rises. 'But you, I understand, sank so low as to fight other nobles within the royal confines of the Citadel, supposedly for your own sport, but in reality for the entertainment of flightless guards who should have been taught to know their place.' Tallis takes a deep breath, relaxing her grip on the arms of her chair.

I glance at Veron. The flush on his face, his tightly compressed lips, show he hasn't forgotten our duel. He is wearing no sword belt today.

'So,' Tallis continues, 'as you entertained them, you may now entertain me. You will fight each other, to the death. If either of you does not compete adequately, you will both be burned. If either of you gives up, or appears to seek an easy death, the survivor will be burned.' She sits back in her chair and crosses her legs. 'What kind of death do you choose?'

Lucien and I look at each other. I don't want to fight him. I can't imagine trying to hurt him. But to burn . . .

Time has not yet softened my memory of the man Patrus had burned last year. The sound of his screams. The smell of his scorched flesh. My stomach heaves.

'The sword. I choose to fight.'

Tallis's mouth twitches upwards. 'As you wish.'

At her signal, one of the guards approaches and removes the manacles binding our arms. I rub my wrists and flex my fingers, wincing as the blood flows back into my hands. The guard hands me a sword. It's heavier than I'm used to, and the edge is notched. Still sharp, though.

Lucien is examining his sword, swinging it experimentally through the air.

For his sake, I have to try to kill him. For my own sake, I have to hope that he tries to kill me too.

Tallis takes a sweetmeat from the dish that has been set at her elbow and pops it into her mouth. 'Begin.'

Neither of us raises our weapon.

'Begin! I will not tell you again.'

I bring my sword up, mouth *forgive me*, and attack.

Lucien isn't expecting me to be so fast. He blocks my thrust, but stumbles backwards at the same time. I push my advantage, attacking again, all the while trying to decide whether I should be aiming for his heart, to end this quickly. Trying to make myself believe that I could ever actually thrust my blade between his ribs –

I land a stroke and the edge of my sword slices across Lucien's chest, splitting the skin like ripe fruit.

Tallis claps and laughs as Lucien gasps, clutching his free hand to the injury. Blood wells between his fingers.

Lowering my blade, I reach for him. 'Lucien – I'm sorry –'

'No,' he snarls at me through gritted teeth. 'You have to keep fighting –' He charges at me, forcing me backwards as I parry blow after blow until I duck below him to aim at his belly. Not quick enough. He steps away and thrusts his sword towards my shoulder –

The pain takes my breath away. I drop to my knees as he yanks the blade free.

Lucien is panting, looking as if he's about to be sick. 'Pick up the sword. Keep fighting.'

My right arm is useless. Blood runs from the wound in my shoulder, dripping from my fingers onto the grass.

Two guards begin to move towards us.

'Aderyn –'

There's so much pleading in his eyes.

I grasp my sword and stagger to my feet. Lift the blade. Swing it down in a wide arc again and again as Lucien gives way before me.

It sounds as if Tallis is still enjoying herself. The crowd watching us, though, gradually falls silent.

I keep attacking. But the weeks of sickness, and the days of torture in the Citadel, have weakened me. My hand is aching with the weight of the sword, my breath hitches with the pain from my injured shoulder, and the tears in my eyes are making it impossible for me to see.

Lucien twists his sword. Rips my own weapon from my hand. I stagger and he catches me. Brings the point of his blade up to rest just beneath my ribs.

I stare up at him. Lift my fingers to brush his tear-streaked face.

'Hack her to death!' Tallis shouts. She's sitting forward on the edge of her chair, eyes blazing. 'Make her suffer, Rookwood, or suffer yourself . . .'

'Let me . . . let me get my sword.' I try to free myself from his grasp, but Lucien shakes his head. 'I'm going to end this. I can't watch you suffer any more. I can't be the one making you suffer.'

'No – she'll burn you –'

A ghost of a smile. 'I can live with that. If there's something after this life, I'll see you soon. If not . . . I love you, my darling Aderyn.'

He kisses me as he draws back his arm –

Too late. Guards take hold of both of us, disarming Lucien and pulling us apart. They begin to drag us towards the stone pillars, while two other guards light torches from the brazier that stands nearby. I struggle in my captors' hands, trying to reach their unprotected faces, to burn them before they can burn me –

Shouts, and the sound of metal clashing against metal, echo

from the shadowy archways that lead to the dungeons and the Dark Guards' quarters.

The guards hesitate.

'Chain them up!' Tallis screams. 'Now! I order you to –'

An arrow whistles past my face and thuds into one of the guards holding me. He groans. Crumples to the floor.

Tallis stares, mouth and eyes wide.

Aron is striding through the nearest archway, sword drawn. 'It's over, you treacherous bitch.' His voice rings through the arena. 'This is the last time you hurt anyone I love.' Valentin is beside him. Even from here, I can hear Veron's gasp. Aron's mouth twists into a sneer as Tallis swings round to face him. 'The time has come for you to vacate the throne, Stepmother, before you are dragged off.'

Tallis's scream of rage is swallowed by a sudden clamour spilling across the arena as people pour from the archways. Dark Guards and archers from Galen battling with mercenaries and a ragtag of guards from Brithys and Olorys.

Fighting erupts everywhere. An arrow thuds into the back of the guard struggling with Lucien. Veron seizes a sword from a guard and jumps off the platform into the midst of Tallis's mercenaries. I reach back with my uninjured hand and dig my fingers into the flesh of the one guard still holding me, until his skin blisters and he screams and releases me. Grabbing his axe, I drive it into the leg of a noble – one of Patrus's relatives, I think – as she lunges towards me with a blade.

Transformed nobles appear in the sky above the Citadel and begin attacking those on the balcony; some of them run inside to escape, some start pulling off their clothes so they can shift shape. Lady Crump is attacking one of the Shriven, shrieking in frustration and shock as her touch fails to bring the other woman to her knees.

And Tallis –

She is nowhere to be seen.

'Aderyn, you're hurt –' Aron is beside me with a sword in his hand. He's breathing hard and bleeding from a cut to his temple, but he looks more alive than he has for weeks. 'Hemeth, get the queen to safety –'

'No! We have to find Tallis. We have to finish this. She can't be allowed to escape again.'

Aron scans the crowded arena as shouts erupt from beyond the fences – the flightless have turned on the guards behind them.

'There –' Hemeth points to a small door set into the wall at the base of the battlements. Tallis is standing in front of it, a Dark Guard's axe in her hand. 'That door's kept secure. She's trying to cut away the lock –' He spins to block a sword thrust from an Oloryan noble and plunges his own sword into the man's gut. 'Damarin! Bring her down –'

But Damarin, distracted by Hemeth's cry, is tackled to the ground by one of Tallis's mercenaries, and Lucien –

Lucien screams. He's dropped to his knees clutching his face, and the man in front of him has raised his sword –

Veron yells and charges, knocking Lucien's attacker sideways and sending the brazier flying. The dry wood piled against one of the stone pillars begins to blaze.

The battle rages around me, screams and shouts deafen me, and everywhere the grass is spattered with blood. I want to go to Lucien, but Tallis has wrenched open the door into the battlements –

'Go –' Aron thrusts his sword into my hand and takes that of the dead Oloryan. 'End it. I'll take care of Lucien –'

End it. With those words, I find the energy to start running.

Beyond the door is a steep, cramped staircase, only just wider than my shoulders, leading up towards the walkway that runs along the top of the battlements. The stairway's mostly in shadow, apart from the light spilling through the doorway and falling through a few narrow chinks in the walls at widely spaced intervals. I start climbing, not waiting for my eyes to adjust.

Tallis is a long way ahead of me.

But I think . . . I think I'm gaining on her. She's struggling with the skirts and train of her gown, tripping every few steps; it looks as if she's scooped the voluminous fabric into her arms and is trying to hold on to that as well as the axe.

The dress I'm wearing, the dress designed to humiliate me, proves no hindrance at all.

I grip my sword hilt. Push myself faster still. Grit my teeth against the ache in my shoulder, against the cramp in my thighs and the burn in my lungs.

Tallis screams a curse at me and hurls the axe down the stairs as I flatten myself against the wall –

The axe tumbles past me, bouncing harmlessly off the stone steps.

She stares at me, her face pale as the moon in the dim light. Turns and flees for the door at the top of the stairs. Bursts through onto the top of the battlements and tries to close it behind her.

But I'm too close. I force my way through.

Tallis runs, making for the door that leads back into the Citadel, trying to rip open the bodice of her dress so she can transform.

'Not this time, you hell-bred demon –' I lunge forward, leaping onto the train of her dress and sending her sprawling. The Crown of Talons slips from her head and rolls across the stone walkway.

Tallis turns and tries to scrabble away from me, pushing herself up and gripping the low parapet that edges the walkway, clinging to the iron rings that have been driven into the stone to hold the ropes strung across the arena. 'Let me go! Let me go!' Her mouth twists into a snarl. 'You traitor to your own kind, you disgrace, you –'

I press the point of my sword beneath her chin, forcing her head back. 'Enough.'

'You dare attack your queen?' She laughs. 'I could have made Solanum great. It could have become the centre of an empire. But now it will fall, just like Celonia. And it will be your fault. You're a failure, Aderyn. And you're going to die a failure. You, and that flightless creature you married.'

From the corner of my eye I see her right hand, sliding a knife out of her pocket . . .

I step back and bring my sword down in a wide arc. The blade bites into her upper arm, slicing through muscle and bone and through the rope beneath until it scrapes against the stone of the parapet. The severed limb drops to the floor. Blood splashes over my legs and begins running in rivulets between the paving stones. Tallis staggers. Howls with pain, clinging on with her one remaining hand as blood soaks through her silver bodice.

'No! No . . . what have you . . . what have you done?'

'I've transformed you into one of those you hate: into one of the flightless. Tell me, *my queen*, how does it feel?' I set my foot on the parapet next to her and position my sword above her heart, forcing myself to look her straight in the eye. 'That was for Odette, and for Aron. And this . . . this is for all the flightless of Solanum, and for all the nobles too. For everyone you've ever hurt. This is for all of us.'

Her eyes widen as I plunge the blade into her chest. When I pull the sword out, Tallis slips and tumbles backwards. For a moment, she lands on the network of ropes strung from the parapet, and lies there staring up at me. But there's a gap in the net now, and she can't cling on. She falls through the ropes and plunges from the top of the battlements down, down into the arena far below. Her body lands half on the blazing wood around the stone pillar. The flames leap up as her skirts catch fire and she begins to burn.

She shrieks – a high, piercing cry of agony that cuts through the noise of battle, until it fades into the roar of the fire.

Tallis is dead.

My sword slips from my hand and I drop to my knees, retching over and over until what little there was in my stomach has been disgorged. I crawl as far as I can manage along the top of the battlements, away from the vomit and the blood and Tallis's severed limb. Sit with my back against the parapet. Close my eyes.

I know I should go back down. Or at least seek the shelter

of the stairway; the fighting is still raging below, and I'm up here alone and exposed.

But I'm too tired and in too much pain to move. If I breathe too deeply, the agonising ache from my injured shoulder turns my stomach. And if I go back down, and find that Lucien is dead, or Aron –

Better to wait up here. Someone will find me soon – one of my friends, or one of my enemies.

Right now, I'm not sure I care which.

'Aderyn?'

I recognise the voice. But I'm somewhere warm and soft. Comfortable. I don't want to open my eyes and have to deal with reality. Recalcitrant nobles, or Lucien and Aron fighting, or Tallis –

But Tallis is dead. I remember her body plummeting from the top of the battlements, her silver skirts catching the wind like a swan's wide, white wings. And Lucien, and Aron –

'Aderyn, my dear . . .'

Aron is leaning over me, sitting on the edge of the bed in which I'm lying. My own bed: I'm back in the royal apartments. He huffs with relief as he smiles at me.

'You're awake.'

'Yes.' I smile back at him. 'You're alive.'

He nods, frowning slightly. 'Four days have passed since the battle; it's the twenty-sixth of Laurus now. How much do you remember?'

'I fought Tallis. Killed her. And then –' And then . . . For an instant, I'm back in that moment, vomiting, my hands

371

slick with blood, the gritty flagstones of the rampart hard beneath my palms. I shake my head. 'Nothing really, after that. Where's Lucien? And Letya, and Lancelin? Please, tell me they're alive?'

'Letya's fine; she's barely left your side these past few days. Lancelin is ill – we found him in the dungeons – but he's improving, especially since I saw him and explained Lucien's part in all this. And Lucien himself . . . he's injured, but he's alive –'

'Injured? How?' I start to push myself up. 'Where is he?'

Aron presses me gently back onto the mattress. 'Careful – your shoulder's been stitched. It's healing well, but you're not supposed to make any sudden movements. Lucien's back in his own room, and he's being tended to.' He grips my hand. 'He's a little altered. But he's going to live, Aderyn. He's going to be fine. You can see him soon.'

I listen for a moment; a clock ticks on the mantelpiece, and birdsong floats in through the open window on fresh, summer-scented air. No shouts, no clash of sword on sword. It's peaceful. 'We won, then?'

'Yes, my queen.' Aron brings my hand to his lips and kisses it. 'We won. There's still some mopping up to do. The rump of Tallis's mercenaries fled south-west; their fleet is still anchored off the Passerine Islands. But Lucien's younger brother – who had been imprisoned in the watchtower in Hythe, it turns out – is leading an Atratyan company to capture the ships. And Arden of Dacia, who's suddenly extremely anxious to be of use, is directing the pursuit of the mercenaries overland. Several of the nobles who supported Tallis and Siegfried have fled, and Eorman of Frianland – to nobody's surprise – has offered them sanctuary.'

I sigh. 'I suppose we will have to deal with him, at some point.'

'Eventually. But Lord Pianet's spies tell me that some of the Friant nobility are less than happy with the prince's behaviour. Perhaps they will deal with him for us. As for the nobles we've already captured, or who have surrendered, they're in the dungeons. Together with the handful of flightless who supported them.' He raises an eyebrow. 'Trials will have to be held.'

'I suppose so. And I suppose justice will have to be served. But let's be merciful too, if we can. Let's try to protect the kingdom without losing ourselves in the process.' I shift position, trying to make my shoulder more comfortable. 'What of those in the Eyria? And . . . everyone else?' I'm nervous to ask about Valentin, now it comes to it.

'The Eyria is emptied. Though I think we will keep it stocked and in good repair from now on, just in case. And Valentin –' he grins, joy lighting up his face – 'Valentin is here too, and uninjured, and the hero of the hour due to his tunnel.' His smile fades. 'Though we got to you just in time. Veron told me –'

'Veron?'

'Yes.' Aron must see the question in my eyes, because he adds, 'He's under house arrest, with a broken leg. When we fought our way into the arena, and Valentin was next to me, I caught a glimpse of Veron's face . . . Well, let's just say that he was convinced to switch sides – again – and fight for us instead.' He shakes his head and smiles a little. 'We'll have to work out what to do with him. Executing him probably wouldn't be the best thing for my relationship with his brother, I suspect, however that develops.'

'We'll release him, I suppose, and hope he decides to work with those now ruling Celonia rather than against them. Although, I'd be inclined to keep a very close eye on him from now on.'

'I agree. He's told me, by the way, about what Tallis did to you. In the dungeons, and then in the arena. When I think what could have happened, if we'd been just a few minutes later . . .'

'But you weren't, so you don't have to think about it.' I pat his hand and smile at him reassuringly. In truth, I can't yet bear to talk about the dungeons, or how nearly it ended in disaster. The memory is too raw. 'How many did we lose? How many of our people died?'

Aron sighs and shakes his head. 'Too many. Verginie of Lancorphys died in the attack on the Eyria. Lady Finch, Lord Shrike, Bran Shadowshaft . . .'

The list goes on, and a lump comes to my throat. So many people I'd become fond of. And poor Nyssa, to lose her mother as well as her betrothed.

'Lord Corvax is gravely ill,' Aron continues. 'He had some sort of seizure when Bran's body was brought in. His heart, I suppose. But I've seen him, and I told him we will honour Lord Bran as a Protector at his last flight. And I thought we might give Brithys to his brother Fane, instead.'

'Of course. What about the Shriven?'

'Three dead. Hemeth is injured, but recovering. Subject to your agreement, I've appointed Damarin official representative for the island of Galen. Lady Yaffle, surviving member of Convocation for Olorys, has objected.'

'On what basis?'

Aron purses his lips, humour glinting in his green eyes. 'When I asked her that, she didn't seem entirely sure . . .'

I smile. 'So the fighting is over for now, but we still have politics.'

'Oh, yes. We still have that . . .'

There's a knock at the door. Aron helps me to sit up. 'Come in.'

Valentin enters the room and bows, saying something in Celonian.

'He says, may the Firebird bless you and bring you swift recovery on her golden wings.' Aron grins again and takes Valentin's hand, drawing him near enough to kiss. 'Valentin's helping me practise my Celonian.'

'Perhaps he can teach me too, one day.'

'I'd be honoured, Your Majesty.'

'Please, Valentin. Call me Aderyn. Or cousin, if you wish.'

He bows again, smiling at me. 'Very well, cousin.'

The door opens to admit Letya, followed by Cora, a tray laden with food in her hands. The savoury scent rising from the covered dishes makes my mouth water. Letya holds the door wide and curtsies pointedly at Aron and Valentin. 'If you don't mind, my lords, Her Majesty is supposed to eat, and then she's supposed to rest. Visiting time is over.'

For once, I am not inclined to argue.

* * *

375

A week has passed, and I still haven't seen Lucien. His doctors told me first that he couldn't have visitors, and then that he didn't want them. So I've had to be patient. And I've been busy; there are only three weeks left until the Feast of the Firebird, the summer Solstice, and Aron and I hope to have most of the repairs to the Citadel completed in time for the celebration. But this evening Lucien is supposed to be joining me in the throne room, where Aron and I are to receive the thanks of the Skein. Apparently, they want to honour us. To reassure us that they will also honour the oath they took in the Eyria.

Excitement bubbles beneath my ribs as my heart swells. An assembly for the flightless, a review of the Decrees . . . I try not to think too hard about what that might mean for Aron and Valentin. For me.

Letya and Cora are trying to find a dress that will fit over the bulky bandages around my shoulder. We settle eventually on a sleeveless taffeta evening gown in gradated shades of green. Seeing my hair in a mirror for the first time almost makes me cry. But Letya manages to tidy up the mess left by Veron's scissors, cropping the ragged curls into a bob. By the time she's placed a delicate gold filigree diadem on my head, I'm somewhat reconciled to my new appearance.

'You look beautiful, Aderyn.'

I study Letya's reflection in the mirror as she stands behind me. 'So do you.' She does – she's put back the weight she'd lost, and has styled her ash-blonde hair in a different way, and she seems to have given up trying to hide the burn on her throat with high-necked dresses. She looks a little older, and more serious.

We've all been marked by the last few months, one way or another.

And then she grins, and she's once again my childhood friend, my sister. 'Here. An early birthday present for you.' She sets something on the dressing table: my Atratyan luckstone.

'You found it!' I pick up the carved green feather and turn it over in my fingers. 'You're amazing, Letya. And thank you.' I'd almost forgotten that I turn nineteen tomorrow. It's nearly a year since I left Atratys, a new Protector, hoping to find out who murdered my mother.

'There's something else too.' She passes me a small leather bag, and I tip the contents into my palm: the ring of Atratys, my coronation ring, and my wedding ring too. 'I thought you might like to wear them.'

I hesitate for a moment, then slip all three rings onto my fingers. Wife, Protector, queen. For once, their weight doesn't bother me.

There's a knock at the door. Letya opens it.

'Aderyn, Lord Rookwood is waiting in the sitting room.'

I glance back at the mirror, strangely nervous.

My friend laughs. 'Go. You've not got long. Cora and I will be in here if you need us.'

I take a deep breath, and walk through the open door.

Lucien is standing by the bookcase. He turns as I come in and smiles at me, warmth in one of his dark eyes. But the other . . . I flatten my palm against my breastbone. I thought I knew what to expect. Aron told me what happened: the eye was lost, damaged beyond repair when Lucien was struck in the face by a mercenary. But seeing him now, the empty socket covered by an eye patch – it breaks my heart.

377

'Oh, Lucien –'

'Aderyn . . . don't cry.' He sweeps away the tears that have spilled onto my cheeks. 'This –' he gestures to his missing eye – 'this is nothing. Just tell me you forgive me.' His face crumples. 'When I stabbed you in the shoulder – I wanted to die. I would have run myself through with my own blade if it hadn't meant leaving you there with Tallis.' He laughs, though I can hear the strain in his voice. 'And I thought I'd already hurt you enough . . .'

'You were trying to save me, Lucien. I knew that, even in the midst of the pain.' I grip his shoulder. 'There's nothing to forgive. The important thing is that we're both alive. Healing.'

'You're right.' He looks down, entwining his fingers in mine. 'The pain is fading. But the scarring, I'm afraid, will be permanent.'

I smile up at him and brush my fingers along the line of his jaw. 'I have a back covered in scars, as well you know. When you first saw them, you told me that I shouldn't try to hide them. That they proved I was strong.' A thought makes me frown. 'Is that why you wouldn't see me? Because of your face?'

'Maybe. A little. But I was mostly worried that –' He breaks off.

'What?' I prompt.

He takes a deep breath. 'I know you, Aderyn. You're strong. You're going to spend the rest of your life fighting for what's right. So I want you to know that I'm strong too. My body may not be whole any more. But I'm still strong enough to be here at your side, if that's where you want me. And even when my body fails, my love for you will remain.' Slowly, Lucien drops to one knee. 'My heart is entirely yours. It will be forever. Even if we can't be together in the way we both want. I remember what you said, about keeping your vows to Aron. And I want you to know I understand.'

'Now that the Skein has agreed to review the Decrees, Aron and I hope that some compromise can be reached – some way we can continue to rule together, and still be happy. Aron loves me, but his heart belongs to Valentin.' I clasp Lucien's hand. 'As for your heart, I'd offer you my own in return, my dearest. But you already have it.'

Lucien kisses my fingers and stands and holds me close. I rest my head against his chest. For the first time in months, I feel completely safe.

The bell of the Citadel begins to toll, summoning the Skein. I pull away and look up into Lucien's face. 'I think I could grow to like the eye patch, by the way. Though –' I tilt my head, frowning – 'I don't know . . .'

His eyebrows go up. 'What? Is it the wrong size? Or colour –'

I shake my head. 'I'm just not sure you wear it as well as Patrus did, that's all.'

He bursts out laughing. 'I think you owe me a kiss for that.'

I lift my mouth and he presses his lips to mine and we kiss with an intensity that makes my legs weak and my heart hammer in my chest. Until Letya, somewhere behind us, clears her throat loudly.

'It's time, Your Majesty. Lord Rookwood and I will see you in the throne room.'

'Good luck,' Lucien whispers, and follows Letya out of the room.

I smooth my skirts. Straighten my shoulders. Aron is already waiting in the audience chamber that links our apartments. He offers me his arm, and together we walk down to the entrance hall, and into the throne room, crowded with flightless and Shriven as well as nobles. Shouts and applause ring through the summer evening air as we reclaim Solanum for the House of Cygnus, as the Crown of Talons is carried ahead of us on a velvet cushion and replaced on its pillar next to the double throne.

The crown is finally back where it belongs.

And so, I think, am I.

Epilogue

Six Months Later

Letya lifts the small blonde-haired child, her brother's daughter, onto Vasta's saddle – 'Hold tight now, Merin,' – and pulls herself up behind her. She pauses, looking down at me, a faint crease between her eyebrows. 'Don't be too late, Aderyn. The ambassador from Ryska will have arrived this afternoon, and you know you're supposed to sign the trade agreements with Galen before you fly back to the Citadel tomorrow.'

I drop a curtsy, say, 'Yes, my lady,' and stick my tongue out at Letya, which makes Merin giggle. I grin at the child. 'You can tell your aunt that I'm glad she's taking her responsibilities seriously.' Letya represents Atratys in the new assembly, and Lord Lancelin is training her to be the next steward. 'But she doesn't need to worry. If I'm ever unsure how to behave, I always ask – what would Lady Crump do? And then I do the opposite.

Letya bursts out laughing. 'I'll see you later then, Aderyn. Come on now, Vasta.' Horse and riders move off, Letya calling over her shoulder, 'But not too much later . . .'

I go back to contemplating the scene before me: Merl Castle, my childhood home, its walls and the rocky promontory upon which it stands stained crimson by the late-afternoon sun. Henga, her reins trailing, nibbles the few remaining succulent leaves of sea tuft growing in the cliffs nearby. The daylight won't last much longer. A cold breeze tugs at the divided skirt of my habit, a reminder that it's winter, despite the blue sky above. Letya's right: I should probably return to the castle.

And yet I linger as the shadows lengthen, lulled by the waves washing rhythmically against the black sands beneath my feet. I remember playing on this beach with Letya. Riding here with her. One ride in particular: the day I was thrown from my horse and almost eaten by a rock dragon.

The day I first met Lucien Rookwood.

As a raven, he killed the dragon. As a human, he picked me up and carried me to safety. Ignoring my protestations. He took me for one of the flightless, a mere child. Mocked me when I told him I was in fact the Protector here, that he was trespassing on my land.

If you're the Protector of Atratys, I'm a princess . . .

The recollection makes me smile. I decided he was arrogant. Dismissive. Possibly ready to kill me. He told me I was reckless, and there have been plenty of times during the course of our relationship that I believed he hated me. He held a blade to my throat not so very long ago.

And yet, in a few days' time, we will finally celebrate our

wedding. For the first time in a thousand years the Decrees have been, if not rewritten, at least amended. Aron and I have had our marriage dissolved, and now we are ruling side by side as cousins, and friends. My firstborn child will eventually inherit our throne, and he – or she – will be able to rule alone, if that is their wish. The Decree that forces the monarch to be married has been abolished.

I place a hand on my belly, wondering what it would be like to be a mother. Not yet, but one day . . .

A pair of arms slides around my waist, and Lucien kisses the side of my face. 'What are you thinking about, my lady?'

I turn round in his arms. I'm used to his eye patch now, and the scar running across his cheekbone; the combination makes him look more like a roguish pirate than the queen's consort. But I rather like it. And he is still my Lucien. I kiss him, enjoying the soft warmth of his lips.

'I was thinking about the day we first met. Princess.'

'I remember. I rescued you, didn't I?' He grins. 'The first of many rescues . . .'

'I think we've both done our fair share of rescuing.'

'I cannot disagree, my queen . . .' He tightens his arms around me. 'Let's go to Hatchlands. There's no one there right now. My brother and father are here, my mother's at court . . .' He winks. 'Just think of all those empty bedrooms . . .'

'We can't do that, Lucien. I have a diplomatic reception this evening. And then tomorrow we have to return to the Citadel for Valentin and Aron's wedding. And then back here, and then –'

He silences me with a kiss.

When we break apart, I gaze up at him. 'That was intensely pleasurable. But also completely unfair.'

'But I want you to myself.' He sighs. 'I know you're the queen. And a Protector. And I'm going to support you in both those things. That's my role. I just . . .' Resting his forehead against mine, he tangles the fingers of one hand in my hair. 'I want to be married *now*. I want the rest of my life with you to start right this moment.'

'A few more days, that's all. Aron's wedding at the Citadel, our own wedding here, and then the coronation.' Re-coronation really, but with the ancient Crown of Talons which Tallis had stolen. 'And then two weeks entirely to ourselves before the Solstice celebrations.' I snuggle against his chest. 'I suppose I should ride back soon. Letya will be waiting for me.'

'I suppose you should.' Tilting my chin up, he kisses me again, and sighs. 'I just wanted to get you alone, at least for a little while.' He pauses, caressing my cheek. 'You look sad, Aderyn.'

'I'm going to miss Letya, that's all. I'm glad she has her new roles, that she's finally being recognised. But it does mean she'll have to stay at Merl most of the time.'

'You just need to make sure you have space in your schedule for frequent visits. You should speak to your new clerk about it. Actually, I'll speak to her about it.' He kisses my hand. 'You look after the kingdom, my queen, and I'll look after you.'

'Oh –' We both jump back as a wave washes over our feet. 'The tide's turned. I'd better get back to the castle.'

'I'll see you there. Here . . .' Lucien hesitates, but only for a moment, before taking off his robe and eyepatch. 'Do you mind? It will save me carrying them.'

'Of course not. But don't transform too near to Henga. I don't want to have to chase her along the beach.'

My handsome betrothed grins, jogs further along the damp sand and, as the setting sun gilds his skin, crouches and shifts from a human into a magnificent, iridescent-feathered raven. He croaks a farewell and launches himself into the sky.

I turn away and walk towards Henga, still intent on her snack.

I wonder when I will be back here. Times change, for kingdoms and for people. My life from now on is going to be busy. Different.

But it's the people I love, more than the places, that are important. Letya will have her work in Atratys, and Lucien will always have Hatchlands, and Aron and Valentin may eventually spend some of their time in Celonia. But together, we'll find a way to make it work. Just as the nobles and the flightless and the Shriven are, between themselves, finding a way to live alongside one another. A way, despite their differences, to become one people.

Just as I am finding a way, I hope, to be both Aderyn and the ruler of a kingdom. Perhaps not the leader everyone expects, but a leader nonetheless.

The people of Solanum are truly my people now.

And I am their queen.

Acknowledgements

We've been living in Solanum – in our heads, at least – for most of the last two and a half years, so our first thank-you goes to the team at Hot Key for enabling us to share our shapeshifting swan fantasy with so many readers. We couldn't be more delighted to have found such a wonderful publishing home for our books. Special thanks to our brilliant and insightful editor Carla Hutchinson; to Talya Baker, Sasha Baker and Melissa Hyder for copy-edits and proofreading; to Amy Llambias, Molly Holt and everyone in the marketing and publicity team; to Alexandra Allden and Steve Newman for a second beautiful, breathtaking cover; to Sally Taylor for the artwork and Solanum's map; and of course to Emma Matthewson for seeing the potential in our writing in the first place.

Thanks (as always) to our fantastic agent, Claire Wilson at RCW, ably assisted by Safae El-Ouahabi, for continued guidance and support.

Thanks to Vic James for friendship and fun and for loving *Talons* enough to give us our cover quote. Thanks also to the YA authors who were kind enough to give us lovely quotes about *Swans*: Bex Hogan, Michelle Kenney, Isabel Strychacz, Holly Race, Mary Watson, S. M. Wilson and Joshua Winning.

Finally, we'd like to give a big shoutout to all the wonderful authors, booksellers, bloggers, vloggers and Instagrammers who have shown *Swans* and *Talons* such love and who have shared that love with other readers. The last year hasn't exactly been the easiest for anyone and, at the time of writing, the pandemic isn't over. But every time we've gone into a bookshop and seen our books there, and every time we've been tagged in a tweet or Instagram post by someone who who's enjoyed reading *A Throne of Swans*, it's reminded us that life can be fantastic. Thank you.

Katharine and Elizabeth Corr

Katharine and Elizabeth Corr are sisters, originally from Essex, now living in Surrey. When they both decided to write novels – on account of fictional people being much easier to deal with than real ones – it was obvious they should do it together. They can sometimes be found in one of their local coffee shops, arguing over which character to kill off next. Katharine and Elizabeth are authors of the spellbinding series The Witch's Kiss.

@katharinecorr
@lizcorr_writes
Instagram: katharinecorrwrites / lizcorrwrites
www.corrsisters.com

Thank you for choosing a Hot Key book.

If you want to know more about our authors and what we publish, you can find us online.

You can start at our website

www.hotkeybooks.com

And you can also find us on:

We hope to see you soon!